PRAISE FOR

THE GIRL IN THE BLUE BERET

"Ushering her readers back and forth across the decades, [Bobbie Ann Mason] perfectly weaves history with fiction. . . . In many ways, the book is a tribute to these unsung civilians whose heroism often was never acknowledged by those they helped. . . . [A] near-perfect war story."   — *USA Today*

"[This book] will send you dashing to the shelves to devour everything else [Mason's] ever written—it's that good. . . . A spellbinding tale of war, love and survival [that] alternates seamlessly between World War II and modern Europe . . . Mason's writing is exquisite. Not a single word is wasted or out of place, and she never drifts toward sentimentality. . . . Not only a remarkable work of historical fiction, it's also storytelling at its best."   —Associated Press

"Mason's lovely tale . . . will resonate for many."
                                           — *Good Housekeeping*

"Mason has given us a portrait of a man from a generation whose members were uncertain about the protocols of letting oneself feel. And she has lovingly captured the tone of bluff assertion still shared by veterans of that war. . . . *The Girl in the Blue Beret* is a work of remarkable empathy."   — *The New York Times Book Review*

"Bobbie Ann Mason has long been considered one of the finest writers of regional fiction—Kentucky is her home and inspiration—but her affecting new novel takes place in France, and she's just as comfortable and insightful there. . . . A story that's luxuriously contemplative, sustained by the depth of Mason's sympathy . . . What a stirring tribute to the Resistance this novel is. . . . Once again, Mason has plumbed the moral dimensions of national conflict in the lives of individual participants and produced a deeply moving, relevant novel."
— *The Washington Post*

"Bobbie Ann Mason raises bracing questions about the subjectivity of memory and history [and] nimbly navigates between the stirring past and the suspenseful present."
— *The Boston Globe*

"A compelling tale . . . a page-turner, filled with sudden reverses and narrow escapes. It is also an act of remembrance and a tribute."
— *AARP*

"A richly told tale that gives its main character a chance to relearn what it means to be a hero."
— *The Christian Science Monitor*

"Renowned American author [Mason] based this haunting novel on her late father-in-law's wartime experiences, and the rich setting, detail, and intimate character nuances ring true. . . . Highly recommended."
— *Library Journal*

"[Conveys], in heartbreaking detail, the suffering of the Parisians and the high cost they paid for freedom. In her fifth novel, the talented Mason offers an emotionally powerful story of the ruinous effects of war."
— *Booklist*

"A fabulous tale . . . Mason's subtle, gorgeous prose keeps us captivated. . . . You occasionally pause to marvel at how real her fictional world seems. . . . Mason can say quite a bit about America just by telling one man's tale." —*BookPage*

"[An] impressive, impassioned new novel . . . The unforgettable story [is] a gripping tale of redemption. . . . Spellbinding and emotional . . . richly crafted." —*The Miami Herald*

"This is a book about then and now, told both in the present and in the past through memories, flashbacks and anecdotes related by characters. This sort of dual timeline has rarely been done as well as Mason does it here. The structure of this book is flawless. . . . It's a masterful achievement. . . . Mason's writing is, as always, rendered in the clear, smooth voice of a natural storyteller. . . . Just another one of the pleasures of reading this very high quality literary work." —Baton Rouge *Advocate*

"Mason writes with empathy and rich language, transforming what might have been a midlife crisis into a middle-aged re-evaluation of life that is full of promise for the future." —*Sacramento News & Review*

"Mason's storytelling manages to juggle two contrasting realities, to rich effect. . . . Mason leads us skillfully from the young, would-be hotshot, who doesn't look back, to the shut-down older man. . . . She treats her characters kindly, even if time and the world have not." —*The Philadelphia Inquirer*

"Ms. Mason has crafted a novel of reconciliation with the past. . . . *The Girl in the Blue Beret* is a work not to be missed; its audience is universal." —*The Washington Times*

"Richly detailed and insightful . . . [Mason's] work is never what it simply appears to be on the surface. . . . The subtle intricacies begin way below the visible layer. . . . *The Girl in the Blue Beret* draws the reader in. . . . So compelling that you might find yourself wishing it had gone on for another hundred pages."

—*The Broadkill Review*

"Well worth reading, exposing a subject that stresses the goodness of humanity, of man serving his fellow man despite chilling consequences."

—*Washington Missourian*

"There's something for everyone in *The Girl in the Blue Beret*. It's part mystery, part quest, part love story, and part nostalgia trip. All the parts are powerful and contribute to an even superior whole."

—*The Manhattan Mercury*

"Mason tells the story of a group often overlooked: the French Resistance. . . . The book feels very real. . . . Not everyone remembers things identically, not every hero is perfect, not everyone enjoyed a 'happily ever after.' . . . A must-read for World War II enthusiasts."

—*San Francisco Book Review*

"Bobbie Ann Mason just keeps outdistancing herself. *The Girl in the Blue Beret* has everything: adventure, intrigue, fear, sorrow, nostalgic ache, regret, romance, and most importantly, love. She writes of the platonic love of one's fellow travelers, along with romantic love—and what a beautiful love story it is, told with grace and elegance from the point of view of a narrator you won't soon forget. I loved this book, and so will you."

—RICHARD BAUSCH, author of *Something is
Out There* and *Peace;* winner of the PEN/
Malamud Award for Short Fiction

"A flight through the gripping, war-ravaged past and the discovery of love—Bobbie Ann Mason's moving novel is written with great clarity and insight."

—KIM EDWARDS, author of *The Memory Keeper's Daughter* and *The Lake of Dreams*

"An elegant and eventually lovely story of war, need and apprehension."

—ROY BLOUNT JR., author of *Alphabet Juice* and *Long Time Leaving*

THE GIRL IN THE BLUE BERET

RANDOM HOUSE TRADE PAPERBACKS | NEW YORK

BOBBIE ANN MASON

THE GIRL IN
THE BLUE BERET

A NOVEL

AUTHOR'S NOTE

My late father-in-law, co-pilot of an Allied bomber shot down by a German fighter plane over Belgium during the Second World War, owed his eventual escape from Occupied Europe to the help he received from members of the French Resistance, including a teenager he would remember as "the girl in the blue beret." Inspired by my father-in-law's wartime experience, *The Girl in the Blue Beret* is nonetheless a work of fiction: names, characters, places, and incidents are the products of my imagination or are used fictitiously, and any resemblance to actual events, locales, or persons, living or dead, is coincidental and unintentional.

Published in the United States by Random House Trade Paperbacks, an imprint of The Random House Publishing Group, a division of Random House, Inc., New York.

RANDOM HOUSE TRADE PAPERBACKS and colophon are trademarks of Random House, Inc.
RANDOM HOUSE READER'S CIRCLE & Design is a registered trademark of Random House, Inc.

Originally published in hardcover in the United States by Random House, an imprint of The Random House Publishing Group, a division of Random House, Inc., in 2011.

LIBRARY OF CONGRESS CATALOGING-IN-PUBLICATION DATA
Mason, Bobbie Ann.
The girl in the blue beret: a novel / by Bobbie Ann Mason.
p.   cm.
ISBN 978-0-8129-7887-2
1. World War, 1939–1945—Aerial operations—Fiction.   2. World War, 1939–1945—Underground movements—Europe—Fiction.
I. Title.
PS3563.A7877G57 2011
813'.54—dc22   2010036861

Printed in the United States of America
www.randomhousereaderscircle.com

9 8 7 6 5 4 3 2 1

Book design by Barbara M. Bachman

DEDICATED TO
MICHÈLE AGNIEL
AND TO THE MEMORY OF
BARNEY RAWLINGS
(1920–2004)

BLISS WAS IT IN THAT DAWN TO BE ALIVE,

BUT TO BE YOUNG WAS VERY HEAVEN!

— WILLIAM WORDSWORTH, "The Prelude"

ESCAPE AND EVASION

DuのRING WORLD WAR II, THOUSANDS OF ALLIED AVIATORS CRASHED OR
parachuted into Occupied Europe. A number of escape-and-evasion
networks helped to hide them and send them safely back to their
bases in England. Thousands of Europeans risked their lives by hiding the airmen in their homes, providing false identity papers, and
smuggling them by sea to England or across the Pyrenees to Spain.
Between 1942 and 1944, more than three thousand British and
American downed flyers successfully evaded capture with the help of
an unknown number of ordinary citizens, who risked being shot or
sent to a concentration camp.

THE GIRL IN THE BLUE BERET

FLIGHT CREW **THE DIRTY LILY**

Molesworth Airfield, Station 107, England

303RD BOMB GROUP, B-17G

SQUADRON 124

MISSION TO FRANKFURT, GERMANY

January 31, 1944

Captain	LAWRENCE WEBB
Co-pilot	MARSHALL STONE
Bombardier	AL GRAINGER
Navigator	TONY CAMPANELLO
Top-Turret Gunner, Flight Engineer	JAMES FORD
Radio Operator	BOB HADLEY
Ball-Turret Gunner	BOBBY REDBURN
Left Waist Gunner	HOOTIE WILLIAMS
Right Waist Gunner	CHICK COCHRAN
Tail Gunner	DON STEWART

AS THE LONG FIELD CAME INTO VIEW, MARSHALL STONE FELT HIS breathing quicken, a rush of doves flying from his chest. The landscape was surprisingly familiar, its contours and borders fresh in his memory, even though he had been here only fleetingly thirty-six years ago. Lucien Lombard, who had brought him here today, knew the field intimately, for it had been in his family for generations.

"It was over there beside that tree, *monsieur*," Lucien said, pointing toward the center of the field, where an awkward sycamore hovered over a patch of unruly vegetation.

"There was no tree then," Marshall said.

"That is true."

They walked through the furrowed field toward the tree, Lucien's sturdy brown boots mushing the mud, Marshall following in borrowed Wellingtons. He was silent, his memory of the crash landing superimposed on the scene in front of him, as if there were a small movie projector in his mind. The Flying Fortress, the B-17, the heavy bomber the crew called the *Dirty Lily*, had been returning from a mission to Frankfurt.

"The airplane came down just there," said Lucien as they neared the tree.

Lucien was elderly—probably in his eighties, Marshall thought—but he had a strong, erect physique, and he walked with a quick, determined step. His hair was thin, nearly white, his face smooth and firm.

"Normally a farmer would not permit a tree to thrive in his field," he said. "But this tree marks the site."

Unexpectedly, Marshall Stone began to cry. Embarrassed, he

turned his face aside. He was a captain of transatlantic jumbo jets, a man who did not show weakness. He was alarmed by his emotion.

Lucien Lombard nodded. "I know, *monsieur*," he said.

In Marshall's mind, the crumpled B-17 lay before him in the center of the field. He recalled that the plane had been lined up with the neatly plowed furrows.

The deep, rumbling sound of a vast formation of B-17s roared through Marshall's memory now. The steady, violent, rocking flight toward target. The sight of Focke-Wulf 190s—angry hornets darting crazily. The black bursts of flak floating like tumbleweeds strewn on a western highway. The fuselage flak-peppered. Slipping down into the cloud deck, flying for more than an hour unprotected. Over Belgium, hit again. The nose cone shattering. The pilot panicking.

Marshall, the co-pilot, took the controls and brought the *Dirty Lily* down. A belly landing on this foreign soil. There was no time to jettison the ball turret. Only as they were coming down did Marshall see that Lawrence Webb, the pilot, was unconscious. The Fort grazed the top of a tall hedgerow and slid in with a jolt, grinding to a hard stop. The crew scrambled out. Marshall and the flight engineer wrestled Webb's slack body from the plane. The navigator's face was torn, bloodied. The fuselage was burning. Machine-gun rounds were exploding at the gun stations. Marshall didn't see the tail gunner anywhere. The left waist gunner lay on the ground, motionless.

Marshall had been just twenty-three years old then. Now he was nearly sixty, and he had come to see this place again at last. He was crying for the kids in the B-17, the youngsters who had staked their lives on their Flying Fortress. He hadn't known he had pent up such a reservoir of emotion, even though he probably thought about the downing of the B-17 every day. He willed his tears to stop.

Lucien Lombard had seen the plane come down near the village, and he rushed to help the crew, but Marshall didn't remember him.

Now Lucien said, "It is like yesterday."

Marshall toed a weed-topped clod of dirt. "The worst day of my life," he said. "Some bad memories."

"Never mind, *monsieur*. It had its part."

Several people were crossing the field, headed toward them. They had arrived in a gray van with the name of a hardware store on the side.

"Everyone from the village has heard of your visit," said Lucien. "You are a hero."

"*Non.* I did very little." Marshall was ashamed.

Lucien introduced him to the group. They were all smiling at him and speaking rapidly. When Marshall could not follow some of their thickly accented French, Lucien explained that everyone there remembered the crash. Three families had sheltered members of the crew, and Dr. Bequet had treated the wounded.

"I'm very grateful," Marshall said, shaking the doctor's hand.

"It was necessary to help."

More introductions and small talk followed. Marshall noticed two men scanning the ground. Lucien explained that people still found pieces of metal there—bullet casings, rivets, and once even a warped propeller blade. Marshall thought of how he had torn up the field when he came zigzagging down that day.

A man in a cloth cap and wool scarf stepped forward and touched Marshall's arm.

"*Oui*, it is sad, *monsieur*," the man said. He regarded Marshall in a kindly way and smiled. His face was leathery but younger than Marshall's. He seemed familiar.

"You were the boy who helped me!" Marshall said, astonished.

"*Oui. C'est moi.*"

"You offered me a cigarette."

The man laughed. His taut, weathered cheeks seemed to blush. "*Bien sûr.* I would never forget that day. The cigarettes I had obtained for my father."

"That was my very first Gauloises," Marshall said.

"You were my first *Américain*," the man said, smiling. "I am Henri Lechat."

They shook hands, the younger man first removing his glove.

"You warned me that the Germans were coming," Marshall said.

Henri nodded. "It is true. You had no French then, and I had no English."

"But I knew. We communicated somehow."

Marshall's voice broke on the word *communicated*.

"We will never forget, *monsieur*."

"You told me to run," Marshall said, recalling how he had stowed the cigarette in the inner pocket of his leather jacket. Now he felt his tears well up again.

Henri tugged on his scarf. "I told you to hide in the woods, and you comprehended."

Recalling the boy's urgency, Marshall tried to laugh. Henri had raced up, calling a warning. Pointing back the way he had come, he cried, *"Les Allemands! Les Allemands!"* Then, pointing to the woods in the other direction, he shouted, *"Allez-y!"* Marshall did not see any Germans, and he would not leave until all the crew was out. The bombardier was wounded in the shoulder, and the navigator had a shattered leg. The tail gunner appeared; he had hopped out easily. The left waist gunner was unconscious and had to be pulled from the fuselage window. Marshall was relieved to see the ball-turret gunner, who was limping toward the church with a man carrying a shovel. Someone said the right waist gunner had parachuted. The pilot was lying on the frozen ground, his eyes closed. Fire was leaping from the plane.

Marshall knelt by Webb, trying to wake him. Nothing. Someone squatted beside Marshall and opened Webb's jacket.

"Docteur," the woman said, pointing toward the village. She pointed in the opposite direction, toward the woods, and said, "Go."

Marshall stood. The flight engineer appeared at his side. "Let's go," he said. "Everybody's out."

Several of the villagers were making urgent gestures toward the road. German troops would be here in moments. Marshall knew that they converged on every fallen plane, to arrest the Allied aviators and to salvage the wrecked metal for their own planes. The German fighter that had downed them was circling low overhead. Marshall began running toward the woods.

Had the Germans shot anyone from the village for helping the American flyers? Marshall wondered now, but he did not want to ask. He had tried to be sure all the crew were out, and then he left the scene. In the years after, he didn't probe into the aftermath. He lived another life.

"We were so thankful to you, *monsieur*," one of the men was saying. "When your planes flew over we knew we would be liberated one day."

Marshall nodded.

A stocky woman with gray, thick hair and a genial, wrinkled face said, "The airplanes flying toward Germany in those days—there were hundreds of them. We rejoiced to see them crossing the sky."

Henri kicked dirt from his leather boot. "I didn't know at that age everything that was understood by the adults. But I knew the deprivation, the difficulties, the secrecy. Even the children knew the crisis."

Cautiously, Marshall asked, "Did the Germans arrest anybody for helping us?"

"*Oh, non, monsieur.*" Henri paused. "Not that day."

Lucien Lombard clasped Henri's shoulder and said, "The father of this one was killed—shot on his bicycle, on his way home after convoying one of your *aviateurs* across the border to France."

Henri said, "I had to grow up quickly. I had the responsibilities then for my mother and my sisters."

Lucien said, "His family hid that *aviateur* in their barn for a time."

Marshall recoiled. He could see the waist gunner lying motionless across the furrows. He saw himself running into the woods. He saw the boy's face. The plane was on fire.

Marshall had decided to return to this place finally, knowing it was time to confront his past failure. He had expected to be alone in the field, and he had not thought anyone would remember. The news of the death of the boy's father jolted him. He had never heard about that. In all these years, he had thought little about the people who had come running to the downed airplane. He had felt such a profound defeat in the war that he had not wanted to return here. During the war, more than anything, he had wanted to be heroic. But he was no hero. He had felt nothing but bitter disappointment that he didn't get to complete his bombing missions against Nazi Germany. And what happened later, as he skulked through France, was best forgotten, he had thought.

Marshall was a widower. His wife, Loretta, had died suddenly two years before, and the loss still seemed unbelievable, but now he began to feel his grief lift, like the morning fog disappearing above a waiting airport.

Dazed by his brief visit to the muddy field in Belgium, Marshall spent the last hours before his flight home walking around Paris. It was a mellow spring day.

He had always enjoyed this city. He bid for Paris flights several times each year, and when he became senior enough, he got them. Climb out of JFK in the evening, fly above the invisible Atlantic during the hours of darkness, and arrive in Paris under a bright sun.

He thought tenderly of Loretta, who had always refused to believe he was anything less than heroic. He wished she could have been with him on this trip.

He watched children on skates zooming alongside the Luxembourg Gardens, near the crew hotel. He thought about the boy in Belgium who had helped him, and he thought about the boy's father—shot for convoying a gunner from the *Dirty Lily*.

On his layovers, Marshall had rarely gone to museums or tourist attractions, but he enjoyed the bustle and anonymity of a city that still had a feeling of intimacy—unlike New York. Or London. He liked being able to understand conversations he overheard. After the war, he had taken courses in French, and over the years he had become fluent enough to get along. He liked to read novels in French.

By the time he reached the Louvre, he realized that during his walk he hadn't been seeing Paris as it was now, 1980. He had been resurrecting 1944. Ghostly images overlaid the scene before him. At the Tuileries, his gaze followed the magnificent view through the gardens and on up the Champs-Elysées to the Arc de Triomphe. Over this sight now he superimposed his memories of being there long ago, when there were hardly any vehicles. He saw images from newsreels and photographs: Hitler's hordes marching in perfect lockstep; later, Churchill and de Gaulle triumphant.

To Marshall's right, somewhere along the rue de Rivoli, was a Métro stop. He and a brash bombardier named Delancey had stumbled up from the Métro, scared, towering like Lombardy poplars among the crowd of much shorter Frenchmen. If they missed their contact, they would be stranded—lost amidst the Germans, circulating around them in their menacing gray-green uniforms.

She was there. He saw her first, sitting on a bench reading a timetable. There was a quietness to the crowd, as if people were on their best behavior. Marshall had doubted that a mere schoolgirl would be sent as their contact, but there she was, sitting with a book satchel and earnestly consulting a timetable.

The agent's directions had been precise. *Find the girl in the blue beret. She will have a timetable and a leather school bag.*

Marshall remembered that moment vividly. She was waiting there, her blue beret standing out like a flower against the barren winter gardens of the Tuileries.

There was still a bench in that area. Not the same bench, he thought, but it was in approximately the same place.

But no, he was wrong. When he saw her on the bench, Delancey hadn't been with him. He and Delancey had first seen her at the train station. Why did he meet her in the Tuileries? Then he remembered.

As he neared the place de la Concorde, he thought of the Concorde—the SST. He wished it would fly over, a happy coincidence, tying history in a knot. Moments of history entwined here— Marie-Antoinette lost her head; the Egyptian obelisk replaced the guillotine; Napoléon dreamed the triumphant arch. Marshall felt his own history emanate from him, as if he been holding it condensed in a small spot inside himself. Reviewing his past was new for Marshall, something that had started as he approached his sixtieth birthday— and retirement. Tomorrow was his final flight.

—

FOR YEARS, MARSHALL had dreaded retirement. Mandatory premature retreat, he called it, infuriated at the federal law. He hated being forced out. He was perfectly healthy, and he had stopped smoking ten years ago. Asking a pilot to stop flying was like asking a librarian to burn books. Or a pianist to close the lid forever. Or a farmer to buy a condo in the city. His mind entertained new metaphors every day.

Retirement would be like the enforced passivity he had endured during the war, after the crash landing. Then, he was a caged bird.

The airline didn't want rickety, half-blind ancients at the controls. *Screw the airline*, he thought now. Roaming Paris, he composed the thousandth rebuttal he would never send in: *Since being let go on account of advanced age and feebleness, I've been forced to adopt a new career. Henceforth, I shall guide hikers up Mont Blanc, and on my days off I'll be going skydiving.*

The pilots Marshall hobnobbed with might talk about investments, or summer homes, or time-share condos, but none of them really cared about anything except flying. One former B-24 pilot golfed, and an ex-fighter jock intended to sail his deep-draft sloop around the world someday, but Marshall thought their pastimes were half-hearted substitutes. He was interested in everything to do with aviation, and he was always reading, but he thought hobbies were silly. Collecting swizzle sticks or crafting model airplanes—he couldn't imagine. Whenever he thought of what to do with his retirement, he drew a blank. Pushing the throttles forward, racing down the runway, feeling the wings gain lift, pulling the yoke back and aiming high into the sky—that's what his pilot friends really wanted. That's what he wanted.

Marshall wandered down a street of five-story apartment buildings. This was the lovely, proportionate architecture he remembered.

The people who had helped him in Paris during the war would be retired now, he thought. The French retired young. Robert? *Roh-behr*. Marshall didn't recall the young man's last name, but he would never forget him. Robert and his clandestine missions. He remembered Robert appearing in the small hours of the morning with an urgent message. He remembered Robert letting his rucksack fall to the floor, then reaching in like a magician to produce cigarettes or a few priceless eggs. Once, he pulled out an actual rabbit, skinned and purple. From inside the lining of his coat came thin papers with secret messages. Whatever happened to him after the war?

MARSHALL ALWAYS ARRIVED EARLY FOR HIS FLIGHTS. HE TRIED to nap in the pilots' ready-room at Charles de Gaulle Airport. He hadn't slept well, his final B-17 mission blending in his dreams with the 747 he would be flying across the ocean for the last time. He read the newspapers and stoked up on coffee and peanuts. In his experience, peanuts balanced the caffeine turbulence without cutting the uplift of the caffeine itself. He wanted that uplift today. The night before, several of the crew had taken him out for a retirement wingding, complete with a late-night frolic at the Folies de Pigalle. He could hardly pay attention to the titillation, for thinking of his visit in Belgium.

Today his first officer, Erik Knopfler, who was twenty years Marshall's junior, caught him trying to nap. "Hey, old man, getting your beauty sleep? That's what you get for staying out late partying."

"Yeah, they're telling me I'm old. 'Happy birthday, here's your burial plot.' "

Carl Reasoner, the flight engineer, joined them. He said, "I know we're always razzing you senior guys, but Marshall, I'd rather fly with you than most of these guys today coming out of Vietnam."

"That goes for me too," said Erik.

"Well, thanks, guys. I appreciate that. I walked all the hell over Paris yesterday, and my heart runs like a top. Yet they say I'm too old."

"Oh, we have to get rid of you, you know," said Erik with a laugh. "We don't want you old guys hogging all of the seniority."

"That's diplomatic," Marshall said. "Just wait till you hit the big six-O!"

In the washroom, Marshall spruced up and gave himself the once-over in the mirror. Loretta would have wanted him to look good on his final flight. *He couldn't be sixty*, he thought.

At the dispatch office, he checked the weather forecast and worked out the fuel load. Then he stopped at scheduling, where he gave the crew his captain's briefing. He tried to be august as he presented the flight plan and ran the crew through routine checks. He dwelled too long on ditching procedures, but he didn't want to slight anything. And instead of leaving it to the first officer, he would do the damn walk-around himself this time, he thought. He wanted to kick the tires. One last time.

After the briefing, Erik ogled an attractive flight attendant in a short skirt as she descended the stairway.

"I'd like to see her twist down the aisle of the plane like that," he said. "But man, the girls on my last flight must have come from the Salvation Army."

"They were better in the old days, huh, Marshall?" Carl was teasing him again. "Everything was better then, I hear."

"Naturally."

Marshall set off for the plane, his travel bag in one hand and his "brain bag"—his flight manuals, maps, flashlight, and hijacker handcuffs—in the other. He felt pleased by the respect the younger guys gave him. "Bus driver!" his son, Albert, then a teenager, had once taunted him.

Marshall was prepared for hijackings, bombings, unruly passengers. He had to be ready with his skill, his *sang-froid*, his instantaneous judgment, his focus. He had learned to make his eyes radiate alertness. He practiced unblinkingness. He could go sixty-four seconds without blinking. He had to ease up a bit when he began to need artificial tears. He hated having to carry a bottle of eyedrops.

He jokingly called the younger pilots whippersnappers. He had been one himself. The one who crashed the B-17. He quickly corrected that thought. He was the one who safely brought down the wounded bomber.

THAT MORNING HE was especially careful in the cockpit, concentrating fiercely on every item as the first officer went down the checklist. It was so easy to make a simple mistake. He wanted to savor the joy of the takeoff, the sweep of the flight, with his mind fully at ease. The 747 lacked the more intimate contact with the ground and sky that he had known in smaller planes, but it had grandeur. It conferred distinction. The captain of such a mighty vessel had reason to be proud. He loved to taxi. He loved to lift. Sometimes he forgot to breathe, he loved it so.

He took off, banked, trimmed, and set the course. He was climbing, due west. Soon he was flying past Rouen, Le Havre, Caen, Bayeux, Sainte-Mère-Église. He was flying above the Normandy beaches. Sword Beach. Juno. Gold. Omaha. Utah. So often when he flew out of Paris or London, he imagined what it would have been like if he could have flown on D-Day. But he never got that chance. He had flown only ten missions, and all his months of expensive training had ended in a fiasco in a bumpy field in Belgium.

Yet the people he met in Belgium remembered him and the crew. They had hidden three of them from the Germans and tended to the wounds of others. They had dwelt on the crash for all these years. It had become part of the local lore, a mythology. The day the aviators fell from the sky. He remembered that field in Belgium during the war with devastating clarity, but the people were unknown to him. And now Marshall knew that one of them had died protecting a young, lost American.

Passing control over to Erik, Marshall sat back. His eyes scanned the instruments automatically, monitoring the machine as he had done innumerable times before.

He had tried to put the war behind him, but sometimes it surfaced. Over the years he thought from time to time about the girl in the blue beret and wondered what had become of her. A twinge of regret fluttered deep inside him now, and this feeling, like his earlier tears, surprised him.

THE FLIGHT HOME was routine, fairly smooth, until they hit a light chop over Newfoundland and Marshall had to speak to the passengers about seat belts. He didn't get chatty, the way some pilots did. *Just fly the goddamn plane*, he told himself.

As they neared New York, the purser got on the intercom to tell everyone that this was the final flight of their captain's career.

"Land, ho," Erik said now. "I guess you won't miss flying in weather."

"I'll take weather," he said. "Gladly."

He had a bad horizon going in, with a carpet of popcorn clouds, but they cleared as the plank shape of Long Island came into view. Now began the most challenging part of any flight—the landing. Marshall leaned forward. They were easing down to lower altitude, and the swamplands of JFK were becoming distinct. Marshall had always enjoyed the low-altitude stages of flight, when details of the landscape became plain. Today the egrets wading in the swamp looked like flags of surrender.

He made the turn toward Long Beach, over the inlets and swamp to the beckoning runway.

The landing was buffeted a little by crosswinds. He turned into the wind, sidling like a crab as he maneuvered against it. They were over the threshold. He pulled the yoke slightly, flaring. They were centered above the runway.

"Forty, thirty, twenty," Erik called out.

Marshall pressed the rudder pedal. The nose swung around just as the main gear kissed the concrete. Perfectly aligned, the big ship settled to earth. Kicking the crab out, it was called.

"Nice," said Erik.

"See. It's still possible to actually fly a plane once in a while."

Marshall heard the intercom click on and then some kind of staticky noise. He began to grin, realizing he was hearing applause from the passengers. He was being sent out on a high note, and he found it gratifying.

4

MARSHALL HAD WANTED TO SNEAK OUT OF THE AIRPORT, but the crew waylaid him with a brief farewell ceremony of plaudits and pranks. The purser gave him a teddy bear dressed in a pioneer flight suit, complete with goggles and a little leather helmet.

"Sure you got all your paperwork done, Marshall?" a junior pilot asked, kidding.

"I'll have nightmares about that," Marshall said.

"That's the thing. More time on paperwork than jiggling the yoke."

"Aviation has gotten so bureaucratic that even us superheroes have trouble," Marshall said. He had perfected an avuncular chuckle as a filler for idle conversation.

It was always strange to enter a new decade, he thought as he closed his logbook. It was as if you were allowed for a moment into the workings of time before easing back into the usual steady pace of life. The disbelief that greeted a new decade was a defense against disappearance. Perhaps after he had passed the hurdle of the new decade, the dread would even out and he would simply continue his life. He had imagined retirement as a looming wall, with a lawn chair parked in front, but now he did a little skip at the end of the escalator, a spontaneous grace note of anticipation. *Screw the airline.*

For the first time in years, he wasn't required to drop off his passport at the scheduling office.

He found his Honda Civic, its silvery gray like an emblem of age, and drove home as if on autopilot. He always found that the wheel-clutching demands of driving a mere automobile were minor trifles. On the four-lanes he could zip around lumbering trucks and keep the accelerator even, but on streets, with their stop signs and inter-mittent shopping strips, he grew inattentive.

"I hope you don't fly that plane the way you're driving this car," Loretta had said once. Most of the time she pretended his driving was like Apollo at the reins of his chariot.

As he passed the garbage mountain near Rahway, glittering with green glass, he remembered Loretta saying it sparkled like the aqua-marine of the Mediterranean Sea. It's garbage, he pointed out. His career had liberated him from the kind of work done by most men. He couldn't imagine himself driving a bulldozer, sculpting refuse. He ascended, bursting through the cloud layers, rising, rising, scoot-ing through the atmosphere, leveling off at thirty-six thousand feet. The jets, the bumping through clouds, the speed—it was like sex, with much more at stake. Sometimes he imagined he could just keep rising until he reached the moon. He thought now about the time, just before *Apollo 11*, when Neil Armstrong was practicing on the flying-bedstead lunar trainer, a framework contraption that hovered. The thing went kerflooie, spun out of control, and Armstrong hit the eject button at the last possible millisecond. Matter-of-factly, he parachuted to the ground, shucked the chute, and was back at his desk in thirty minutes. He didn't even mention the incident to his office mate. Just another day on the job.

ALTHOUGH BASED AT JFK, Marshall lived in New Jersey. From the air, the landscape made sense to him, but on the ground the suburbs were a meaningless hodgepodge of deadpan houses and noxious shopping centers. Loretta had flourished in the suburbs. She knew the neighborhood of the school and the streets where she took Al-bert and Mary to harp and flute lessons when they were growing up. Yet she remained devoted to Cincinnati, her hometown, and she had gone there often, with the children, even after her parents were dead. His own parents died long ago, and he had lost touch with all other kin in Cincinnati and down in the Kentucky mountains.

The Stones' house was a two-story, green-clapboard colonial hedged with boxwood. The interior was feminine throughout, except for his wood-paneled study, with its somber barometer and photographs of DC-3s and the beloved old Connie—the Constellation, the most satisfying airplane he had ever flown. He had always been like a special guest in this house, someone who dropped in every week or so. Loretta played her part as hostess. Home life had an air of pretense, as if staged. When he was away, did she strike the set?

Whenever he thought about his role in the family when the kids were young, he teetered off balance. What a fraud he was! What did he know about parenting? He was the dad who took the children to get the Christmas tree, the dad who carved the turkey, the dad who drove the station wagon on summer vacations. On holidays when he had to be away, Loretta simply shifted the date. The turkey waited. Santa too.

Loretta greeted him sunnily each time he returned. The transition was disorienting. In an airplane, he was perpetually alert, energized, a cat watching a mouse hole. On the ground, his real self floated away. Home was a maze of costumes and allowances and bicycle tires. He stayed in his den for hours on end, absorbed in the ancient Mayans or Viking explorers or Georges Simenon mysteries—in French. He read anything he could get his hands on. He jogged around the high-school track.

Yet he had held fast to the contract. This home life in New Jersey was what all the sacrifices were for—the training, the war, the job. His nuclear unit ensconced in this fine colonial two-story was his *raison d'être*. He had no complaint. As a 747 captain, he was a success, and his family was proud of him.

Now Marshall entered the deserted house, carried his bags up to the den, hung his uniform jacket in the closet, and set his hat on its accustomed shelf. The scrambled-egg brim of the hat seemed to be saying something, but he shut the door on its grin. He opened his carry-on bag and pulled out the gift teddy bear by the paw. Its ridiculous little flight suit made a mockery of him. He threw it into the closet, where it landed among a jumble of shoes.

At his base in England, in his leather flying jacket, he had jokingly called himself the Scourge of the Sky. Then he met those deadly Focke-Wulfs. He had always felt anguish over the loss of the bomber. A B-17 cost a million dollars, big money back then. And it cost forty thousand dollars to train a pilot. That he didn't get to fly more missions was like a cruel coitus interruptus. He had never gotten over that disappointment.

He sat in his den, the most comfortable place in the empty house. A tape ran backwards in his mind. His final airline flight, and before that, embarrassing himself in the field in Belgium, and long before that, crash-landing in that field. Once again, he peered through the B-17's windscreen as he brought the bomber in. The Belgians seemed fixated on the memory of the plane coming down in their field, so close it could have plowed into their church.

Now something had shaken loose. The distant past was no longer behind him, something to be shoved behind while he forged ahead; now it was in front of him.

HE HAD TO FIGURE out what to do with the house. Sell it? Turn it over to his kids? He didn't want to rent it out. That could be a disaster. He wanted to ask Albert to live there, but he doubted Albert would take care of it. Albert's idea of upkeep was giving himself a biannual hair trim. The house needed some repairs. Loretta had always cautioned against letting the house become an eyesore in the neighborhood. It was on the verge. Marshall sprang into action. The day after his final flight he hired some odd-job guys who promised to come at the end of the month to work on the gutters and windows.

For several days he reviewed the war. In the mornings, he dashed through the *Times* crossword and went for brisk walks in the neighborhood, or he jogged around the track. On his birthday he ordered a pizza, and when it was delivered he was surprised to see that the sun was setting. He hadn't opened the drapes all day. He had been absorbed in a history of the Mighty Eighth Air Force and was especially engrossed in the section on the Hell's Angels, his bomb group.

He ate the pizza while watching a TV special about Hollywood's early days. Nothing else was on.

During the next few days he plunged into his aviation library— the flight magazines and books, the videotapes, the clippings. He would get lost in the forties. He found Loretta's big-band albums and played several of them straight through. As he listened to Artie Shaw's ecstatic "Frenesi," he realized that he knew every note by heart. He recalled days when he was waiting to ship out, when he and Loretta were sharing Cokes on silly, frenetic dates, or jitterbugging to the music of Blue Barron and his orchestra at the Castle Farms ballroom in Cincinnati. The yearning notes of Doris Day singing "Sentimental Journey" brought to mind the end of the war, when he married Loretta.

He kept the music going while he pored over maps of Occupied Europe and books about the air campaign against Hitler. He traced the route of his B-17's last mission. He traced his route from Belgium to Paris.

He remembered an afternoon in Paris in 1944 when bunches of daffodils arrived in a bicycle basket from the country. Coming out of his long hiding, he saw flowering bushes in the park, and even though he had rarely given thought to flowers except for knowing that women liked them, he knew at once that the dancing floral displays amidst the sickly swastikas and dull green uniforms were a defiant sign of hope. He remembered seeing the girl rest her nose in the trumpet of a daffodil.

HIS DAUGHTER, MARY, had called on his birthday, and now she was calling again, checking on how the retirement was going. He had not mentioned his plans.

"I've been thinking," she said. "Is there anything I can do?"

"What?"

"Is there anything you need?"

"Don't worry about me."

"Well, Albert and I are both worried."

"Why?"

"Well, if you don't have flying—"

"Afraid I'll go off the deep end?"

"Listen to me," she said sternly. He could hear her talking to her dolls—a scene from twenty years ago. "If you don't have flying, what will you do?"

"I'm brushing up on my French," he said.

"Say something to me in French."

"*Tu es une bonne fille.*"

"A good girl?" She sighed.

"A good daughter."

He waited for her to say he was a good father. He told himself she was trying to think of the French word and had drawn a blank.

Marshall regarded his children with mingled awe, amusement, respect, and alarm. He knew young people were headstrong, and he had intentionally granted his children the freedom to go their own ways. He had been an arrogant youth himself—stubborn, always butting heads with authority. Mary worked on a newspaper in Boise, Idaho, and Albert was still unsettled, working part-time in Manhattan while studying for his second master's degree—first math, now design. They never told him much.

He never told them much either, but now he told Mary about his visit to the crash site and his notion of going to live in Europe for a while.

"I'd like to retrace the trail I took through France in '44," he said.

"That's neat, Dad. A little trip to the past. That could be fun."

The conversation came to a standstill. Marshall realized he was kicking at the doorstop between the kitchen and the dining room—a weighted, fabric pioneer girl with a churn. He said to Mary, "Your mom would kick me across the room if she could see what sad shape her churn-girl is in."

Mary laughed. "Throw that thing out, Dad. It's probably breeding germs."

ALBERT AGREED IMMEDIATELY to house-sit. He could come the first of June, when his rent was due, he said when Marshall telephoned. Marshall hadn't been able to figure out how else to find an occupant, and he knew Albert had little money. As an inducement, he threw in use of the car as part of the deal. But when Marshall stressed the need to look after the place and make any necessary repairs, Albert hesitated.

"I'll pay the expenses," Marshall said.

Albert had a contrary streak. He always resisted if Marshall made any demands. Albert had been a rebellious kid, and by his college years he was, in Marshall's view, a hippie protester. Marshall was always thankful that Albert had gotten a deferment during the Vietnam War. But it separated him further from his son. Their experiences had been so different.

"You O.K., Dad? Are you O.K. with the retirement?"

"I'm dandy," Marshall said.

After they hung up, Marshall reflected that both Albert and Mary had expressed concern for him. He was annoyed but also grateful. They were good kids, really. Maybe he and Loretta hadn't done such a bad job.

His mind zipped back to the year when Loretta was first pregnant. She had done up her hair in a wavy mass that was supposed to imitate Hedy Lamarr's rolling tresses in *White Cargo*.

Loretta said, "You can name the boy, and I get to name the girl."

That was the plan. A boy and a girl. And it worked out. Albert was first. Loretta liked the name Marshall chose.

"Is Albert a name in your family?" she asked.

"No. It's just a name I'm fond of," Marshall said. He added, "It's a name for courage."

When the girl came along, Loretta announced that the name would be Mary. "I'm naming her for you," she said.

"I don't know how you twisted Mary out of Marshall," he said.

IN A PLACE NORTH OF PARIS, a man and his wife dressed in dark, loose clothing were hovering over a radio, listening for a coded message from the BBC. In a corner, the boy was reading his lessons.

The message came, and the boy translated it for him. *Blue tit birds will be nesting at twilight.* Marshall could not make sense of it.

But the couple raised their heads, triumphant and tense. There was a bottle of wine on a worn wooden table, and a cat curled indifferently by the fire.

The boy's father, Pierre Albert, disappeared into the night. A long two hours later, a muffled boom sounded in the north, and from the dark backyard Marshall could see in the distance a blaze erupting bright enough to show its angry smoke.

5

IN A SHOE BOX (LADIES' PUMPS) TAGGED "FRANCE," IN LORETTA'S curlicue handwriting, Marshall found several letters and photographs, some French coins, a map, and some memorabilia from the war years. In the bottom were the letters he was looking for—two from Pierre Albert, one in English, one in French.

ALBERT, PIERRE
PAINTER
CHAUNY (AISNE) FRANCE
6 FEBRUARY 1947

Dear friend,
I am sending you a little word to ask you what are you doing and to tell you that we are going very well and hope that you are the same since we see you. Here, everything is going very well. I am always in the peinture and my boy works with me. He is now a young gentleman and I am very glad to have him. My wife go very well too.

I hope that you are now with all your family and all the hard days that you passed are now finished.

Here in France, the situation is always very hard. We always have the ration but it's going a little better than the time the Germs were here, but it's not tomorrow that we will have like before the war. I think that we will have to waite 2 or 3 year before that everything go all right.

My wife and I would be very glad to have some of your news. I

join here some photographs. I am your friend, and I send you all my
best wishes from my wife and Nicolas.

Pierre Albert

Marshall remembered answering Pierre's letter in French, laboriously, freeing the Frenchman to respond in his own language,
which Marshall could read more easily now.

CHAUNY 3 APRIL 1947

Dear friends,
I received your letter with joy. I know that your return was not
known without difficulty, but at last we are very happy that you
have returned, in sum for you the war has ended.

We would be very happy to receive your visit and also your wife
and your little son Albert and for us to count you among us again
sometime, in order to speak of our old memories. At home you know
we often speak of you. I will give you some explanations about my
work with the Résistance, after you left. I made connection with the
escape networks in Paris.

I profit some at the same time to make you know that Nicolas,
my wife, and I wait in order to receive each the distinction "Medal of
Freedom" by the American authorities.

In response to your questions I would tell you that the coffee,
sugar, ham, soap, butter, rice, tobacco, are very rare, also the clothes
and shoes. On the other page, we give you the dimensions for Nicolas,
who is very large.

In the expectation of reading you and of seeing you, receive dear
friends our good kisses to your little Albert from all our family.

Best wishes to you and your family and le petit Albert.

Pierre Albert

P.S. I beg you to pay attention for there are some thieves in course of the parcel's route. Don't forget to write how much money it will cost for all you will send.

Marshall was dismayed. He had answered Pierre's first letter, but had he bothered to answer this second letter? He had been so eager to get on with his sun-kissed American life—new wife, baby, airline job—that he had neglected his French friends. He had never returned to Chauny. He didn't even know if he had sent the goods Pierre had requested. Yet how well he remembered Pierre and Gisèle! And their son, Nicolas.

Nicolas: "Gary Cooper!"

Marshall: "*Je ne suis pas* Gary Cooper!"

Nicolas: "*Tireur, tirez!*" Shooter, shoot!

The child's gestures had made Marshall homesick for western movies. With his revolver—something he should have ditched when he began his trek into hiding—Marshall had attempted a fast draw and a twirl, to sensational acclaim and pleas for repeats.

Nicolas: "Howdy, pard-ner."

Marshall remembered secret bustlings, hurried dinners, and nighttime tappings on the door. Pierre went out to fight a war, while Marshall glumly played cards and tried to read Maupassant in French.

"The neighbor says she saw you peek out beside the curtain this afternoon. That neighbor is good, but I don't know if all the neighbors are good. You can't trust. Stay away from the windows." Pierre's voice had been severe, Marshall remembered.

Le petit Albert. It dawned on him that news of Marshall's son signaled a great achievement for the Frenchman. Pierre had risked his life to help Marshall survive the war and start a family. Marshall's own son knew nothing about the source of his name—the Albert family, Pierre and Gisèle and Nicolas, who had been so important to Marshall for a few weeks long ago. He had given them his aunt's Cincinnati address, and they had written it in a ledger. He remembered that little book now. Pierre had squirreled it away behind a small cupboard that had loose slats.

Marshall lectured himself, *You weren't that ignorant and unfeeling. You knew enough to name your son Albert, and evidently to write at least one letter to a family who took care of you.*

He remembered Loretta saying, *You can name the boy, and I'll name the girl.* Marshall wondered now if he had chosen the girl's name, what would he have chosen? Gisèle?

If he went to Chauny again, he might find the house where he had hidden. Maybe it would be immediately familiar, like the field where the *Dirty Lily* had crashed. He could imagine Pierre and Gisèle still in their same house, their son living down the block.

Le petit Albert: the words shimmered.

Restless, he found some ice cream in the freezer and scraped the ice crystals off. It tasted old. In wartime France, ice cream was scarce, he remembered. No one had ice. The same word worked for both. *La glace.*

"In the war he couldn't get ice cream," he had heard Loretta explain to someone about his love for ice cream.

They used to have a hand-crank freezer, and when he first tried it, in his attempt to be efficient, he turned the crank as fast as he could and then let it rest a moment, then cranked it again at full gallop.

"That's not the way you're supposed to do it," Loretta said several times. He paid no attention. When the cream began leaking out, he learned that he had made whipped cream, which had swelled quickly.

"I tried to tell you," Loretta said, laughing. "But you always have to haul off and get the job done. Sometimes I think about offering you a hammer."

The twenty-three-year-old kid disguised in a Frenchman's peasant outfit invaded his mind again now, like a pop-up cartoon character. It was the fatuous youth he had seen when catching his reflection in windows.

That night, he dreamed he saw the girl in the blue beret strolling up the Champs-Elysées with a book satchel slung over her shoulder. When he awoke, the dream puzzled him, but then he remembered eating ice cream with her—a small cardboard container of black-market ice cream, smuggled in newspapers and straw.

What had happened to her? Did he have any chance of finding her and her family again? And Robert, who had brought the ice cream on his bicycle. He remembered Robert speaking in hushed tones with Marshall's host family in Paris. He teased some papers from his coat lining, and the husband and wife studied them for a long time, whispering exclamations. The woman crumpled the papers and tucked them in the stove. Marshall remembered Robert's bright young face, the meaningful laughter that punctuated what seemed to be a serious discussion. Marshall longed to go out with him, to be of help. Anything. He envied Robert, who went off on hazardous missions, while Marshall was fastened up like a fattening calf.

6

MARSHALL, WAITING FOR JUNE, LIVED ON TV DINNERS — A slab of meat loaf, mashed potatoes with a stagnant pool of dirt-brown gravy, peas, carrot cubelets, and a cubbyhole of apricot cobbler. Airline food, one of life's staples. He recalled the scarcity of food in France during the war, the way a family shared its meager rations. He remembered a large carrot, baked in ashes and sliced into five pieces, each piece enlivened with several dusky flakes of an herb.

Sometimes in the evening when he watched an old forties movie, he drank a beer, but his pilot's discipline still restrained him. Twelve hours from bottle to throttle. He didn't like to cloud his mind. His brain bag was gathering dust, and his uniform was drooping in the closet. He imagined it hanging there a hundred years in the future. Numbly, he stared at the global map on his wall, Paris gleaming like the North Star.

He still wore his wrist chronometer, set to Greenwich mean time. He was reviewing his French books.

He slept on the studio bed in his den, where he had escaped so many hours over the years—reading books, writing on a portable typewriter, studying French. The kids' bedrooms, down the corridor in line with the den, were like abandoned stores, still full of merchandise. Like someone studying for exams, Marshall spent his days and nights with the war—books, tapes, and the movies and documentaries on TV. One night he stayed up until two to watch *Twelve O'Clock High* again, and he couldn't sleep after the movie ended. It was set at an air base in England like Marshall's. When he closed his eyes, he was flying over the English countryside, low over the patchwork of fields and the white scar along the Channel. Winter-brown fields and hedgerows and clusters of trees enclosed the base, peacefully, as stoic as the English people. When the airmen traveled into Kettering, the quiet village seemed safe and snug until they saw the ration lines and the blank shelves of a grocery.

During a layover in London a few years before, Marshall had returned to the airfield at Molesworth. He took a train to Kettering, then a bus to Thrapston. The train was blue, more modern than the dusty green wartime coach that he recalled. He found the base deserted, with weeds growing through the tarmac, and he recognized the scene—Dean Jagger in *Twelve O'Clock High* returning to his old base and hearing the B-17s roar to life in his memory. So much in the world was predictable, a celluloid cliché, Marshall thought. Like Jagger, he could feel the throbbing of the B-17s, their bodies sexed up and loaded with their bombs. The crews had decorated the noses of their planes with alluring women, cartoon characters, snappy quips. *Dirty Lily* was scantily garbed in black, with raven hair and red puckered lips. She was their figurehead, their cheerleader, their whore and mama all in one. All the guys were ready to fly, bomb the Jerries, be heroes.

The old base was bare and neglected, surrounded by barbed wire, with warning signs. As he stood gazing through the fence, he could make out a distant cluster of trees next to several rows of Nissen huts that had formed the hospital. They appeared derelict. Beyond them, through the trees, he could see one of the stately homes of England, Lilford Hall, a seventeenth-century manor. He remembered how from the air its stonework, with ornate chimneys and split-level roofing, gleamed white, and the sheep in the surrounding fields seemed like connect-the-dots.

THE BASEMENT WAS STUFFED. Marshall burrowed deep into the closets, sniffing out ancient relics, and pulled out some boxes of letters. A postcard tumbled out. It was a *kriegie* card— *Kriegsgefangenenpost*, a POW postcard.

Dear Marshall, Well, it is not easy to find something to write about. Just wanted to tell you I haven't forgotten you. I am getting along alright. No news that I can tell. Hope to see you soon. Tell all the folks hello for me. Always, Tony

The card was dated March 2, 1944, only a month after they went down, but it had not been postmarked until March 24, 1945. Tony Campanello was the navigator. He and Al Grainger, the bombardier, and Bobby Redburn, the ball-turret gunner, had been captured by the Germans and were MIA for a year longer than Marshall was.

Loretta had saved all his letters in a box tied with a green velvet ribbon. Marshall thumbed through the early letters from the Texas air base where he trained, now and then losing himself in a description of the barracks or some practical joke the guys had pulled. In a separate packet he found the V-mail letters he had been looking for, letters he had written her from England, and he set those aside, intending to read them at the right time.

He found some addresses in Loretta's address book, and he began to write letters to the surviving crew about his trip to the crash site and about the boy's father who died helping one of their gunners. He asked about their own escapes after the crash. Don Stewart, the tail gunner, had died in a Cessna in 1959. Marshall didn't know how to reach Campanello, so he asked Grainger. "Since you bunked together in that German resort hotel, I figure you might still be in touch with each other," he wrote, then wondered if he was too flippant. Marshall looked again at the *kriegie* card from Campanello. He didn't get stateside till June 1945, and he remained in a hospital for many weeks. As far as Marshall could recall, none of the three POWs had ever talked much about life in the stalag.

7

Marshall thought the family who hid him in Paris was named Vallon, but in the Resistance, people often took false names. Robert was often there, bringing news and supplies. He bicycled out to Versailles one weekend and brought back a freshly killed goose hidden in a carpetbag. The farmer who sold him the fowl had declared it would be safer for him to carry a slaughtered bird, its honker silenced.

The apartment was alive with feathers, which Mme Vallon carefully saved for pillows. Marshall helped with the plucking. Since the rich smell of roasted goose would attract neighbors, maybe even suspicious German soldiers, Marshall had to be prepared to jump out the back window and to enter the neighboring apartment in case of a heavy knock on the door. The Vallons and their guests enjoyed their goose and their conversation, with a gaiety both genuine and frantic. Amidst the laughter and good will, they insisted that Marshall eat extra, heaping his plate. What was that guy's last name? Marshall remembered him so well. Robert was good at cards, had a high-pitched laugh but little English. Marshall remembered hearing his bicycle in the vestibule, the two-toot signal of his arrival.

The girl was called Annette. He remembered her laughing. She was standing by the window, half hidden by the lace curtain, with springy spools of brown hair dangling beside her cheeks. She said, "Don't look, but there are two German officers down there. Their uniforms are so silly! They look like ballerinas in those big pleated coats. Oh, I can't say this, it's too embarrassing, but they were walking where the neighbor's dog was walking and one of them—oh, his boots!" She laughed. "They deserve that!"

At the time he had felt faintly humiliated to be guided through Paris by a girl. Marshall, an American bomber pilot, Scourge of the Sky. But now what she had done for him struck him differently. She was only a young girl, but she had bravely battled the Nazis, to aid high-and-mighty, grounded, hapless Americans like him.

He didn't know if she was still alive.

8

THE FAMILY PICTURES ON THE WALLS DISTURBED HIM. HE WAS startled to see Loretta staring at him, or to see the young children smiling, frozen in time. On impulse, he began taking down the pictures.

At a loss for storage space, he decided to stack them in the master bedroom. He had avoided that room for months, but now he forced himself to peek in. The bed was made, and nothing was loose—books, shoes. He had forgotten that on the bedstand on her side of the bed, Loretta had kept a framed photo of him in uniform, taken the year he was promoted to captain. He turned the picture facedown, then noticed the photograph on the wall near the dresser, a publicity shot taken for the airline during the heyday of the Connie. There he was, the co-pilot, with the pilot and the flight engineer, followed by three stews in gray suits and pert little caps. They were crossing the tarmac, and the magnificent Lockheed Constellation was shining in the background. They were a team, the essence of aviation's glamour. That was what they were selling, and he had been proud to be in the picture.

On the dresser was an earlier photograph: Marshall in his Air Corps uniform and Loretta in a snazzy broad-shouldered suit and an upswept hairdo. She was clutching a purse, and her toes peeked out of sassy pumps. He was her handsome hero; she was his glamour girl, his Loretta Young, his young Loretta.

ALBERT CALLED, TOUCHING BASE about the house. June was approaching.

"Have you figured out how long you'll be gone?" he asked.

"No idea. I'm just going to go with the flow—isn't that what you're always saying?"

Albert was quiet. Then, in a disturbed tone, he said, "Well, I guess you know what you're doing." He paused again. "Is there something special waiting for you there?"

"I don't know what you mean."

"You might as well tell me, do I have any other brothers or sisters?"

"What in the world? Good grief." Marshall's anger flashed through his normally rigid reserve.

"It's O.K. if you do," said Albert. "I don't mind."

Marshall, uncomfortable, stifled the impulse to hang up. He had always avoided contention by leaving.

Dear Albert,
I know we've had our differences. I know I wasn't always around.
That was my job—to go away. I don't know what to do about it. I'm
sorry your mom had to shoulder most of the burden of raising you.
The schedule was brutal, but I wasn't living a double life. I was
flying. Now I can't fly. So I'm going to try something else.
Love, Dad

He thought this letter but didn't write it.

An unspoken dab of doggerel, a message to Albert, kept going around in his head:

You owe your existence
To the French Resistance.

Le petit Albert. That phrase shot through his mind from time to time, but he couldn't explain it to his son.

MARY WAS PLEASED that Albert would look after the house. On the telephone, Marshall assured her that her mother's things would remain undisturbed and that she could have whatever she wanted.

"Where are you going to stay over there?" Mary asked.

"I'll stay in a hotel until I can find a place. I'll let you know."

Mary was silent. He heard her sigh then. "When are you going?"

"You know me. My bag is always packed."

She was silent again, but then she said, in a small voice, a child's, "When will I see you again, Dad?"

THE ODD-JOB GUYS had been working on the house—caulking, repairing windows and the roof. As Marshall mowed the yard with the gas-powered push mower, he realized that Loretta's rosebushes and all the shrubs and flowers needed attention. He didn't expect Albert to care any more about the yard than Marshall ever had.

The Garden Angels descended upon the place one day, working fast and chattering over loud music on a portable radio.

"It looks good," he told them at the end of an hour.

He arranged for them to come every week and keep the yard in shape.

"I'm the man," said the chief Angel, a young bronzed guy in a sun hat with a sort of halo wobbling on a spring.

When Marshall picked up his dry cleaning, Mr. Santelli said, "How's the wife? I don't see her anymore."

Marshall said, "Oh, she's getting along."

Farewell.

The gas station. The insolent pump jockey in a T-shirt worn outside his jeans, no belt. Kids in France didn't dress so disrespectfully, Marshall thought. Probably not, anyway.

AS HE WAS reorganizing his file folders from the war, his eyes fell on two photos of the Albert family. He remembered now that the Alberts had sent these pictures. They had been placed in the wrong folder. Here they were: Pierre and Gisèle, a romantic portrait of them, posed lovingly. It wasn't a wedding picture. They were older, but still in love.

The other photo was a snapshot of the young boy, Nicolas, in long stockings and short pants that ballooned at the knee. He and two other children posed with a goat tied to a cart. Marshall studied the shaggy yard—a tangle of vines, the outbuildings, the fence, long tufts of grass that hid the children's shoes. He had spent hours in that yard, mostly after sunset. He would recognize the place instantly.

9

THE NIGHT BEFORE HE LEFT FOR PARIS, MARSHALL DREAMED he couldn't pass a check ride. He made goof after goof. He stupidly called out that the reciprocal for due east was 230 degrees. He woke up, kicking off the covers.

Dreams like this were common for many pilots. Marshall would dream he was being tested for his pilot's license, or his captain's certification, and everything would go wrong. Numbers etched on his brain did cartwheels. As he lay in bed, he thought about Neil Armstrong, who had commanded the first orbital docking mission. His Gemini capsule had spun out of control. He and his crewmate were spinning so fast they were about to black out, but Armstrong figured out that a thruster must have stuck and made an instant, intuitive move that stopped the spinning. He had to make an unscheduled splashdown in the Pacific, but he prevented a catastrophe and became a national hero.

Looking at himself in the bathroom mirror, Marshall wondered what his own first words on the moon might have been.

"Sorry, folks. I hate to say this but the moon is plug-ugly! We spent twenty billion dollars to come here?

"And where are the moon pies?"

He showered, shaved, ate a bowl of Total, and drank the last of the orange juice. He knocked off the *Times* crossword in fifteen minutes. Then he washed his bowl and tried to think of what he had forgotten. He had half a day to kill. He repacked his two large bags to make room for his portable typewriter, and he stuffed his brain bag with his French books and some of the letters and photos from the war. Reciprocals kept going through his mind.

—

MARSHALL, ALWAYS DIGNIFIED on an aircraft, wore dress pants, a blue blazer with brass buttons, and a dark tie. He was seated in row 21, next to two overweight tourists in blue-jeans. It annoyed him to see passengers in jeans. As a pilot, he might have deadheaded in the cockpit jump seat, but now, flying standby, he sat in coach—an aisle seat without even a view of the horizon. He told himself he didn't need a window. He had crossed the Atlantic so many times, he knew all the coastlines intimately. He sometimes imagined he knew the shapes and textures of particular places in the ocean, the angles of sunlight and shadows on hidden deeps.

When he first joined the airline, the journey to Paris took twenty hours on a Connie, with stops in Newfoundland and Iceland. The pilots slept in shifts, in bunks behind the cockpit. On a 747, the flight was about seven hours. A 747 captain could fly high above the weather on elegant, precise great circle routes. But a Connie flew at fifteen or twenty thousand feet, right in the weather. Marshall would take a Connie between clouds, around them, or sometimes above. He felt that he could maneuver the sky itself to keep the flight smooth. In one of his recurrent flying dreams, he was sitting in an easy chair atop a gleaming metal wing, steering the wing through the sky by thought control. *Bank right.* The huge wing dipped right, just as he wanted. *Straighten. Climb. Accelerate.* The magic machine obeyed precisely. He was alone in the sky, master of flight.

The sun was low when the plane was pushed back from the gate and began its crawl to the taxi lane. He couldn't see the wing flaps from his seat, but he heard them coming down. Whenever Marshall had deadheaded, he was an alert back-seat driver. He could hear each sound the plane made. He could always hear mistakes.

Captain Vogel's takeoff today wasn't bad. Marshall loved the speed, the rush, the power of a takeoff even when he wasn't in charge. He loved racing down the runway. His mind went through all the moves—easing back the yoke, feeling the wings lifting. You were the plane, the bird. You were soaring, rising, guiding, turning. Breathless. A plane wanted to fly; takeoffs were its natural bent. You trusted yourself to the machine. You *were* the machine. You maneuvered so smoothly that the passengers would think they were sitting in their living rooms. Now, as a passenger, Marshall could hear every note of the ascent. He could feel the engines spool. He could guess the cruising altitude when they reached it. Thirty-six thousand feet, he thought. The heading was about forty-seven degrees east.

The passengers began to squirm after the plane leveled out and the seat-belt sign went off. A woman across from him asked for a blanket.

"Would you like something to drink, sir?" A flight attendant with bulky arms and blowzy hair trundled her cart just past his row and braked it.

"A ginger ale, thanks."

She scooped the ice with a plastic cup, her fingers touching the ice. The other stew had wrinkles. The airline business was going to hell, he thought. He had to admit their job was hard. Only the stews, on their feet, up and down the aisle, would feel the strain of the 747's peculiar three-degree nose tilt.

The flight was smooth enough. Airliners had to be flown without flair. In the B-17 sometimes you were bouncing like a child on a rocking horse. The yoke would be vibrating like a jackhammer, and you held on, on a wild ride, better than anything a carnival ever offered.

The man next to him tried to talk about the Mets, but Marshall immersed himself in the packet of V-mail he had written to Loretta from Molesworth Airfield in England.

10

THE LETTERS WERE PHOTOSTATS OF MICROFILMED V-MAIL—
a compact stack of five-by-seven pages of miniaturized handwriting.
His eyes lit on random passages as he flipped through the stiff little
pages, all written between November 1943 and the end of January
1944.

Dearest Loretta,
Last night I stumbled through the blackout to a small town nearby.
Was almost killed by derby-hatted Englishmen tearing along in the
dark on bicycles with no lights! At a pub I had a glass of English
beer—which cost me two bob, six pence, along with some kind of
meat pie.

*

Hello, sweetheart,
Today is typically an English day—in other words, it's raining
lightly, and it's damp and cold. Our barracks are made of brick and
stone, as are nearly all structures in the Isles, due to the scarcity of
wood. There are four of us to a room, and we have double-decked
beds. There are two lockers and two small "chester drawers," as my
mother used to say. We eat in a mess hall similar to the one in the
States. However, we use our mess kits and canteen cups to hold the
food and coffee, and fall in a wash-up line at the end of each meal.
At the Officers' Club here we may buy English ale between 6 and
10 in the evening and see a free picture show. Yesterday I went over
but was unable to get a seat.

*

Today was wet and cloudy, and there is no moon whatever tonight.
On our way to the mess hall in the blackout we manage not to bump
into each other by rattling our mess kits.

*

Our room has a coal stove with a terrific capacity for fuel, and it
keeps a guy busy throwing coal into it. I think the hardest thing I'll
ever have to do in the line of duty is getting out of bed in the
shivering morning to build a fire in the little monstrosity! Luckily I
have my long-handled G.I. drawers. Yesterday, I very ingeniously
bored a hole in His Majesty's floor and installed a piece of pipe on our
wash-stand, so that now, instead of having to go outside both to get
and dispose of our water, we merely go out to get it. Also built a
wooden contraption which I'm using as a clothes-line and wardrobe,
but which I'm going to use to hang myself from if I don't get a letter
from you soon!
    Love you to death, baby!

He could have been writing from Boy Scout camp, he thought.
Such schoolbook phrasings! Of course he couldn't tell her much
under the censorship rules. And he didn't want to tell some things.
The dull smack of enemy shells hitting the plane. The noise up there
in the sky when the guns opened up. The giant yellow and orange
and red flowers bursting open far below—the beautiful blasts of the
bombs his plane dropped.

Dearest Loretta,
Hootie, Tony and I hopped the bus into a town in this vicinity last
night, and after shaking, bouncing and shivering for an hour (the
"bus" is a plain old G.I. truck), the driver stopped and said, "Here
we are, men—the 'Target for Tonight.'" Believe me, it was a matter

of taking his word for it! It was strange to walk through the fairly crowded streets of this town, hearing voices but seeing only vague forms and shadowy outlines of buildings.

We found the Red Cross and had a cup of coffee and asked about the nightlife of the metropolis—said nightlife consisted of a skating rink, two cinemas, and a few pubs. We chose the best-recommended pub, got directions, and found it, with a few sneaky blinks of my "torch," as a flashlight is called here, and divine intuition. It was a barn-like pavilion with a bar and dance floor and a band. The band, let me tell you, wouldn't worry Harry James very much! During the evening they played "Missouri Waltz" and "Pennies from Heaven"—highly corned-up versions, too.

The high point of the evening was a raffle. When the fellow came around selling the tickets, due to my uncanny ability to get mixed up on the English language and monetary system, I gave him two half crowns, thinking that would buy two tickets. Instead of two, he gave me thirty-six (!) tickets, so of course I won the damned prize, which was a bottle of Scotch whiskey! That sure beat the pub's weak beer.

We had to leave at ten o'clock to catch the truck back "home," and we made it just in time. We had one of those famous fogs last night, and that plus the blackout really obscured the streets and houses. It was a very cold ride, and did it feel good to be warm again!

*

Honey, I've been a seamstress tonight, patching rips in the blackout curtains. Say! Let's not have black drapes in our dream house, baby. Let's show we have nothing to hide.

*

Tonight coming back from the mess hall I learned that war is dangerous! I was absent-mindedly walking on what is the "wrong" side of the road here, and was knocked ears over appetite by a

blacked-out bus—it was only a glancing blow and merely injured my
"dignity," but it surely messed up my only clean pants!

Hootie is standing in the door, letting all our nice cold air out,
and letting that nasty old warm air in from outside. I'm thinking of
spreading a little water on our floor and using it for a skating rink
in the morning.

Marshall recalled with some fondness those dark, breakneck,
nighttime forays and the foolhardy bike races to the mess hall in the
early-morning blackness. After a while he had developed a sixth
sense about walking in the dark. He tried to act like a keen animal.
He learned to relax his pupils to take in more light. He grew sensitive to the nuances of darkness, how the eye could be trained to interpret shapes in the dark. In deep darkness, he learned to move with
his arms out ahead. In good moonlight, the landscape was en-
chanted. And if there were drifts of mist about, sometimes passing
across the moon like advertisements trailing behind a small plane, he
might feel he had entered another world. The flimsy, scattered mists
were pleasant, but the thick fogs smothered and enclosed the base
with tooth-chilling cold. The fogs glowed with light borrowed from
the moon, a light so dim the eyes could not penetrate it.

Darling, I've said it before, honey, but—once more—please don't
worry a lot about my work here. I was optimistic enough, I think,
about this business before I came in closer contact with it, but the
outlook at closer quarters is even more reassuring. Plain statistics are
very comforting, and when you add to them my undeniably
outstanding ability as a Hot Pilot (?!) the future looks absolutely
rosy! The only thing I'm afraid of is that the thing will get to be such
a snap that the Big Operators will boost the score from 25 innings to
a hundred!

Of course, I plan to personally throttle Adolf Hitler if I get a
chance. Aside from the heavy humor, I AM very much impressed by

the record and achievements of this outfit, and I know damned well
that I'm fortunate to be with it. They're a great bunch of lads.

Twenty-five missions was the goal. And his score turned out to be
only ten. Plain statistics were shit, he thought as he flipped through
the pages. Sixty Forts hadn't returned from a raid to Schweinfurt
one bleak October day, a few weeks before Marshall arrived at
Molesworth.

Bob Hadley came in from a mission the other day and had a fever
and a bad cold. He reported to the Dispensary and was sent up to the
General Hospital. The rest of us here in our pneumonia hole are in
pretty good shape—with this eternally damp weather. It seems nearly
impossible not to have a constant case of the sniffles.

It was hard to write her after he came in from a long, tense flight,
weak-headed from breathing straight O$_2$ for hours, his body taut
from leaning in to the throbbing yoke of the plane. The fatigue
could not be cured by a two-day respite. Hadley had been hospital-
ized with a touch of anoxia, oxygen deprivation. Alone, Marshall bicycled through the English countryside, the domestic patchwork of
fields only here and there revealing the wartime crisis with the barracks and control tower of an air base. He remembered discovering
the remains of an old Roman road, then finding it on his map. He
had written about it to Loretta in one of the V-mail letters, and he
saw now where that detail had been censored out in heavy black ink.
The blackout was pervasive, like the fog. Sometimes he was a worse
censor than the official censors.

He did not say that the English girls were so desperate for sex
that they would have braved machine-gun fire to get to the GIs.

Thought I'd forgotten your birthday, didn't you? Well, I didn't, so
Happy Birthday, Darling! Wish I were there with you. I'd spank

you on one end and kiss you on the other! You know, honey,
sometimes I have the feeling that in one or two minor details I just
might be falling short of the perfect man for you. One of those minor
details is that even when I'm 80 years old and beginning to lose the
bloom of youth, I'll undoubtedly still get caught short on Christmases
and your birthdays. So will you please forgive me for not giving you
something for your birthday this year and get your present for you
for me? (Should that be "for me for you"?) Preferably some of them
swell black things with the black trimmings. When you put 'em on,
think of me, and I'll think of you putting 'em on.

   And on your next birthday I will attend to all that there stuff
myself.

Marshall was stunned. He didn't recall writing such lovey-dovey
letters. When he looked back, it was mostly aviation stuff he thought
about.

But he remembered the English girls.

"These girls are wild!" said Al Grainger. Grainger had been cor-
nered by a big-boned cutie at the dance the weekend before Christmas, when busloads of English girls arrived. Marshall quickly
selected the first pretty girl he saw and zoomed across the room
toward her, with his wing flaps down. She saw him coming and
opened her arms. It was as if they were long-lost lovers reuniting on
a railway platform. She was Millie, with a brother in the RAF, and
between dances, they chatted about bombers. Then the phantom of
Millie's sweetheart off in the infantry on the continent of Africa
came between them, and he saw that she wished he were her
Christopher and not a lanky Yank. If it had not been for such
thoughts, Marshall and Millie might have had a spontaneous cou-
pling right there on the dance floor, while the band was playing
"Frenesi." It astonished him that anyone would attempt to imitate
Artie Shaw on the clarinet. Some of the girls jitterbugged to "Frenesi" in a frenzy, whirling their skirts with abandon, burning off the
gin they gulped between dances, trying to forget their faraway

sweethearts. Marshall and Millie danced to the end of a slow song, bodies pressed tightly together, and he said, "Thank you. He'll come back. Trust me." They parted, and a bit later he thought perhaps she would interpret his words as Yankee arrogance—now that Uncle Sam's flyboys were there to win the war for the English, she could be sure her boy lover would return.

Ma chèrie,
J'ai une femme et cinq fils!
    How am I doing, honey, with my French lessons? My college French is coming back to me. I've got a couple of pamphlets that I'm going to spend some of my spare time on, hoping, of course, that my linguistic accomplishments will be merely cultural and not of practical value.

*

Hello, honey,
I just got back from the show here on the base. It was "Palm Beach Story," with C. Colbert and J. McCrea. I thought it was pretty good, although a bit risqué for these ingenuous blue eyes of mine! This makes two nights in a row that I've patronized the post flickers.

*

I took some swell pictures today, baby, and I hope to be able to send you some prints. Just got off work a little while ago and I am dog-tired, plum worn out and exhausted. I'm going to make a quick trip to the mess hall and come back and climb into bed, and I hope no one wakes me until noon tomorrow.

He took his old camera on one of the missions. He remembered patching a couple of pinholes in the bellows and polishing the lens. He wanted to get some action shots, but there wasn't much action that day. He snapped Webb at the controls, then Webb snapped him, cigarette dangling from his lips, his helmet flaps loose. Out the window other planes in the formation were visible, like blackbirds. He didn't know what happened to that picture.

Hootie got 137 shillings out of a slot machine in the Club tonight. That's about 29 bucks. Hootie has all the luck.

*

I made my debut as an extra in the motion picture business today. There's a training film being shot here called "Target—Berlin," and a bunch of us walked up and down (self-consciously) in front of the camera. Supposed to be crews going from briefing to the planes. I have to be up early tomorrow, so I may have a busy day.

Marshall pored through the letters, trying to adjust his memories to the evidence. What a sentimental stripling he had been! What a stone-face he became later on. It surprised him to encounter that younger guy, cooking up sweet talk. After he and Loretta were wed and settled, maybe he thought he didn't have to compose endearments anymore. He wondered if it had seemed no longer necessary then to try to go deeper in his heart. At Molesworth and during flight training, he was sociable enough and loved high jinks, but after the war, he tended to stand apart. He always told himself that the sobering responsibility of flying for the airline and raising a family required a certain discipline.

He thought again of Neil Armstrong. From what Marshall had read, Armstrong seemed to be the ultimate pilot. When the lunar lander's computers failed, and it was running low on fuel, and the landing zone was unexpectedly full of huge boulders, Armstrong calmly maneuvered over the rocks to a safe spot. Armstrong's attitude was *Give me the job and I'll do it. O.K., I did it. I landed on the moon. Here's your moon rocks. Now leave me alone.* Marshall liked that.

—

HE THUMBED THROUGH the letters, recalling the pleasure of receiving word from Loretta, her chatter sustaining him from day to day. Her picture, propped on an upended fruit crate in his room, was like a poster of a movie star selling war bonds. Before each mission he tried to memorize one feature—her temples, a downy shadow on her cheek, her bangs, or her rolled-under hair, the top upswept and fastened with a barrette. Her upper lip had a slight kink on the left, like a deliberate sign of flirtation, but he knew it to be a scar, just a nick from flying glass, a broken glass on a kitchen floor when she was a girl. He had had to reassure her many times about the scar. It didn't detract from her looks. It gave her character.

In that cold, shoddy room in England, it was hard to look at her photograph, to be reminded of the sweet softness waiting for him stateside. It distracted him from the urgency of his job, fighting the damned war.

His mind ricocheted between the movielike quality of the life he had reported in the letters and the life he remembered. Each time he read about an early rising the next day, he knew exactly which mission it was. An early rising meant staggering out in the predawn chill to the mess hall for the special mission-day breakfast with genuine eggs. Then came the briefings, followed by the jeep rides to the check stations. Memorizing maps. You never knew for sure that you were going on a mission until the runner tapped on your door and said simply, "It's 0400 hours, breakfast at 0500." But sometimes you had an inkling the day before that you were "going out amongst them," as the saying went.

The weather was so bad on his first mission, in December, that they had to land through the clouds and rain by the aid of magnesium flares on the ground. On that mission, his adrenaline shot up like nothing he had known before. Each mission had the same effect, more or less. On his third mission two planes were lost, and he remembered the feeling of emptiness when the stragglers didn't appear by tea time. He hung around the runways with the other crews, scanning the sky. At mess, a frantic cheerfulness hid the dread. The winter darkness closed in on the empty, silent sky.

The planes that didn't return became abstractions. Guys he knew had simply disappeared, and he didn't think about them again. Pilots sat far removed from consequences, anyway. Bombs didn't really miss their targets and kill children at a skating rink, or dismember mothers in a park. You didn't see bodies flying apart or hear the shrieks. You flew along, dropped your load, and flew away.

THE ENGINES OF THE 747 were droning comfortingly in the night, as the passengers settled down to watch the movie. The captain made a brief visit seatside for obligatory pleasantries. "Glad to have you on board, old-timer." The B-17 could have almost fit inside this luxury bus, Marshall thought. The bomber's waist windows were open, and the fuselage rattled and shook. Riding through the formation's churned-up air was like jouncing along a creek bed in a rattletrap Model A Ford. Cruising speed was about two hundred miles an hour, and it was a long way from England to the heart of Germany.

Marshall flipped through the V-mail again. What a youngster he had been. He saw that at each stage of life a person reassessed the earlier stages, and a new perspective, almost a new identity, took form, as if the shifting views of the past were museum dioramas before him. He felt the power of ignorance, the drive of youth. Only oversexed young men could have fought that war. He was feeling nostalgia for a terrible time, and he didn't know what this meant. He had gone to war with a willing heart. What did he want now?

At Molesworth, he truly felt he was the hotshot pilot Loretta believed in. He *knew* the Messerschmitts and Focke-Wulfs wouldn't get him. Other guys—immediately nameless and faceless—got shot down, but he wouldn't. He believed this. He had to believe it, or he couldn't have flown the next mission.

After a mission, the Doughnut Dollies appeared, American girls in their Red Cross Club-mobile, their dull-green bus that paid its good-will visits to the flak-weary bomber crews. The girls' hair was breathtakingly seductive, and with their cheerleader voices and plush warmth they were as alluring as any of the stars in the movies he saw at the Officers' Club. All the crews ran for the hot coffee, the doughnuts—their reward, lovely girls offering their wares.

One evening he was at a rooming house in Kettering with one of the American girls. "The Red Cross girls aren't supposed to step out like this," she said, giggling.

"What your mama doesn't know won't hurt her," he said.

The girl, nameless in his memory, wore something lacy beneath her skirt. She cuddled with him for a long while before they went ahead. She said, "It's good; it doesn't matter. It's all right, baby."

"Hold me close."

"Sure, baby."

He wanted her warmth. He wanted to be enclosed, blanketed with her soft flesh.

"This is stupid to say," he said, "but you're soft like those dough-nuts you bring. And sweet too."

She only giggled and didn't mind. She smoothed and admired his shoulders; she deposited little breathy kisses all over his stomach. She sat up, hands on her hips, and said, "Let me be the girl on your bomber nose. You do have a girl on your plane nose, don't you? You all do."

He laughed, but he wouldn't utter the name *Dirty Lily*. She didn't pry.

When it was time to leave, she pulled on her stockings carefully, snapping them to the belts, straightening the seams, checking her look in the mirror. He thought he would not see her again. He was going to bomb Hitler to hell, and she was giving him energy for the job, obtained without regret or guilt or pain.

She said, "Come to the Rainbow Corner whenever you get your

pass to London. Ask for me. There's always something going on there. And so much dancing! Some of these guys can dance all night. Ask for Miss—"

After a mission to Bremen, he went to the Rainbow Corner, the Red Cross canteen, but he did not see her anywhere in the crowded room. He asked for her, but she wasn't on duty. He gathered with the crowd around the radio for the news—nothing good. The news from the Pacific was abstract. The news from the Italian front was mostly about the ground war. It did not seem real either. He smoked a Woodbine cigarette with a girl named Julie. He had a Coca-Cola and a sandwich, talked to several Red Cross girls, then walked around London. The crowds were trundling along, busy and quiet. Umbrellas popped out a couple of times, but he strode on in the cold mist, past Saint Paul's, Big Ben, the Parliament. Here and there he saw the unmistakable damage from the Blitz, and he wondered who might have been standing there as the Luftwaffe swung over, raining explosives. Seeing the destruction, he felt no qualms about bombing the bejesus out of Germany. As he ambled through St. James's Park, near 10 Downing Street, he saw that the streets around Buckingham Palace were blocked, and he detoured over into Regent's Park. Later, at a small tearoom, he noticed the pasty faces of the malnourished and sleep-deprived, hunched over their tea and biscuits. He felt disembodied, juggling several realities at once. He was an American pilot, among friends, allies; he was a stranger, yet a friend, with an overlapping history. He noticed admiring glances. But RAF pilots were jealous of the American flyers. One called out to him, "Hey, Yank!" Out in the slow traffic, the tall red buses seemed comical. He passed girls bundled in tired tweed, their hats worn close, their stockings thick and wrinkled. It was a cold day, one that made him wish for his soft fleece-lined bomber helmet, but he knew he appeared snappy in his Air Corps uniform, with his lieutenant bars, his smartly creased trousers, his shined winter shoes, his overcoat slung over his arm.

He was self-aware, charged with purpose. That's how he remembered his younger self, anyway. He was in the midst of the greatest undertaking in human history. He was in the middle of either the greatest victory or the greatest catastrophe ever known. Or both.

NOW, ON A JUMBO JET to Paris, he wasn't sure he remembered his youthful self any better than he remembered the Doughnut Dolly.

Albert had denigrated Marshall's war. He said America was imperialistic, that Truman shouldn't have dropped the atomic bomb. On one occasion, Albert casually remarked, "Everyone knows the U.S. is the worst country on earth. I'm thinking of going to live in some foreign country where everything is real. Someplace in South America. Or India." Marshall recalled staring with amazement at his son, who was on spring break from college.

On that January day in 1944, when Marshall walked through St. James's Park, the war was raging. The skies over Germany were filled with death. But in a way, Marshall and his buddies went to war as cavalierly as Albert entertained moving to Nepal.

A scene arose in his memory. Years ago, when Albert and Mary were children, they were roller-skating up and down the sidewalk in front of their house in New Jersey. Rain began falling, and Marshall rushed out to close the windows of his car.

"You'll get wet, kids," he said, but they didn't seem to mind the rain.

They rolled on down the sidewalk as though he were invisible and they were protected from him.

MARSHALL WAS NO LONGER sure whether he had first been untrue to Loretta before Christmas that winter at Molesworth or after. He recalled an evening in Brington, on a pass after a mission to Kiel. He found himself in a room above a pub with an English girl, who didn't volunteer her name, and he finally asked. Madge. It was an icy night, with icicles glinting in the fog. She had a brown paper parcel tied with string, something for "me mum," she said. Under the dim light of a blackout bulb, they undressed each other clumsily. The poor illumination made her more attractive than she probably was.

After January 11, the mission to Oschersleben, it no longer seemed to matter if he was untrue to Loretta. But he hadn't even flown that day. Marshall and his crew did not go out because the *Dirty Lily* had a fuel-line problem. They watched forty-one B-17s depart, and for the rest of the day they sweated out the mission with the ground crew.

By tea time everyone's nerves were on edge.

As the first returning planes began to roll in, the jitters only intensified.

"What's the count?"

"Twenty-seven, I think."

They watched and listened, long past tea time, but no other planes came. Four planes had aborted early. Ten planes were missing.

Marshall imagined the lord of Lilford Manor having his tea, whether or not the planes returned. He shared his fancy house with a flock of nurses. Marshall had been to the place for a nurses' dance. Long-legged Nurse Begley—where was she now?

At mess, they heard a familiar rumbling, then the siren of the ambulance. They rushed out, mouths still full, to see who was coming home. It was not one of theirs but a Fortress from another base, a straggler that couldn't go any farther.

"At least somebody made it," Marshall said when they returned to their quarters. "Whoever the hell they are."

One of his roommates, Al Grainger, threw his boots at the wall and said, "If I get back to the States alive, I'm going to fuck the first fifty girls I see, including the Statue of Liberty."

"Is she carrying a torch for you?"

"I think so. I've lost my torch."

"It's under your bunk."

Grainger rummaged beneath the bed and retrieved his flashlight.

But all light was forbidden outside at night. He dropped the light on his bed, and they headed to the Officers' Club to get drunk.

"Where the hell is Oschersleben anyway?" asked Grainger.

That night Marshall wrote to Loretta, *Same old same old today. Trying to do my job. I'm starting to like English tea. I polished my shoes; etc., etc. Miss you badly, honey. Lights out now.*

"HIT ME," MARSHALL SAID to the dealer. The *snap-snap* of cards distracted him from the roar in his ears left over from his pleasure jaunt over Bremen the previous day. He had been in the lead plane of his squadron, and he felt cocky. The losses on January 11 had made him angry, and he suspected that Webb was scared. Webb sat at the yoke mostly in silence, and he seemed unnerved when they neared the target. When he handed off control to the bombardier, he pressed his trembling hands on his knees. The landscape below was a dusty white, patches of snow below.

Hootie couldn't stop talking about a pilot named Gorman, who hadn't come back from Oschersleben. Hootie, furtively regarding his cards, said, "What do you think—he could have escaped and gone over to someplace safe, some nice island with a white beach, nice sand. Good landing strip, long flat beach. He could be there, with women in little swimming-suits made out of feathers, and they could be gobbling coconuts and oranges."

"Ambrosia," said Marshall. They looked at him. "Coconuts and oranges. My mother made it. It had bananas in it too." He was recalling a dish so special, so rare, that it was like a taste of paradise. Ambrosia. Only at Christmas.

"Yeah, bananas. A banana tree right there. Gorman would pick a banana and peel it back and put it in her mouth just so—" Hootie was demonstrating, but the laughter around him was hollow.

"Knock it off, Hootie." He was a goofball, always going off on a mental tangent.

"You'll get grounded, you keep rattling your mouth like that," said a radio operator, a glum guy who never cracked a smile.

"Who's in?" asked the dealer.

Guys like Gorman left and didn't come back. They disappeared. A magic act—*poof*. There one day, gone the next. No one saw or heard what had happened. *Poof*.

Marshall studied Loretta's portrait, the flat, two-dimensional inanimate thing made of light and shadow, and wondered how he could possibly hold it dear. It wasn't her. He should save her for later. If he succumbed too deeply now, he could be spiraling toward a tropical beach, with Gorman. He needed the sharp edges of his mind. He turned her facedown, like a playing card, on the rough wood of the fruit crate.

That weekend everyone was drunk. A load of WAAFs was trucked in for the officers' dance at the manor. They were auxiliary for the RAF, working with the crews on one of the nearby bases. Those women drove trucks, worked the radio, manned the check-in stations.

"We do everything but drive the plane," one told him. "But we steal flips—when a pilot's going up at night for a little ride and wants to take somebody along. I always go. It's grand."

"She's got a stomach of iron, that one," said a frowsy brown-haired girl. "I'm glad I've got my two feet planted."

Marshall danced with a tall gal called Sal, who was wearing her mother's old rabbit wrap, with her hair slung up in a truck driver's regulation pompadour. The American nurses danced in their jazzy uniforms. They had changed out of their bloodstained brown-striped seersucker nursing dresses.

MARSHALL HAD BEEN scheduled to fly on January 29, but the fog pushed down on the planes as if it were a heavy weight, grounding them. It didn't lift until nearly noon. The mission was delayed for two days.

The morning of the thirty-first was clear, but the courier running from the weather station reported clouds toward Frankfurt by afternoon. In truth, you couldn't think logically that far ahead. Marshall was eager to go. His mental wings were flapping like a migrating goose.

The commander was Hornsby, a short, no-nonsense man with bulging eyes like a pug dog. Marshall had observed him coming out of the Officers' Club late one night, pulling on his leather gloves as if he had a job to do that instant. He was walking with deliberation, almost scurrying, as if he couldn't keep up with himself, as if his thoughts were racing ahead, his plans and schemes already airborne. He was a man who could envision and execute a swarming.

For a swarming was what it was, when thirty or forty planes took off from Molesworth, one by one, and then circled and began to swirl into formation. Soon the crews could see other swirls around them, as other formations from other bases in England began to join in. Squadrons joined squadrons, becoming sixty-ship combat wings. Before long, there were nearly a thousand planes, from all the air bases in England, the Mighty Eighth Air Force of heavy bombers with their loads. It was intense, impossible to exaggerate, enormous. And later, when their fighter escorts arrived, hovering above, it was a truly colossal force.

It was a sight the world would never see again, Marshall thought, those redoubtable goose-flock Vs hell-bent toward their target. Hundreds and hundreds of aircraft, *clouds* of them. The flyboys rode through the tangled currents of slipstreams for as long as eight hours, their adrenaline levels shooting sharp. The shudder and shake of the yoke—the little boy on his rocking horse, the high-hearted man mounting the anonymous woman.

The men on the plane that day: Cochran, Campanello, Ford, Grainger, Hadley, Redburn, Stewart. Stone. Lawrence Webb. Hootie Williams.

Hootie! The name still ripped his guts.

———

WHEN HE RETURNED from the war and saw Loretta again, she expected him to propose to her in an old-fashioned way. He had arrived in Cincinnati on a troop train from Philadelphia, and she had taken the bus to Union Station. The grand dome of the station was so immense he felt like a toy soldier beneath it.

"You're the handsomest thing I ever saw in my life," she cried. "Sweetheart, you're all mine!"

Her warmth flowed through him, promising to erase the recent past. He felt it slipping away, like a spiral movement in his mind.

Her flirtatious manner seemed exaggerated, the bow on her hat whimsical, her giggle girlish. It was jarring, seeing this innocent, naïve girl. He was overwhelmed with joy to be with her, on U.S. soil again. The last months were fading into a dark dream. Yet she was a stranger, like somebody's kid sister, altogether too silly and carefree to take seriously. He had not seen a woman behave this way in months. This girl Loretta might have been going to taffy pulls.

At the nearest soda fountain, crowded with GIs and their families and sweethearts, they had Cokes and he ate a genuine hamburger. The sumptuousness of the hamburger, paired with its sweet carbonated companion, sent him into a reverie. Here was this girl showering him with devotion. She was swinging from side to side on the spinning stool next to his. Her dress was white, with red polka dots, and the skirt flounced at the hem. She crossed her legs and deliberately showed her knees. She wasn't petite like the French girls, he thought. He held her waist and stopped her singsong swinging. She sucked the straw of her Coke, leaving lipstick. He had kissed off all her lipstick, but she had reapplied it. It was bright red, for the polka dots of her dress.

FROM CINCINNATI, HE MADE an obligatory visit to his relatives down in the mountains. The bus ride to Harlan was a strange, grim little trip. He found an uncle dying of lung disease and his wife unable to grow her garden because she no longer had the breath to climb the hill behind their dog-trot house. Marshall hated this place where the coal mines had destroyed his parents and grandparents. He had never wanted to go back there.

If they had been worried about him during the war, no one said. They all said Marshall looked older. They wouldn't have recognized him. No one wanted to hear about the war. His Uncle Jimmy refused to believe that Marshall had been a bomber pilot. His cousin Herman tried to get him to come back and work in the mines. One of his aunts accused him of gallivanting and pleasuring himself while his kinfolks needed him. His Aunt June Bug insisted on living alone after her stroke. His cousin Dan had moved to Richmond and was working at an ammunitions depot—doing what, no one could say exactly.

Marshall knew he had been an oddball in that family for years because his parents had moved north to Ohio. After they died, he had lived with Aunt Shelby in Cincinnati and learned proper English in school. He would never have tolerated being teased the way some of the backwoods boys in the Army were. Marshall never apologized for seeking an education. He went to college for a couple of years before the war. What he wanted in Loretta was everything he didn't find in his relatives. She listened to the Metropolitan Opera on the radio. She liked museums. She lectured him once on the historical significance of the gargoyles on the buildings in downtown Cincinnati. He liked seeing Loretta parade her culture. She had class. When he saw gargoyles on Notre Dame in Paris, they seemed almost like old friends.

11

Captain Vogel had begun his initial descent into Paris in the early-summer dawn. It had been dark only briefly during the night, and Marshall dozed, Molesworth memories swirling in his mind. He always had trouble sleeping on an airplane. As soon as sleep shut down his hearing, he would awake with a jolt, thinking the engines had quit.

When both his seat mates left for the lavatory, Marshall leaned across to the window, to see if the plane was flying over the Channel, as he had guessed. Spotting England's familiar shore, he yearned for Molesworth. Molesworth was where he had lived up to his ideal of himself. Before everything fell apart.

The morning they took off on the mission, their tenth, Marshall was making a secret bet with himself on how far he would get with Nurse Begley when he returned. Her front teeth were like Chiclets, shiny and squared off, and she framed them with bright lipstick the color of cherries—not pie cherries, but whiskey-sour cherries. She tasted more like pie, though. He was a fool. She was from out west, with bony hands and long legs and thick, radiant hair, and she had a habit of slinging her hip in a shooting stance. Her name was Annie, but the flyboys called her Nurse Begley because of her name tag bouncing on her chest. The formal name made it easier to mock their own lust for her and her great bazooms. Her name tag bobbed squarely atop the left one. Nurse Begley was Rita Hayworth in chestnut hair.

Marshall had had his chance to impress Nurse Begley the night before. She had agreed to meet him outside Lilford Hall, where the nurses bunked. Lord Lilford hunkered in one wing of his place.

"He's probably down to a butler and three footmen," Marshall joked.

"We heard he sits in his basement with earmuffs on," Nurse Begley said.

"What? He doesn't like airplanes outside his window?"

"The noise of us nurses is probably worse," she said with a laugh and a Hayworth toss of her hair. Her chest jiggled.

"We take off right over his house." Marshall grinned. "From the air, it looks like a toy palace in a train set."

"That's nice, to think that his house might not be so grand," she said. "Depending on how you look at it."

Nurse Begley was in her off-duty skirt and jacket, and her trench coat was unbuttoned. He backed her up against the ivy-covered wall of Lilford Hall, their bodies curving close.

"What do you like to do at home?"

"Do we have to talk about home?" she said, fondling his lapel.

He kissed her deeply, jamming her into the rustling winter ivy.

"Say—you want to give me a good-luck charm to take with me? Ten to one says I go out in the morning."

"What?" She was rummaging in her shoulder bag. "I need my hair clip, my lighter . . . Hmm."

"Knickers," he said.

Her giggles aroused him.

"In the winter the English girls wear something they call woollies to keep them warm," she said. "An English girl gave me some."

"That would be swell."

Thrilled, he watched as she wriggled out of the woollies, sliding them down her bare legs, crumpling them into a wad, and with a slight caress of his frontage, she tucked them into his pocket.

"Good night, flyboy," she said. "Good luck tomorrow."

He slept with his face in her woollies, and indeed they stayed roasty-toasty. In the morning, he stashed them in his leather flight jacket.

—

"DROP YOUR COCKS and grab your socks, boys," said the runner at 0400 hours. "Breakfast at 0500 hours."

The mess sergeant barked, "Combat eggs for breakfast. Load up, fellas. And pick up your sandwiches before you go. Nobody wants to be hungry in Germany."

"I'm not going to be *in* Germany, pal," said Hootie. "I'm going to be *over* Germany."

Next, the Nissen hut with the big maps on the wall. The Nissen was a makeshift structure of corrugated metal where all that day's crews crowded to learn the "Target for Today." The room steamed with the body heat of flyers duded up in their leather jackets and bulky flight garb as the top brass unveiled the flight plan and the weather guy added his two cents' worth. The big chalkboards listed each plane.

When the target was revealed, there was a shocked silence, then nervous jokes and groans. As usual.

"Send me to the rest home right now," Grainger said to Marshall.

The flyers watched the general with his pointer, the commanders, the couriers rushing in with news.

The flyers rode to the equipment room to gather gear—chute pack, Mae West, flak suit—a bag of stuff big enough for a two-week vacation. Then the jeeps and trucks carried the flight crews out to the hardstands, where the ground crews were loading the bombs and making last-minute inspections.

Next, Cupid's leap—the contortionist act required to board a B-17. Marshall swung himself upward into the hatch opening of the *Dirty Lily*. Grab the rim with both hands, kick your legs up and in, then slide forward on your ass. One of the ground guys called, "See you at 1500 hours, Lieutenant."

The takeoff from Molesworth in the dawn was a spectacle. The planes lined up nose to tail on the taxiway and headed for the turn onto the runway. The flashing reflections off the planes taxiing ahead sometimes blazed like machine-gun fire. The roar of the engines was lyrical, like the thunder of a herd of young horses, spirited and healthy. Engines revving, the planes sashayed out in a long, slow file, waddling side to side. B-17s were tail draggers. For a better view over the noses, the pilots wriggled the planes sideways—left, then right, left, then right. Under other circumstances, it might have seemed comical.

As each plane reached the top of the runway, it turned, still rolling. Throttles went forward, the engines bellowed, and the ship raced into the air, following those ahead, with more coming just behind. Liftoff after liftoff, one every thirty seconds. They climbed out of the ground gloom into brilliant sunlight and began circling the field, maneuvering to establish their formation, each bomber slipping into its assigned slot.

Marshall believed the B-17 was an elegant aircraft. He had been so young, so cocksure, he took it for granted that hundreds of heavy bombers could squeeze together in tight aerial patterns and fly long distances with no collisions, no peppering one another with all their bristling machine guns, no smashing one another with their long streams of deadly bombs. In training, he hadn't yet grasped how stupefyingly harmonious a full operational mission would be—a thousand bombers hurtling through the sky as a single, immense, layered entity, a unified airborne fleet.

The flight to Frankfurt was steady and routine—that is, nerve-wracking and physically exhausting. Marshall loved it. He loved that exuberance that came from the closeness of other Forts. Riding in the turbulence from the planes around them was exhilarating. He and Webb took turns holding position on the west ship's wing tip. The physical effort to hold their plane in formation was like roping a steer and pressing it down for hour after hour. Working the throttles, constantly adjusting and readjusting speed, flicking their eyes from the instruments to the sky and back, kept them from thinking about the cold. The contrails from the planes ahead and above blew past in steady streams, chalk marks etching the sky. They were in the dazzling midst of a beautiful deadly force. Marshall was on the alert for unusual moves by the fighter escorts, the "little friends," or some looming Nazi bastard. He needed the eyes of a fly, omnidirectional.

The roar of many thousands of engines was a thunderous symphony. The air was North Pole cold, but the sheepskin-lined helmet and his leather jacket were cozy, and the cockpit had some heat. Farther back, the waist gunners shivered in the open windows, but they wore electric flight suits. In battle they could warm themselves with the heat of their busy guns. Hootie claimed he never noticed the cold.

At ten thousand feet, they donned their "Halloween masks" for oxygen. They were up too high to smoke, too high to breathe—just when Marshall could have used a cigarette. At twenty thousand feet, he saw the ground as an abstraction, a schematic of peaceful farmland, brown like faded, worn-out rugs. As they flew farther north, snow cover started to appear, until the ground was a patchwork of whites, like overlapping tablecloths of varying pale shades.

Time passed, the timelessness that takes over when every split second is eternal. It was peaceful—until they met some Messerschmitts he did not care to remember.

Near target, Al Grainger crawled past the cockpit on his way to the bomb bay to pull the pins.

"Al's dressing his eggs!" Hootie yelled through the inter-phone as he always did.

Webb, the pilot, issued his routine reprimand. "Cut the blab, boys."

He transferred control to the bombardier at the IP, the initial point on the approach. As always, Webb said, "O.K., bombardier, you got it." Easing back from the controls, he joked to Marshall, as always, "Now it's relax time."

Grainger leaned into his bombsight, making only the slightest adjustments of their course. Here in the heart of enemy territory, they stopped all their evasive maneuvers and plowed ahead, straight and level, as if begging the German flak gunners to pick them off.

Just when they needed to twist and skitter most, they renounced defensive maneuvers. They drove toward the target until the eggs finally streamed from the *Dirty Lily*'s belly and the pilots could take control again.

Marshall heard Grainger call "bombs away."

As the bombs—M-17 cluster incendiaries—fell away, the plane lifted like a balloon. Suddenly lightened, she soared with relief.

12

Charles de Gaulle Airport was belligerently modern, with bleak, functional terminals and hangars, but today the morning mist gave the place a touch of mystery.

I can start life over, Marshall said to himself as he marched through the jetway. He had to, he thought. What else should a retired pilot do but effect *un grand changement?*

He hitched a ride into the city with the crew. Captain Vogel had insisted, since Marshall had reserved a room at the regular crew hotel. Accustomed to carry-on bags, the crew had waited for him while he detoured into baggage claim, and after enduring some small talk and inane senior-citizen jokes, here he was again at the familiar place. It was a modest hotel with breakfast in the basement.

"*Bienvenue,* Captain Stone," said Charles, the clerk, an old acquaintance, at the desk. "You fly your airplane to us again."

"No, no more." Marshall touched the sleeve of his blazer. "No uniform this time."

"Vacation?"

"No. I'm *retraité.* They say I'm too old to fly now."

"That is good, Captain! Now you will enjoy yourself."

"But flying is what I do, Charles. I'm really a bird!"

Marshall was pleased that his French was good enough to keep Charles from switching to English.

His room wasn't ready. He left his bags with Charles and set out, intending to force himself to stay awake all day by walking the spacious city. On layovers, he usually wandered for hours or went to the movies. He tried to stay on East Coast time, so he was often up late, reading in his room. But now he was going to be on Paris time.

He walked along the Seine, a long gray stripe through the city, toward Notre Dame. It was a fine June day. He had a kink in his leg. Ever since his wallet was stolen in London a few months earlier, he had been stashing his money in a contraption that fit beneath his trouser leg, even though he suspected it was conspicuous and that every thief knew precisely where to look. It came loose once today, when he was in the *toilettes*. He readjusted the strap, which now pinched.

The quai Saint-Michel was crowded, and he hurried to a quieter area. He noticed the fluttering lights and shadows in the young trees on the boulevard. At a sidewalk café he ordered a coffee, and when it came he ordered a sandwich. He had learned to order coffee first. Otherwise the waiters would not bring it until he had finished his sandwich. He always enjoyed his layover routines. He often sat on one of the boulevards at a place like this and read the papers. Smoking used to be essential. Marshall was still tempted at times by a whiff of European tobacco in the street, but sometimes the smell reminded him of the odor of a mangy dog. After quitting, he learned to divert himself by watching people, but they were usually smoking. Today a teenage couple, locked at the waist, sauntered by, each brandishing a cigarette with the free outside hand. He chuckled, thinking of life in a cockpit—the captain and the first officer used the outside hands for the yoke, the inside hands for the throttles. He wondered at the blithe confidence of mothers crossing the street with baby carriages—there were two in sight. He watched well-to-do women in their glad rags, walking dogs smaller than their purses. Young professionals wove among babbling bunches of unself-conscious tourists. A caricature from a Fellini film—heavy make-up, beehive wig, feather boa, platform shoes—paraded past. He liked the way the crowd meandered. They were going to lunch. They were talking. The lone women were conversing with their crazy little dogs.

He realized that he was scanning the crowd for familiar faces. Fat chance. It bothered him that he couldn't remember Robert's last name. He thought he would recognize him if he were to pass by now, almost four decades older but still himself.

"Désolé." Someone bumped into his small table. Marshall, glancing up, saw a stooped man with a battered black valise, hurrying on past Marshall's table.

Désolé! He was sorry, too. He was always amused that the French were desolated if they were late or jostled you in a crowd or dropped a pea from a fork. He was in a period of desolation, he thought, then quickly checked himself.

HE DIDN'T KNOW where to begin. In all his years of flying to Paris, he hadn't been back to the zoo. He hadn't lingered at any of the train stations. He had never tried to find the Vallon family. He wasn't sure where they were living when they sheltered him in the spring of 1944. As he walked through the city now, his mind turned the noise and color into tense, quiet, bleached-out scenes, garnished with grim red-and-black flags, the swastikas cartwheeling in the breeze, the ubiquitous cow-manure color of the German uniforms standing in stark relief. One afternoon after school Annette had taken him on a zigzag tour of the sights of Paris. With most of his time spent indoors, he found Paris that day fleeting and bewildering—the grand plazas, the ornate, ancient buildings, the bizarre long-necked Eiffel Tower wearing a gigantic Nazi flag like an apron. Or did he remember that flag from a photograph? He wasn't sure.

Annette guided him on other walks close to his hideaway, the Vallons' apartment. He remembered being careful not to put his hands in his pockets, as Americans did. *Don't jingle your change!* he was told. He did not smoke in public, for fear of holding his cigarette the uncultured American way, fingers outstretched, instead of with an insouciant, inward-turning grip of thumb and forefinger. He wanted to smoke, no matter how he had to hold the cigarette, but often there weren't any. Not even the bitter Gauloises.

Annette walked in front, and he followed, ten meters behind. If she stopped at a news kiosk to thumb through the magazines, he was supposed to keep going and saunter over to the other side of the street. When she resumed her walk, he could resume his. In this peculiar stagger, she managed outings for him. Away from the center of the city there were fewer German soldiers, more day-to-day lives—people waiting in lines for food, some seeking the extra morsels to feed a large American pilot hiding in the closet or a forbidden live duck kept in the bathtub.

His snapshot memories of the Paris streets: There was an air of normal city life. People managed to look fashionable, if slightly shabby. He remembered women in high hats or scarves wrapped on their heads or tied under the chin. They carried baskets and bags for the marketing. Now and then a frolicking child seemed to paint a dash of color on the drab urban canvas.

AFTER SETTLING INTO a meager but sufficient single with floral walls and a television with a broken knob, Marshall went to visit Jim Donegan, a pilot he knew who lived in Paris. Jim, who had retired two years before, had urged Marshall to call whenever he was in Paris. He had married a Frenchwoman after divorcing his second wife. During the war Jim piloted a B-26 Marauder; he was in the first swarm on D-Day.

Jim and Iphigénie lived in the Seventh Arrondissement, and Marshall decided to walk there. The day was warm, with a soft glow, fuzzy through the lush early-summer trees. The coffee had briskly reset his mental clock. He wanted to live on Paris time, and he thought beating jet lag was a matter of will. Denying his need for sleep, he set out from the hotel and detoured over to the Eiffel Tower, where he muddled through throngs of tourists.

He always thought the tower was like something from *The War of the Worlds*, this gangly giraffe of an alien. He had been to the top only once, with one of the stewardesses, Melissa Littleton, during a long layover years ago, when he flew 707s. Where was she now? He never saw her again after their return flight to JFK. He couldn't remember what else they did in Paris, or where they stayed.

He quickly fled the wild hubbub beneath the tower.

"MARSHALL, OUR CONDOLENCES on your wife," Jim said.

"*Désolée*," said Iphigénie.

"Your wife, a beautiful woman," said Jim, hugging Marshall's arm. "Much too young."

"*Merci*," Marshall said, staring at the parquet floor. "It was merciful," he said. "The suddenness. She didn't have to suffer." He hated saying that. He had said it so much it had begun to seem like the truth.

Marshall was speaking French, in deference to Iphigénie, but she quickly switched to English. Jim, a couple of years older than Marshall, had a new paunch. Iphigénie, who worked in fashion design, was unsmiling, and she was dressed up in a chic outfit like someone about to go to a reception at the Hôtel Crillon.

"Retirement is a whole different ball game, Marshall," Jim said.

"I can't imagine it yet." Marshall laughed. "I'm liable to hijack a jumbo—if I could find someplace to park it."

"I'd go with you, but Iffy wouldn't let me."

Iphigénie caressed Jim's cheek. "He calls me this questionable sobriquet—"

"Only because I love you, *ma chérie*," Jim said.

Jim insisted on showing Marshall the view from the bathroom window—the head and shoulders of the Eiffel Tower.

"The view from the bidet," Iphigénie said with a wry smile when they returned.

"I knew a bidet had to be good for something," Marshall said.

Jim laughed. "Last year some Americans rented the apartment next door for a few weeks, and they used their bidet to wash potatoes!"

"That seems logical to me," Marshall said.

A memory hit him. He had washed his feet in the Vallons' bidet in 1944.

Later, as they were having coffee, Marshall told Jim and Iphigénie that he intended to follow the trail he took in 1944 and try to find some of the people who had helped him. He explained about the two families whose names he knew. "But the Vallons aren't in the telephone book. I know where the Alberts lived, in Chauny, but of course they may be gone."

Iphigénie shuddered. "I would not want to go back to that time."

Jim said, "Iphigénie's family had it rough during the war."

"It was nothing but pain, Marshall," she said.

Marshall thought he might soon regret this visit.

Iphigénie said, "You won't find anyone who will talk about the war."

"Wouldn't people in the Resistance talk?"

"They are not in the telephone book under '*Résistance*'!" she said dismissively.

"But there were Resistance newspapers. Maybe the libraries—"

"The true names wouldn't be known," she said. She pooched her lips out disdainfully. "They had code names."

She began removing the coffee cups. "People don't talk about the war," she repeated.

JIM WALKED WITH Marshall toward the Métro. Marshall was getting tired. He apologized for having upset Iphigénie.

Jim said, "She was a little girl during the Occupation. She was sent away to her grandparents' house in the country, so she was separated from her parents."

They walked down the block, then paused by a news kiosk. Marshall said, "I always regretted that I didn't get to fly on D-Day."

"The point is, Marshall, you were part of the whole thing. The big picture."

"And you?"

"Well, that morning flying across the Channel never leaves me. And as we got near the beaches—it was wall-to-wall ships down there."

They walked on. At a street corner they waited for the light. Jim said, "I wouldn't have missed it for anything. You know, I don't think I could have done what those guys did, the ones who waded to the beach. Imagine. There's a thousand Jerries with machine guns in bunkers, and the Army hands you a rifle and tells you to go on up that beach. I mean, God almighty." He paused. "All *I* had to do was bomb a bridge. I could turn around and go home."

"I know what you mean."

Marshall and Jim crossed the street with the light and stopped on the corner.

"What do you miss most about flying, Jim?"

"God, everything." Jim scratched his head and looked straight ahead.

Marshall didn't say anything.

Instead of taking the Métro, he decided to walk. By the time he reached his room, he couldn't resist a nap.

JET LAG HIT HIM by surprise. With no airline schedule, he gave in to insomnia and naps. He was hungry at the wrong times. He had always been efficient about his job. He could see what was needed and block out the rest. But now everything had changed. Old, jobless, wifeless, in a foreign land. He felt suspended, as if on a permanent layover.

For the next two days, as he walked through his fatigue, he tried to get his mind straight about what he was looking for. He wanted to find the Albert family in Chauny and the Vallon family in Paris. They might all be dead. Or retired to the Riviera. There were others, too, who had helped him along the way. But he had forgotten their names. Their false names, he corrected himself.

———

ONE MORNING MARSHALL woke up on Paris time and felt sufficiently rested.

"Lights. Action," he told his reflection in the mirror as he shaved.

After a coffee and some cornflakes in the petite breakfast room, he took the Métro to the Gare du Nord and boarded a train to Chauny. He remembered Gisèle Albert in an apron, wiping her hands, her son, Nicolas, tying a shoe.

The train made several stops. He gazed out the window at fresh fields, villages, and intermittent stations. He saw a man on a mower, a woman with her apron full of something abundantly green gathered from her garden; a girl in a spotted kerchief on a bicycle.

HE KNEW THE STREET name from Pierre Albert's 1947 letter, and it didn't take long to find that street. From the station it was a straight line, a turn, a dip down, a veering to the left.

There it was. He knew the house. It was brick, the local style of brick laid in decorative crisscross patterns. There was less greenery now, more sidewalk and pavement, and the tall wooden fence in the back had been replaced with a low brick wall. The barn was gone. The room where he had been hidden was at the back of the house, with a window on the side. Now, from the street, he could see his window, with its overhang.

He remembered bicycling from here to the train station the day he left for Paris.

He was hesitating about going to the front door when a couple with a dog passed by and glanced at him curiously. He started to move on. Then a small gray Renault pulled into the driveway. The driver emerged and headed for the house. He was carrying a yard-long baguette and a plastic grocery bag.

"Nicolas?" Marshall said.

The man turned. "*Oui?*"

13

MARSHALL GAVE A LAST GLANCE AT THE NOSE ART BEFORE he ran for the woods. *Dirty Lily* would have to take care of herself. She was still on fire. Bob Hadley was panting, but Marshall didn't dare slow down for him. "Come on, come on," he whispered sharply, urging him into the woods. Marshall wore his leather sheep-lined helmet and his A-2 leather jacket, with his escape kit in a leg pocket. They had shucked their parachute rigging, but the catch on Hadley's jammed and he had to cut himself loose.

The woods were sparse on the edge, but dense deeper in. The terrain was brushy, with occasional large trees. Marshall scouted for climbing trees. He saw evergreens, a bank of them, and slowed down. When Hadley stopped to throw up, Marshall said the dogs would be after them.

"What dogs?" Hadley said.

"There will be dogs," said Marshall. "And they like puke."

"Webb was dead, do you know? He was dead, I could tell."

"We're not dead. Let's go."

Marshall thought Hootie was dead, but he wasn't sure about Webb. He knew Grainger's shoulder had been hit and Campanello's face was bloody. The Germans would be there soon, scavenging the mangled Fort like buzzards.

The girl on the bicycle had disappeared. She had told him to wait while she went to find civilian clothing, but he had run into the woods. Their squadron mascot was patched onto Marshall's leather jacket—Bugs Bunny placidly eating a carrot and resting his foot on a bomb. Only two days ago, Marshall had boasted that he was the Scourge of the Sky in brown leather. Now he was a marked target.

The day had turned gray, and they twisted and turned several times in their dash through the trees. Marshall didn't want to get lost in the woods. They had to seek help from some willing farmer. Marshall groped for his compass, squirreled away in one of his zipper pockets. "North's that way," he said, gesturing through the evergreens.

"Are you sure?"

"See the old patches of snow on one side of the tree? That would be north." He zipped up the compass. "Look at the sun, goddamn it!"

Hadley relieved himself behind a tree. Marshall remembered something from escape-and-evasion class. *Empty your bladder and bowels first. You'll feel better and you'll be prepared for the next crucial stages of your evasion.* He said this to Hadley.

"That's the only thing I remember from evasion class," Hadley said. "And I figured tossing my cookies counted. What country do you think we're in?"

AT SUNSET THEY MADE a shelter beneath the swooping boughs of an evergreen. They nibbled bits of chocolate and Horlicks malted-milk tablets from their escape kits. Hadley wore a heavier B-3 shearling jacket, much warmer than Marshall's, and with no Bugs Bunny. They huddled together that night in a way Marshall had never expected to do with a man. He couldn't abide Hadley's fretting, his restless sleep punctuated with long sighs. The night was bitter, but the low-slung green boughs stopped the wind. Marshall could not identify the trees, but years later when he took his children to get a Christmas tree he decided they were some kind of spruce. Once, Loretta said innocently, "We'd better get spruced up," and he cringed, remembering his long night in the Belgian woods.

They slept fitfully, and Marshall buried his face in Nurse Begley's woolly-drawers, inhaling her sweet smell. He berated himself for paying so little attention in evasion class.

During the night, he thought about winter visits to his uncle's house in the mountains, where he slept with a newspaper-wrapped hot brick. The windows were single-glazed, and the cracks around the windows and doors let in small zephyrs. He slept in a feather bed with some cousins, who sometimes tried to steal Marshall's brick. There was often tussling over the covers and the bricks. "Stop your squirming," his aunt would call from across the room. "You'll let all the hot out."

In the morning, the sunrise gave them their bearings. Hadley climbed a tree and reported a road leading to a village to the west. To the south was another road, with some farms set back beyond trees and fields.

"South," Marshall said. "To Grandma's house we go."

Soon they emerged from the woods and saw the road, beyond a large field. Hadley insisted on traveling west, to search for a boat across the Channel, but Marshall argued that the only way back to England was south, through France and over the Pyrenees to Spain.

"But we'll never make it, Marshall. I don't care what they told us in evasion class. It's too far, and it'll be Germans all the way. If we go west and just hide out, sooner or later there'll be a way to get across the Channel. Or if not, the invasion will be coming soon and we'll be home free."

"Germans are here too, Bob. Look."

Ahead, a convoy of military vehicles was speeding down the clear, wide road. On a smaller, intersecting road, a man with a donkey and a cart plodded along. After studying the silk maps included in their escape kits, Marshall decided they had inadvertently crossed the border and were probably already in France. They continued south, but after an hour of arguing about the best route, they decided to split up. Marshall preferred being alone anyway, making his own decisions, and he was sure Hadley was wrong about the invasion. They parted on a ridge where they could see a clear juncture of west and south.

"Don't lose your map," Marshall said. "Put it in your coat lining."

Thick, tall hedgerows separated the fields, and here and there farmers were at work. He tried to pick his way parallel to the main road, while keeping concealed, hiding in a ditch or among some trees when he heard vehicles approaching.

A truck convoy passed. He could see the German cross on the doors. He didn't know if he was afraid. He knew he would have to find shelter this evening and each evening to come.

He walked at a fast pace, stumbling over the uneven terrain, keeping close to the trees and behind hedgerows, away from the road. In a thick evergreen copse, he found a stream that seemed clear. He filled his collapsible flask and dosed it with a water-purifying tablet. He rested for a while, thinking it was a good refuge, but Spain was far away, so he rose and stumbled on. He skirted a small village, passing close enough to see a flag flying—the swastika, spidery arms akimbo.

He kept moving till dusk, trudging through the countryside. Now and then he heard voices, but each time he crept away. He came to a large stone barn. He watched a man guide a cow into the barn and fasten the door. He did not see dogs. After sundown, Marshall entered the barn and sank into a pile of hay, exhausted. He ate a tablet of Horlicks and wondered how to milk a cow.

Next morning, he jerked awake. The farmer was standing over him, gripping a raised scythe. Marshall found himself silently maneuvered out the door and across the barnyard. The farmer waved the scythe threateningly, shooing him away. Marshall ran into some nearby trees, regretting that he hadn't grabbed the cow's teats during the night for a warm drink. When he stopped to catch his breath, he saw how he was shaking.

IT WAS LATE AFTERNOON. He had walked about eight miles, he thought. He approached a farm with a barn adjoining the house. Behind the barn some rectangular hay bales were stacked in a neat cube. There was an opening big enough to hide in, even sleep. Poking inside, he found a hen's nest with one egg. He cracked the egg against his knuckles and opened it carefully. The yellow center was beautiful, like a sun sunken in a bowl of honey. He swirled it in his mouth and swallowed. He rummaged around for more eggs, but there were none.

Easter eggs. An incongruous memory came back as he lay amidst the bales. Marshall and his cousins were searching for bright, dyed eggs under the bushes and in the crannies of the corncrib and the cow shed. He was a small boy then. His grandmother saying, *Get them all. Don't waste.* But they invariably found an egg a week past Easter, and they ate it anyway, the hard yellow center gone green on its surface.

It was too early to sleep. He carefully left his hiding place. In the barnyard he stared at the pig trough, then the chickens' water pail. He didn't want to waste his halazone pills on those. If the farmers were out in the fields, the women would be in the houses, he thought. Slinking behind the barn, he made for the back door of the farmhouse. He knocked once, lightly. A short, middle-aged woman opened the door. Fear flashed across her face.

"*Je suis un aviateur américain,*" he said in what he knew was a laughable accent. "Please, I need help."

She put her finger to her lips, then pointed to the barn. "*Là-bas! Là-bas!*"

He slipped into the barn and hid behind some machinery. She arrived soon, with some milk and a piece of bread, which he wolfed greedily but gratefully. She had a warm face, with wide-set dark eyes. She wore a dark dress and a bonnet. She motioned for him to stay, and then she left. He sank into some loose hay, suddenly exhausted. After dozing for a while, he heard her come in again. She brought some peasant clothing for him—a coat and some balloon pants of a thick tweedy wool. After she left, he pulled the pants over his flying pants and found that they fit well enough. They were short, but his flight pants dropped down like cuffs. Loretta would laugh. The coat fit too snugly over his flying jacket, but he was unwilling to get rid of his leather jacket in winter.

Loretta. When would she know that he hadn't come back to base? How long would it take him to walk to Spain on back roads, hiding in barns?

The door opened and two middle-aged men speaking in loud voices roused him. He had been told in evasion class that most Frenchmen collaborated with the Germans. There was a reward for turning in downed airmen. Speaking gruffly, the larger of the two men grabbed Marshall by the collar. He wanted proof that Marshall was an American *aviateur*. Marshall showed him the U.S. Army label inside his flying jacket. Following regulations, he had not brought anything in writing with him. No names, no addresses, no photos. His dog tags were in his boots.

The men scrutinized him carefully, then whispered together, keeping their eyes on him. Leaving, they signaled that he should stay in the barn, and they latched the door behind them. Marshall wasn't sure what to do. In a few minutes, the woman returned, bringing him another piece of bread, some cheese, and a corked green bottle with some wine in it. She put her finger to her lips and left.

Marshall thrashed in the loose hay, trying to sleep. Later, well after midnight, the two men reappeared, this time with a third man, who shook Marshall's hand and addressed him in English. He grinned, showing uneven teeth.

"We will help you, but it is necessary to verify your identity and send it to London to determine if you are a spy."

Marshall relaxed slightly. "Why would I be spying on you in an American flight suit?"

"The best disguise of all, perhaps. Where did you come down?"

"I don't know. North of here. I don't know if it was in Belgium or France."

The interrogator studied him. "You will stay here until it is time to move you."

"What are you going to do with me?"

The trio whispered to one another, then all smiled warmly at Marshall. The man who spoke English said, "We will move you to where it is safe. There is great risk in sheltering you. If you are not who you say you are, you will be shot. If you reveal who we are, we will all be shot. We will aid you, but only if you can prove to us your identity."

Marshall volunteered nothing. He suspected that the man knew about the crash. What if he was a German agent? Or a Frenchman ready to capture him and turn him over to the Germans? Marshall was confused. But he knew he needed help. The man told him to remain in the barn, and that someone would be on guard so that he would not get away. "We will take care of you," he said. Marshall wasn't sure how to take that.

"Your identity tag, please. We will verify with London."

Marshall took off his right boot and handed over one of the two dog tags hidden inside. Getting the boot off was a relief, but he pulled it back on. He needed to sleep in all his clothes, ready to run.

The man wrote down something. "We will see if you are a *boche*."

He asked a series of questions. The name of his mother, his sweetheart. His height, weight. Marshall realized that a German would have hesitated, his mind running through conversion tables. Reluctantly, he answered.

"What is a cockpit?"

The place where I feel cocky, Marshall thought.

"Who won the World Series last year?"

Marshall was relieved to answer that. He was a Yankees fan.

The questions ended abruptly. He wondered if he had passed the grilling or if he would have to bolt.

IN THE MORNING, a different woman appeared with his breakfast. She was heavyset and wore work garb, a canvas jacket, and clog shoes. Speaking in heavily accented English, she explained that her sister had answered the door the day before.

"This is some real coffee," she said. "We have saved it for two years, for a special occasion."

"Thank you."

She gave him some bread and some jam.

"There is no butter. The *boches* took our cow."

The bitterness in her voice made him trust her somewhat.

"How do you know English?"

"I used to know an Englishman."

"Am I in France or Belgium?"

"France, *monsieur*." Her eyes were hazel.

She said, "We will take care of you until the *Résistance* arrives. You are safe here, but you must stay hiding. Do not make a sound."

She brought him a jug of warm water, a razor, and a sliver of soap. Later in the day she brought him newspapers and books and kept him company while he ate bread and cheese.

"I will teach you my language, a little. *Un peu.*"

"I know a little."

"Say '*s'il vous plaît.*' Please."

"*S'il vous plaît.* I know that much. *Merci.* I know that."

His college French had been in books. Pronunciation was guess-work.

"Say my name. Jeannine. *Jan-neen.*"

"*Jan-neen.*"

She offered him a French grammar book, and the next time she came, he had reviewed the verb forms. He heard her doing the barn-yard chores, feeding the hens and ducks. Her sister cooked him a duck egg, which was delicious. Years after the war, he asked Loretta why she never bought duck eggs. Why always hen eggs? She laughed so loudly. "I never heard of people eating duck eggs," she said.

HE SPENT THREE DAYS in the barn studying French vocabulary. *La table, la fenêtre, le canard.* Table, window, duck. Sometimes the words in the lessons were sad. Teapot. Fireplace. Pillow. Tender words that could spontaneously pierce his heart like shrapnel. *Jeune fille. Bébé.*

"My son is in Germany," she said. "Say *la guerre*."

"*La guerre.*"

She lowered her eyes. "The boys cannot fight the war," she said. "They are in the work camps."

She did not ask about his life in the States or about his plane crash. She brought him a piece of bread fresh from her oven. She had hoarded some flour for special occasions. He savored the bread, its chewiness a challenge.

He rested in the nest of hay. Outside a goose honked. He watched dust motes in the crack of light across the dirt floor; in them he imagined he could see swarms of aircraft. In the night he heard RAF bombers, and soon after daybreak he heard a lone B-17. The familiar sound was unmistakable. He tried to see through the cracks in the barn walls. He couldn't spot it, and the sound faded. It was another straggler, another crew in trouble. He fantasized being rescued by it. He listened for a crash, but he heard nothing, and he did not mention it to Jeannine.

On the third night his interrogator reappeared.

"We checked you thoroughly with the English authorities, and you are Marshall Stone, of the 303rd Bomb Group. I am happy to say that we will help you get back to your base in England."

"Excellent. Thank you." Marshall was elated. The coil inside him began to unwind. "Can I get over the mountains to Spain?"

"I do not know the next stage. I know only one stage." The man handed Marshall the dog tag. It was still warm from the man's trouser pocket. Marshall held it tightly in his hand, as if it were a good luck charm and he suddenly believed in magic.

The man said, "Tomorrow you will be driven to a safe house."

A WOMAN WAS HURRYING up a winding stair. The cramped house had uneven floorboards, perhaps centuries old, with a threadbare carpet. He could see her hand at her bosom, holding her dark shawl tightly together, her black scarf tied beneath her chin. She came swiftly up the stairs, signaling for him to retreat from his room into the hiding closet. Grabbing his bedding, he crawled into the dark, hidden recess, and she pushed a chest in front of the small, low door. Dogs were barking on the street. Several heavy vehicles drove by. After a while, she mounted the stairs again and moved the furniture aside, releasing him.

The room contained one bed. Marshall was shut away like an attic child with nothing to do. On the walls were a crucifix, a picture of the Madonna and child, a pastel landscape of something that looked like misty mountains, and a photograph of a young man in a double-breasted suit. There was no chair, only the chest, the narrow bed, and a tiny mat on the floor. Each morning he heard a certain whistling from the street. Was someone so happy, or was it a signal?

The first morning, a shy adolescent girl brought him down the stairs into the kitchen, where four women in black garb were bent over large wooden bowls. He imagined they were widows or mothers from the first war, women aging with painful memories of young men. The women were working with cheese. The woman who had shown him upstairs the previous evening rose from her work and poured him a cup of coffee from a pot on the wood-stove. The small cup was fiercely hot, and the ersatz coffee was bitter and strong. She did not offer milk or sugar. Through the window he saw a tan mutt, its ears alert, facing the street.

Behind Marshall a low murmur of voices rose as the women resumed their tasks. The tallest of the women spoke to him, and from a cupboard she removed a piece of hard bread and gave it to him. She seemed to be apologizing for the lack of butter.

A heavily dressed man opened the door, and the tan mutt rushed in with him and a woman dressed in pale green. A babble of energetic French followed, and Marshall sensed seriousness but not immediate danger. The man left then, with the dog.

After he ate the bread, Marshall was shown where to empty his chamber pot. The woman in green dipped hot water from a cauldron on the stove into a handled jug, and she gave him something like a dishcloth that he understood to be a bathing towel. There was soap and a razor in the room upstairs. He took the jug and the towel upstairs and gave himself a spit bath. Later he brought down the chamber pot and emptied it. The women looked up from their work, stared at him as he passed through, then bent their heads again.

Marshall had nothing to make the hours pass. Over and over the plane slid into the field. Over and over he ran through the woods, smelling the smoke from the plane. He couldn't remember when he knew he was afraid. He thought he was more afraid now, looking back.

The red-cheeked boy, dressed in brown baggy pants and a cap. The cigarette. Webb and Hootie lying on the ground. The plane burning.

Everything Marshall owned now was in his pockets. There was the yellow card with a few French phrases to use in case he was shot down in France. The silk map, the first-aid items, the tube of condensed milk. Because he wasn't supposed to be caught with the map, he worked at memorizing it. It was so intricate, the print so small. He needed better lighting. He sat on the floor against the wall, staring at the blue floral bouquets of the wallpaper. He tried to focus his mind by counting the bouquets.

He heard shouts in the street. He heard a horse clopping along, dragging a cart of some sort. Through the tiny window he could see an arc of the street and a wedge of open field. He could see the traffic pass. Occasionally he saw a group of children walking by. Their spontaneous giggles and laughter charged him with a bit of hope.

IN THE EVENING the women closed the shutters and drew the dark drapes to conceal the candlelight of the kitchen. He was brought downstairs to share a rabbit stew with the eight family members— the four older women, two young girls, and their parents. Reticent,

Marshall observed them. His knowledge of French collapsed under the rush of their conversation. He learned to interpret tones if not their run-together words. He saw their skeptical looks, the gestures they made over their food. He could tell when they were talking about the Germans. The Germans apparently took the family's goose for their Christmas. The Germans gorged on chocolate! Chickens! Butter!

The women in black had an authority that made the girls and their mother cower. There were no young men. The women barely spoke to Marshall, but when he tried to draw them out with his makeshift vocabulary, they modestly but eagerly queried him about America.

"*FDR? Connaissez-vous FDR?*"

"Shirley Temple?"

No one in the family revealed their names except for the man, Reynard. He was short and slender, with knobby hands. He pulled a leather wallet from his pocket and showed Marshall his identity papers. He pointed to his photograph, his name, his occupation, his citizenship. He flipped through the papers quickly.

"*À Paris,*" Reynard said. "In Paris you will obtain the *fausse carte d'identité.*"

"*À Paris,*" they all said, nodding in assent.

They were saying he would need a false ID card.

Every evening he heard German soldiers marching through the village on night patrol, singing a mournful song that sounded like homesickness itself. Warmth from the evening fire drifted up the open stairway door to his garret. He crept out and sat on the stair.

Sometimes he heard the Luftwaffe overhead, a nasty roar that he could feel in the pit of his stomach.

At night the face in the cockpit of a Focke-Wulf 190 visited him, a fighter pilot who had suddenly, briefly, flown alongside the stricken *Dirty Lily.* Their planes were so close, like cars on a street.

He replayed his mission, instant by instant. He didn't want to forget it, but neither did he want to relive its most terrible moments.

He was heartsick; he didn't know the fate of the crew. They had lost the plane.

He had been in England kissing Nurse Begley, and suddenly here he was in a claustrophobic hidey-hole, waiting, waiting, in a house of strangers jabbering gibberish, women in shapeless black garments plodding through their days worrying with food, fragments of food, roots from a cellar. He was a helpless pipsqueak. When he went down to empty his chamber pot one morning, he saw the girls' mother come in from the garden with a green leaf. She waved it in his face and chattered excitedly.

France didn't seem as cold as Cincinnati, from what he could gauge by the quality of the unheated air, the chill in the house.

He heard voices downstairs during the night, and footsteps ascending the stairs. *"Monsieur, monsieur, des Américains! Américains! Aviateurs!"*

He opened the door and there stood two men—disheveled, large, haggard, sleepy-looking.

"Des aviateurs!" one of the women in black—the tallest—said. She was carrying a small candle.

"We were shot down," the taller one said sheepishly.

"You *suis américain* too?" Marshall asked, startled.

"Yeah boy!" said the other. "I've been on the run, like a wild pig rooting around in the woods. Four days. Then I met some friendly guys who took me to a farmhouse and I got grub, and next thing you know I met Pete and they brought us both here."

"Pete Drummond, 403rd," the tall one said. "Waist gunner. Our Fort got hit on the way back from Frankfurt, and I bailed out. Let me tell you, that was some ride."

The woman left, and for a time the flyers filled the room with their stories. Marshall was glad to hear English. Probably one of these flyers was from the Fort he had heard flying low a few days earlier. The guys gabbed until another of the women climbed up to their hideaway.

"Chut!" she said, entering the room with a tray. "Hush."

She had brought them each a cup of ale and some pieces of bread.

"Man, this cock-sucker French bread is liable to tear out all my fillings," said Pete.

The other flyer, Nelson Avery, a tail gunner from the 305th, gnawed his bread steadily. "Excuse me, I'm still starving." He licked the crumbs from his hand. "I don't know what happened to our plane, our crew. I got out, but it was on fire and I reckon they're all goners."

He spoke as if he were talking about a distant event that did not concern himself. His emotions hadn't registered yet, Marshall thought. Nor had his own. He didn't know where he was or what he was supposed to feel. It was some small comfort to have two more flyers there with a language in common, but they also intruded on what had been his private garret.

"Where's your flight suit?" he asked Pete, who was dressed like a laborer.

"I robbed a scarecrow."

The pants were filthy and ragged, too short, and the sleeves of the jacket rode up his arms, exposing his GI wristwatch.

Marshall joked, "Next time, I'm going to pack a sandwich and a French peasant outfit."

"Always be prepared, huh?" said Nelson. "Well, the Boy Scouts don't teach you how to bail out of a blazing bomber."

"I got the piss knocked out of me when I landed," Pete said. "When you hit the silk there are two big spurts. First, you're out the door, WHOOM! Then WHAM! The chute opens. Then you're falling, like your ears have gone deaf. Or you're in heaven. Then WHAM-BAM! You hit the ground."

"It's so peaceful till you hit," Nelson said.

Hearing about their flakked and burning bombers and their heavenly parachute descents intrigued Marshall. He almost envied them. They could just float down to the ground, and then they were on their own. They didn't have to see their crewmates lying dead. He shivered. The *Dirty Lily* slammed into the ground again.

"What do you think comes next?" Nelson asked Marshall. "Is the Underground going to get us out?"

"You never know who might be friendly or not," said Pete. "I tried to ask a man on a bicycle for directions, and he just kept going. He muttered some frog grunt I couldn't understand, but you could tell he didn't want to be bothered."

"They're afraid," Marshall said. He sipped his ale, trying to make it last.

"But this family is going to help us."

"How long have you been here?"

"Three days. Every day they say I'm going."

"I think the invasion is coming any day," Nelson said. "I kept hearing that on base."

A step on the stairs. The signal Marshall had learned, the *chut!* sound and *Allo Allo.*

The woman had brought two blankets. Pete thanked her. *"Merci,"* he knew to say.

"Mercy bucketsful," said Nelson, grinning as he took the blankets.

Marshall understood from the woman's gestures that Pete and Nelson would have to sleep in the hiding closet, to stay concealed. He helped her move the chest away from the small door. There was some bedding inside.

"Both of us, in there?" Pete said. He and Nelson laughed.

Marshall tried to make them understand the seriousness of the house rules.

"Not a sound," he said.

"I hope I don't fart," Pete said, with a glance at the woman. "She doesn't understand *fart,* does she?"

"She'll know it when she hears it," Marshall said angrily. "And so will the Germans if they show up here. So knock it off."

"O.K., O.K."

"Seriously. No laughing. No snoring. Nothing."

The woman stayed. She straightened the photograph on the wall.

"That's her son," Marshall explained. "This was his room. He was sent off to a work camp in Germany."

Pete and Nelson made sheepish noises then, and Marshall was glad he had caused them discomfort. He was feeling like a veteran at evasion.

"She wants our cups," he said.

After the woman left, he reiterated all the cautions. "These folks are laying their lives on the line for us," he said.

Marshall offered his bed, but the other two would not take it. "We'll take turns on it if we're here very long," he said. "I hope we get out of here in a day or two so we can go get a forged ID. I don't know who I am anymore."

His attempt to joke fell flat.

HE LAY ON THE SMALL BED thinking about Webb and Hootie. Hadley was a fool, maybe a POW by now. Chick Cochran, the right waist gunner, had bailed out. Or had he? Hadley said he did. Maybe Chick was in the wreckage. Where were Grainger, Redburn, and Campanello now? They couldn't have gone far with their wounds. They could be hiding and getting treatment, but if they had to go to the hospital, they might have had no chance at escaping. He knew Ford and Stewart had headed for the woods, in a different direction from Marshall and Hadley. He counted nine. And Marshall made ten.

14

"NICOLAS! NICOLAS ALBERT?"

"*Oui.*" The man with the baguette turned toward Marshall. "*Américain?*"

"*Oui.* I was here in the war."

"*Un aviateur américain!* American flyer!" Nicolas banged on the door.

Marshall's sudden reunion with Pierre and Gisèle Albert and their son, Nicolas, made him think of a boisterous litter of puppies waking up from a nap. Yes, Marshall was going well. How was Pierre going? How was Gisèle going? They were going well. Nicolas too. Marshall's French was going excellently.

The twelve-year-old boy was recognizable in Nicolas the man. Marshall remembered him eagerly bringing in daily reports of the aircraft he had spotted, the whereabouts of Germans in the streets, activities he had seen around the train station or the post office or the school. The Germans had requisitioned his school, occupying one half of it and crowding the boys into the other. Marshall recalled that Nicolas had been earnest and intelligent, full of questions about America.

"Do you still have your American maps?" Marshall asked him now.

"You remember? *Bien sûr.* I have a weakness for geography, but I have not yet traveled to your country."

Nicolas was a school superintendent, and he often had lunch with his parents. He and his wife lived in a suburb of Chauny, and their two daughters were attending a university in Nancy. Gisèle insisted that Marshall join them for the meal. There was plenty, she insisted.

She was tiny, with a narrow forehead, bushy eyebrows, and strong hands. Pierre had thinning hair, a thick neck, nostril hair, and an occasional boom in his voice. He was perhaps a decade older than Marshall, but his grooved face seemed hardly older now than it had in 1944. He assured Marshall that the clothing he had asked for long ago had arrived. Marshall thought Loretta must have sent it, but he didn't say this. Gisèle told him they had kept in touch with many of the aviators they had sheltered during the war.

"I'm not much of a correspondent," Marshall said, explaining that his failure to answer Pierre's letter was a faux pas that jumped over the years.

"*C'est la vie.* Nevertheless, it gives us great pleasure to host you in our country again. Gisèle, get the Calvados."

Pierre poured the aperitifs. He raised his glass. "A toast to your son, *le petit Albert,* and to your return to your friends in France."

"You remember." The phrase *le petit Albert* was still fresh in Marshall's mind from rereading Pierre's old letter.

"That gave us such joy when you wrote of your marriage and your son. Do you give the French pronunciation—no, of course you do not."

"They don't speak much French in New Jersey," Marshall said. "And I'm afraid Albert is not much interested in the meaning of his name—or in the war."

"Ah, the young. Give him time."

"It is the greatest honor to us that you give him our name," said Gisèle, who began gathering dishes from a cupboard. "Don't derange yourself. You know that I don't accept help in my kitchen."

Marshall hadn't thought of offering help, then was sorry that he hadn't, then relaxed, knowing any exertion would have been inappropriate.

Gisèle laid out dishes on an old wooden table that was sticky with sugar crumbs and spills. "We have a simple lunch," she said. "But Nicolas demands his favorites."

"Maman is the best cook in France."

"Angeline is a superior cook!"

"My wife," Nicolas said to Marshall.

In a while, Pierre uncorked a bottle of red wine, and Gisèle served slices of a vegetable terrine adorned with bits of radish. As they ate, Marshall told them about his life after the war.

"I've had a cushy life," Marshall said. "Cushy—*facile, luxueuse?* The worst thing that ever happened to me was crash-landing the B-17." Immediately, he thought perhaps he should have said the loss of his wife.

"Marshall, you were very frightened when you came here!" said Gisèle. "You were so disturbed about your airplane and your friends."

"You flew the grand airplanes," said Nicolas. "In the war and after too!"

"I wish I could have flown more missions," Marshall said. "I really regret that."

"Everyone has his part, Marshall," Pierre said, finishing a tidbit of toast.

Gisèle cleared the plates and served a heavy stew, with the baguette.

"It's a feast," Marshall said.

"This is no longer wartime, dear Marshall!" said Gisèle, spooning stew from the bulbous tureen into a dish for him. "There is much food now."

"People forget the deprivation," said Pierre. "Marshall, you know that after war there is a grand forgetting."

"That is normal," said Gisèle.

"But now the people of our country have forgotten too long." Pierre poured wine and recorked the bottle.

"All of France has amnesia," Gisèle said, gazing out the window.

"It has to be finished," Pierre said. "Oh, you know France has had a terrible history. Terrible."

"The *collabos* know who they are," said Gisèle bitterly.

Pierre said, "Too many of those—but they have to live with their shame."

"You made a *tarte Tatin*, didn't you, Maman?" asked Nicolas.

"*Bien sûr.*" She nodded. "I have beautiful apples," she said to Marshall. "Remember the apples we ate in 1944?"

"Yes, I believe I do."

"We had few apples, and we had to make use of every small part." Gisèle wrinkled her brows.

"You were generous with me," Marshall said, the warmth of the wine easing him.

Pierre shrugged and tore another piece of baguette. He said, "When the fleets of the B-17s went over, with the streaming rows of cloud like breaths on a cold morning, we rejoiced. We loved the sound. When we heard the bombs drop on the munitions factories and the aerodrome at Laon, we knew there was danger for us, but there was more danger if nothing was done."

Nicolas said, "It was very exciting to see the planes, and to hear the roar of them filling the sky. We were always watching for parachutists."

"Nicolas saw a parachutist die," Gisèle said.

"An American? Did one of our bombers crash around here?" Marshall stiffened.

"It was a man from a B-24, the Liberator, which fell somewhere to the east," Nicolas explained. "We were outside at school, at the time of the recess, and we heard the noise of the plane high above, but we could not see it. Then we saw the man in the harness, floating down so peacefully, below a canopy. We began running. He was not far away. Then as he floated down we saw a German soldier on the bridge shoot him. We could see the man's body jerking. He dropped behind a dairy near my school. Naturally we ran toward him. We had our little pocket knives—my friends and I had them for cutting parachutes! And now there really was an *aviateur* coming from the sky. He was not far from the school, maybe half a kilometer. Other people were running, and they told us to go back, stay away. Of course I was a boy and I wanted to be involved. There may have been six of us boys, all running. And the *aviateur* was shrouded in his parachute. People began tearing it away, quickly, cutting the lines, and I could see him lying there, bloody and lifeless. I remembered all the *aviateurs* we had harbored in our house, men who had parachuted or who had survived crash landings—like you, Marshall—and I was very disturbed, because I realized that this young man would have a family, maybe a girlfriend, probably dear parents who were worried about him and who would grieve. I knew that the Germans would bury him in a way that if the man's parents knew, they would be mortified. Oh, the thoughts I took with me as we hurried back from recess to our classroom, where we must sit perfectly still all afternoon and recite pluperfect verbs!"

No one spoke as Gisèle cleared the dishes.

"I was lucky," Marshall said then. "Without you, what would I have done? Out on my own, I would have been dragged to a stalag very soon."

Pierre raised his glass. "To friends from two countries, to the friendship of two countries."

"The same for me," Marshall said, not finding the right words. His voice choked.

"*La tarte Tatin—voilà!*" said Gisèle, setting the dessert on the table.

"*Merci, Maman,*" Nicolas said.

The apple tart was so delicious that everyone fell silent. After it was finished, Gisèle removed the plates and served coffee.

"This is real coffee!" she said. "It is good, is it not?"

Marshall laughed. "I remember the wartime coffee! What was it—mud and sticks? What was the secret?"

"An exclusive ingredient from Germany," she said, touching his arm gently.

Marshall nodded. "It was a hard time."

"Yes, very difficult," Gisèle said, trading glances with Pierre.

AFTER THE COFFEE, they showed Marshall the back room where he had hidden. Now it was a laundry and storage room, packed full, so that it appeared even smaller than Marshall remembered. He recalled Gisèle crooning to a baby crying in the kitchen. A commotion outside. Someone running down the street. Later, a gunshot in the distance. A fire in the neighborhood, a house burned. Gisèle told him to crawl through an opening in the back of the armoire into a narrow lair behind the wall and not to come out until she signaled. He heard sirens, blasts.

Now he listened as Pierre and Gisèle explained that the Germans had found *résistants* three houses from them. They arrested the adults, shut the children in the basement, and set fire to the house. Neighbors rescued the children, and Gisèle cared for the baby until a grandmother in the country could be located.

"I heard the baby crying," Marshall said. "I never knew what was going on. But I wasn't supposed to be told anything."

"It was better that we keep you closed behind the armoire!" Gisèle said.

Marshall remembered hearing about the bombing of the aerodrome at Laon. At night he listened to the German soldiers marching in the streets, singing.

"Remember the Germans singing at night?" he asked.

Gisèle shuddered. "That detestable music," she said.

15

AGAIN AND AGAIN, DURING THE SIX WEEKS OF HIDING IN CHAUNY, he had tried to imagine the crew's whereabouts. He alphabetized the guys and staged imaginary escape scenarios. On the feather bed in the back room, or stuffed in the little dugout behind the armoire, he wondered if any of the guys stuck together, if any of them had been turned over to the Germans. Maybe they were hidden in the church basement. He imagined a hidden door behind the church organ. He saw Hadley crossing the Channel on a fishing boat—torpedoed. He thought of a hundred ways to escape. And a hundred ways to be captured. He imagined a POW camp.

He thought about the *Dirty Lily*'s nose art and how they had all celebrated the artist who painted it, a Molesworth mechanic with a flair for pinups. The crew sprayed beer on the plane to christen her. And they sprayed beer on Webb, who had known a certain Lily in London.

People came rushing through the field, as if on wings themselves. He guided the *Dirty Lily* down onto the mud-brown field. She pointed toward the village, a huddled grouping of gray buildings with a deliberate church spire. It seemed that every resident was startled onto the field. They were waving. He saw them even as he was descending. The *Dirty Lily* stopped short of the nest of buildings at the end of the field.

Then he was in the woods, away from the field.

A girl on her bicycle saw him through the trees and signaled to him. She was small and thin, in a light wool coat and scarf. Maybe twelve years old. Or fifteen. Her shoes were heavy and worn. Her bicycle had a small bell. She warned him, *"Monsieur, les Allemands!"*

She spoke a little schoolgirl English.

"Your clothing," she whispered. "You must hide it. Stay here. I will bring you other clothing." She put her finger to her lips. "Shh."

If she came back, he would ask her which country this was, Belgium or France. He could hear vehicles approaching. The local residents would not be driving, petrol was so scarce. He retreated into the woods as the sounds came closer. The voices and vehicles clustered around the dying plane. Where was Hadley? Hadn't they run to the woods together? Webb, he thought, was dead. But they had hauled Webb out. Folded next to him in the cockpit, not responding. Blood in his lap.

"Everybody's out," said Hadley, appearing at the edge of the woods. Or maybe he had been there all along.

"Is Stewart out?"

"Accounted for."

Where was Hootie? Hadn't he seen Hootie lying pale and lifeless in the field?

Over and over, in hiding, he replayed the crash scene, wondering if the girl on the bicycle ever returned with clothing for him.

"I BROUGHT YOU HERE from my cousin Claude's," Pierre was saying now. "Do you remember?"

"Yes, that wild bicycle ride in the dark!"

"We were on the bicycle together," Pierre said with a laugh. "You pedaled while I sat on the handlebars."

Marshall outlined for the Alberts his erratic journey from the crash in Belgium to their house in Chauny—the farmer with the threatening scythe, the three nights in a barn while the Resistance checked him out, then several nights in the home of the women in black, where he hid in the upstairs room.

"Then the *Résistance* took me to Claude's, but the convoyer who was supposed to meet me there didn't show up, and they dumped me out in the field! I thought I had been betrayed."

"No, that was correct. They didn't want to be seen with you at Claude's."

"They pointed to the barn, I remember, and I ran through a field in the dark and fell down a couple of times."

"And then you were safe in the barn."

―

MARSHALL HAD HIDDEN UP to his neck in a pile of scratchy, dried weeds and grasses, his nose dripping from a sneezing fit. The noise of his breath on the hay was raucous in his ears but to other ears perhaps no louder than a wisp of dried grass rustling. A shadow passed over him, and he heard two voices mumbling angrily in French.

"*Les Allemands,*" said the older one, with a guttural spitting sound of contempt.

"*Va-t'en!*" the other man said.

A cat jumped up on the hay and landed virtually on Marshall's face. The tail swiped his face, and then the cat rubbed against Marshall's head and purred. In the shadows the men did not see the cat's discovery. The cat, a bushy, ragged, pied thing like a mop head, drooled on Marshall's hair, then rubbed its face in it. Marshall didn't dare free his hand to move the cat, who was purring loudly.

"*Qu'est-ce que c'est, Félix? Tu ronronnes comme un train!*"

The lantern whipped toward the corner, and Marshall's eyes were blinded by the glare. The French voices rose in alarm as he crawled out of the hay, the cat swirling around him. Standing, he held his hands out to the men.

He had been given a password, a phrase that might be innocuous if these men were collaborators, but meaningful if they were expecting him.

Carefully, he said, "*Il y aura de l'orage demain.*"

"*Comment?*"

He repeated the phrase he had memorized.

"*Oui, oui,*" they said. He had passed.

"*Je suis américain,*" he said haltingly. "*Aviateur.*"

"*Aviateur?*"

Their excitement purred like the cat. "*Chut!*" they said to the cat. Be quiet.

"*Je suis un aviateur américain,*" Marshall said.

The older man repeated the French words. Marshall always remembered his own poor pronunciation—a hayseed stab at a phrase that was elegant in a Frenchman's mouth.

The older man was Claude, and the younger one was Pierre. They were cousins, Marshall learned later, and the farm belonged to Claude. They wore rugged work clothing, heavy wide-legged trousers and tight jackets. Their clothing was patched, their shoes were dirty, and their berets were heavy and dark. Marshall's clothing by then was similar, though ill fitting. He still wore his U.S. Army boots and his flying jacket. One of the women in black had ingeniously sewn a layer of coarse linen onto the outside of the jacket.

Pierre pointed to the house just beyond the barn and touched his stomach, then his lips.

"*Vous avez faim? Soif?*"

Marshall nodded eagerly. Pierre gestured for Marshall to stay hidden in the barn. When Pierre and Claude left, the cat bounded down from the hay and followed them. Marshall thought he heard the men teasing the cat, saying the Germans would catch him and have him for supper.

Long after dark, Pierre returned, bringing bread, cheese, an apple, a bit of fatty ham, and some wine—a quarter of a bottle. Marshall devoured the food. "*Merci, merci,*" he kept murmuring.

In patient, slow French, with some inventive gestures, Pierre explained that the Germans were bivouacked in the village a mile away. Marshall could catch some of the words. If they found him hiding here, Claude would be shot—Pierre clutched his heart and drooped for effect—and his wife would be sent away. The American had to be silent.

After Pierre left, Marshall relieved himself outside, burying his waste like a cat. During the night the cat found him and curled up beside him. Nurse Begley's woollies warmed Marshall's neck, and he drifted through sleep, his dreams sending him on bombing raids to Germany. A crashing sound awoke him—the cat, leaping off the hay. Later, the cat crunched his way through a mouse meal. Afterward, Marshall could hear the cat licking his fur. Marshall had not had a real bath since he left England.

Near dawn, in an adjoining section of the barn, someone snapped a cow into her stanchion. Marshall heard the sound of milking, hard squirts on metal. Through a crevice he saw a woman in a scarf and a heavy coat leave the barn with the pail of milk—and the cat. In a short time, Claude appeared, with a hot breakfast wrapped in a towel in a basket. A boiled egg, some ersatz coffee, some hard bread. Claude had acquired a few English words during the night.

"Tonight you go to Pierre. The house of Pierre, yes? The son has English. Today—" He made gestures for Marshall to stay hidden.

Letters from Loretta would keep coming to Molesworth. Here he was, lost, hidden, having dropped from the sky like a bomb.

"I REMEMBER A CAT at your cousin's barn," he said now to Pierre and Gisèle. "Félix."

"Félix!" said Gisèle. "I remember old Félix. He was a smart cat!"

"We were pals," said Marshall.

"Why would I remember that cat?" Gisèle said, puzzled. "There were so many."

"I must return to school," Nicolas said, glancing at his watch.

"I remember you in short pants and a necktie, rushing off to school," Marshall said.

Pierre stood to embrace Nicolas. "My son is a great success," he said. "He is school principal."

"He was my professor and translator in '44," Marshall said.

"Your French, Marshall!" said Nicolas. "Now you know our language. You have learned well. Please allow me to help you in any way possible while you are here. *Au revoir*, Marshall!"

Nicolas drove away, and Gisèle directed Marshall to a divan in the sitting room.

"Make yourself at home," she said.

16

MARSHALL SPENT THE AFTERNOON REMINISCING WITH PIERRE and Gisèle. Some retirees might play golf or sit on the porch, but he would drink wine in a French home with people he knew in his youth.

He ventured, "I know that you were out at night on important missions when I was hiding here."

Pierre grinned. "It's good the Germans were not as observant as you."

"I will show you his medals," said Gisèle, jumping up and rushing from the room.

The medals were framed under glass—the Medal of Freedom, the Légion d'Honneur, the Medaille de la Résistance, and the Croix de Guerre.

Marshall examined them while Pierre fetched another bottle of wine. After he had poured the wine, he began, in a disjointed way, to gather his memories.

"I don't get to speak of it often," he said. "You perhaps know that I was the chief of our group here, and I kept the arms for all the *secteurs* of the region."

"In your house here?"

"Oh, no, no. Gisèle would never permit that. No, a neutral place. We planned the sabotages, and everyone involved had to have invincibility—how do you say in English, innocence?"

"Deniability?" Marshall said, thinking of Watergate.

"Oh, the sabotages we planned against the *boches*! Every day we did the telephone lines. On several occasions we blew up the railroad tracks—and the canal locks."

"And the alcohol *distillerie*," Gisèle said.

"Yes. And the bridges on the highways, as well as those across the river. After you left here, we accelerated our clandestine activities, anticipating the *débarquement* of the Allies." Pierre sipped his wine and was silent for some moments. "But after the Allies arrived on June 6, things grew worse—open combat with the *boches*. When the Allies came to Normandy, you understand, the *boches* were in panic for their marvelous Reich. I delivered all the arms to the *secteurs* and asked my men to leave their jobs and be prepared for widespread action against the enemy. More than ever, our efforts were necessary. This became very bad, for the Gestapo was on alert against all *Résistance* activity. This was especially hard for me, for many men came to the house and I had to be ready."

"We received a warning," Gisèle said.

Pierre had to go underground, to a friend's house, seven kilometers away, for fifteen days, while Gisèle and Nicolas stayed at home. Gisèle was certain Pierre would be arrested.

"And you comprehend what this would mean," Pierre said. Grinning, he drew his finger across his throat.

"But I was careful. I was thinking up here." Pierre touched his forehead. "I was a step ahead of the *boches*. They were strangers here, but I knew the place. I knew what they might do next, where they might go."

"He said that again and again, until I maybe believed it," Gisèle said.

"You and Nicolas were my eyes and ears, too. You did your part."

"I remember Nicolas and his reports," Marshall put in. "Always busy."

Gisèle, twisting her hands together nervously, said, "You will never know this ordeal, Marshall."

"It turned out well, *chérie*!" Pierre said.

"I was happy to shelter the *aviateurs*. The rest was *horrible*."

Pierre acknowledged the dangers, but then he laughed.

After his period underground, he was given another assignment—to investigate in his region of Aisne all the munitions and fuel depots for airplanes, the German army headquarters, and the railways. He had to mark these targets on aerial maps for American bombers.

"I traveled to Paris three times in two weeks to deliver these maps. They were taken to fields where couriers in small planes from England came for them. This was very gratifying to me. All of it was for bombing by your bombardiers!"

"Pierre was very brave," said Gisèle. Pierre squeezed her hand.

"After Paris, I went into combat again with the Chauny organization, and our task was to prevent the *boches* from crossing the bridges. After setting the charges, I intended to reassemble my group, who had the weapons we had distributed. But when I set out alone on the Soissons road, I found myself facing maybe a hundred enemy soldiers! I was—how is it said?—shaking in my boots, but I did not reveal this. The lieutenant was only ten meters away. He called to me, and he lifted his rifle and aimed at me. *'Raus!'* he said. *Mon Dieu!* But then someone interrupted him and he forgot about me. More and more the *boches* were disorganized. And so my life was spared!" Pierre smiled broadly.

"You were a lucky man!" said Marshall.

"I returned with my men to town, but we could do nothing there, for we were watched. Then two hours later the bridges blew up, and in the confusion we managed to get our weapons out of hiding—just in time to see the avant-garde *libérateurs* of Patton's army! The rest of our work was to guide their way through town and to do away with the isolated *boche*, and to watch the roads to let our Allies make their triumphal advance toward Belgium."

Marshall listened intently, "the isolated *boche*" echoing in his mind. "I want to say something," he said, lifting his glass. He paused, trying to find words, knowing they were inadequate. "Thank you, Gisèle, for providing so well for me. Thanks to your son, too, for helping me with my French. Thank you, Pierre, all of you, for risking your lives. I propose a toast to you, my second family. *Merci beau-coup*."

Marshall was amazed at himself. He had never offered a toast in his life until this moment. He felt warm from the wine, strangely happy, and slightly askew.

LATE IN THE AFTERNOON, Nicolas returned, bringing his wife.

"Angeline wished to meet you, Marshall, so I went home and re-trieved her," he said. Angeline spontaneously gave Marshall a two-cheek kiss. She was sturdy and neat, with a fluffy blue scarf arranged over her blouse.

Pierre leaned toward Marshall. "My son and his wife have no son. I do not have grandsons to carry my name, but perhaps there is no need." He lifted his glass. "Again, to your Albert."

Angeline brushed her hand against Nicolas's shoulder. "Don't forget, Nicolas," she said.

"*Ah oui.*" Nicolas opened a large shopping bag he had brought. "Do you recall, Marshall, that you gave your *aviateur* jacket to me?"

"Yes. I was afraid to keep it." The Alberts had supplied him with warm civilian garments, and Marshall, who was fond of Nicolas, had given him the flying jacket.

Nicolas pulled the Bugs Bunny jacket from the bag. "*Voilà!*"

Speechless, Marshall held his old flying jacket. He caressed the worn leather and ran his hand inside the pockets.

"I wanted to preserve it for you if you ever came back," Nicolas said.

"Nicolas displayed this jacket when we first met," Angeline said, smiling. "He was very proud of it!"

"I was the envy of all my classmates after the war concluded and we could spill our secrets."

The leather was cracked now. Bugs Bunny still looked sarcastic, his foot on the bomb and the carrot dangling from his hand. "Eh, what's up, Doc?" Marshall said in the best Bugs voice he could manage, and everyone laughed.

AFTER GISÈLE HAD SEATED everyone in the small, overfurnished front room, Pierre said to Marshall, "Nicolas can help you find some of those persons who helped to shelter you before you arrived to us."

Marshall had told Pierre and Gisèle about some of the nameless people he remembered, and now he told about the family in Paris who had hidden him after he left Chauny. He explained his admiration for the young daughter, who led Allied pilots through the city.

"It was hard to believe that a schoolgirl would be a guide for American aviators," Marshall said.

"Oh, it was normal, Marshall!" said Pierre loudly. "The Germans would never suspect a schoolgirl. Therefore, many young girls were employed."

"There were many girls in the *Résistance*," said Angeline. "My aunt flirted with the Germans to distract them while her friends slipped food from the back of the supply truck! They were sixteen, she has told me, no more."

"Be thankful, Marshall," Gisèle said. "Your countrymen have never known such times, when children must become combatants."

"I was hoping someone here would remember some of the contacts in Paris," Marshall said. "There was a young man I remember especially. He came several times to the place where I was hiding, bringing messages and supplies, and he went south on the train with me. He was called Robert, but I have no idea what his last name was! I want to say it was Julien, but I don't know why. Maybe that was his false name, his *nom de guerre*? I don't even know if the family I stayed with in Paris was really named Vallon."

"But you knew our names," Pierre said. He explained that Vallon was more than likely correct. "The code names were usually a first name, used only for clandestine acts like sabotage. I was Emile." He laughed. "Gisèle teased me, calling me Emile!"

"Dear Emile!" she said, patting his arm affectionately. "My secret lover!"

Nicolas offered to check with some local sources for information about the regional escape lines. "I will search for records of Vallons in Paris. And I would like to find those women in black for you," he added.

Pierre said, "The chief contact for the *Résistance* in this area, the captain, who took his directions from London, is unfortunately disappeared—deceased."

"His family may have a logbook or something," Angeline suggested.

"I wrote nothing down," said Pierre. "The work I did—all was in my head. It was dangerous for people to put names in writing. To put anything in writing."

"We kept the address book of the *aviateurs*," Gisèle reminded him.

Pierre served some homemade cider from an amber bottle with a clamp top. The cider was rich and strong, and Marshall sipped cautiously, remembering a pint of moonshine from his youth.

"We didn't serve this on the airline," he said.

Pierre smoked a cigarette and talked on about the war.

"To get a potato for supper was a clandestine act, but here in the country the farmers had more. When we heard the American tanks, and we saw the Germans on the street, standing around, confused, we grew bold. They knew it was all over, and we could not help taunting them even more than usual, asking them if they would eat their potatoes cooked the French way. We said, 'You must be looking forward to going home! See the wife, the *Kinder.*' " Pierre stopped to laugh heartily, then continued more soberly. "Of course we knew and they knew that they might go to a prison when the Allies prevailed, or they might find conditions at home even worse than here, for us. We knew their country was bombed to hell. But we enjoyed saying, 'Oh, it will be so grand to see the wife and the *Kinder* and go to the circus and eat nice strudel.' We were cruel. We didn't care. It was a joy. How could we restrain ourselves? But they still could have executed us all!"

He nodded contemplatively. "What causes this? Such barbarity. A war. All these horrors, when men sink lower than beasts. How did it happen? Can it happen again? This is why I encourage Nicolas and Angeline to inform their daughters. I never stopped informing Nicolas. Of course he was there. He saw it. But we must tell. We must tell."

"I didn't see everything," said Nicolas. "But I've been thinking about it ever since. I am so fortunate that my parents and I survived."

"Not Cousin Claude," Pierre said.

"Oh, the man with the farm, where I hid?" Marshall asked.

"Oh, yes. Maybe I did not mention it when I wrote you—at the end of the war? Claude was killed in his barn. Blown up by accident—one of our own explosives. It was a terrible thing."

"I will never forget that night," said Gisèle. "That's when we tried to protect Nicolas, and not let him see."

"I was at his funeral," Nicolas said. "I saw him dead. I knew what happened."

Marshall pictured the barn. And Claude. And the cat. Félix.

NICOLAS AND ANGELINE offered to take Marshall to his train. As they prepared to leave the house, Nicolas handed the flight jacket to Marshall.

"For you."

"Oh, no. It's yours."

"But I kept it for you, that you may have it again one day."

"But I gave it to you, and your wife likes it! I have no use for it. I really want you to have it."

Angeline seemed pleased, and Marshall was glad to relinquish the jacket again, but he thought later he might have misunderstood Nicolas's offer. *Damn my French*, Marshall thought.

HE BOARDED AN EARLY-EVENING train at Chauny, and watched out the window as the growing twilight gradually dimmed the gray-green fields. The train paused at Noyon and Compiègne, stations he couldn't recall. When he was on that train to Paris in 1944, he had been given precise instructions, but riding as a French worker had been difficult. He was wary and hesitant. Another flyer, the bombardier Delancey, was being sent with him, but they did not sit together. Marshall didn't know the ordinary behaviors of French people on their daily business. Some women in mesh head wraps were laughing, but the rest of the car was quiet. At Compiègne a rush of people boarded the train, and a gray-haired man in a dark jacket sat by him, mumbling a question—probably "Is this seat taken?" Marshall thought his one-word reply had a scared-rabbit tone. He was sure he would be found out when he stood up, over six feet tall among the modestly sized Frenchmen. He was aware that the train could be bombed at any moment—bombs from the Allies, bombs from the Underground.

The particulars of experience often escaped him, but the outlines and the shapes of landscapes and skyscapes lingered in his mind. It was a discipline gained from flying, in always knowing where the North Star was, where the horizon lurked, which way was up. He had learned the outlines of airfields, the configurations of runways, the placement of hangars, the skylines of cities, the gentle curve of the ocean horizon, the wheeling constellations overhead.

From his seat on the train now, he watched as the farm fields yielded to ragged outskirts, which melted into factory buildings, which gave way to the switching yards of the Gare du Nord. It had been a long time since he had wanted to spend a day talking and laughing with a group of people. His stay with the Alberts in 1944 overlapped his visit now, as if he had jumped over time and might still be hiding behind an armoire or in a haystack with a cat. The shadowy figures of the brave people who had saved his life—in barns, in hidden rooms, on bicycles—were coming clearer, almost reachable. He welcomed them. After the ease and pleasure of returning to Chauny, he could almost believe that the girl in the blue beret would be waiting when the train pulled in to the station.

17

BACK IN HIS PARIS HOTEL, ALTERNATING BETWEEN INSOMNIA and waking dreams, he could hear Annette Vallon's singsong French, her playful teasing. During those three weeks in 1944 he thought he saw the soft baby fat of her cheeks grow thinner. Her mother insisted on giving him the largest portions of food. "You are large, *monsieur*," Mme Vallon told him. "We do not need so much."

"I don't want this," Annette said, moving a carrot on her plate. "You may have it."

Perhaps she still needed the nourishment of milk, he thought. She needed meat. The milk ration, for children only, was for her younger sister, Monique. Food had been more plentiful in the country, on the farms and in Chauny with the Alberts.

He remembered the way Annette and her mother hugged so casually. He could see in them a happiness that persisted despite the hardships of wartime. Mme Vallon had embraced him too. She was small, and she had to reach up, but her warmth momentarily blotted out the war. He thought of his own mother, when she was a young woman, before she got sick.

Marshall had hardly ever paid attention to cooking, but in Paris food was so scarce it became a fixation. He watched Mme Vallon practice her art. With a small piece of chicken, a dab of saved butter, and some elaborate fussing with the pots on the wood-stove, she made a terrine, a sort of chicken Jell-O with a yellow layer at the bottom. She flavored it with bits of dried herbs.

"You need your strength for your journey," she said, giving him a second helping.

He didn't know when the journey would be, or how.

He offered them some francs from his escape kit. He had two thousand francs, oversized bills like pages from a book. The portrait of the woman in a helmet was Joan of Arc, he learned years later.

They would not take his money. "We do this gladly," Mme Vallon insisted. "It is our necessity."

"But you could buy a rabbit and some eggs," he argued.

One evening she cooked a pot of tripe—the only item the butcher had left, she said. Marshall was revolted when he saw her scrubbing and soaking the hog's entrails that afternoon. He ate sparingly, but M. Vallon treated the dish as a delicacy, making soft groans of appreciation.

"With more butter and some cream, this would be almost divine," he said, but everyone knew he was pretending.

Annette nibbled. Monique did not speak at the table. Marshall hardly remembered her. A child of eight or ten?

They spoke English with him. Annette listened carefully when the adults spoke. Then she tried to offset the anxiety in their voices with her own girlish chatter. Her mother indulged her, he thought. He could see in her mother's face what Annette would become. Mme Vallon wore her hair swept up, with long hairpins holding a pile of it. In the corner of the sitting room she sometimes brushed Annette's hair, twirling it with her fingers. Annette's hair was medium length, dark brown with curls framing her face. She wore no lipstick. Her clothing hung loosely on her thin frame. On Sundays she washed and ironed her blue smock for the school week. It was what the girls wore to protect their clothing, she explained, and it was a sort of uniform.

He remembered her sitting at a table, working with the buckles of her cowhide school bag, which she called her *vache*. She placed her books and papers inside purposefully—like a pilot packing his brain bag, he thought now.

In the morning, Mme Vallon went to the market early, and M.

Vallon left soon after for his office. Marshall did not remember now where Monique had been.

"Time for your French lesson," Annette announced.

The large apartment was cold, and Marshall was wearing three sweaters.

"Pronunciation, *s'il vous plaît*," he said. "I'm lost."

"My English teacher thinks I have a 'bad' accent," she told him. "She tries to teach the way they say in England. Tomato—we say *tuh-maht*, they say *tuh-MAHT-oe*; that's easy. But you say *toe-MAY-toe*. I have fear that my teacher will recognize where I am getting an American accent!"

She made him a tea of herbs, plentiful because the Germans detested herbs and had not appropriated all of them. She rubbed a piece of leftover bread with some mint and a little oil and warmed it on the stove. He had built a small fire with some chips of coal and paper so that her mother could make coffee, a substitute made of acorns—or perhaps cockleburs and birdseed. Marshall didn't know.

"Perhaps Maman will bring an egg. I will cook it for you in this fragrant oil."

"*Mais non.* You and your mother should have it."

"No, you have half, and Maman and I share half." She wiped the pan with a lump of bread she had saved. She smiled. "Perhaps Maman will bring some butter. And cinnamon."

"And cornmeal."

She didn't understand, and when he explained she turned up her nose.

"One doesn't eat that," she said. "Food for the animals."

"Then maybe she will bring some more of those delicious pig guts we had last night!"

"*Les tripes! Mmm. Bonnes. Bonnes.*"

They laughed.

She made him pronounce all the words they had discussed. The words for corn and cinnamon and butter. Eggs. Bread.

"Perhaps I make us too hungry," she said apologetically, reaching to pull up her limp white sock that was sagging into her shoe.

"It's all right to talk about food," he said. "I think about food every day!"

"We should speak of other things," she said emphatically. "Now, let's learn flowers."

"Do I need to know flowers? I was never any good with botany. *Botanique?*"

"Well, then, trees. It is necessary to know *les arbres.*" She led him through a list of trees, then some animals. "At our summer house in Normandy, we had geese and chickens. We could have stayed there since the beginning of the war, when everyone suddenly left Paris, but we returned. Maman insisted we were in more danger there than here. My father had to be here, and I must be here to do what I can to help," she said.

"Do your parents hide many aviators? How do you feed them?" He wasn't supposed to ask his helpers questions, so the Krauts couldn't force anything out of him if he got caught.

She shrugged. "We manage."

"And what do you do?" He knew she went somewhere Friday afternoons after school.

"You are not to know." She smiled. "The Germans, if they are on the bus, I put my books beside me and occupy as much space as possible. I enjoy making inconvenience for them. Also, it is amusing to drop my books at their feet. In a way they are gentlemen. 'Oh, mademoiselle, I must assist you!' and in another way they are ready to make the arrest. But they do not, not the schoolgirls. So they think they are kind and helpful, but we are laughing at them. Every little bit of trouble we can cause, innocently—'Oh, it is only the schoolgirls'—is a way to express our frustration."

"Should you be provoking the Germans?" he asked. "It sounds dangerous."

"I know. But how can one resist?"

Mme Vallon was at the door, with her groceries, mostly rutabagas.

"Your usual catch," Marshall said, but he could not make the expression understood.

"If this war ever ends, I will never touch another rutabaga!" Mme
Vallon said, depositing the bags on the kitchen table.

"Did you find anything else?" Annette asked, poking into the
smaller bag.

"I have ten grams of butter—very precious. I have the sugar. We
must get along without even ersatz coffee. Tomorrow, they said. No
bread, of course. All the farina is going to Germany. Maybe our men
working at the factories will get some of it." Mme Vallon rummaged
deeper in the bag. "One cheese ration."

"Let me imagine," Annette said. "Tonight, baked rutabaga with
cheese. A soupçon of butter."

"A tiny pinch of sugar with the butter," her mother said with a
smile. "I have some herbs."

THEY WARNED HIM to stay away from the dining room window,
which gave onto the street, but he could watch from a side angle
through the lace curtains. He saw only an occasional vehicle—a Kü-
belwagen or a Mercedes-Benz flying a small flag with a swastika on
it. The building was on a corner, and his bedroom overlooked a
small side street. The blackout curtains at night cocooned him. He
heard few traffic noises. People were out in the mornings and flock-
ing home late in the day, after dark. He watched them, did exercises
to keep his muscles from cramping with inactivity, and studied
French. For months as a pilot trainee he had studied mechanical
manuals: hydraulic pressures, lift angles. In January he had been
keeping house in his barracks, writing lovesick letters to Loretta,
trying to squelch suspense over the next mission. During the day he
attended lectures and flew trial runs, and ten times in two months he

had been out on wild sky rides, lugging bombs. A few times he had visited the villages near the base, and once he had been to London. Now, he was trying to talk French and reading Verlaine. He was almost twenty-four years old. He had stepped into an alternate life, like Alice in Wonderland, down a rabbit hole—but without his Bugs Bunny jacket.

There was hardly anything he could do to help Mme Vallon. He envied Robert, the good-humored young guy who came by bringing fresh meat wrapped in paper. He brought cigarettes. Marshall listened for his bicycle, arriving in the downstairs foyer. Robert was slender but powerfully built, with thick hair and dark eyes. He always seemed to be on urgent business. Marshall imagined him as a daring Resistance agent out gathering intelligence or transporting explosives, while Marshall himself sat out the war behind lace curtains.

Annette teased Marshall for lolling around the house while she worked so hard at school. She teased him for his efforts at French, even while she patiently coached him. And she teased him for the rude outfits he had to wear—the layers of old sweaters, the too-short pants, the rough socks, the cloth slippers with the seams loosened to make room for his huge toes.

At the table the family managed to make their meager dinners last for hours, regaling one another with jokes at the Germans' expense and family stories that Marshall thought must have been often told.

"The wine makes us convivial," said Mme Vallon. "We forget the difficulties."

M. Vallon did not speak of his work at the city hall, but Marshall observed that he came home with extra ration books.

"If they fail to account for the number, who is to know?" Marshall overheard M. Vallon say—but in French, so Marshall wasn't sure.

Once M. Vallon said to Marshall, "I am an honest man. I have always been an honest man. It is for honor, for patriotism, that we take care of the *aviateurs*."

"We are not violent," said Mme Vallon. "But we can do this."

"The Germans were a people of culture," M. Vallon said sadly. "I do not permit myself to believe that every German connives in this conquest."

"We are ancient enemies," Mme Vallon said.

From time to time, hints of despair broke through the Vallons' determined tranquility. But they quickly assured themselves that de Gaulle and his Free French troops would liberate Paris soon. Any day the *débarquement* of the Allies would begin. In the evenings the family played card games and conversed. At nine o'clock, Annette's parents tuned in to the BBC on the wireless for the news of France. *Chut!* Shh!

One night, they were awakened by explosions followed by sirens. In the chilly dark they were all out of bed, peeking from behind the curtains.

"It is not far," said Mme Vallon. "The smoke is across the park."

"Whatever happens, I will not consent to leave Paris again," said her husband. "The exodus in 1940 was shameful. We will not descend to that again."

18

Marshall dined with Jim and Iphigénie at a quiet bistro and told them about his visit to Chauny. He tried to avoid discussion about the war that might upset Iphigénie, but today she seemed more relaxed with him and asked questions about the Alberts.

Marshall saw that she adored Jim. He noticed that Jim's hair was thinning.

"Retirement's a hell of a thing, Marshall, but you might say I've got a new career here in Paris," Jim said, touching Iphigénie's cheek affectionately. "It's like picking up a new route I haven't flown before. Remember when we added the New Delhi route?"

"Oh, do I."

The crew of a Connie might be away for as long as two weeks, flying from New York to Madrid or Paris, then resting a couple of days before picking up the next leg to New Delhi. They stayed in New Delhi two or three days before turnaround.

"What a life," Jim said.

For a while, they rehashed the glory days of air travel, but then Marshall declared that sometimes he had fewer regrets than he had expected.

"Deregulation is going to ruin the airlines," he said with a momentary flash of anger.

"We got out at a good time," Jim said. "I try to tell myself there are other things in life. Tell Marshall about our trip, Iffy."

Iphigénie finished a delicate maneuver with sauce, potato, and a fragment of duck leg before speaking. "My niece is getting married, and we're going for two weeks in the Dordogne." She became animated, flicking her ring-studded fingers outward. "It will be a very nice country wedding."

Jim patted her hands down. "Iffy's going to see her whole family, and—*oh, la la!* My God, Marshall, you sit with these Frenchies and their feasts all afternoon and you can't understand why they're not all blimps. Iffy is loyal to her family, but then she comes back to Paris." He lowered his voice to a mock-conspiratorial tone. "She's very French, very chic. She won't wear pants, none of those jeans that American women wear."

"Disgusting," said Iphigénie. "Disrespectful."

"I'm with you there," Marshall said. The waiter refilled his wine-glass.

Jim went on. "Iffy wears those heels that make her ankles so slim and sexy, you know what I mean. I've known her for five years and she always surprises me."

All the while Jim was speaking, he was looking at Iphigénie, teasing her, judging her reactions (she was pretending not to hear him), congratulating himself for his taste in women and, Marshall thought, insulting Iphigénie in an underhanded way. He tried to remember if he had treated Loretta this way. He thought about Annette and her mother, and after a lull in the conversation he began telling Jim and Iphigénie about hiding in the Vallons' apartment.

"I keep thinking how brave they were," he said. "I really didn't give them credit for the risks they took. It's only becoming real to me now. Strange, isn't it?" He swallowed some wine. "I'd love to find them again."

"They may want to forget the war," Iphigénie said, her eyes down. "But they were very kind to you."

"Retirement takes you full circle," Jim said. "A lot of people want to go back to their young days. Maybe that's true with the people you're looking for."

"Who knows what might have happened to them?" Marshall said. "They could be in Timbuktu. That goes for all of the people who helped me escape. I'd like to find them, to thank them. But I don't know. Maybe it's not a good idea."

"You were fortunate to find the persons in Chauny," said Iphigénie, touching a napkin gracefully to her lips. "And fortunate they were happy to welcome you again. As for the others . . ." She waved her hand ambiguously.

Later, as they parted on the street, Jim said, "We'll be back in a couple of weeks, but here's where you can reach us if you need to." He wrote the number on a bit of paper. It was Iphigénie's parents' home near Brantôme.

"*Au revoir*, Marshall," Iphigénie said, pecking his cheeks lightly.

Marshall tucked the paper into his trousers pocket and walked to the Métro, wondering whatever could possess him to call Jim Donegan in the Dordogne.

MARSHALL FOUND HIMSELF circling Napoléon's Tomb. The thing was like a sleigh, or a giant baby's crib with a lid on it. It was highly polished stone, the color of roasted chestnuts. Freestanding in a circle under the Dôme des Invalides, it was downright weird. Inside— a man once, now disintegrated. And he was packed into a set of coffins nesting one inside the other like Russian dolls.

A vague memory had drawn him here. Napoléon's Tomb was a safe house, he recalled someone saying. He didn't know what that meant. Did Nappy have room inside his cave to hide a scared airman with his dog tags in his boot? Marshall wondered why so many people got the idea that they were Napoléon in a past life. *Reincarnation—what crap*, Marshall thought. But Napoléon was always good for a laugh.

He had come here once with someone. With Robert on his bicycle?

NICOLAS WAS ON THE TELEPHONE with news. Marshall had just returned to the hotel from apartment hunting. It was too expensive to remain in the hotel. He was still breathing hard from his walk up five flights of stairs. The elevator was small and busy, and he had grown impatient with the wait.

"I've learned a few things," Nicolas said. "But I don't yet know what to do with this information. As you know, the people who helped you before you got to Chauny would be very difficult to locate, but we can start with the family you knew in Paris. My father told me something about the network in Paris that picked up the flyers from this region. It was one of several escape lines. It was called the Bourgogne."

"I don't remember anyone ever mentioning that name."

"You recall my father spoke of going to Paris to do the maps for the intelligence service?"

"*Oh, oui.*"

"He made a connection with a *convoyeur* from the Bourgogne on that trip."

Nicolas explained that the escape-line organizers had trained with the Free French in England, then sneaked back into France to find people to establish safe houses, to make the false IDs, and to act as guides. The Bourgogne network led the flyers from Paris south to Pau or Perpignan and linked them there with other guides for the rest of the journey. "All that is very familiar territory to you, Marshall."

"Yes and no. I was mostly kept in the dark. After I returned, I was debriefed in London, but I couldn't tell them much. And after the war, I just wanted to forget it. It was over."

"Yes, I understand," said Nicolas. "But now you want to know. That is normal. I'm trying to contact the man who was principal in the Bourgogne, and I'm waiting for him to answer my call."

"Well, I appreciate this, Nicolas. I'll have to give you more than a Bugs Bunny jacket this time."

Nicolas laughed. "It is my pleasure and my duty, Marshall. It would be an honor to me to help you in this quest."

"Of course they could all be dead, or citizens of New Caledonia by now."

"Ah. Life is an adventure, Marshall."

"So it is."

"I'm going to check more in the libraries. I may take the train into Paris one day and check some holdings in the National Archives or the *bibliothèque*."

"I could do that, perhaps?"

"It is no problem to me. Besides, Marshall, you may need better French for research at the very proper and bureaucratic Bibliothèque nationale! I mean no offense."

"I understand."

"I'll be in touch."

MARSHALL BOARDED A TAXI with his luggage and a bag of laundry. He had found a suitable place in the Fourteenth Arrondissement, south of the Montparnasse Cemetery. The concierge, who lived on the ground floor, was a laconic country woman from the north. Her husband had returned to their village for the summer to help his aged father with his fruit orchard.

In the lobby of the apartment building two chairs sat in a tiled nook with a potted plant and a wall telephone with buzzers. Marshall had rented a two-room furnished apartment up two flights. He squeezed his belongings into the Tom Thumb elevator and dashed up the stairs to meet it.

The apartment was spacious enough, with a large living area overlooking a small park, a minimalist kitchen, a shower, and a plain bedroom with a narrow but long-enough bed. There was even a bidet.

Exploring the neighborhood, he found a small market on the rue d'Alésia and stocked up on supplies, everything from cornflakes to toilet paper. He toted his bags back, then tried to figure out bedding. He had never bought sheets in his life. Where did one buy them in Paris? The concierge was out. Should he call Jim in the Dordogne?

A pleasant woman at the counter of the neighborhood *tabac* directed him to a department store near the Denfert-Rochereau Métro, and without—he hoped—seeming too stupid he selected a pair of sheets, a light fuzzy blanket, and a flat pillow. In the apartment, he arranged his possessions. He set his brain bag and typewriter on the table that would be his desk and stowed his clothing in the plain, massive armoire, which smelled like old shoes.

He examined his place. The wood floors were worn, the radiator was dusty. There was no TV, no radio, no clock. All he could hear was the murmur of the small refrigerator and the occasional sounds of traffic. This, he realized, was the only home he had made for himself since he arranged his corner of the barracks at Molesworth.

He was alone. No one back home knew where he was.

WIDE AWAKE IN THE MIDDLE of the night, he did a preflight walk-around, then ran through a preflight checklist in the cockpit. Instead of counting sheep, he tried to count and name all the switches, controls, and dials in a 747 cockpit—tachometer, fuel-flow indicator, radar altimeter, autopilot trim indicator, airspeed . . . flap position . . . hydraulic-system pressure . . .

He had to get his bearings. The search for long-lost friends from the war was beginning to seem absurd. He wanted to find Robert and the Vallons, but maybe finding the Alberts was enough. Marshall was officially an old man, booted from his job. Yet here he was, traipsing around France, indulging a pointless nostalgia. Trying to speak French was ludicrous. The Alberts must still be chortling over his awkward American drawl.

As dawn approached, he sank into slumber at last.

Late in the morning he bought a telephone, but there was nowhere to set it except on the floor by the window. In search of hardware, he wandered the neighborhood until he came upon an odd little shop that he had passed once or twice before. It called itself a *librairie-papeterie*, a bookstore-stationery store, but the windows displayed cases of small items—clothespins, light bulbs, shower caps, transistor radios, doll clothes, candles, hedge clippers.

"*Bonjour, monsieur,*" said the man behind the counter. He was wearing the typical long blue work smock.

"*Bonjour, monsieur.* I see that you have a little of everything here."

"*Oui, monsieur.* Just ask me for anything."

It took Marshall a moment to summon the French words. "Shoe polish."

"*Oui.*"

"Clock radio."

"*Bien sûr.*" The man tapped the counter confidently, his gold ring clicking.

"Hammer. Nails."

"You are a good client! The Americans are the best clients, because they want always everything."

"You have everything I need here," Marshall said. "This is the Everything Store! *Le magasin de tout?*"

"It is a *bazar,*" the man said, smiling. "*C'est le bazar ici.*"

Marshall left with all the items on his list, and also a notebook, envelopes, a supply of batteries, a flashlight, an extension cord, a small table for his telephone, and an antique postcard of Napoléon's Tomb.

THE CONCIERGE WAS astonished that Marshall's telephone service was hooked up in two days.

"People wait and wait," she said. She was sweeping the floor and smoking. She mumbled something about the weather.

He called Albert, to let him know where he was, and asked him to call Mary for him.

"Mary was sick last week," Albert said.

"Oh, what?"

"She had food poisoning—salmonella, I think. She was really sick for about four days, but she's over it. I never trusted her cooking."

"Should I call her myself?"

"No, I'll call her. She's O.K."

Albert reported that a tree had come down in a thunderstorm, but he had called the Garden Angels, who had dealt with it promptly. It was the tree in the back outside Marshall's den. Marshall would miss the shade—if he returned to New Jersey. At the moment, he couldn't quite imagine living there again. What was there for him in New Jersey?

"I'm sorry to hear that, Albert. But thanks for dealing with it."

"It missed the other trees, and it missed the shed. So I guess we're pretty lucky."

"Yeah. Don't forget to send me the bill."

"I forwarded some mail for you to the American Express."

"Thanks, Albert." After an awkward pause, he said, "Well, gotta go."

"Wait. How's it going over there, Dad? Did you find those people you were looking for?"

"Some of them. I found the family that helped me in that little town. They were still there, same house, all these years."

"That's good."

"It was great to see them again."

"Great. What else are you doing? Going to museums?"

"Not much. I haven't had time. But that sounds like a good idea."

"Don't worry about the house."

"O.K. I appreciate it. Take it easy, Albert. And tell Mary I'm glad she's O.K."

Marshall left a message for Nicolas, giving his new number, and another one on Jim Donegan's answering machine.

Later, as he was walking through the parc Montsouris, he looked up to see a 747 above the city, on its way out of De Gaulle. The gear was up, the wings clean, the nose jacked high. Things would be quieting down in the cockpit, the crew squaring things away, getting ready to hand control over to the autopilot. "Let George do it," they used to say.

19

A SMARTLY DRESSED WOMAN SAT AT THE SMALL ROUND TABLE next to his on the sidewalk at a corner brasserie on the rue d'Alésia, where he was waiting for Nicolas. Struggling with the diabolical crossword in *Le Monde*, he was aware of her sitting with her hands resting lightly on the table, a demitasse before her. She had shoulder-length blond hair. Her skirt was short, riding up her thighs. Her legs were crossed, and she was wearing stiletto heels with dark stockings. She was sitting there, doing nothing. She had been there perhaps twenty minutes. When he glanced her way, she looked away. He knew he was still attractive to women, at his age, even without his flight uniform. He wondered if she was waiting for him to speak to her. He heard her let out a sigh. She was waiting for someone who wasn't coming, he thought. He was stuck on a seven-letter word for *échelonner.* The crossword was impossible. Abandoning it, he read news from the States. Mount Saint Helens was still belching, and the hostages languished in Iran. Marshall was still angry with President Carter for failing to rescue them. The woman next to him was attractive, and he thought perhaps she was an actress, studying for her role as a woman of the café scene. Or waiting to be discovered by a film director.

Nicolas appeared, having taken the train in from Chauny, and they did the two-cheek. All smiles, he brought greetings from the family and a gift of damson jam from Gisèle.

Marshall wanted another coffee, but the waiter, who had seen Nicolas arrive, began clearing another table.

"I'm too impatient," Marshall said to Nicolas. "I'll never learn your easygoing ways here."

"You are so fast, Marshall. Quick to the draw!"

Marshall forced a smile. "Gary Cooper, that's me. But you know, when I went back to the States in '44, still gung-ho to fight the Nazis, I was sent to Texas to train bomber pilots. It was a letdown."

The waiter interrupted, and Nicolas chatted with him about an impending football match. Marshall wished he had a gift for small talk. He saw the woman at the next table pay her bill and walk away, not even wobbling on her stilts.

"I made an interesting discovery, Marshall," Nicolas said after they had ordered coffee. "There was a youth fascist group who wore the blue beret."

"Are you serious? How could the schoolgirl who helped me escape have been a fascist? It doesn't make sense."

"I know." Nicolas laughed. "Perhaps it is the French beret that is the problem—it is like a symbol, it can mean anything anyone wants it to mean."

Marshall stared at a pigeon eyeing a chunk of baguette the woman in high heels had dropped on the cobblestones. The pigeon came strutting across a large manhole cover wrought in the pattern of a star.

"Nicolas, I've been thinking. I can't really imagine what it would have been like if America had been occupied and stressed to the limit the way the French were. What would we have done?"

"You would have risen to the occasion, Marshall."

"I don't know." The pigeon seemed to be looking at him. He said, "I can't imagine my children doing what the young people here did." He wondered about Loretta, what she would have done. "What about your daughters?"

"I would like to think that they would be strong." Nicolas smiled. "We speak often of this question."

A flock of nuns passed by, and the pigeon skittered away.

"Do you recall a Robert Lebeau?" Nicolas asked. "Robert Jules Lebeau?"

"No. I don't recognize that name."

"Lebeau may have been the one who was with you in Paris."

"The guy I knew as Robert? I don't think I ever knew his last name."

"I have run across Lebeau's name in association with the Vallons, and I believe it's probable that he came to the apartment where you were sheltered. He worked for the Bourgogne line."

"Do you know where he is now?"

"He owns an *épicerie* in Saint-Mandé. A small grocery. I have just been there, but he was in Provence, inspecting crops. I don't know how long he stays, and his daughter at the shop would not say."

"Why not?"

"I had the sense that she did not want to expose her father to a stranger. In any case, we must wait a few days for him to return."

When the waiter brought a press-pot of coffee and a pitcher of hot milk, Nicolas offered more pleasantries. He was no doubt popular with his students, Marshall thought, for he had an easy, jocular manner. Marshall regarded the short-cropped dark hair and brown eyes of the slim Frenchman. He was wearing dark pants, a blue shirt, and thin leather shoes. His long, delicate feet matched his graceful hands.

"So who was this Robert Jules Lebeau?" Marshall asked when the waiter was finished. He hadn't imagined Robert as a shopkeeper. He had thought Robert might be a diplomat. Or a journalist perhaps.

"He was a *convoyeur* who met *aviateurs* north of Paris," Nicolas told him. "I'm guessing that he was the contact for the Vallon family and very possibly the youth you remember coming to them on his bicycle."

Nicolas gave Marshall a brief history of the various escape networks for downed airmen. After the largest one, the Comète, was infiltrated by the Gestapo and nearly destroyed, the Bourgogne smuggled airmen from Paris to Spain.

"Did you ever hear of Dédée de Jongh?"

"I don't think so."

"She was a young Belgian woman *très forte*, very strong, very courageous. She began the Comète and escorted many *aviateurs* herself across the Pyrenees. She was just a girl. But never mind. You could not have known her."

Nicolas sipped his bowl of coffee and winced at its heat. Marshall liked the idea of drinking coffee out of a bowl, but he had poured in too much milk, making the coffee too weak. A loud bus whooshed past, flooding them with fumes. Nicolas waited for the noise to subside, then reported some findings about the chief of the Bourgogne network—Georges Broussine, a well-known journalist.

"One of Papa's old contacts remembered Broussine, and he knew that Lebeau had been to Chauny to meet flyers, and then Papa recognized the names. So I think it is likely that they are links between Chauny and the family you stayed with in Paris."

"Your father said he didn't know any names."

Nicolas shrugged. "Papa knows more than he allows. Anyway, the Bourgogne chief still lives here, but he does not answer me. He may be out of the country. Perhaps in the meantime we will find Monsieur Lebeau and get our information."

Bells in the nearby church were ringing the hour. Marshall had walked past that church, at the intersection of Maine and Leclerc, several times on his way to the Métro, but he had paid no attention to it.

He said to Nicolas, "That church has probably been standing there for time out of mind, tolling its bell. I never took time to notice things like that before. Not since I was in hiding during the war."

Nicolas said, "Marshall, the churches did not ring their bells during the Occupation. You heard no church bells then."

20

Marshall walked around the city aimlessly, his head in a muddle. He was in a detective story, yet he wasn't the detective. He was the reader, or an innocent bystander caught up in an intrigue. He was tempted to chase down Robert Jules Lebeau the *épicier* himself, but he recognized that Nicolas wanted to help, and Marshall didn't want to deprive him of that satisfaction.

Nevertheless, a couple of days later, he found himself in the nearby suburb of Saint-Mandé on the *épicier*'s block, a short street of small shops off the avenue du Général de Gaulle. The fruits and vegetables were in bins outside the shop. It was a simple grocery store. At the small counter inside stood an attractive young woman in an Indian tunic and jeans, her limp hair tied in two loose hanks. He selected a plum and went inside to pay.

"*Bonjour, madame,*" he said.

"*Bonjour, monsieur. C'est tout?*"

"*Oui.*" She was occupied with tying some string on a package, and he waited to ask about Lebeau. He paid for the fruit, then hesitantly asked for water to wash the plum.

"It is clean!"

"*Vraiment?*"

"*Vrai.*" She was shooing him from her shop.

"O.K.," he said, wondering which one of them had been rude. Maybe his French was at fault.

At the door, he turned. "Is your name Lebeau?" he asked.

"*Non.* He is not here."

"Monsieur Lebeau owns this market?"

"*Non.* It is mine."

"Where is Monsieur Lebeau?"

She shrugged and began furiously punching some numbers on her small calculator, dismissing him.

"I believe I knew him during the war," he said. "I'd like very much to find him again."

"I know nothing of him and the war."

"Do you know a family named Vallon?"

"No."

Anger erupted in him, and he turned away quickly. "*Au revoir, madame,*" he said, his back to her. He thought she grunted a perfunctory *au revoir.*

She seemed young, but Marshall couldn't judge age anymore. He didn't feel old himself. Physically, he felt no different from ten or twenty years ago. He frequently searched his face in the mirror for signs of age. He didn't have wrinkles, just a few vague sags. He touched his face now. His skin was rough and his beard was scratchy. He needed a new razor.

He returned to the Métro, where several streets met and angled off in different directions. Still irritated, he paused near the stairway down to the trains and surveyed the busy intersection, with its bountiful trees and striped crosswalks. Nicolas had suggested that Saint-Mandé was where Marshall had hidden with the Vallons, but Marshall did not recognize this space. One building opposite the Métro was shaped like a crescent, and he thought he would have remembered that, but he didn't.

AT AMERICAN EXPRESS he collected his mail—a letter from Mary, a newsletter from the airline, some financial statements, letters from his crewmates Tony Campanello and Bobby Redburn, and a letter from an address in White Plains, New York.

He decided to walk over to the Madeleine, a neoclassical church that Nicolas said had been a meeting place for aviators stashed in Paris. It was easy to find, Nicolas explained, and the men simply blended into the crowd on the steps in front. Marshall had not come here when he was hiding in Paris, but now he sat on a step and read his mail. The open sun warmed him, and the crowd disappeared from his consciousness. Mary's gentle inquiries touched him. She didn't mention her food poisoning.

Marshall was glad to hear from two of the three crewmates who had finished the war in a POW camp. Bobby Redburn, the ball-turret gunner, wrote from California:

> *You asked what I remembered about the crash. I remember scrambling up out of that bubble when Webb said bail out, but then Hootie stopped me from bailing out. And that was after Cochran had already flown out the door. Chick was always impulsive—he had a hair-trigger reflex. That's a great gunner for you. But I grabbed the chute pack and was ready to dive. I guess I'm glad I didn't. It tore me up what happened to Hootie—and he may have even saved my life.*

Marshall found Redburn's letter painful to read. The mission seemed to be there again—the plane descending, crew scrambling, the tumult that followed. He folded the letter and turned to Tony Campanello's letter. Tony was the navigator.

> *I called your house and your boy told me to write you in Paris. He said you'd retired and become French. Couldn't get enough of it, huh? When I got out of the stalag I never wanted to go to a foreign country again in my life. And I haven't.*
>
> *But I'm kind of misty-eyed about what you told me about going to Belgium. You know, I never thought back. I just hated those Krauts so much and wanted to get out of that hellhole camp I was in and get home. I thought I'd finally gotten that behind me. Truly, it*

made me feel proud to think of those people in Belgium remembering
us, so many years later. A very nice family took me to the hospital.
They knew the Germans would come and get me, but my leg was
busted so bad they couldn't have hidden me. I think Ford or Hadley
might be able to help you out with your questions about the
Underground. . . .

It would be mighty fine to see you again. I've done pretty good for
myself, working at Boeing. Real good money, Marshall.

Marshall continued reading about Tony's job in Seattle, his house
on the beach, his children and grandchildren, the club he belonged
to, all of it remote and almost meaningless to Marshall now. He felt
like a rare bird. What did he think he was doing? He had always had
a tendency to set out on his own, without advice or help. During the
years of his career there had always been a family attached, like a flying buttress, a visible support. Now that he was truly on his own,
being a loner had a different meaning. He wished his search for
Robert and the Vallons could be simpler, that he could just turn a
corner and meet Mme Vallon, holding out her arms to welcome him
back to Paris.

The last letter was from Gordon Webb, Lawrence Webb's son.
Marshall had written to the pilot's widow about his visit to the crash
site, and she had passed the letter along to her son. Marshall had a
fleeting memory of a rambunctious tyke with a grieving mother after
the war when he and a couple of the crew went to Baltimore to pay
a condolence visit. Now Gordon Webb wrote that he was flying for
Pan Am, out of Kennedy, and that he often flew to Paris. He wanted
to meet Marshall, to hear firsthand about the incident that took his
father's life. Marshall didn't like the idea. He replaced the letter in its
envelope and surveyed his mail.

It was too warm in the sun. He stood and made his way down the
steps past a pair of picnickers and a woman with a baby stroller
parked precariously on a step. The plum in his pocket had grown

soft, and it was staining his jacket. He examined the plum, fingering the squishy, bruised spot. He crossed the street and dropped it into a waste bin.

Glancing up, he saw an L-1011 head into De Gaulle, its gear down. For the guys in the cockpit, the adrenaline was starting to pump. Get your heading right, sink rate right, speed right. Line her up, compensate for the wind, bring her in dead center, flare, kiss the tarmac, ease in the thrust reversers. God, he had loved it.

21

IN THE MIDDLE OF THE NIGHT, WITH STREETLIGHTS AND NOISE streaming through the cracks of the shutters, Marshall tossed with his whirling thoughts. Words and images reverberated— Bourgogne, Lebeau, *épicerie*, rutabaga.

Bright lights spilled through the cracks of the dilapidated shutters. He needed curtains. He remembered putting up curtain rods for Loretta, screwing metal pieces to the window facings and hooking together the metal tabs of an infernal system of brackets and flat, corrugated rods. He didn't want to do that again. He could call Mary for advice. But he didn't want to think about curtains. Or Loretta.

Next morning, he decided to go to the Gare du Nord and try to visualize it in the gray tones of 1944. The station was newer, busier now—no German officers in their olive-drab greatcoats, ballooned trousers, and menacing jackboots. He did not know what track he had arrived on, but as he roamed across the wide expanse of the station, heading toward the trains, he remembered more clearly his first sight of Annette when he arrived from Chauny. She was studying a timetable. On the train he had seen a workman wearing a blue beret, and he was concerned that there might be more than one female in a blue beret and he would follow the wrong one. But she was clearly the *girl* in the blue beret. Her white socks were slouchy, her shoe soles worn thin, her hair tousled. She wore a wool coat, buttoned up tight, and carried a book satchel. She glanced in his direction but did not acknowledge him or the other airman—Delancey, the navigator from Nebraska. At the end of the platform, she turned and crossed the large atrium of the station, then skipped down some stairs. Marshall and Delancey followed as she led them up and down other stairways and out into the street, then finally down into the bowels of the Métro.

She had zigzagged like a rabbit, Marshall thought now as he tried to re-create that journey.

After stopping for a pack of mints at a kiosk on the main level, he made his way back into the Métro. At a main juncture for train #4, a jazz ensemble with horns, a saxophone, and drums was playing a song he thought he recognized. But there was no reason he should know a popular song, unless it was some unlistenable noise he had been forced to hear from his children. Thinking about his children's alien, alienating music saddened him. He stood listening to the musicians, young people from a music school identified on their placard. His habit had always been to walk unresponsively past sidewalk acts and beggars. Now he wavered. He made a resolution. If he listened for more than a minute, then he owed them something. He scattered his change onto the square of dark velvet in front of the musicians. A twenty-franc piece jumped the edge, and he stooped to retrieve it. The trumpet started then, blasting Marshall's ears. He recognized the song now—"Night and Day," from the forties. Then, as the trumpet soared, it occurred to him that when he arrived here at the Gare du Nord—scared, wearing a Frenchman's ill-fitting work outfit—his first sight of Annette had formed his chief impression of her, the one that stayed with him. It was her confidence, the way she strode across the crowded station, gliding past German soldiers. It was her carriage, the way she sported her beret as if it were high fashion, not a mundane piece of a school uniform. It was her liveliness, her self-assurance. And yet she was so young. He had immediately felt that he should protect her, not vice versa.

From the Gare du Nord, he took the Métro, changing at Châtelet for the #1 train. He wasn't certain, but he thought the stop he wanted was the Palais Royal-Louvre. After emerging at the large square, he made his way to the colonnaded shops along the rue de Rivoli.

There had been a *photomaton* among those shops. One day Annette had guided him there. It was a cubbyhole on a balcony within a department store. He remembered Annette speaking to the woman there. He had practiced his mug shot, in his French dress clothes, and learned *"regardez-moi."* The woman placed him against a white wall and aimed the camera at him. *"Regardez-moi,"* she said. Then, nervously, she packaged his photos in a cellophane sleeve and added a receipt, handwritten elaborately, with several notations. Marshall was eager to leave, but Annette was in no rush. Self-possessed, she exchanged a burble of French jabber with the clerk. Marshall admired Annette's nonchalance. Finally, with a cheery *"Merci, au revoir,"* she left the shop ahead of him. He was to walk along the Colonnade, then cross the street and find the bench where she would be waiting in the Tuileries.

Outside, he remembered now, the sun was shining so brightly that the sandy surface of the winter garden, with its bare shrubs and twisted tree limbs, hurt his eyes. He had worn a suit of M. Vallon's for the occasion. Even though it was tight, he had felt comfortable in the suit jacket, knowing the Germans would not expect an American to wear a French suit coat and tie. He had combed his hair at the *photomaton*. His photo was rakish, he decided later.

As he approached the bench, she stood and made her way, *sans souci*, toward the Métro.

At the flat later that day, Annette and her mother worked with the photos, creating a fake ID card for Marshall. Their equipment was kept in a carpetbag, which they were prepared to toss out the rear window in an emergency. The bag contained numerous stamps and specially printed forms to produce work-identity cards. They changed Marshall's age so that he would be too old for the obligatory work service—the labor camps in Germany.

"It's hard to think of so many new names," Annette said with a sigh, as she pored over the telephone directory. "How about François Baudouin? No, there *is* a François Baudouin. There's no Julien Baudouin, though."

"It will be good for a stonemason," said her mother. "You are a stonemason!"

—

"HOW DID IT GO at the *photomaton*?" asked M. Vallon when he returned that day.

"It went well," Annette said quickly before Marshall could speak. "The photo is handsome. He is a true Frenchman!"

M. Vallon was a fastidious man, well dressed, calm. Marshall had noticed how he brushed his suit every morning before leaving for work, and he carried an umbrella on rain-threatening days.

M. Vallon said, "I was on the rue de Rivoli this morning, before you were there. It was just before noon. There was an unusual quietness, but then in the distance I could hear the German soldiers begin their march. Their marching and their music drifted all the way down the Champs-Elysées." M. Vallon marched across the room, imitating the Nazi goose steps. "If only they knew how ridiculous they appear to others, they would retreat in humiliation."

Mme Vallon said gently, "But my dear, if they see you making fun, they will not be amused."

"One must make fun nevertheless," said Annette. "Play the innocent! Confuse them with a perfect stream of beautiful French words. '*Monsieur*, you are in France. In France, one speaks French!' "

Annette's mother worked on Marshall's work-permit card after dinner. Marshall practiced writing his new name, Julien Baudouin, on a sheet of paper before signing the card. He was Julien Baudouin, a stonemason, a *tailleur de pierre*, born in 1917 in Blois, residing in Montreuil.

That night they heard a commotion in the streets again—a heavy, distant sound, then a siren.

Mme Vallon, regal in her robe, stood with her family in the center of the living room floor. Marshall watched from his doorway. "We have to do something more," she said. "They only strengthen our resolve."

M. Vallon embraced his wife and daughters, and they stood together, listening. The siren waned, and then the streets were quiet.

"It could have been anything," he said.

No one was ready to return to bed, so they sat together for a while in the dark at the dining table. M. Vallon said, "When I was on the rue de Rivoli today, I had to pass the Hôtel Meurice. I was not allowed to walk in front of it, where there is the white barrier, so I walked through the Tuileries for some distance. It sickens me, the enemy headquartered in such a magnificent place, in the heart of the pride of Paris."

He slammed his fist on the table, an unexpected gesture from this elegant man, Marshall thought.

In the morning Marshall chatted with Annette as she and Monique prepared for school.

He said, "Your parents are magnificent. You too. You're all very brave."

"No. We have to be careful, but we must help you. You are our cause. If we don't help the *aviateurs* and get them back safely, then we have done nothing."

He remembered he was sitting on a divan. She leaned over and gave him a quick two-cheek kiss. Then she lifted her satchel and headed for school.

"You are very nice," she said, turning at the door.

THE *PHOTOMATON* WAS NO longer there. In its approximate place was a souvenir shop selling gaudy silk scarves, postcards, plastic Eiffel Towers, even berets. The legendary Paris that had been saved from obliteration was now burlesqued by tourist-happy gay Paree. Marshall walked down the Colonnade, past the swank Hôtel Meurice, M. Vallon's anguished tone echoing in his thoughts. At the place de la Concorde, the view before him was vast and open, like his ardent heart.

22

He WAS LIKING THE WIDE-OPEN SPACES OF PARIS, THE EASE of movement, the pace. One afternoon he strolled through the Jardin des Plantes. Annette had taken him and another aviator to see animals in a large park, but today the layout of the menagerie at the big botanical garden did not seem at all familiar. He stared at the sad apes and headed for the exit on the rue Linné.

"*MONSIEUR GUY, BONJOUR!*" he said with exaggerated good cheer when he arrived at the Everything Store. Guy was his best friend in this city, he thought rashly.

"*Bonjour,* Captain, how do you go today?"

"I go just fine today. And you, Guy?"

"*Comme-ci, comme-ça.* A little of the gallbladder."

"*Quoi?*" Marshall didn't recognize the French term.

"Next to the liver."

"Too much rich food, Guy?"

Guy shrugged. "It is necessary to eat."

Marshall enjoyed poking around the store, gabbing with Guy about his stuff. He seemed to be a pack rat. Marshall had recently discovered some artifacts from the forties among the piles of out-dated merchandise. He pored through postcards and photos of war-planes and old sheet music, a miscellany scattered among batteries, shower attachments, art supplies, nails. Guy knew that Marshall was a pilot who had been in France during the war and was seeking the past, but he had volunteered little of his own. He had said, "I was only a little child."

Today Guy pumped him for the story, and Marshall stayed for a long time, telling Guy about hiding out in Paris during the war. Guy listened as though he was turning over a problem in his mind.

Finally Guy said, "I have often heard the older people say to the younger ones, *'Il vous faudrait une bonne guerre'*—you need a good war. They meant so we could understand the hardship of life. But the ones who were *résistants* would not say that. They were disgusted by war." He paused and stared into the labyrinth of his store.

"I would not wish a war on my child," Guy said.

WAITING FOR NICOLAS'S NEXT REPORT, Marshall passed a few days uneventfully, watching himself settle into some vague routines. In the mornings he ate cornflakes or eggs in his kitchen, then went to the *tabac* up the street for a *double express*. He liked it better than his own experimental brews. He bought bread from the *boulangerie*, lugged his laundry to a woman down the block, explored the neighborhood. He walked through the corner church whose bells he heard so frequently. It was the Saint-Pierre de Montrouge, at place Victor Basch. The names were just words to him. He made a circuit of the pews and altars, but he did not know what to look for. He explored Montmartre, ate a *croque monsieur* at a sidewalk table, and mounted the steps of the Sacré Coeur but didn't go inside. After buying a small TV from the Everything Store, he found a news-debate program he enjoyed and was pleased that he could more or less follow the fast-talking Frenchmen. He rediscovered jumping jacks and push-ups. He couldn't find anywhere to buy a pack of peanuts.

At the bank, he changed another two hundred dollars into franc notes. Then reluctantly he arranged to meet Gordon Webb on his next stopover in Paris.

23

WHEN THEY MET IN THE LOBBY OF THE PAN AM CREW HOTEL, Gordon Webb saluted Marshall and invited him for a drink in the bar. Wearing khakis and a polo shirt, he looked ready for a round of golf. At first Marshall didn't notice a resemblance between Gordon and the resolute pilot of the *Dirty Lily*, but later he heard Lieutenant Webb's voice in Gordon's guffaw. The kid had a loud laugh, just like his father.

"Well, Marshall Stone," Gordon said after they had been served drinks. "I tell you, right now I'm bored with airline flying. I miss all that shaky-do flying I did in 'Nam! I bet you miss those Big-Ass Birds."

"The B-17 wasn't very shaky-do, not like you mean in a fighter."

"You're putting me on. I've seen films of 17s damn near doing rolls."

"Well, maybe," Marshall said. "But you can bet those crews needed to wash out their shorts when they got back to base."

"That's a joke," he added when Gordon didn't respond.

Gordon said, "I'm thirty-eight. I did three tours in 'Nam. I signed on with Pan Am five years ago. After flying reconnaissance, the airline is like milk runs. Pretty dull."

"Times have changed," Marshall said, smearing water from his glass around on the table.

"I flew the fastest. I flew recon. I flew the Voodoo, the One-Oh-Wonder." Gordon made sweeping, swirling motions with his hands, a bird angling and diving.

For a while, Gordon described his hairiest flights in the F-101, and Marshall found himself both envious and eager to quit the subject. He glanced intermittently at the TV screen—the largest he had seen in Paris—that hovered above the zinc bar. Gordon's voice drowned out the TV and the quiet conversations of the others in the room. The waiters scurried past unobtrusively.

At last, with his second drink, Gordon asked about his father's last flight. Marshall remembered how he had taken over the plane because he thought Webb had the jim-jams. This was not what he told Gordon.

24

IT WAS A TENSE MISSION, BUT MARSHALL WAS GEARED UP FOR IT. Rocking and swaying, he rode the rolling air as the formation of nearly a thousand fully loaded heavy bombers clawed their way to Frankfurt. The *Dirty Lily* behaved herself. The formation was so huge—a great dragon, a sky serpent, miles and miles long—that no single bomber was in much danger. Enemy fighters could maul a squadron far in front or far behind, they could blast the guts out of bomber after bomber, but your own squadron might sail along undisturbed.

With all their guns, B-17s truly were flying fortresses, Marshall believed then. He remembered the strangeness of flying with stacked bombs at his back and gunners all around—pickets on duty, manning the ramparts. The pilots sat high in the cockpit like kings on thrones, commanding their airborne castles.

As the *Dirty Lily* advanced into Germany, a swarm of Messerschmitts appeared in the distance. They whipped through a high squadron far ahead. Marshall could see the winking lights of machine-gun fire.

An Me-109 came closer, diving toward a nearby squadron.

"Bandit at two o'clock," the right waist gunner called to the crew. Hootie's tone was as nonchalant as if he were offering a passing hello to a ground crewman.

Now other crewmen got on the inter-phone.

"Where's our escort?"

"They're coming."

"We need P-51s," Webb said.

Marshall didn't see any friendlies.

As usual, the chatter was nervous, self-mocking, and incoherent. Webb had never succeeded in imposing discipline.

"Uh-oh."

"Adjust, adjust."

"No, we're clear."

Marshall was imagining what he would write to Loretta. The enemy fighter was like a devilish insect tormenting a cow in a herd. Up close, the interceptors were more like vampire bats. No, not that at all.

"Can you see, can you see?"

"Oh, say can you see."

"There's more of them—"

"There's a Mustang—a little friend!"

"That one's ours all right."

"This is tight. . . . Hold on."

"Stop it, guys," Webb said. "Pipe down."

An Me-109 was spiraling, aflame. The sky ahead was chaotic, with tracers and shell bursts scratching the blue like an electrical storm. Strange colors and breezes whirled aloft. It was not real. It was a show. *We know what we're doing*, Marshall thought.

He had been such a smart-aleck, he thought now.

Several Me-109s were tagging one of the planes ahead. Webb was jiggling and shimmying, to spoil the fighters' aim, although they weren't shooting yet. Some were getting closer, but nothing to worry about yet. In the *Dirty Lily*'s nose compartment, the bombardier and the navigator were working their guns. In the rear, machine guns hammered sporadically. The plane shook with the recoil. Marshall vibrated in his seat, which he had reinforced with a piece of metal from the repair post.

Then the fighters melted away. The squadron was approaching the target—the grid of factory buildings, the roadways the crew had been told to expect.

"She's yours, bombardier," Webb called to Al Grainger. Webb eased back from the yoke.

The flak guns down below opened up. Batteries of 88s filled the sky with exploding fragmentation shells—great puffs of greasy black smoke with crimson fire in the center, bursts of lethal metal splinters whistling through the air. The agitation from the shells whipped up the already tempestuous sky, but the *Dirty Lily* bored straight ahead through the black blotches, held steady by the bombardier. This was anus-puckering time. The flak seemed close enough to touch. Jerry flak was accurate, as flak went.

Marshall pictured Al Grainger leaning over his bombsight and gently maneuvering the *Dirty Lily* with slight twists of his control knobs. The pilots could only sit and wait. There were no atheists on a bomb run, Grainger always said.

When the bomb-bay doors opened, a rush of freezing air blasted the crew.

"Shut the door!" Marshall called, as usual, waiting for Grainger to toggle the bomb switch. Sweating out the bomb run seemed to take hours.

Grainger called, "Bombs away!" and the *Dirty Lily* lifted, suddenly lighter and buoyant. Webb instantly grabbed the controls again. The front of the formation was bending back. The huge dragon was slowly wheeling around to begin tearing and pawing its way homeward. The sky was graying, but the weather would hold. They could see below them tracer smoke and then the multicolored smoke blooms from the falling bombs.

There was more flak. Marshall heard bits of it hitting the fuselage. It was raining metal.

Then the plane jerked. Something heavier had hit them. It didn't register for a moment. Marshall saw smoke puff from the #4 engine. The engine began to sputter.

"Shut down number four!" Webb commanded. "Feather the prop!"

Marshall yanked the throttle and punched the feather button as quickly as he could.

"Done," he said.

Underpowered, the *Dirty Lily* was sluggish again, and they were unable to keep up with the other Forts. The drag on the starboard wing was severe. Losing speed, she was dropping from formation. Marshall struggled to trim the plane, while Webb pushed the yoke forward and descended. They needed to get away from the action, where they wouldn't be noticed. They hoped the *Dirty Lily*'s olive-and-gray camouflage paint would make them inconspicuous. Alone, a straggler, she would be easy prey.

"We can get back on three engines," Webb said, stating the obvious.

Webb was too calm, Marshall thought. That was because this wasn't really happening.

Marshall didn't know what had hit them. Probably flak. But maybe it was a chunk of metal blown off a Fort. The sky was a pandemonium of random debris, shells and fragments, ragged junk, pieces of airplanes.

This wasn't what he had imagined back in flight school. This was all wrong.

WHEN THEY WERE LOW enough to doff their oxygen masks, Webb sent Marshall back to the waist to inspect for damage. The waist gunners were scanning the skies through their open windows. Marshall noted some flak rips in the plane's skin, but nothing serious—a few punctures, a couple of jagged metal bits of flak underfoot. The fuselage was cramped, crew jammed together ass to elbow. But the light coming through the windows was dazzling.

Then, as Marshall turned back toward the cockpit, the light flickered. A wisp of cloud washed past. Then another. Marshall hurried forward. Through the cockpit windows he saw a lovely drift of whiteness in front of them. Clouds. Webb burrowed into the mass. The lighting dimmed. They were inside a soft gray haze, concealed from sight.

"Thank God," Webb said, as Marshall slid into his seat. "If this cloud-bank goes far enough. . . ."

He didn't need to say more. If they could work their way west hidden within clouds, Jerry wouldn't spot them.

They flew on, steady and cold and watchful. They alternated. Webb flew for a while, then handed off to Marshall. From time to time, they dipped below the clouds so the navigator could get a peek at the ground, to correct his position coordinates. The crew was grim and silent. Marshall refused to believe they might not reach base. The trip home should be simple now, a steady push into the west. Slow, maybe, but they would get there. They were having steak and ice cream at mess that night, rare treats.

"Webb, I need you to drop below again." It was Campanello, the navigator.

"Roger."

Webb took the controls from Marshall and eased back the throttles. The plane sank gracefully toward brightness below. She floated downward into the clear. Marshall was counting the seconds till they could climb again.

They depended on Campanello to guide them home. On the way over, there was no need to navigate. They had played follow-the-leader, the sky full of Forts all going in the same direction, and Campanello could take it easy. But now, with his compass, ruler, and a pencil, and only a few glimpses at the world below, he had to take them home by dead reckoning.

Lily lifted up into the clouds again.

THEY HAD BEEN FLYING more than an hour, disbelief masking dread. They were still swaddled in clouds when a Focke-Wulf 190 suddenly appeared alongside Marshall's starboard window, materializing out of the gray mist. Marshall and the German pilot spotted each other at the same moment, and each froze. The Jerry's leather helmet was pushed back, exposing a patch of bright blond hair. Then the FW-190 flipped and vanished.

"Bandit starboard!" Marshall yelled on the inter-phone just as he heard the guns open up.

"Where did that come from?"

"Did you see that guy?"

"Let's get the hell home," Webb said, muttering half to himself, half to Marshall.

How did the 190 find them? He would circle back, if he could. Marshall called to the gunners, "Don't blink!"

It must have been sheer, lousy chance, he thought. Fighters were looking for them, but the chance of finding them in the clouds was one in a million. And finding them again, unlikely.

But the FW would alert others. More German fighters would be looking for them now. A straggler. A defenseless Yank.

"Those big Fritzes get ambitious when Goering threatens to send them to the Russian front," Marshall said. "He promised them an Iron Cross for every Fort."

They flew on, Webb maneuvering only a little, a slight zigzag in the clouds. There was a nervous babble on the inter-phone for a while, but it died down.

The silence of the inter-phone then was like the crew holding its breath. When Marshall wasn't scanning the cloud-clogged skies, he steadied himself by methodically reviewing the compass, the altimeter, the airspeed indicator, making a constant inventory of the instruments. Could we speed up? Could we trim better?

Webb, exhausted, handed off to Marshall while he wrote up the data in his log. They seemed to be flying in slow motion. It was eerie, timeless. They pushed through the enveloping grayness, at times seeming not to move at all. Marshall's eyes were stinging. He had to remind himself to blink. He had hardly noticed when they came down out of the sub-zero cold.

Slowly they groped their way, fighting the yoke and rudder pedals, trying to pile up the miles behind them. An hour of this. Or was it a day? Or a week?

The hands of the chronometer crept ahead but didn't seem to have any meaning. The *Dirty Lily* skulked through the grog. They were slinking toward home.

We won't die, Marshall said to himself. *We might not die.*

Then the clouds began breaking up. *Damn.* Adrenaline pulsed higher. The vapor around them thinned, broke apart, and gradually evaporated. They were in the open.

It must be Belgium down there, unless they had angled down over France. No sign of the Channel, unless it was the blue haze on the horizon.

Farmland, a river, a village—a mile or so below. Marshall could make out a stone church. More villages and fields.

Campanello was calling through the inter-phone the name of the river below when a Jerry fighter bore in on them from dead ahead. Grainger yelled out, "Attack! Attack! Twelve o'clock level."

—Grainger was shooting.

—The plane jolted.

—The Plexiglas nose cone shattered.

—Bullets smacked the back of the pilots' control panel.

—Top turret opened up, then the waist gunners.

—The FW raced under them and was gone.

Wind screamed through the opened fuselage, and the *Dirty Lily* bucketed and shuddered. Marshall and Webb both grabbed their yokes, fighting a plane almost out of control. Their air speed was dropping dangerously.

Webb motioned downward. He and Marshall both pushed forward on their yokes. The crippled plane nosed down.

The top turret gunner called, "I think I got him!"

Tail gunner: "No, you didn't."

"Al's hit!" Campanello yelled. His voice was thin and distant in Marshall's headset. "Shoulder. And me. My leg."

Webb yanked the yoke to the right. They pulled through a diving turn, then hauled back. Straining, muscling, Webb and Marshall leveled the bomber at about five hundred feet, maybe less.

"Bandit, ten o'clock high!" Top turret.

The guns were hammering again.

The FW—silver with red markings—raked their port side, nose to tail.

Hadley, the radio man, called out something that sounded like "running board."

Chick Cochran was on the inter-phone from the waist. "We've got a fire back here!"

"Bail out, bail out!" cried Webb.

"No!" Marshall cried. "Too low!"

Webb leaned back and reached for his chute pack. Marshall clung to the yoke.

Marshall called to the crew, "I'm bringing it in."

Marshall said to Webb, "It's my airplane."

He saw fields next to a village. He was going straight in. He yelled on the inter-phone for the ball-turret gunner to crawl out.

They crested a line of trees, then sank toward the dirt. As the plane skidded onto the field, the props ripping the ground, Marshall saw Webb slumped, head resting on his chest as if he had just nodded off for a quick snooze.

25

MARSHALL HAD RARELY TALKED ABOUT THE PLANE GOING down, and he hadn't told Gordon all of it. He had never felt like taking credit for bringing the plane down safely. Webb was unconscious, perhaps already dead—exactly when, Marshall couldn't say.

"An FW-190. A mean fucker," Gordon was saying.

Marshall squirmed. "Your father had been hit. He was slumped over by the time we stopped moving."

Gordon shook his head. "Damn." He surveyed the room blankly. "That's what's called a bad day," he said, forcing a laugh. He flexed his fists.

"Nothing was anybody's fault," Marshall said. "Your dad did one hell of a job. Nobody could have done better."

Gordon called to the bartender, "*Garçon*—what do I have to do to get a refill?"

The bartender raised his eyebrows and turned his back. He made a show of dawdling before bringing the bottle.

"There's certain things I've got against these Frenchies," Gordon said to Marshall, after the bartender left. "Why they didn't do the job in Vietnam. Why they hate us for doing the job they couldn't do. We saved their ass in the World War Number Two, but they forgot about that. They have convenient memory. I tell this to my wife, and she says, 'Gordon, you're like a dog worrying a bone. Bury that bone and let's go add another garage to the split-level.' Or some other crap." He laughed again, apparently struck by his own wit.

"Have you been married long?" Marshall asked.

"Linda and I got together after I came back to the States in 1970. Now, that was a bad scene for you, 1970. All those protesters, spitting on GIs coming home." He swallowed an eye-popping slug of Scotch. "I had some problems with that war from the start, but I did my job. That's American values." Webb turned serious. "We had military discipline when I was a boy—lights out, reveille, spit-polish your shoes. When I saw my stepfather in the hall on the way to the goddamn bathroom, I had to salute! He was a career Army man, a colonel. I don't know when he met Mom."

He paused. "Then you see what I did to repay him—joined the Air Force!" Gordon rubbed his hands together. "The One-Oh-Wonder! Man, I was one afterburning bastard."

Gordon asked Marshall a few questions about his father then—how he did takeoffs, what he liked to do on his time off. Marshall tried to paint a lively portrait, but he was flummoxed. It was hard to come up with stirring stories about Gordon's father.

Then he remembered that he had bicycled into the English countryside with Lawrence Webb and a couple of other crewmates after a tough mission to Bremen. They had made a day of it, biking through peaceful country, racing on flat stretches.

"He was a speed demon on a bike," Marshall said. "A One-Oh-Wonder."

He declined another drink. After promising Gordon he would be in touch, he left. He walked to his apartment in the early twilight, shedding the alcohol and feeling his eyes grow clear again.

26

HIS MAIL CAME TO HIS APARTMENT NOW. IT ARRIVED IN A locked cubbyhole in the lobby. Mary sent photographs of a trip she had taken to the Olympic Peninsula, and Albert sent drawings of a landscape plan for revising Marshall's backyard with ground covers. No one would have to mow! he explained. Loretta would have had a fit, Marshall thought. Ground covers bring snakes, she would say.

He had received a couple more letters from the crew, in answer to his letter about visiting the crash site, and today he heard from Bob Hadley, his erstwhile escape partner. Hadley wrote from California, saying it had never occurred to him to return to the crash site, but he was glad that Marshall was searching for his helpers. Hadley wrote, "I didn't know the name of the family that sheltered me in Paris. I didn't stay there long, because everybody was starving in Paris." He had no reaction to Marshall's account of the boy's father who was killed. But he was wondering if Marshall had written to Hootie Williams's family. Hootie was single, and no one in the crew had kept in touch with his parents. Marshall thought about the Hootie he had known at Molesworth. He could whip the pants off everybody at poker. He could hold his liquor. He could sew. He could probably do magic tricks. Hootie always came up with something unexpected—and the last thing anyone expected was that he would lose his life.

Marshall opened a small package from Kansas, thinking it was from another of his crewmates, the flight engineer, James Ford. But the writer was James's daughter, Sonia.

> *My father is ill and cannot reply to your letter, but he wanted me to send you this tape recording he made about his experience in France*

after your plane crashed. It wasn't until last year, when he was told
he had lung cancer, that he decided to make this recording for my
brother and me. When he was able to share his account it brought us
closer together as a family, and we wouldn't trade anything for this.
I'm a nurse in a psychiatric ward and all I hear all day is far-fetched
stories. But this tape tells a story that is both fantastic and true, and
it is one I cherish. My mother did not live to hear it, but I have a
feeling she did know some of it before she went. Dad sends you his
best wishes, and he remembers with gratitude how you pulled him
out of the plane.

Marshall did not remember pulling Ford from the plane. Webb
was lying in the dirt. Ford and Marshall together had hauled him out
of the plane. Marshall had been over these memories so often that
they had become only memories of memories.

He wrote a brief letter to Sonia Ford. He tried to remember if
Ford was a smoker. They all were. He couldn't listen to the tape
recording until he added a tape recorder to his Parisian furnishings.
But maybe he didn't want to hear another version of the tale. The
rendezvous with Gordon Webb had been unnerving, and it was
playing in his mind still.

He was settling into his new, perhaps temporary, life. He made
small talk with the grocer, the laundress, the butcher, the guy named
Guy at the Everything Store. He tried to remember to carry a string
bag for his purchases. The baker kindly sawed a loaf in half for him,
saying a single person would let the bread go stale. Marshall had not
always paid such attention to the small tasks of daily life, but it
pleased him to economize. He remembered the Depression. He
didn't like extravagance. He was making nearly a hundred thousand
dollars a year before he retired, and now with his pension and without Loretta, he had more than he needed.

But what did he think he was doing? He walked and walked. If he
was really serious about finding Robert and the Vallons, he should
be out doing research, he told himself. Instead, he was depending on

Nicolas. He didn't know what to do. Gordon Webb was flitting back and forth across the Pond and acting like it was a dipshit job. Marshall would have been happy to be in that seat, even as a co-pilot.

On the boulevard Montparnasse he saw an aged woman with pinched eyes and a doughy face holding out a bowl for coins. She was swathed in black, stooped, breathing with difficulty, agony on her face. She could be a war widow from World War I, he thought. And she would have lived through the Occupation. He recalled the women in black who had taken care of him. What this woman could tell him! He found change in his pocket and dropped it into her bowl.

Don't put your hands in your pockets! Don't jingle your change! That is what Americans do. Did his guide on the train warn him about that? Lebeau?

He didn't speak to the old woman, but walked on, troubled. He saw so few beggars, just the cluster of *clochards* by the Seine.

NICOLAS TELEPHONED TO REPORT abysmal luck with the National Archives and the library.

"All day I searched. The *Résistance*. The Bourgogne. The RAF, the Free French, the U.S. Army Air Corps. It is just as I feared—everything I wanted is classified! Even now, after so long a time." Marshall could visualize Nicolas's boyish gestures, his hand tapping his head, flailing the air, forming a fist toward the ceiling. "They have buried our history, Marshall. We are adrift."

Marshall was apologetic. "I don't mean to waste your time."

"No matter. It should not be so hard to find a *résistant*," Nicolas said. "They're so proud of what they did. But the *collaborateurs*— *pfft*—no!"

Nicolas had learned nothing more about Lebeau or the Bourgogne line, so he urged Marshall to try the *épicerie* in Saint-Mandé again. "I have a strong suspicion he is the person you remember at the Vallons. Good luck with talking to the daughter."

"I'll try to be more courteous this time," Marshall said. He wasn't sure he was ready to face that spitfire again.

The picture in his mind was growing clearer. A young guy riding a bicycle into Paris from the country, a goose hiding in the basket. The breeze ruffled his hair as he pedaled past a German convoy. He was singing.

"Whenever you find your *résistant*, I am certain he will welcome you," Nicolas said. "Meanwhile, Marshall, I will search more around Chauny for people who might recall something about those who helped you before you came to us."

"The women in black."

"*Oui.*"

27

Mission to Saint-Mandé. depart at 1400 hours. all systems ready. Marshall was on the case now. No more dilly-dallying. He had slept well the night before. And he had downed two expressos.

He could have walked, but the Métro was convenient—Alésia to Châtelet, changing to the #1 train for Château de Vincennes, exit at Saint-Mandé. The *épicerie* was in a middle-class neighborhood, on a side street of old apartment buildings and a few small shops.

The woman he had tangled with previously was not in sight. Marshall bought a banana from a kid in a long apron who was slapping a towel at flies. When Marshall asked for Robert Lebeau, the kid tossed a long, dark lock from his forehead and said he hadn't seen him in a long time.

"Could I reach him by telephone?"

"Beaucaire is a long way, *monsieur.*"

"I can afford a long-distance call."

"He has no telephone."

The kid pointed to a minuscule notepad next to a basket of apples.

"Write a note to my cousin," he said. "She runs things."

Marshall scribbled a message, with his telephone number. A small dog—an animated mop-head—appeared from a nest beneath the counter, yapped at Marshall sleepily, circled, and tumbled back into his basket.

"*Merci. Au revoir,*" Marshall said to the kid.

Marshall was unworldly, ignorant about the real preoccupations of the people around him. He had tried several times to strike up conversations with various people about the war but got nowhere, except with Guy at his shop. After seeing the old woman on the boulevard Montparnasse, he began to think he saw a sadness in the faces of older people on the street.

He strolled on through Saint-Mandé, looking for anything that might prod his memory of 1944. He didn't recognize the shops on the main avenue. Nicolas suspected the Vallons had lived here and that the Bourgogne network had been active in this area. That spring, the Bourgogne had become the main channel for transferring fallen aviators from Paris to the south. Marshall tried to imagine the clandestine activity that occurred here, when people lived out their secret, seething anger. This was an ordinary neighborhood—busy, but American flyers being shepherded down the street would have been as obvious as astronauts at a hoedown, he thought.

The Vallons' flat was expansive, with airy, bright rooms off a long parquet corridor. After six weeks of confinement in the small house in Chauny, sometimes sleeping behind the armoire, Marshall luxuriated in the spaciousness of the apartment in Paris. More and more American bombers were falling from the sky, and the airmen were streaming into the city. Some of them came to the Vallons for false IDs before going to ground in scattered safe houses. He heard murmurs about the snow melting in the mountains; waiting for the right connections; waiting for a particular message concealed within the French news from the BBC. Robert came every couple of days, often bringing a flyer in need of a new identity. Robert was an earnest youth in a heavy overcoat, with a rucksack, from which he drew money and news and papers. Marshall had envied Robert. Damn, he had those wheels. On his bicycle he could go anywhere. Marshall imagined him checking designated "letter boxes" for secret messages or biking to outlying towns to finagle with secret suppliers. Mme Vallon had said Robert's ability to gather scarce foodstuffs was a miracle. He brought olives and almonds. Once he brought a chicken.

Marshall walked from Saint-Mandé to the Bois de Vincennes, remembering that Annette had led him and three other aviators on a long walk through a park, for exercise. It was probably this park, he thought as he crossed the street. They were not to acknowledge her, or talk to one another. They had to remember what they had been taught about the French way of smoking. It was better not to smoke. They had no change to jingle in their pockets, and they would not have dared to buy something at a kiosk even if they had. They followed this sprightly, fearless girl, who walked along, carrying her book satchel through the park as if she was on her way home from school. She would pause sometimes to look at a plant, or pet a dog, or sit on a bench to consult a book or write on a scrap of paper, allowing the flyboys to saunter in different directions for a few moments, so that they weren't a conspicuous troop moving together.

Now, near the entrance to the park, Marshall knew with certainty that this was Annette's neighborhood. He recognized the enormous boulder across the street. The zoo was there, right where he remembered. This was the zoo Annette had taken him to, not the one at the Jardin des Plantes. Just inside the entry was a rock mountain rising out of the earth, several stories high. It was for the mountain goats. He remembered seeing a pair of German soldiers who were looking up at the giraffe and did not realize there were American B-17 crewmen in their midst. Marshall held his breath. He was thrilled. Being up in the sky in a bomber was one sort of unreality—one form of surreal dislocation—but moving among the enemy as they strode around in their hostile regalia was even more improbable. His life had become a weird drama he could scarcely comprehend.

Turning back, he crossed the busy street and tried to get his bearings—the space, the shape of the place. Annette had led the airmen to the Bois de Vincennes from her apartment. He thought he would recognize the building. Saint-Mandé was a long main avenue with dozens of other streets running into it. He decided that the correct direction was to the left. He walked down a long road parallel to the avenue. He turned onto a street at random, saw an unfamiliar church. He tried the next street. The apartment had been on a corner. Maybe it was two blocks in. He walked past abundant trees, along small streets, toward the *centre ville*.

For an hour or more he crisscrossed the streets. From time to time he thought he recognized an intersection, a set of windows, a small alley. But something would seem wrong and he would try another street. Memory was a bitch, he thought. The Vallons' apartment was probably not here at all. But he was sure of the zoo.

A group of children was entering a small park behind a blond woman carrying a green canvas satchel. He came to a corner, turned left. Another corner. Was it here? He studied a pale gray stone-block building with green frilly ironwork on the tiny pigeon-walk balconies. It was an attractive building, solid and clean. This could be it. He stepped back, considering, remembering how he had stood far away from the lace curtains but could see a triangular section of the street. His heart lifted. This could be it.

Maybe they had an unlisted telephone number and were sitting at home right now.

IN HIS MEMORY, perhaps exaggerated, the Vallons had treated Marshall as a privileged guest—their privilege as much as his. He had confidence in them. They could get him safely to his next hideout, farther south, farther on to Spain. Despite air raids and the possibility of the Gestapo dropping in unannounced, they seemed unafraid. Their company was so pleasant that he would not complain.

He had wanted to do something to repay the Vallons, but he could only watch and wait. One day from the window he saw a couple hurrying along the street, heads down, talking worriedly. He could see some French police and two German officers down the block. He was alone in the apartment. He knew what to do if he heard jackboots stomping up the stairs. He was to retreat through the kitchen window onto the balcony and into the kitchen window of the next flat. M. Gilbert lived there, "a nice man who will take care of you." But what if the jackboots were coming for M. Gilbert? No, they assured him. This could not be.

He watched the uniforms advance down the street. He was sure he could not be seen from below, but he was careful not to touch the curtains. The man and woman walking ahead of the police paused, the woman clasping the man's arm. The Germans marched past, but the French police stopped the couple, and Marshall could see the pair rummaging for their papers.

A black Citroën pulled up beside them. The police directed them into the backseat, as if offering them a lift. The car drove off.

THE CONCIERGE ANSWERED when he rang the doorbell. She was a sweet-faced woman, maybe in her forties.

"*Excusez-moi, madame, je cherche les Vallon.*" He explained more than he needed to, his words tumbling out.

There were no Vallons. She shook her head. She had never heard of Vallons here. She had lived here fifteen years. If there had ever been Vallons, they had moved away before she arrived. He thanked her, and she wished him *bonne journée.*

He went on his way. When he passed the *mairie*, the city-government building, he thought he could inquire about death certificates. But he hadn't the heart.

THE YOUNG WOMAN had returned to the *épicerie*. She was alone, and for a moment Marshall observed her standing dreamily behind the counter. She was nice-looking. Her little dog jumped out and barked ferociously as Marshall entered.

"*Bobby, arrête-toi,*" she said.

He stooped to greet the dog, turning his palm out for the dog to read his benign intentions.

"*Bobby, bon chien.* Good dog." He tried to pronounce "Bobby" the way she did—*BOE-bee.*

"*Bonjour, monsieur.* You are here again."

"*Naturellement.* I'm a steady customer." He chuckled, in what he hoped was a pleasant manner.

"I apologize for before," she said, surprising him. "I had too many tasks that day, and I had lost my head."

"In English, we would say, 'I would lose my head if it wasn't screwed on.' "

She laughed, and he said, "But I was the rude one. I came, in part, to apologize."

She smiled. She had on an embroidered blouse and long earrings like a hippie, but she wasn't grungy. Her short skirt revealed shapely legs, smooth knees. When she raised her eyelids to acknowledge him, he caught a glimpse of color on her upper lid, just a tinge of lavender, the shade of her blouse. She was very pretty. He realized that she was regarding him with interest, which pleased him.

"Do you like dogs, *monsieur*?" she said.

"I haven't been around them much."

"My *petit chien* is so bored. I must take him for a tiny walk." She called through a door to the back, "*Michel, vas-y.*"

The kid appeared with a broom. The woman bent down to lift the dog, her knees flashing.

"*Bobby, mon petit artichaut.*"

She held the tan fluffy dog in her arms, hugging him. Then she let him down. As she fastened his lead, the dog wagged his entire body. Marshall did not recognize the breed, but the pooch was about half the size of his brain bag.

"Michel will take care of the store for a few minutes," she said. "Bobby is so good. He works with me all day. But he needs some air. Come along, *monsieur.*"

"My name is Marshall," he said, following her from the shop.

"And I am Caroline."

"Did I guess correctly that Robert Lebeau is your father?"

Nodding slightly, she said, "Come, Bobby."

They walked on the side streets, the dog sniffing happily along the way while Marshall ambled beside Caroline. Her perfume was strong, and her brown hair was shiny in the sun.

"*Viens, Bobby, allons-y.*"

The dog picked up his pace, and Marshall found himself quickly explaining his search—the shot-down aviator seeking his past. As before, she told him she had never heard of a family named Vallon.

"I think I may have known your father," he said. "He may have been one of the *Résistance* agents who helped me get out of Paris and back home. I didn't have names, and I have very little to go on."

"But surely you are not so old?" she asked.

"I am sixty."

"I was born after the war," she said. "I have heard that my father was *résistant*, but I have not much to tell you. He never talked to me about the war."

"Did you ever ask?"

She stared ahead. "He was not the type to talk," she said.

"Weren't you ever curious?"

"No."

They were passing a small park, where children were cavorting on slides and teeter-totters. One section of the fence came close to the edge of the narrow sidewalk and made passage difficult. They had to walk single file—dog, Caroline, Marshall. When the sidewalk widened, she stopped, leaned against the fence, and gazed through the iron bars at the children.

"I never really cared about the war," she said. She turned to him. "It is the past. Let's talk of something else. Tell me about the United States."

28

"MY FATHER HAD TEN CHILDREN," CAROLINE TOLD HIM THE next evening. She had met him at a café-restaurant she had suggested, near the Sorbonne. "He had five with his wife and five with his mistress. I am one of those from the mistress." She lowered her head for a moment. "I detest to think of my mother like that. It makes my father less to love. It has been a misery knowing this. I do not even know my brothers and sisters who are from his wife. They grew up in Montreuil and were respectable and went to the Catholic school."

The room was large and comfortable, with wicker furniture and plush cushions, pastel colors, soft lighting. A peek at the menu confirmed his guess—this was an expensive restaurant. They were sipping aperitifs, something amber in small glasses. She was wearing a low-cut embroidered blouse tight on her breasts. He tried not to stare.

"Let's order the langoustines!" she said, giving the menu only a glance. "A specialty."

"Sure," he said, wondering—and not caring—if langoustines might be pig snouts, or some obscure organ meats. They were the most expensive item.

The waiter came, and Marshall ordered the langoustines for both.

"I like this place!" Caroline said with a smile that illuminated her features. "I come here with my friends whenever we have something to celebrate—not so often! But there are birthdays."

Her mouth turned up in a crooked half smile—a hint of flirtation. The waiter asked about wine.

"It's all the same to me," Marshall said to Caroline. "I'm woefully uncultivated."

"I'll choose it," she said. "It is no bother."

She said something unintelligible to the waiter, who agreed vociferously.

Marshall asked her, "So you grew up with your mother in Saint-Mandé? Your father did not live with you?"

She nodded. "It is near my father's other family. He must have wanted to keep his two women close so he wouldn't have to travel far between them!" She laughed flippantly. Marshall was charmed.

She said, "My mother accepted the arrangement, but when he was at our apartment, it was an obligatory appearance only. This we understood. He didn't supervise us. He left that to my mother. Maybe he thought he didn't have that authority. I do not know. My mother kept some distance from him, for she had dignity. She did the cooking for him when he came, and he took care of her, in his fashion. I think she was afraid of him. *I* was afraid of him." She stopped, concentrating on tearing a piece of bread.

"Afraid he would hurt you? Hit you?"

"No. But he was a stranger. He was there but not there. I don't know what played in his mind." She shuddered.

Marshall was uncomfortable, thinking of his own home life. Albert and Mary would chatter about school or friends or games, and he would gaze out the window.

The wine arrived, and he sampled it carefully. It was dark and rich.

Caroline sipped some wine, then continued, "His mother, my *grand-mère*, refused to listen to anything bad. I did not know her well. On the point you want to know, about the war, my *grand-mère* would refuse to listen. 'Don't bring it up,' I can hear her say. She's dead now, but I can still hear her say so clearly, 'Robert, your wife doesn't want to hear that, that other woman doesn't even have a right to hear it, and I don't want to hear it; that time is past. It's over, *fini*. You have to think about providing for all those little ones. That is the only thing that should concern you.' "

Caroline leaned over the side of her chair as if to check on her dog, but she had not brought him. Marshall supposed it was some kind of reflex action, or perhaps she just wanted to expose her cleavage.

She said, "His mother, my grandmother, called my mother 'that other woman' in front of me! They did not know each other. Maman didn't want to hear about the war either. All she asked for was financial support. She dutifully made his dinner on Wednesdays, and he gave her a pile of franc notes, not always the same amount. She never knew if there would be enough."

"Did he have the *épicerie* then?"

"He had a business at Montreuil that was in his family for many years, and then he bought the *épicerie* for my mother. He did have the decency to provide us with the shop."

"Do any of your brothers and sisters work there?"

She shook her head. "My brother Jean, my brother Claude—they made apprenticeships in construction. My two sisters married. I was married too—for about five years. Not now."

"Children?"

She shook her head. For a while she talked about her marriage to a lazy machinist obsessed with horse racing. Marshall did not mention Loretta, and she did not ask him personal questions. From time to time he spoke up, to slow down her French or to ask her to repeat something. He didn't know most of her slang. He was not sure she understood what he wanted. The Robert she was describing did not seem familiar. He knew he was prying, but he liked her voice, the way her breasts moved with all her gestures.

The langoustines appeared—a pile of what looked like overgrown crawfish, or baby lobsters.

"They resemble *homards*, do they not?" she said with a little laugh.

They hit a language barrier. He couldn't give her a French word for crawfish, and he didn't understand *homards*. The langoustines lay on a bed of rice, in their weird red shells, with long feelers and bug eyes. He had to follow her lead in breaking the shells and slipping out the slim slivers of pink-tinged flesh.

"Take the time," she said, as she delicately extracted a morsel from the tail and brought it to her lips.

For a while they worked on the food, which seemed more like a surgical operation than a meal. Marshall was sitting with a view of some old black-and-white photographs, perhaps from wartime, on the wall behind her. He couldn't keep from looking at them, as if he might recognize someone. Caroline obliviously tackled her pile of crusty sea creatures. Earlier, as she told about her mother, he was studying a photo of mothers leading children across a cobblestone street, mothers in head-scarves tied in a triangle. Loretta wore a scarf that way in the forties, he recalled. That photo was between a picture of a line of people outside a *boulangerie* and a picture of a crowd of young people dancing in the street.

"He gave my mother the *épicerie*," Caroline repeated. "And now it is mine—since she died."

"Does he ever come into the shop?"

She wiped her lips with her napkin carefully, then said, "No. He is never there."

"Then how can I find him?" he asked impatiently.

"I don't know."

"The kid said he was in Beaucaire."

"My cousin—Michel."

"Is your father in Beaucaire?"

She shrugged. "I haven't spoken to him in five years."

There was a trace of sadness in her voice, but also bitterness.

"I really would like to find the Robert I knew," he said. "Maybe I've got the wrong one. Don't you have a picture of him?"

"He was no father to me," she said.

—

THEY FINISHED THE MEAL chatting about other subjects. She wanted to know about California and New York, and he told her about flying 707s cross-country. She ordered coffee and chocolate cake, but he declined.

"Coffee is for mornings," he said. "It's the insomniac's enemy."

"Nonsense. One cannot conclude a good meal without some coffee. And of course some cheese or a sweet." Her mouth turned up in a crooked half smile.

"I'll pass," he said. But he caught her smile and peered into her eyes.

Walking from the Métro at Alésia, rounding the corner past the dark hulk of the church, he thought about how her skin had glowed, how she laughed as she broke the little tails of the shellfish. Before they said *au revoir*, she had invited him to dinner at her apartment, in a week, and he had said yes. She offered to look for some old photographs of her father. He would have said yes even if she had said photographs of her ex-husband.

THE NEXT MORNING, a cloudy Saturday, Marshall telephoned Nicolas.

"Can that be true?" Nicolas said. "He has disappeared? Something odd is going on. She told me he was in Provence."

"She said her father's family had lived in Montreuil, so maybe that's a clue. I'm looking at a map. Maybe I could find the other business he owns. Maybe he's there."

"I checked on that and found nothing."

"I can't connect the guy she described to the Robert I remember," Marshall said. "And where is he?"

Marshall had the map spread on the bed, tracing his finger from the Saint-Mandé Métro stop to the zoo. "There's intrigue here,

Nicolas! Maybe he's one of those guys who thinks the war is still going on, and he's gone underground. Pardon me, I've been reading too many French mystery novels."

Nicolas laughed. "Maybe you should get on the Métro, Marshall, to seek him underground. Or the sewers of Paris, perhaps."

"That reminds me—what was the station I left from to go south, toward Spain?"

"The Gare d'Austerlitz. The trains go south."

"I don't think I've been there since the war."

"That's where you would have departed with your guide, who could have been Lebeau. And, Marshall, you must know—it is the station where they sent the Jews out."

"Isn't Germany north?"

"They were sent to internment camps in France first."

"I see."

"Maybe you don't. The *French* interned them."

He paused. Marshall didn't know what to say.

Nicolas said, "Don't worry, Marshall. I will make some more inquiries, hoping to hear things Bourgogne. I will busy myself."

"I appreciate your help, Nicolas. Here I am in Paris, an old guy on the loose. Sometimes I feel pretty mixed up."

"Don't worry, Marshall. You have friends here. One day, perhaps, you will be content. Don't forget my parents are expecting you here again in Chauny for a grand Sunday at their table. Maman will invite you."

"I haven't forgotten. *Merci, Nicolas. Au revoir!*"

29

A LETTER FROM AL GRAINGER WAS THE ONLY MAIL IN THE BOX. Marshall was relieved to hear from him finally. Grainger, always the straggler.

Dear Marshall,

I was on vacation in Branson when your letter came. I was bowled over. Long time no see! 1963, was it? I'm sorry to hear about Loretta. She was the life of the party, I remember! Always saying something cute. Well, that's a heartbreaker, and now you're retired. Two big things at once, I guess you're thinking. But I know you, Marshall. You'll grin and bear it, keep a stiff upper lip. God never gives us more than we can bear. We know that from experience, don't we?

Whew. The account of your trip back to the final resting place of our old machine filled me up. Not to mention the resting place of our pilot. And I keep thinking about Hootie. That Hootie was a stitch. That was about the worst thing I took with me into captivity—the sight of that funny, twisted kid laying on the ground. He looked so peaceful! I was sure he was dead. And I tell you I was scared seeing him like that, with all those people rushing at us. They got me off to somebody's house, and there was a doctor, but my shoulder was so bad they had to take me to the hospital, and that's when the Germans started to watch over me till I got better, and then they hauled me off to their fine country where the scenery—thanks to our guys!—was a lot of wreckage, things blown up, piles of stones and rubble. I kept giving thanks to the Lord that I was alive and that our bombers were just tearing them up. I knew the Jerries couldn't last, so that gave me hope.

While I was in Stalag Luft I, I found my strength in the Lord,

and He helped me through the worst days. I'd say prayers every time
we had a pinch of something to eat in that hellhole, or whenever we
got mail and Red Cross packages. I think the others I bunked with—
I was in with Campanello, you know—got tired of me making a fuss
over Jesus. I'd say we had to share our rations with Jesus, and all
sorts of stuff that must have sounded like claptrap, but I swear it got
us through. Oh, we didn't dig any escape tunnels, but we figured
how to defeat our enemies by giving all the credit to Jesus. Man, that
was a time.

After we got out, I was sent back to Missouri, and my shoulder
had healed a little funny, so I had several operations at St. Louis. I
think it turned out OK, just aches a little when it's real wet. Life has
been pretty good since. I got established with my business out in
California, but I get back to Missouri, even though my parents died
long ago. I've got so many relatives. My two sons live there, and my
daughter's in California. They're all busy producing babies and
they're all doing well. This was the American dream, huh,
Marshall? I can't complain. We did good.

It's sad to learn about the man who lost his life helping our crew,
but it pleases me to hear how fondly the Belgian people remember us.
I hadn't given a whole lot of thought to them over the years, but now
I see that they have been thinking of us ever since. It would be good
to see you again, Marshall, and see the old crew, what's left of it.
Remember, the eyes of the Lord run to and fro.

Yours in Christ,
Al

Marshall lay sleepless in the heat, tossing on his new sheets,
which were still stiff, even though he had had them laundered. They
wouldn't stay tucked, and he found himself wallowing on the bare
mattress. Evidently he had bought two top sheets. Grainger's letter
preoccupied him. Al had dropped those bombs on their targets so
gleefully. Hitler's Focke-Wulf works was his favorite. Marshall had

been surprised when Al became a lay pastor. Al, the evangelist bombardier.

The sheets were damp and twisted around his legs. He wondered whether Gordon Webb had ever panicked in an F-101. His father had panicked and Marshall had taken over. Only Chick Cochran obeyed the order to bail out. Marshall was glad Gordon hadn't been very curious about his father. Marshall had seized control of the plane in a mutiny that lasted about twenty seconds—until he saw that Webb had been wounded. Marshall saved the crew. He was proud of that. But any good pilot could have belly-landed the thing. Webb was dead.

Marshall saw lightning flash, followed on the count of ten by muffled thunder. He imagined sitting in a cockpit, waiting for takeoff, watching the storm, waiting for clearance. Lightning hit his plane once, but it didn't hit the fuel tanks. He remembered Saint Elmo's fire dancing on his wings a few times. He liked spotting a glory in the clouds below—a rainbow ring with the plane's shadow in the center. He heard himself as pilot, the instructor, telling the passengers, "Folks, on the left side of the aircraft you will see a magic rainbow." It was a circle, seen from above. Telling Loretta. Her boundless enthusiasm.

The advantages he had had in his life as a flyer were still a marvel to him, but now he had no schedule. He had no flights, no logbooks, no maps to study, no uniform to keep in pristine condition. He didn't know what to wear. He was trying new things—a load of langoustines. Caroline bothered him. Her pop-out breasts. And the fact that he was still thinking about her slim, seductive hips in those deplorable blue-jeans.

He turned the light on and sat up against the wall. The rain had stopped. His watch said 4:11.

Who was Robert? Surely not a man who was mean to his children. Marshall was getting nowhere. In the turmoil of his nighttime thoughts, his wakeful dreaming, he thought he had been trying to find the young man he wished he had been. As a time traveler, he could jiggle the outcome. He could be a hero after all.

"You jerk," he said aloud.

30

HE ATE SOME CORNFLAKES AND THEN STOPPED FOR AN *EXPRESS* at the *tabac* down the block. He was growing to love the strong French coffee. Quickly, he had another. Then he headed to the Everything Store, where Guy had just the tape recorder Marshall needed.

For a change of scene, Marshall sat on a bench in the parc Montsouris, trussed up his ears, and listened to the tape James Ford had made for his family. In the direction of the rue d'Alésia, a police siren was yelling out its high-pitched hee-haw. A 747 flew overhead. He couldn't make out its markings.

> *You know, I never wanted to talk about it. I didn't want to brag. And I didn't want to wallow in self-pity either. It went both ways.*
>
> *I went into the Army Air Corps in 1942 and trained in Texas. I qualified for flight engineer, and if I had to shoot a gun, the top turret was a pretty good place to be—much better than in the tail or the belly. I was sure thankful I didn't have to be the belly gunner. The waist gunners were more exposed too. But on the top, I could duck down from my bubble.*
>
> *When it came time to go to England, we shipped out on the* Queen Elizabeth *luxury liner! Of course we were crammed twenty to a stateroom, but that ship was so beautiful, and we had the run of it. That was sure a fine trip. I always said Martha and I should take a trip on that ship—now they've got the QE-II. Well, never mind.*

Marshall listened to Ford describe Molesworth and then the missions. Matter-of-factly, he told at some length how the plane was hit on the mission to Frankfurt.

It may surprise you to know, but when a fighter comes at you from the side, you don't aim ahead. You always aim between him and the tail of your own plane because your own speed will add to the speed of your bullet, so you aim off to the side. And how do we do that? Skill and practice!

At some point I knew we were going down. I didn't hear when the pilot said "Bail out," but I'd been firing and firing and didn't always hear everything. Then, first thing you know, I turn and see somebody bail out! It was Chick Cochran! Oh, he was so quick. He'd be across the finish line before you said "go." I was still on the lookout for the fighter that had hit us twice, so I didn't know what Webb and Stone were up to. I just kept my eyes on the job, but then I saw the ground coming, and I tried to brace myself. It wasn't too bad really. Then all hell broke loose. I think Webb was dead then, and the bombardier's shoulder was hurt, and Stone and I were rushing every which way getting people out. We pulled Webb out, and then laid out one of the waist gunners on the grass—a funny guy we called Hootie.

Marshall did not recall helping Ford with Hootie. Hootie was lying there pale as fog. Marshall's mind drifted back to the crash, while on the tape Ford was describing a long period of hiding in a French town called Ham, an experience similar to Marshall's own evasion. Then Ford was sent by train to Paris.

When I got to Paris I was met by a young couple—sweethearts, I believe. The guy wore a thick overcoat and workman's shoes. We didn't speak, and I don't remember now what our signal was, but they led me through the train station and onto a subway train out to a neighborhood sort of place with a lot of apartment buildings. The young girl went off somewhere, and the young man took me into a building. He rang the bell and a woman let me in.

I stayed with that family in Paris for a week. The young man at the train came to the apartment two or three times, and he gathered with the family in the kitchen and they talked in low voices. I think he was the person they got their instructions from, and I understood his name to be Robert Lebeau. It took me a long time to figure out the name because they pronounce Robert "Robert" without the "t" on the end.

I don't remember that family's name, but I never forgot his. Robert Lebeau was the one who took me—and about six others—on the train down to near the Spanish border and hooked me up with the guides who led me across the Pyrenees. In the time I was around Lebeau, I was fascinated by how committed he was. He was very devout, a loyal Catholic. He was polite. He was a dashing figure! He was a very courageous young man! Devoted to his country, his mother.

Marshall's mind had been wandering during Ford's long hideout in Ham, but he was jolted when he heard what had happened in Paris. Robert Lebeau! He had to be the Robert Marshall remembered. Who was his girlfriend? Annette? Marshall thought about Annette's thin wrists, the limp lock of hair lying against her cheek as she poised her pencil above a problem.

He could hardly listen to Ford's account of the arduous crossing of the Pyrenees (slow going, snow). He was thinking about Lebeau. Who was that family who hid Ford in Paris? Maybe Ford would remember. Marshall was eager to learn what else Ford knew, but he hesitated to impose on a dying man.

He paced along the small lake in the park, calculated the time in Kansas (still early), and then headed back to his apartment.

By the time he reached his place, he had decided it would be entirely natural to telephone the former flight engineer on his deathbed. Maybe Ford would be glad to hear from him. He should express his concern for Ford's health, let him know the old crew was thinking of him. Marshall thought through his rationalizations. If he was sick himself, would he want the crew crowding around, watching him die, interrupting his reveries with small talk on the phone? Probably not. But most people would, he reasoned.

—

"HELLO. ARE YOU JAMES FORD'S daughter? Sonia? This is Marshall Stone. I got your letter and the tape. Gosh, I'm really sorry to hear about your dad. That's terrible. I remember him so well. He was the best top-turret gunner a B-17 crew could have. And he could have flown the plane himself, he was such a good flight engineer."

Sonia said, "He wanted you to have that tape. He made it some time ago, and then he was so surprised and happy to hear from you."

"How is James doing?"

"Well, he has good days and bad days. Today's not too bad."

"Listen, do you suppose I could talk to him a minute? Say hello?"

"Let me see. Can you hold on?"

Waiting, Marshall rehearsed what to say to James as quickly and as efficiently as possible, so as not to tire him.

Sonia spoke again. "I'm sorry, Mr. Stone. Could you call back later? We're having thunderstorms, and I'm afraid we have to get prepared for tornados! You may not know how it is in Tornado Alley. Is that all right? Dad wants to talk to you. Call back tomorrow about this same time, O.K.?"

Marshall was left to imagine Ford lying ill, being hauled somehow out to a storm shelter and down a hatch. He remembered Ford tearing along on a bicycle from the barracks to the mess hall one cold, dark morning. Something about the way he aimed the front wheel of the bike, as if it was his ammunition and weapon and vehicle all in one, had struck Marshall that day. Marshall remembered having deep confidence in Ford at that moment.

31

IN HIS INSOMNIAC STRETCHES, MARSHALL REPLAYED HIS ESCAPE-and-evasion adventure through France, dredged up new characters in his long-gone drama, and finally reached Paris, where the girl in the blue beret met his train. She was alone, the toss of her head leading him to her parents' apartment, where her mother cranked out his false ID as simply and skillfully as if she were sewing costumes for a school pageant. Robert came and went—always purposeful, always mysterious.

Half-asleep, he let his mind wander over Ford's taped memories—Ford hiding in Belgium, getting to Ham, then to Paris. At the Gare du Nord a girl and her boyfriend met him. Annette, no doubt, and Robert Jules Lebeau—one of those dashing, darkly handsome guys girls can't resist.

He didn't remember Annette and Robert as a pair of sweethearts when he was with the Vallons. Had Ford been there before or after Marshall arrived? Did they fall in love after Marshall left?

Caroline could be the daughter of Annette and Robert, he realized. Annette may have become the mistress who bore Robert so many children. The energetic, joyous girl he had known became the weary, neglected woman Caroline had described. It seemed incredible. Just as Robert's shift to a loutish, inattentive father seemed incredible.

The sun was already seeping through the cracks of the shutters when he opened his eyes, repeating *Robert Jules Lebeau*, the words jarring him awake. The good-natured young man he remembered had energy and brains—and commitment. Of course he and Annette became sweethearts. In retrospect, it seemed inevitable. Then he thought that Annette more likely was the wife, not the mistress. Either way, it seemed sad.

"DAD HAS BEEN ASKING about you," Sonia Ford said on the telephone. "He complained that I made you wait so long to call! I wasn't sure how long the tornado watch would go on yesterday, and we had a doctor's appointment later."

"Did you have a tornado?"

"Not this time, but you never know."

"I've been thinking about James and the old days. How's he doing?"

"Dad—are you awake? I've got your old friend here. Marshall."

James's voice on the line was shaky, but his midwestern cadences were familiar, and Marshall found himself talking easily with the former top-turret gunner.

"I can still picture you standing up there in your greenhouse, James," Marshall said. "Aiming that gun in every direction at once."

James laughed, a thin rasp. "Marshall, your letter was the best thing that's happened to me since I got sick."

After more chitchat, Marshall explained his move to Paris and asked about Robert Lebeau. "I don't know for sure, but I think he may have been the guy who helped me too. Do you remember the family you stayed with?"

"No, not very well. They went off to work and left me in a little room, so I didn't see them much."

"Was there a daughter?"

"Might have been."

"Annette? The Vallon family?"

"No, that doesn't ring a bell."

"I'm trying to find the family I stayed with. There was also a guy who was there a lot. I think he might have been Lebeau."

"I don't even know why I remember his name. But he impressed me a lot."

"You said he had a girlfriend."

"He had a girl with him at the train. I thought they were sweethearts, because they seemed so interested in each other I wasn't even sure they saw us flyers. But I don't remember seeing her again. When he came to visit the family I stayed with, he was alone. I think he came over with information, what they were supposed to do and so on."

"The guy I knew didn't speak English," Marshall said.

"This boy didn't either . . . but somebody translated for me. That's how I knew something about him. He talked about church a lot. I guess he was Catholic."

"Do you remember where in Paris this was?"

"Oh, a ways from downtown, I think." James's voice broke, and he began to falter. "I just can't remember."

"You said he was dressed in heavy country clothes and workmen's boots?"

"He dressed like he was going to cross the mountains himself."

"I'm glad somebody had good shoes," Marshall said.

They laughed together. "That's the truth!" James said. "I never thought I'd live to think that was funny, but I had these shoes that were like bedroom slippers! I cried for my good old A-6 flying boots, but I'd gotten rid of them."

"Yeah, all of us Americans with our big feet and GI boots."

James laughed again, but he sounded weak. "I'm sorry, Marshall."

"I'd better let you go," Marshall said, regretting that he couldn't continue his relentless probe.

"I'm so glad to hear from you, Marshall. Maybe I never told you this, but you did a damn fine job landing our Fort."

"Thank you. You could have done it yourself, James. You were a flight engineer second to none."

"I don't know about that."

"See you, old buddy."

Marshall felt guilty, pouncing on James's last good moments, moments that belonged to his family. He wasn't sure he had learned anything worthwhile. He was wandering through a land of ghosts, slivers of memory, clues floating like summer midges.

32

CAROLINE'S NARROW STREET WAS ONE SPOKE IN AN INTERSEC-
tion of five streets. It reminded him of an *étoile*, like the design one
could see from the top of the Arc de Triomphe. Marshall had picked
up more tourist lore in his past few weeks in Paris than he had in all
the years of flying in and out of the city. Then, he was thinking only
of his next flight, or reviewing his last flight for mistakes. Now, he
was surprised to notice occasionally that he hadn't been thinking
about flying. It had been twenty-two days since he had been at the
controls of any vehicle. Instead, he had been zipping around on the
Métro, the subterranean opposite of the limitless friendly skies. He
liked the speed of the trains. He liked the way the train to Saint-
Mandé twisted and turned just before it reached the station.

At the intersection he passed two drugstores, a *tabac*, and two
small cafés. He detoured around a minor motorcycle accident—a disheveled, shaken biker, his mangled *moto*, two police cars. Caroline's
building, a stone structure with pale blue shutters, was a block from
the accident. She had told him to ring number 3A. There was no
name listed. After she buzzed him in, he walked up the three flights,
proud of his sturdy heart and hardly out of breath.

Caroline was waiting on the landing outside her open door.
She was wearing a short, silky Indian dress in a soft pale green color.
Her lipstick was slightly off-center, accentuating the slant of her
smile.

"Please be comfortable," she said, settling him on a hard divan.
Her dog slept through his arrival.

"Bobby is getting old," she explained, caressing the dog's head.
"He must have his little naps."

"People are crazy about dogs in the U.S.," Marshall said. "And cats."

"Did you have a pet?"

"No. Well, my children did, but I never had one that was my own pet."

She gave him an aperitif, something sweet and gingery. Her apartment was chock-a-block with bric-a-brac, hanging beads and bells, and curling posters of movie stars and impressionist painters. There was an atmosphere of musty old Paris in the room. He couldn't take in all the gewgaws.

Sitting down with the dog between them, she said, "Tell me about the United States! Tell me about your home, and where you were born."

"I started out in Kentucky."

"Kentucky! Oh, I want to go to Kentucky. What a marvelous word. My life's dream is to go to the United States."

"Really?"

"I used to know an American who said he would marry me and take me to the state of Minnesota, but he was teasing me. He never meant it."

The talk meandered. She seemed less nervous with him, more aware of him. He was aware of her legs, her smooth knees, her lips, her clinging dress. Her earrings struggled inside the flow of her hair. But as she talked, he examined her features for hints of Annette. The slight curl in her lip? The same shade of hair?

At her insistence, he described the life of an airline pilot. He avoided the technicalities, skipped the frustrations with the management, skirted the stews, and probably made the whole enterprise seem as glamorous as she wanted it to be.

"I flew to Rome five years ago and got airsick on the way back," she said with a frown. "Did you get airsick when you crashed your bomber?"

"No. When you're in a situation like that, you don't pay attention to your body."

"Like opera singers," she said. "I always wonder if they *péter* when they are singing. A good time to let go without being heard!"

Laughing at her own crude wit, she went to a shelf and seized a wooden cigar box next to an arrangement of porcelain poodles.

"This is what you came to see. I had to search for this, and I almost did not find it." She opened the box and plucked from a pile of loose photographs a scallop-edged snapshot of a young man.

"That's him!" Marshall held the picture under a lamp. "I remember him. I knew your father! He *was* the agent connected to the family I stayed with."

"I never knew any of that," she said. "But these photos are from that time."

Marshall studied Robert's face—the small, sharp features, the dark, rough-cut hair. Robert stood on a road near a trimmed waist-high hedge. Beyond was a field, with no identifiable plants, a low cover crop of some kind. It seemed to be winter, judging by the young man's coat—dark, heavy wool with a thick collar, perhaps of mouton. He was hatless, his abundant hair shining. A rucksack dangling from one hand appeared to be empty. The camera caught him in a slant profile, not facing the camera with an obligatory smile but deliberately posing as the serious revolutionary.

Marshall wondered if Robert had been in the Maquis, the Resistance fighters who camped out in the wilds. Pierre and Nicolas had told him that young men often took to the Maquis to escape the obligatory work-service in Germany. Marshall studied the photograph, observing the country setting, with a shed or barn in the background. He recognized the young man, of course. He even recognized the coat. He strained to recall if there had been any signs of flirtation between Robert and Annette. No, not under her parents' eye, he decided.

"I owe him a great debt for helping me," Marshall said now to Caroline, who sat down beside him, tucking her legs under her on the small divan.

"He was a terrible man," she said.

"I find that so hard to believe." Marshall told her what James Ford had said—what a fine person Robert Lebeau was, how he owed his life to this young man in the picture.

She shrugged and dug in the box. There were more photos of him, with a crowd of siblings and his parents—a stocky, mustachioed dad and a squat, dark mother.

"How do you happen to have these? You said he *was* terrible. Isn't he still alive? Where can I find him?"

She didn't answer, and he wondered if she was going to cry.

"Aren't these the kind of pictures that would belong to his wife?" he asked quickly, to forestall the waterworks.

Caroline shook her head slightly and said, "Maman told me that his wife wanted to know nothing about his past. She drew a line through it. Everything before her entry into his life was *pfft!*" She zipped up the past with a quick hand gesture.

"So he gave them to your mother?"

Caroline nodded. "Maman didn't really want them either. She found it too painful to think what he used to be and what he became."

"What was that?" Marshall was confused. Was Lebeau a good man or not? What were his crimes? "Just a minute," he said. "First, I have to know something. What was his wife's name?"

"Hortense. Why?"

"What was your mother's name?"

"Emma Romain. That is my name. Romain. We never had his name. This is her photo."

Caroline's mother had a high forehead, dark wings of thick hair, and a soft but careworn face. Marshall detected the resemblance to Caroline in the nose and the oval shape of the face.

He was glad that Caroline excused herself then and began to rattle dishes in the kitchen. She wasn't Annette's daughter. Annette didn't marry Robert. He was relieved, but he remained transfixed with the box of pictures. Robert Jules Lebeau, in all the early photos, was young and handsome, heartthrob enough for a wife and a mistress.

The later photos of Robert—with Caroline's mother and with their children—were few, mostly showing occasions at a dinner table. In some of the pictures he wore the traditional French workman's blue smock. In one series of photos there were Christmas presents and a small tree on a table. The older Lebeau had a faded, sad aspect. His thick hair was swept back, revealing a high forehead. He sat at the table with the children, but he did not seem to be involved with them. He was not even looking at the camera.

CAROLINE SERVED DINNER on a small table in a nook between the kitchen and the divan. The wine was light and dry, and Marshall enjoyed the food, the first home-cooked meal he had had in some time. Since lunch with the Alberts in Chauny, he remembered. Before that, he had no idea.

"I recognize this potato from your store," he kidded.

"And you will the fruits too," she said.

By the time she brought out oranges and strawberries, he had told her everything he could think of about Cincinnati, Kentucky, and New Jersey, and he had become thoroughly informed about her wholesalers, orchard suppliers, and favorite customers—the guy with the tattoo of the Virgin, the old couple with the Great Dane who pulled them everywhere, the homosexual couple with a fondness for artichokes, the matron who offered frequent updates on her fibroid problem. Caroline rose to fetch a sharper knife for the fruit. Returning to the table, she brushed his arm with her hand, and he pressed his hand on hers, almost involuntarily, as if the gesture were a part of speech. But it was momentary.

While she was clearing the table, he ducked into the bathroom, where he faced lingerie hanging on an ornate collapsible rack. Dainty things—placed there deliberately? The bidet looked like a good place to give a small dog a bath. He steadied himself by gazing at his hard, lined face in the mirror. His unblinking eyes.

It pained him to remember how mechanical and inattentive sex had become with Loretta in the last couple of years of their marriage. He had, however, shared a few passionate nights with a flight attendant he saw on some of his London trips. She was a purser, somewhat older than most of the attendants. Her name was Penny, and she was planning to retire from the airline and start a florist's shop. She took him to the Coventry flower market, where she bought flowers for her room—something she always did, she said— and she pressed a small white flower into the lapel buttonhole of his jacket. At Loretta's funeral all the flowers made him remember Penny, and he wept.

He had rationalized infidelities to Loretta by telling himself that his sporadic overseas flings were an alternate reality. He believed she would understand that. He could come home and enter into her world as if he had never been away. He was a false-hearted fool.

He studied Caroline's lingerie. He imagined slipping such garments off her youthful body.

But the image was off-kilter. It would be like seducing a friend's daughter, he thought. Robert Lebeau, the buoyant, active *résistant*. How could he have become the sad man in the photos, the bad father to Caroline?

If Annette had not survived the war, she could not have become either Robert's wife or his mistress, he thought.

"CAN'T YOU STAY?" Caroline asked when he emerged and checked his watch. "I will make coffee."

"I have to get my beauty sleep," he joked. "And I have to make some phone calls to the States." A lie.

"Don't go yet," she said.

They sat on the divan with another glass of wine, and then the dog began whimpering.

"Go away, Bobby. Wait."

The dog padded out of the room. But he quickly reappeared, whining insistently.

"I must take Bobby out. He cannot hold himself long." She eased into her flung-off sandals.

"I'll go with you," he said. "I need to leave."

"*Non, non, et non!* Come with me and then we will return."

She fumbled with the leash, murmuring to the dog as if she was sharing intimate secrets. The sounds blurred—her key in the door, the jingle of the leash, her whispering to Bobby.

Her walk was something of a prance, the self-aware gait of a woman who had a man's attention. It was dark in the small park they passed. Marshall found himself praising Bobby's absurd little *merde* production. Robert Jules Lebeau was going through his mind, flip-flopping images of hateful man and good man.

"It's too early for you to go home," she said.

"I'm an old man. I get tired," he said.

She touched his arm. "I would make you coffee."

"No. Thanks. Really."

"Are you bothered with me?" she asked as they turned down a broad street.

"I'm sorry. I'm just finding it so hard to get the story about your father straight in my mind."

She didn't reply for a moment.

"He was not a father to me," she said.

"No."

"Let's stop at this café," she said, tugging his arm. The tables were not crowded, but on the sidewalk a woman with a stroller of twins in pink rolled by, almost nipping his foot. It seemed late to see babies being strolled.

Marshall and Caroline sat at a sidewalk table in a splotch of neon light. They ordered two coffees. Her face seemed brittle in the glare. He thought he could see a trace of Robert in her features.

She smiled up at him. "It is very nice here, no?"

"Yes."

"Marshall, I realize I have been very mysterious on the subject of my father. I don't think about him. He is not important." She sighed. "But I will tell you what you want to know."

The coffee arrived. Marshall tested his, but he didn't want it. He would never get to sleep. Caroline's hands covered her face. The dog, in her lap, moaned and tried to wriggle between her hands, to lick her face.

"There is such bitterness, *monsieur*," she said to Marshall.

"Not so formal," he said. "I'm not an old man."

"You just said you were?"

"I didn't really mean it. I am an innocent in a foreign land."

"And you want to dig up the past." Her eyes avoided his.

"I apologize. I've been much too forward." He tried to soothe her. He reached across the table, at the risk of being snapped at by Bobby. The light on Caroline's face was harsh.

"I'm sorry," he said. "I've troubled you. Drink your coffee, and we'll talk another time."

Caroline sipped her *café noir*. She said, "No. Let me tell you about my father right now. Let us conclude this matter."

33

"IT WAS SO LAMENTABLE," SHE SAID. WHEN SHE WAS YOUNG, HE was kind. He came every Wednesday evening, like a Father Christmas, bringing oranges or peaches or asparagus, something in season. He presented them as gifts, twisted in newspaper inside an old basket. He came in singing, and he petted each of the children, in turn, according to size. She was the middle child of the five, and as the family grew, his basket became larger. He drew amusing pictures for them. He taught them songs, for he was always singing, and he knew the children's songs, the folk songs, the *chansons*, the religious songs. When they grew older he recited poetry—Verlaine, she remembered.

When he sang "Dans le silence de la nuit," he might have been a choir angel, the melody in his voice was so sweet. But he drank too much, and his behavior was unpredictable. Gradually, his visits became erratic and unpleasant. She couldn't say when the change began. He gushed over the children and sloshed his wine on everything, including their heads. Late one evening when she was about ten, he arrived very drunk. The younger children were in bed, and she was reading. He entered her mother's bedroom. She heard shouting and crying. She was used to their loud noises, but this was different. Her mother was crying, and Caroline could make out some of the words. Her mother was insisting that he couldn't do something or other, pleading. "No, no, no," she said. Caroline's young mind trembled in fear of her father, who had sung the *chansons* so sweetly.

She heard her mother say, "I beg you, tell me how I can live with this."

"You have nothing to do with it!" he cried in a high voice.

"You cannot go on like this."

"This is the way I am."

"No, it does not have to be."

Caroline went to comfort her two little brothers, who had awakened. The cuckoo clock on the wall had not worked in years, but suddenly, as the voices in the bedroom grew louder, the cuckoo strutted out of its hole and gave two loud cuckoos, as if to say *"Chut!"* Shut up.

Caroline believed the cuckoo was an omen. As her parents continued to argue, she could bear no more, and she burst into her mother's bedroom. Her father stood there, on one side of the bed, with her mother on the other, against the wall. They were fully dressed, and when she entered, their faces dropped, their voices lowered, and her father said, "Hello, my little artichoke."

"Yes, did you say your prayers?" her mother said.

Her father patted her on the head, waved goodbye to her mother, and left the apartment.

After that night, he came less often. Then his visits stopped altogether. On Wednesdays the boys asked where the basket of surprises was. It was a long time before they discovered that their mother had been going to visit Robert in the hospital. She would not take the children to see him. His wife and their children visited him on Sundays, and Caroline's mother visited on Saturday afternoons. Caroline heard later that it was a psychiatric hospital, where he had shock treatments to dull his skewered mind, but her mother would not confirm this rumor. After he was released, she managed to keep him away from the children. There was a calmness around the apartment then.

A year later, Caroline was in the apartment one evening with her two little brothers when her father appeared, drunk. He was haggard, mumbling, apologizing for coming without a surprise basket.

"Where is your mother?"

"She's at the shop."

"She was expecting me."

His hands were trembling. He was agitated. He found some wine and poured himself a glass.

"Let me teach you a song I learned."

Caroline didn't understand all the words, but in the school yard she had heard something naughty about a woman's *belle chose*, and he was singing this to her. She remembered him grinning as he sang, enjoying the trick he was playing on her innocence. She refused to learn the song.

"The cuckoo clock—did it ever talk again?" he asked.

She shook her head. "It needed to speak only once. To warn us, to inform us what was going on."

"What was going on, my *petite*?"

She prayed for her mother to arrive. Her father, once handsome but now overweight and worn, stood before her with something glinting in his eye that made her afraid. She resolved to shield the two younger ones from this man.

Marshall reached to touch Caroline's arm, but she didn't respond to his gesture. She kept talking, as if she had to empty a vessel.

"I don't know where he is. He went away after my mother died, a few years ago. I felt she died from the strain—not a legitimate wife, all those children, his drunkenness. I think she loved him, but he wouldn't marry her and she always felt cast aside. So after my mother died, there was no connection, and I did not need to see him again."

She no longer acknowledged her father, she said, and she had not wanted to answer Marshall's questions about him.

"How did you and your brothers and sisters support yourselves?" Marshall asked. He rubbed his eyes, as if that would help.

"We had the shop, and my brothers had work. But we did not exist for his family. We do not have his name."

"How do you have the grocery?"

"He gave the *épicerie* to my mother long before. She made it a beautiful place."

"Your father wasn't all bad, if he gave her the store."

"I recall the terrible times."

Caroline turned her head aside, then bent over the dog and stroked him.

"I'm sorry," Marshall said.

Then, for a while they sat together silently. Marshall tried to sort out what he had heard. Robert had spiraled downward—but why? In 1944 he had seemed so capable. What had he seen and done after Marshall knew him?

"The war . . . ," he said. But then he could find no more words. He wasn't sure what he wanted to say.

ON THE WALK to the Métro, he felt empty and hard-hearted. Caroline hadn't insisted that he stay, but she seemed disappointed. She had grown up in a divided home, not an easy thing. When they had said goodbye, with a quick double peck, he wasn't sure he would see her again. She gave him a small, wan wave as he left her door and turned toward the stairs.

He waited at a crosswalk for the light to change. Ahead, the neon green cross of the pharmacy was blinking, as if wounded.

The train was due in two minutes, and riders were gathering on the platform, many dressed for late-night shifts. Marshall sat on a bench, his mind dulled. The train arrived, disgorging a motley batch of people. Marshall slipped wearily into a vacant window seat, and as the train twisted through the deep tunnel he gazed through the glass at dark, grimy tiles and thick, snaky wires.

34

"I HAVE FOUND ANNETTE VALLON," NICOLAS SAID ON THE TELE-phone.

Marshall, jangled awake by the ringing, became entangled in the cord and dropped the receiver. He fumbled to restore the connection but had to wait for Nicolas to call back. Marshall had slept late again—insomnia lasting till dawn—and had been dreaming of cranes migrating, their necks stuck out straight like jet fuselages.

Robert must be dead, Marshall had decided. If his body was still alive, his spirit was gone. Marshall was sure Caroline had told him the truth. And he was repelled by the thought of pursuing the broken wreck of the gallant young man he had known, if only fleetingly. Marshall knew he was overreacting, but the wave of revulsion was overwhelming. It was pointless, perhaps even perverse, to keep hunting for people he had known long ago, in a wholly different world. He should stop, pack up, go home. Home?

"She's alive? Annette?"

"It is true."

"I'm . . ." Marshall cast about for words. "I don't know what to say. How did you find her?" He hardly knew if he was awake.

"We were searching in Paris, but she lives in a village southwest of Angoulême, in the Charentes. Her name now is Bouyer."

"Bouyer? Are her parents still alive?" Marshall couldn't collect his thoughts.

"I don't know," said Nicolas. "I spoke to her, but she didn't mention her family. Listen, Marshall, she is eager to see you. At first she seemed hesitant, and I wasn't certain that she remembered you, but she spoke with great eagerness after I explained to her how my fam-

ily knew you. She was very gracious then, as if I had used a password!"

Two days earlier, Marshall had telephoned Nicolas about the dis-
appointing end to his search for Robert Lebeau. He didn't feel like
tracking down someone at a mental institution, he had said. Now he
said, "Nicolas, you are like a magician pulling a rabbit out of a hat."

"I should have accomplished this much sooner, but I foolishly
followed some false trails."

Marshall rose from bed and stood by the window. Across the
street several similar cars nested in a row. A small truck was backing
into a narrow space. He took a deep breath. He was awake now.

Nicolas apologized for limiting his search to Paris. "I found her
through another *résistante* in the Bourgogne line, a woman who
knew her and had seen her in Paris a few years ago. She should have
been easy to find, because so many *aviateurs* have stayed in touch
with the people who helped them. I must tell you that I was deeply
afraid the Vallons had met a bad fate, and I was overjoyed to locate
your Annette."

Annette had suggested that Marshall come on Wednesday afternoon for tea, and Nicolas had the directions for getting there.

"The train to Angoulême is simple," Nicolas said. "I would drive
you, but it is necessary to tutor my pupils."

"Thanks, Nicolas. Don't worry. I think I'll rent a car down there
and go exploring."

Marshall scribbled down Annette's telephone number and
promised to come to Chauny soon for Sunday lunch.

35

I T FELT GOOD TO HANDLE A VEHICLE AGAIN. FROM THE TRAIN station at Angoulême, in a boxy Citroën with a balky choke, he headed toward Cognac, an affluent town near the Atlantic coast. After Angoulême, the expanse of vineyards opened out—the grapevines responsible for cognac, the fine brandy that Marshall never drank but that was plentiful in the dollhouse bottles served to airline passengers. The vines were in full growth, twisting and hugging close together, supported by wires and pruned at the top into flat hedge roofs. Grapes. How did anyone take an interest in something so specific and yet so broad? Of course he knew that for the workers vineyards were like the coal mines—not a choice, usually, just an ineluctable fate.

He was afraid she wouldn't really remember him from 1944. In a brief conversation on the telephone the day before, she had been cordial, and although he still pictured her as the girl in his memory, her voice was high-pitched and unfamiliar.

Following the directions she had given him, he left the main route to Cognac and drove south a few miles to the sign for her village. It was a small farming community, with no trace of commerce or wealth. Slowly, he followed several turns until he found the street, then parked at #4, a large wooden portal, arched at the top. There was a smaller door with a bell rope. After pulling the bell and hearing its distant interior clang, he glanced around. It was a quiet street, like a back alley. He saw a field and a couple of gardens. Opposite, a lone white dog paced inside a fence.

A young woman wearing an apron and carrying a rake appeared at the door. Mme Bouyer was expecting him, she told him as she let

him in. A large, regal brown dog appeared, barking until the woman
quieted him. The dog sniffed Marshall's hand, then bowed gracefully.

Marshall was in a large courtyard, enclosed by several small
buildings joined together. At the far end was a two-story stone
house, covered with large-leaved ivy. The walkway was stone.

"Watch your step, *monsieur*."

The buildings seemed disused, the courtyard a bit shabby. Bees
buzzed through the thick ivy, and a bird flew out of it as Marshall approached the house. The place seemed to be a run-down farm, in the
process of renovation. Gardening implements, a wheelbarrow, and
various storage bins were scattered about the courtyard. Two men
were working with a pile of stones. The woman with the rake rapped
on a door of rough wood, leading off the terrace. Then she moved
toward the workers and began to rake the gravel of the driveway.

When Annette opened the door he did not know her right away.
Her features had filled out, and her figure was mature. She gave him
an enthusiastic three-cheek kiss—left, right, left. He bent to her, her
soft cheek pressing his lightly. Her scent was something fresh, an
herb of some kind, he thought, not the cloying sweetness of perfume.

"Do you really remember me?" he said, employing his best
French.

"Of course I do! But we never knew if you returned home safely."
She spoke in English.

He hung his head slightly, and she touched his arm. He tried to
explain—the war was over. He went back to the States. Flying. Not
a letter writer—and he didn't know where to write her.

"It doesn't matter," she said, dismissing the subject with a wave.

Her manner and her clothing—a long-sleeved blouse, long
pants, and sturdy brown shoes—were unpretentious. Her medium-
length waved hair was still dark brown and lustrous. He could see
her mother in her lively eyes, her delicate eyebrows. She wore her
age well, he thought. She was attractive.

A great smile broke over Annette's face as she stepped back to survey him.

"The first pilot who appeared at our apartment in Paris was such a surprise. I came home from school one afternoon, and there at the table, eating some soup, was an enormous boy, a young man, with blue eyes and blond hair. I thought at first—a German!"

"The Gestapo dropped in for tea?" Marshall said, laughing.

"He was an American! My first American. I was entranced. I have forgotten his name. He stayed only one night. Of course I wanted to know everything about him, and all about America. I was smitten! He was an *aviateur*, and his plane had crashed, and my parents were hiding him. And so it began. And then, one day, you." She smiled.

Her vibrancy was what he remembered.

"You have a fine head of hair," she said. "And the gray sides are so distinguished."

Reaching, she touched his hair. Then, turning, she led him into the house, through a small hallway to a dining room.

"Champagne first," she said. "It is necessary."

She had the bottle waiting, in ice, on a small side table, and he volunteered to pop the cork, even though he was unaccustomed to the task. It worked, to his relief. The bottle didn't spew, like those in the movies, and he hoped she wasn't disappointed.

"Let's not have it here," she said, smiling. "Let's sit on the terrace. We must toast to our reunion."

Details of her appearance began to fall into place for him. Her teeth—the lower canine that jutted out at a slight angle, the uncommonly even uppers. He had forgotten them until this moment.

"Do you live here with your family?" he asked, after they were settled on the stone terrace in sling-backed deck chairs, separated by a small, lopsided table covered with a blue print cloth. The dog settled near her chair.

"My son is often here on weekends. My mother comes from Normandy when she is able, or I go there. She lives near Saint Lô. My daughter lives in Cognac and is here almost every day, but she is in Saint Lô now with her children. I will join them later this week for Maman's birthday."

"I remember your parents so well," he said.

She nodded, smiling faintly.

"They were like parents to me," he continued. The champagne almost made him sneeze. "Your mother is in good health?"

"Yes, she is well. I would like for her to move here from Normandy. Saint Lô is too far." She turned her head away. "But my father—oh, he died many years ago."

"I'm sorry. He was a good man."

"*Oui.*"

Marshall hesitated. He said, "I remember him cursing the *boches*!"

She smiled. "My mother will be very happy to know I have seen you."

"I remember how kind she was," Marshall said.

Annette lifted her glass. "You remembered me as the girl in the blue beret," she said. "This is what Monsieur Albert told me. Is it not so? But our signals varied. Sometimes I wore a Scottish scarf. One of the *aviateurs* wrote me, and he remembered me as the girl in the red socks! The beret was a thing I had to wear to school."

He laughed. "The girl in the red socks. It doesn't have the same ring to it."

"During the war we couldn't get stockings. We wore socks, usually white or red. Oh, how I hated them."

The two workmen and the woman with the rake were leaving, and Annette crossed the courtyard to speak with them. Marshall could not hear their words distinctly. She was friendly with them, and he saw them all laughing. He sipped more of the champagne. The workers left, and she rejoined him, apologizing for the interruption.

"The work on this place is without end," she said, laughing.

"It's very grand," he said. "I'm surprised to find that you're a country woman now. You knew Paris so well."

"My husband and I bought this place twenty years ago. It had been a working farm until 1950, and then it fell into ruin, but we saw the possibilities. This has been a slow, evolving project. We restored the barn and the granary. And the *distillerie* across the courtyard we made into a food-storage place—like a cold place? For winter? We renovated the house enough to make it livable. Let's see, we lived in Paris until 1960, but his family is of this village, so we bought this. Oh, it is not luxury, I can tell you truly." She laughed. "No central heating until about ten years ago. We had only the fireplaces. And you remember from the apartment in Paris what it was like with no heat, or maybe a few lumps of coal for that stove we had in the front room. I remember in Paris when there was no heat at all." She seemed to shiver.

"Pardon me for asking, but where is your husband?"

"He is no more. Maurice was a veterinarian. He had his practice over there, in what was once the granary." She pointed across the courtyard to the center building. "He was very happy here. He had his animals, his treatment rooms, his kennels."

"What happened to him? Or am I out of line?"

She set her face, erasing her radiating smile lines. "It was an accident. Kicked by a horse. The hard shoe hit his skull in the most vulnerable place." With a flash of anger, she said, "He took chances. He was the type of person who could walk into the middle of a dogfight—or thought he could—and stop it. He was so used to working with animals that he thought they trusted him. He thought he could reason with them." She shook her head sadly.

"I'm sorry." Marshall murmured what he hoped were the appropriate comments. "How long ago?" he asked.

"Five years in November. It didn't have to happen, but it did. I can accept it. That is that. Some things happen that are neither just nor unjust. They are part of the nature of the universe."

Marshall noticed that she had blamed her husband for his fate while deciding on the indifference of the universe. But there was nothing to argue.

"So you have a daughter and a son?" he asked.

Her face lit up again. For some time, she spoke proudly of the accomplishments of her children and the joys of her small grandchildren. He liked the way she used her hands so expressively as she talked. They were like little ballet dancers.

"And you, Marshall? Please tell me everything."

Marshall told her about his career and his family, trying not to dwell on the disappointment over retirement. As he told about Loretta, Annette reacted sympathetically, then poured him some more champagne.

"Were you happy?" she asked.

"I thought we were." He paused, wondering what to say. "But after she died, I've been asking myself what that meant—to be happy."

"You go through self-examination, I know. When someone dies, you start rearranging everything. It's what we have to do, and you are behind. I'm ahead of you."

She gazed directly into his eyes. He moved his glass around on the wobbly table.

In a swoop, he told her how his retirement had led him back to the crash site and then to France, in search of the people who had helped him during the war.

"And I am here!" She clapped her hands and laughed gaily.

Her sweetness, her vitality, had survived the years.

WHEN SHE EXCUSED HERSELF, he sat there in a champagne buzz. A bird stirred in the ivy, and a light breeze made the ivy vibrate. He felt as though he were inside a network of ivy, throbbing. He saw the dog rise, turn around, then settle down again. Nearby, a striped gray cat was washing its face.

Annette brought a tray of cake and chocolate, with a pot of tea.

After she had arranged their plates and poured the tea, he asked her how she became involved in guiding airmen through the streets of Paris.

"Oh, I am delighted to tell you this. My parents were outraged by the Occupation. Every evening there was intense political discussion, and I heard all of it. They were fervent Gaullists—that is, for France. And Charles de Gaulle—appropriately named!—was the symbol of France."

Annette's smile broke out. "It was easy to play the innocent schoolgirl, and it was amusing to confound the Germans. They tried to treat the schoolgirls with politeness. If you were on the train and they wanted to sit, you were supposed to stand and let them sit, so one always took the opportunity to make that difficult. When they asked for directions, we liked to send them the wrong way. Once, an officer was looking for Napoléon's Tomb, and I sent him to the Père Lachaise! And when they weren't looking I liked to draw the Croix de Lorraine everywhere—you know, the symbol of the Free French.

"Then in 1943, my parents began working for the *réseau* Bourgogne. You must understand that at the time people in the *Résistance* didn't know there was a *Résistance* beyond two or three names. We had no way of knowing how extensive the network was, or even if it was succeeding, but my parents believed they had to do something, and this was a way to be *résistant* without violence.

"Then I began to participate as a *courrier.* I took the train to friends in Versailles and brought back tracts for clandestine distribution. I hid them inside my schoolbook bindings and inside the seams of my book sack—my *vache.* I found this little job very thrilling. I grew more serious then, and I was more careful about teasing the Germans."

ALL AFTERNOON MARSHALL and Annette continued to catch up on their lives and to reminisce about wartime. After the war, she taught school in Paris, and later in Cognac; her children had married well; her sister, Monique, taught music in Paris. Annette's manner was warm, filled with laughter. He felt at ease with her. He could sit there indefinitely.

Eventually, he couldn't help asking about Robert. He told her about searching for him through Caroline and recognizing him in her box of photos.

"I remembered him so well, but that story seems to have a sad ending."

Annette nodded. "Yes. Robert is a sad story. I can't settle that in my mind. But yes, the time he worked with us in the Bourgogne—that was a challenge for all of us."

"Is he still alive?"

"I assume so. But I do not know where he is at present."

"I always pictured him out on daring missions for the Resistance," Marshall said. "I imagined him having secret meetings with *saboteurs.*"

"Oh, no. He was only a *convoyeur* for the pilots," she said. "The Bourgogne line strictly limited itself to helping the *aviateurs.* Robert's parents were grocers, and they were forced to supply the Germans, but Robert was able to get food from them to help us feed the *aviateurs.*"

"His daughter should know this," Marshall said.

"It was very risky, but we depended on him. He probably was your escort on the train."

"My memories are vague, but yes, I think he led me south from Paris. He seemed so mysterious, like he was involved in major operations."

"There was no mystery about Robert. He was too much *not* mysterious, truly. I always trembled for him. He was often in danger."

"Tell me about him."

Hesitating, she offered him another piece of chocolate instead. Marshall was afraid he was asking for too much information, but then she began, slowly.

"At first, he made the false ID papers for the *aviateurs.* We fed the evaders and hid them for a short while, and then he escorted them on the train to Perpignan, where they would cross the Pyrenees with a local guide. But one day Robert arrived at our door, desperate and anxious. He had been arrested on his return from Perpignan. The French police on the train became suspicious of his papers."

"Did he carry a fake ID for himself?" Marshall asked.

"Oh, yes. As you know, all young French men—age twenty to twenty-four—were sent off to the work camps in Germany. He was about twenty-one, but he contrived to look older.

"That day he arrived to us, badly shaken.

" 'Hide me,' he said. 'I was arrested!'

" 'But how did you escape?' asked Maman.

" 'I jumped from the train down the embankment. But no one shot at me. I took two different trains until at last I arrived here.'

"The French police had kept his papers. He was disturbed, but he hadn't lost his courage. He thought the police had let him go in spite of their suspicions. That happened sometimes, even with the Germans. Once he and my father were escorting *aviateurs* from Belgium, and he noticed that the German police seemed to recognize that there were *aviateurs* with them. But then the Germans looked the other way! Maybe it was too much trouble to arrest them. Or maybe it was only that they were looking forward to their beer and sausage. Still, it was all very dangerous.

"After Robert's misadventure, the chief of the Bourgogne stopped him from going to Perpignan. He instructed Robert to bring the identity-card equipment to our apartment, and my mother began to make the false papers, as she did when you were there. Then I began guiding *aviateurs* to the *photomaton* at the Louvre to get the photos for the false identities.

"That is when I began going with Robert to escort *aviateurs* coming down from the north. We would meet them at the Gare du Nord and guide them to their shelter family, then later we put them on the train at the Gare d'Austerlitz for their southern journey. I went on Friday afternoons, after school."

Marshall said, "When I was trying to find you, I started thinking how amazing it was that a young girl would be out on such a dangerous mission."

She laughed. "Oh, there were many occasions that could have been the end! Once, we were with a group of five *aviateurs* at the Gare du Nord, when we passed five others at the stairs to the street! We recognized they were Americans by their large boots and, of course, their height. We didn't dare acknowledge them, and our group had been instructed not to notice anyone, not to respond or react. What a job! The *aviateurs* did not always take it seriously, and the Americans were likely to produce their chewing gum—*mon Dieu!* Or ask for a fire for a cigarette. Oh, they weren't stupid, but we had to teach them not to smoke in public! You remember that."

"A Yank is a Yank," he said, laughing. "It's hard for us to wise up."

"The Germans did not always pay attention. I think they were just happy to be in Paris. They thought they had already won the war. The French police were more likely to notice the large boots. When Robert and I went north on the trains—what chances we took! It was an advantage to behave as a romantic couple—flirting, holding hands. We weren't suspected. Oh, I had a *petit penchant* for him, *bien sûr*—"

She paused, gazing at a bird rippling the ivy. "Robert . . . It's very sad."

LATER, AFTER THE CHAMPAGNE had worn off, she suggested a walk.

"Do you ride?"

"Ride?"

"I have horses."

They walked outside the courtyard to see the horses.

"My son and I hike," she said. "Sometimes my daughter. And all of us ride, so I keep their horses here with mine. My husband always had horses. You noticed the chickens. There used to be a goat, a donkey, a pony, all kinds of wounded things that we rehabilitated. An owl used to live in the rafters over the terrace, but I have not seen any owls there in three years."

They walked down the street to the small field where the three horses grazed. The dog came with them, playfully running ahead.

"Bernard," she called after him. "Don't be a child."

"I've never been on a horse," Marshall admitted.

"You wanted Pegasus," she said, smiling. "But is it true you are not permitted to fly anymore?"

"Not on the airlines. I could rent a plane and tool around. Or I could buy a plane if I had the money. But the airline tells me I'm too old to fly for them."

"But you must fly! If you rent a plane, I will go with you! You must not give up what you love."

He grinned, immediately imagining the two of them on a sky jaunt, performing barrel rolls and nose-dives. The horses had come running to her, and she held out some carrots for them. She stroked them and called them by name—Peppy and Fifi and Charleroi, or something similar-sounding. Marshall enjoyed watching her caress the horses. She was more than fifty years old now, but she still seemed youthful. She had ample, well-formed breasts, and her skin was smooth and fresh.

They walked down a road to the river, passing stone dwellings that could have been there for centuries. The vegetation was thick along the side of the road, and gardens were bursting with tomatoes and squashes. It had been a long time since he had paid attention to anyone's garden. His grandmother had grown vegetables in the holler below the mountain, and he remembered her singing as she worked her slanted patch of ground. He remembered her shelling a basket of beans.

Blackberries grew in profusion by the side of the road. "My grandmother picked wild blackberries in the mountains of Kentucky," he said. "I picked them too when I visited in the summer, but I had to be forced to do it. I loved to eat them though." He laughed, as if he were unfamiliar to himself.

"These are not ripe yet," Annette said. "Oh, look."

Resting on a blackberry leaf was an unusual brown-and-yellow butterfly with ovoid wings.

"I have always loved these butterflies," she said.

"I don't think we have that kind in America."

"A butterfly is born to fly, just as you were," she said, smiling up at him. "But the butterfly flutters and takes its time to see the sights."

"It doesn't burn jet fuel," he said. He remembered once flying through a swarm of butterflies during a takeoff. A flash of color, a cloud, gone before he truly saw it.

They passed a field of what appeared to be corn. "It grows nicely," she remarked.

She called out some greetings to a man and a boy fishing from the riverbank. "They bring me fish sometimes," she said.

They walked on, making idle observations. He didn't want to go back to Paris. He could sleep behind her armoire, he thought.

SHE INVITED HIM to return the next day. After that, she would be in Normandy with her family for a week. She recommended a modest hotel in Cognac, on a street of ancient stone structures. After checking in, Marshall walked around in the fading light. Cognac seemed both ritzy and ruined. At a sidewalk café he ate a fish of some kind, just off the boat. He didn't want any wine. A light rain fell briefly, then cleared.

He managed to sleep in the hot, tattered room above the hotel bar, and the next morning he read the newspaper in the cramped breakfast room. The United States seemed remote, caught up in provincial political squabbles. He would be happy to get rid of Jimmy Carter—the jerk still hadn't gotten the hostages out of Iran—but electing an actor seemed far-fetched. There were few details on the election campaign, so he devoted himself to a great deal of information about the upcoming Olympics. In his mind he was with

Annette. Her youthful purity had lasted with her, but her womanliness surprised him. No husband. A preposterous coincidence, he thought.

He went for a walk along some narrow streets. On the main boulevard two girls on bicycles, baguettes in their baskets, whipped past him. He could almost feel the warm breath of the freshly baked bread as they went by. A fast car passed him from behind, the sound of its horn trailing in its wake.

36

HE FOUND ANNETTE GROOMING THE CHESTNUT HORSE IN THE small field next to the compound. Bernard came running to him, barking joyfully. Marshall said *"Bonjour"* to him. Bernard was a briard, she had told him, a French breed of herd dog. She waved, and Marshall made his way through a wooden gate toward the shed, a shelter for the horses. Next to the field was a sizable garden, with bald cabbage heads, thin sticks supporting bean vines, and some sprawling vines of melons or perhaps pumpkins. He recognized tomatoes.

After greeting him warmly—the two-cheek kiss this time—she explained that she had ridden down to the river on some back trails. He decided she smelled like lavender—as if he knew his scents.

"Go on, Charleroi," she said affectionately to the horse, who had a splotch on his forehead shaped like Great Britain.

Charleroi galloped off, and Annette and Marshall trotted to the house.

While she was changing her clothes, he wandered around the courtyard. The chickens were scratching in the dirt. Bernard, enthusiastic and attentive, accompanied him, like a guide pointing out the sights. Marshall exchanged *bonjours* with the workmen, who were repairing the stonework of some of the small buildings. He did not see the woman with the rake. He peeked into the small stone henhouse, observed the roosts, smelled the heavy aroma. He recalled his grandmother's ramshackle chicken house, which he had not thought of in years. He remembered reaching under a hen to steal an egg, his other hand pushing her head aside. He remembered his grandmother giving chickens grit for their craws, a gravelly stuff with tiny seashells in it. Why did they need grit for their craws? He had no idea.

"I wish you had gone riding with me this morning—it was so lovely!" Annette said, finding him examining some old farm machinery. He guessed that the rusty implement he was studying was a harrow, to be hitched to horses. It was structured with intricate tines.

"As a boy I rode Shetland ponies at the fair. They were about the size of Bernard." He gave the dog a vigorous pat. "You're right. I wanted Pegasus."

She laughed. "Of course. That was the way with you boys. Your airplanes were so romantic."

"Until they crashed," he said.

"The war was very hard for everyone, as you know. But if it weren't for our 'visitors,' it would have been even more bleak." She waved her hand in front of her face, as if to erase the thought. "I'm so happy you returned home safely!"

She was a stylish, confident woman—not girlish like Caroline, in those Indian getups and jeans. Annette was wearing dark slacks and a long-sleeved white shirt. He felt she was making no statements. She was just being herself.

SHE INSISTED ON SHOWING him some of the scenery of the region. She drove her car, so that he was free to look around. He had always thought the French were notoriously daring behind the wheel, but she drove sensibly. The windows were down, and the rush of wind reminded him of the early days flying in an open cockpit. It would not have occurred to him to sightsee this way, he explained to her. He had always seen the landscape from above, where fields and rivers became abstract—elements of a painting. Now it was as though he were in a labyrinth, circling and winding and backtracking—with no headers or gauges or timetables. Without ailerons and throttles, riding became a pleasurable drift.

Annette's husband had practiced in a wide area—driving to people who owned large farm animals, going out on calls at dawn or late at night, any time of day—and she still kept in touch with many of the clients. She stopped at a vineyard, where she bought some bottles of wine from a man who had a pair of friendly briards. Then she drove to another village to take flowers to an ailing man who kept geese.

"Now, a surprise," she announced, as they pulled back onto the main road. "I have a friend who is passionate to meet you. She is another who helped to hide pilots in the war, and her experience was so much more dramatic than mine. She had a great deal of courage. I want you to hear what she did during the war. It is extraordinary."

The friend, a schoolteacher, lived in a town near Angoulême. Their common past aiding Allied aviators had drawn Annette and Odile Durand together.

"I thought you and your parents were pretty extraordinary," Marshall said.

Annette laughed. "Oh, we did what was necessary," she said. "Nothing more." She slowed down to make a turn. "Odile's daughter married last year and has gone away on some type of global adventure with her new husband. Odile is troubled—there are so many dangers in the world."

Annette turned into a street so narrow they nearly scraped the walls on both sides. Expertly she pulled into a tiny apron of stone in front of a small stucco house with a red-tile roof. The door flew open immediately.

The women exchanged kisses, with affectionate hugs.

"*Voilà*, my pilot!" Annette said.

"*Monsieur, monsieur, bienvenue.* I am delighted."

Odile grabbed him and bussed both cheeks. She was small and wiry.

"Odile, I have brought you some eggs," Annette said. "My chickens engage themselves in a contest, to lay so many eggs!"

"*Merci beaucoup, Annette. Tu es très gentille.*"

They sat in the small garden behind the house. It was quiet except for the chatter of the women. Odile said her daughter had written from Bangkok and had ridden an elephant. "*Mon Dieu*, what next!"

"Remember, Odile, what you were doing at her age. She will be all right."

"Elephants I trust, but she and Giscard are on airplanes so often, and I do worry about that. Tell me, *monsieur*, am I right to worry?"

"Travel today is simple, madame," he said. "Airline travel is safe."

"Did you ever have a crash?"

"No, no, not in the airlines."

"Sometimes they crash."

"If you were to look at a timetable, madame," he said, like a professor, "you would see how many flights there are in one day just on one airline—thousands. And they all arrive safely."

"Marshall knows everything about airplanes," said Annette assuringly.

Marshall enjoyed watching Annette with her friend. Annette's good humor balanced Odile's sober nervousness.

After Odile had served them some of the wine Annette had brought, Annette urged her to tell Marshall about her pilots in the war. Odile jumped up, grasped both of his hands, and gazed hard into his eyes for a moment. She was close to his age, he thought. Her hair was gray, with springy curls running willy-nilly up her temples.

"I am so glad you have come," she said. She let go of his hands and sat down.

Quickly she launched into her tale, as though she had been waiting for the chance to blurt it out. Her voice was raspy, as if she was getting over a bad cold, but her French was clear, easy for Marshall to follow. Annette sat comfortably in a straight-backed chair, and Marshall cocked his chair onto its two back legs, rocking a bit now and then.

Odile had been a very young teacher during the war, on her first teaching assignment, in a coastal village above Bordeaux. The Occupation there was relatively peaceful. The Germans, worried about the British and the Americans, kept a nervous watch on the beaches. Odile liked to walk along the seashore, but the Germans patrolled it and had put up a barrier. She could see their bunkers five kilometers down the shore. The school stood between the beach and a large forest, crisscrossed by many local paths. When the weather was good she liked to take the schoolchildren to a clearing in the forest, where there was a certain high rock. They could find berries in the woods and have picnics on the rock.

The school was one large room. She lived with her aunt in the other wing of the building, on the first floor.

Odile's voice grew dramatic. Marshall leaned forward, settling his chair on all fours.

"One Sunday, a knock came on the door. It was a handsome German officer! He was very polite, and he spoke good French. He introduced himself, Hans Wetzel. He was very well-mannered. Very correct.

"I must emphasize that they were always well-mannered, but my aunt had fear that there was a cauldron of wickedness stirring. I hated the Germans because my Jean was at their labor camp, far away. Jean and I were engaged for only six months when he was sent away.

"The German addressed my aunt and me, '*Mesdames*, I come to requisition the school. We need this building to lodge our officers.'

"I drew myself up to my full height and faced this young officer— and I refused! 'Where would the children have their lessons?' I asked. 'The nearest other school is nine kilometers! These children are all from this village. You can't force little children to walk nine kilometers!' I bargained with him. I said he could live upstairs, above our living quarters, and the school could go on. To my aunt's amazement, the German agreed. He clicked his heels, bowed, and declared he would take the rooms above the school for his own lodging and let the school proceed. He said he would find other facilities for the other officers.

"My aunt had fear that the Germans would then take advantage of us, billeting in quarters near our own, but I was determined not to deprive the children of their education."

"You were very brave to challenge a German like that," Marshall said.

"I am not surprised," said Annette. "Of course Odile could handle him!"

Odile continued. The German officer moved in upstairs. He was an aristocrat, educated at the Sorbonne. He displayed pictures of his wife and two small children. The aunt, despite her fearfulness, enjoyed vexing the German. Out in the corridor, she hung a portrait of her young husband, who had died in the first war. She draped black silk around the frame. The German officer spoke to her of the young French officer in the portrait. Then he clicked his heels and saluted.

"Each time he went through the corridor he saluted the portrait!" Odile cried with laughter. "We heard him come through the back door at night, walk quietly down the dark corridor, and then we heard the heel-clicking when he got to the portrait. This gave my aunt enormous pleasure!"

The wine relaxed Marshall. He enjoyed watching Annette's delight in her friend. He was listening attentively to Odile, but his thoughts of Annette formed an undercurrent, a warm tide that pulled him. He fiddled with some broken twigs that had fallen onto the table, arranging them into idle patterns.

On January 5, 1944, a sunny afternoon in winter, Odile was outside for recess with the students when Allied bombers flew over, just beyond the forest. Suddenly they saw three parachutists floating down above the trees. The week before, two parachutists had landed in a nearby village, and some citizens had handed them over to the Germans for reward money. She had promised herself that if she ever saw parachutists, she would try to help them. And here they were. They landed among the pines, only two hundred meters from the school. Quickly, she asked the oldest student to get the children inside and to keep them busy.

"Of course the students always obeyed the schoolteacher!" Annette said.

"*Bien sûr*," said Odile. "At that time, the authority of a schoolteacher was incontestable."

A German patrolling on his bicycle on the street in front of the school saw through the window that school was in session. As soon as she was sure he would remain in front, on the road, young Odile enlisted the help of a neighbor. They scurried into the forest, where they found one of the aviators tangled in a bush.

A man had already reached the site, coming from one of the other paths into the forest.

"*Stupéfaction!* I knew this man!" she cried. He was a *donneur*, one of the men who had turned a parachutist over to the Germans the week before for the reward.

"I said to him, 'I'm taking care of this, *monsieur*. You return to the village.' Once again, as the teacher I commanded respect, so the *donneur* left!"

"What about the parachute?" Marshall asked. The twigs he had been playing with scattered on the stones.

Odile and her neighbor helped the American gather his parachute and hide it in some brush. They insisted that he hide in the thick bushes until dark, and they promised to bring clothing and food.

"On the way back to the school, I encountered a workman who was pushing an American, slightly wounded, in a donkey cart. He was taking him to the factory to turn him in. I said, 'You can't do that!' I stated that it would be treason to France if he turned the man in for money."

"Odile was very courageous," Annette said, turning to Marshall.

"The workman left," Odile said. "And I hid the second American with the first. They were glad to see each other, and they let out a few loud sounds. I hushed them. Then they began to search for their cigarettes. I cautioned them—no, no, *messieurs*! It is dangerous!

"I did what I could with the flyer's wounds. He had a little first-aid box with some medicine and patches. I told them, 'I'm going to leave you here right now, because we cannot take you into a home in the day. The Germans will be looking. If their dogs sniff you out, do not resist. If you do, you will be killed. If you do not resist, the worst that can happen is that you will be a prisoner of war. Be silent. Remain hidden. Do not smoke.' I instructed them carefully, repeating my cautions, especially because I was uncertain of my English."

While the schoolchildren went home for lunch, Odile, her aunt, and the neighbor gathered supplies and contacted people who could help harbor two Americans. When the students returned, a boy was crying, telling her that his parents had seen the third parachutist hanging at the top of a pine tree, with a pool of blood at the bottom.

"I instructed this boy very carefully. 'You must go home right now,' I said. 'Tell your parents to cut that tree down and rescue the American before he loses any more blood.' So this child did just that. His parents cut down the tree, but they declared him to the authorities because he needed hospitalization. If they had cut the tree earlier, he might have survived. His arm was torn almost off. I went to their house immediately, but by then it was clear he was dying from the loss of his blood. His last word, I will never forget, was 'coffee.' "

Marshall had been listening intently. The arm, the falling pine tree. He could easily imagine coffee being his own dying request. But landing in a tree, hanging there, his arm wrenched . . .

"I will never forget the Germans who came to take him to the hospital," Odile was saying. "They came into the house, saw he was dead, and one lifted him by the arm and head, the other the feet. They swung him through the house as if he were a heavy sack of potatoes, and they threw him onto their vehicle, on top of some green canvas bundles. He landed facing the sky, limbs spread, his eyes still open. They drove away without a word. They would salute a portrait of a stranger long dead but treat a fresh body like this! I was trembling with furor and fear. I knew we had a difficult job to undertake."

"Were the other two all right?" Marshall asked.

"In the night I went to get them. They were still in the bush, and to my relief I did not smell cigarettes. They had not smoked. I stowed them in a barn, and the next night I found a room for them with a factory worker. Several people helped me to move them. They spent nights in different homes. One night they were in our kitchen! The German officer went down the corridor, as usual, and we heard him salute the portrait. The Americans were crouched behind the flour barrel in the storage pantry. My aunt decided that one night was all she could bear of having Americans and Germans in such close quarters. The next night we smuggled them out to another home. Everyone in the village knew! They cooperated because I was the teacher. I think the students all knew, but we did not speak of it at school.

"We had much work to do to get clothing for the *aviateurs*. The shoemaker in the village produced some coarse work boots, and I measured them for vests and trousers. I remember there was a beret that we had to stretch."

In the end, the baker drove the airmen to another village in his car. He was allowed a car and a pass into the forbidden coastal zone, for he had to deliver his bread to the Germans. By then the Americans were dressed as French workers, with false papers. The baker knew a group that could arrange their passage across the Pyrenees.

"I was so nervous. I thought we would never get all the details to work. On the Sunday before they left, I went to the house where they were staying to give them some instructions, and a German spotted me on the road.

" 'What are you doing, miss?' he asked. 'You usually go home to your parents on the weekends.'

" 'Oh, I couldn't go this weekend,' I said. 'I had schoolwork to do. What are *you* doing here, *monsieur*?'

" 'I am looking for my lost dog,' he said.

"The *aviateurs* returned to England safely. The *Résistance* received a message through the BBC. But after the war, the *aviateurs* never answered my letters. I kept their American dollars for them. I had told them they must not be caught with American dollars. I didn't know what to do with the money. I kept it until 1947, and finally my mother suggested I give it to charity."

Odile took a sip of her wine, set the glass down, and folded her hands neatly in her lap. Marshall was moved, identifying with the parachutists, remembering being dressed as a workman and plunked down in someone's car, being driven along dark roads.

Annette said, "Thank you, Odile. You see, Marshall, here is courage."

"The parachutes—we gathered them, and after the war we sewed them into clothing. I made my wedding dress from one of the parachutes." Odile smiled. "My Jean returned to me."

Annette, her voice slightly unsteady, urged Marshall to tell about his own evasion.

He gave Odile a truncated account of his escape from France, making light of his own actions while praising the families who had helped him.

"I might not be alive if it weren't for people like Annette and her family," Marshall said.

"*Bien sûr, monsieur.* It is my effort to make all the witnesses of that time go out to the public and speak about it, but Annette has not been ready to do this yet." Odile nudged Annette affectionately. "At the school I am able to talk about it, although some of the parents might prefer I did not. I don't frighten the children. I merely talk to them of history and what France endured when our country was assaulted, when it was taken over and we were robbed of our resources. The children take notice. They sense that there is something in the past, a great storm cloud hanging over us. They know this from home."

"Tell us about the boy who drew the swastika in his notebook," Annette said.

"*Oh, mon Dieu!* I said, 'Do you know what that is, young man?' I was very stern. He was terrified and he said no.

" 'It is the Nazi symbol of hatred, of all the darkness that was rained down upon France.' I told him this with much severity! I made him hold out his palm for the ruler. It made him cry, and it is necessary for the boys to hold their tears." She sighed. "I was filled with remorse later, but I decided that what I did was correct."

"So many don't know," said Annette. "It is too painful for their parents to tell them."

"Yes. And now there are attempts to change the history, to say the worst atrocities never happened." Odile's voice grew shrill.

"The *négationistes*!" Annette said.

"Annette teaches art classes. That is perfect, because she could instruct the young ones about what it was like during the war, but perhaps she hasn't the heart. I am trying to persuade her." Odile's voice dropped.

"I might not be here if she hadn't helped me in 1944," Marshall reiterated.

"I see how eagerly you listened, and I feel you are a friend. You can imagine the three men who parachuted into my schoolyard that distant day."

"Yes."

"It makes me enormously unhappy that I never heard from them again. I wrote to them. They had given me their addresses, but they never responded."

"A lot could have happened to them on the way home."

"I know they reached England, although I'm sure they suffered from crossing the Pyrenees when it was still winter."

LATER, WHEN ANNETTE and Marshall said their goodbyes, Odile implored Marshall to locate the two American flyers for her. "I will write their names for you."

"I'll do what I can." Marshall wasn't confident, but he said he would try. He thanked her for telling her memories.

Odile clasped both of Marshall's hands in hers.

"Please help me to find my pilots," she pleaded.

37

IN THE CAR, THE REST OF MARSHALL'S OWN STORY TUMBLED OUT.
He told Annette more about his landing in France during the war,
about hiding in barns, about sleeping behind an armoire, about
Pierre Albert's Resistance work. Even the boy Nicolas was a local
scout, he said. She listened, nodding attentively. He told her about
returning to the crash site in the spring. He described finding the Alberts again.

"I was a child when the war began," she said abruptly. "Papa sent
us away from Paris a few days before it fell to the Germans. That in-
famous day—June 10, 1940. He stayed behind, hoping to keep his
job in the finance ministry, and we went to our summer house in
Normandy. A few weeks later, Papa decided we should return to
Paris. The travel was abominable—my mother with two children
and innumerable possessions. Monique must have her dolls, and I
must have my books. We arrived at Paris, and the sight of the Nazi
flags on the rue de Rivoli—it made the stomach sick. We *hated* the
Germans! It was insupportable that we should be ruled by these detestable people in their ugly uniforms, the color of mold and ash.
Monique was lively and I tried to play games with her, but I was serious about my studies, and I was alert to my parents' views. They
had friends for dinner many times, and all were inconsolable over
the plight of France. The Germans had tried this twice before.
Could they not see that we were never going to give in to their brutal aggression? It was all *horrible*."

"It still seems very real to you."

"*Bien sûr*. But we made the best of it. Papa lost his job but managed to get another position in the *mairie*, the city government. Maman had difficulty getting enough food. She was outraged that the Germans should make the French go hungry, when it was certain that the Germans would not appreciate *foie gras* or a fine sauce *à la bordelaise*."

Annette was concentrating on her driving. Traffic was increasing now.

"I'm sorry I never tried to find you," he said.

"No, no, no. I did not contact you either. The boy who wrote— I did not answer."

"I still think I must have seemed ungrateful all those years."

"And so did I," she said, turning to smile at him.

It was late in the afternoon, and the sun was behind them. She turned to the last road into her village, eased down the quiet street, and pulled up to her doorway. He got out and opened the large double door to the courtyard. After she parked, he closed the door and greeted Bernard. The workmen were gone. Marshall's rented car stood there, waiting to take him back to the train. He didn't want to leave. Then he had an inspiration. He waited for her to get out of her car. As she shut the door, he said, "Let me take you to dinner tonight."

"I would like that."

"I'll drive," he said, patting the rented car as if it were Pegasus.

SHE CHOSE A SIMPLE place on the river. They sat at a table with an umbrella and watched ducks and geese waddling up the riverbank for bread crumbs. She laughed, holding her wineglass daintily. She talked about her husband's work as a veterinarian. Annette had assisted him very little, for it broke her heart when an animal suffered. She raised the children, kept pets, fed chickens, gathered eggs, helped raise lambs.

"I rejoiced when the animals got well, but I did not have the sensibility, the stomach for enduring the losses! I was a coward, I think! One day I will never forget, a woman came in with a small white dog in her arms. She was in tears. Her large shepherd dog had killed the little one, it was apparent, but she was disbelieving. Very kindly, Maurice took her and the little dog into the examining room, and in a few minutes they emerged. She was weeping uncontrollably, and the little dog was in a cardboard box. It should not have been done—trusting the large dog with the little one. She just did not believe it had happened, or that it had been her fault."

"That's sad."

"I cried," Annette said. "That day my husband said, 'No more. You cannot be the assistant.' He was being good to me, not forbidding me. So I found other occupations! The children, always. And work in the schools. Art teaching. Now I am a floating teacher. I go from class to class, school to school—like the troubadours of old, I suppose."

She smiled, as if seeing herself as an itinerant bard, in a traveling costume.

The waiter poured more wine for Marshall. He was getting used to wine. He liked seeing her across the table, her face lighting up.

"I remember you drawing in your notebook," he said. "You were at your parents' table, drawing, and working over your school lessons in the evenings when I was at your house. You were the most cheerful person I had ever seen."

"One had to be, you know, Marshall." Her eyes went down.

"And I remember how happy everyone was when Robert came on his bicycle."

"Robert—yes." Annette was contemplating her hands, which rested firmly on the table, one on either side of her plate. "An interesting young man." She paused, turning her head aside. "He was very brave during the war," she said. "A good person."

"So I've heard."

On the lake, a goose was taking off in the water, flapping and skidding and finally getting lift. Some lights were coming on in the distant houses. The birds were disappearing, roosting for the night. The last duck quacked.

"Could you come again?" she asked. "Would you like to go hiking after I return from Saint Lô? A real hike into the wilderness?"

"Yes. Sure. I'd love to."

"Do you have some good boots?"

"I'll get some. I've worn out my shoes walking all over Paris."

"Be sure to break them in."

"Where do you hike?"

"There are many places, but I will take you to a good trail, where we will see magnificent scenery."

"I should be in good shape," he said. "All the walking I've done."

"Good. Do you have to be in Paris?" she asked.

"Oh, no. I can be anywhere."

"You should get your boots in Paris. I will tell you where to go."

THE WAITER REMOVED their plates. It was growing dark, and the thrumming insects had struck up a symphony.

She drank more of her wine and began laughing. "I look back on those times, and it was exhilarating. It was amusing to torment the Germans! They occupied half of my school, as they did many schools—like Odile's. Once, I chose the precise moment to let my books fall from my arms onto a German's feet. The *vache* buckled at the bottom, so you could let it fall open and the books would fly out. Robert told me later I could have been arrested for that! But the pleasure of seeing that German forced to pick up my books, as though he were my servant, was worth the risk."

"You and Odile took a lot of chances."

They laughed and he finished his wine. He had rarely had so much wine in one day.

"It was an exulting time, something I've thought about very

much since. Everyone felt intensely alive—expressing joy much more readily than has been possible since. For us, it was *jubilatoire*." She paused, smiling broadly.

"You were young," he said. "When you're young you can feel that."

"But it was the same for Maman! Everybody felt this. I do not mean we were happy, you comprehend? We were in misery. But each day handed out possibilities of little victories. Each time you passed a German and could assert your Frenchness, it was a little triumph. Or if you had a dear friend with you and could show your pleasure with each other, to the soldier's face, it was a little triumph."

The waiter was bringing some sort of dessert of soft chocolate.

"I remember sharing some black-market ice cream with you," Marshall said.

"We did not resort to the black market!" she protested. "We went to people we knew."

She took a spoon of chocolate and savored it.

"Only the children were allowed rations for chocolate," she said. "I was too old, but Monique wanted to share her chocolate. We wouldn't allow it."

He tasted the chocolate and tried to picture Annette's little sister.

"The moon is coming up," Annette said. "It is near the full. I never want to miss the full moon. It is one of my principal joys!"

38

PARIS WAS WARM AND MUGGY. THE SKY FELT CLOSE, THE AIR HEAVY with coming rain. A storm cloud was like a piñata waiting for thunder to whack it, Marshall thought, but he knew that thunderstorms were infrequent in Paris, so he walked to his apartment from the Gare Montparnasse with his small duffel. He told himself he was getting in shape for his hike with Annette, but the weight unbalanced his shoulders, and he began to wish he had taken a taxi. He arrived at his apartment sweaty and feeling lopsided.

Marshall was moving around his own apartment as if exploring it. The bedroom was stuffy, so he pulled open the windows and leaned toward the street. Children on the playground were hurrying away as large drops of rain began to fall. The dark, heavy shadows of pigeons rushed past the windows. He could feel the breeze pick up.

He closed the windows halfway, and the rain splashed against them while he read his mail. Al Grainger had written again, suggesting a crew reunion at the crash site in Belgium. "It was my wife's idea, and I have to say she was right on target. After what you wrote about going back there and meeting those people, it just seems right to go and thank them in a proper way. And we could have a great time seeing each other, catching up, reminiscing. Couldn't we round up all the surviving crew? Their families could come too."

O.K., but no preaching, Marshall felt like replying. He tended to answer letters in his head instead of on paper. Marshall the Procrastinator. Thirty-six years.

After the rain let up, he telephoned Nicolas and reported on his trip.

"Marshall, maybe I have found the house where you stayed before we sheltered you in Chauny."

"The women in black?"

"Yes. I don't know if any are alive, but there is a daughter."

"Good work, Nicolas."

Marshall thanked him and agreed to come to Chauny for Sunday lunch after he returned from his hike with Annette.

Later, he telephoned Mary and found himself confiding that he had located an "interesting" woman who had been a girl when he came through during the war.

"Her family took care of me when I passed through Paris back then," he told his daughter. "Now I've looked her up, and we had a good time reminiscing."

He couldn't continue. He was thinking of Loretta. "A good time" perhaps wasn't the right phrase.

"Dad, it's O.K. if you have some women friends."

"Thank you. Your old dad is still alive and kicking."

"That reminds me—I heard that Albert has a girlfriend! I was blown away. Don't tell him I told you."

"That's good news," Marshall said. "I always thought it would just take time. Maybe this one will work out."

"That's what I thought," said Mary, with only the slightest hesitation in her voice.

"How about you, Mary?"

"I've been going out with a guy at the college—an economist. He's really interesting, and he has some theories about inflation that baffle me."

"Well, let me know if you find out what causes it. How about this—I'm planning to go hiking, and I'm going to buy hiking boots tomorrow."

"Well, far out, Dad!"

"I guess so. But it was never my ambition to become an old fuddy-duddy, you know. I can still get around."

She laughed. "Remember how you and Mom would take us for picnics at a state park when we were kids? Nobody thought of going hiking in those days, but I've gotten more interested in fitness. Everybody has. Maybe we can go to a park again sometime. We could go hiking this time."

"Well, let's do that," Marshall said. "I'll have the boots for it, anyway!"

MARSHALL, COMFORTABLE IN PARIS NOW, no longer carried his cash in a safety pouch on his leg. He gazed at the window display at the Everything Store: fishhooks, a cheese grater, a doll made of seashells, and a Hemingway novel with a faded cover.

"*Bonjour, monsieur l'Américain! Ça va?*"

"*Je vais bien, merci.* And you, Guy?"

"*Comme-ci, comme-ça.* How does your search go?"

"Ah, Guy, I've found her. I was looking in the wrong place. She was in the Charentes!" Briefly, he told of his visit with Annette and the hike they planned together.

"A *rendez-vous* for a *randonnée*," Guy said, smiling.

"Exactly so!" Marshall fingered some leather bags hanging from the wall. "I'm looking for a backpack, a small one for hiking."

Guy produced a leather rucksack that resembled something a mountain climber of the nineteenth century would carry. The French farmers in 1944 carried such rucksacks, slung over their shoulders. Robert Lebeau had one. Marshall had one himself, holding his meager supplies on the train out of Paris.

"I'd prefer something more modern, Guy."

"More American, you want to say."

Guy revealed a cheap blue zippered pack that seemed suitable. Marshall paid and made small talk about his trip to the Charentes. Then he remembered that he needed a curtain of some kind to keep out the streetlights. For some time he examined the crop of dusty bamboo blinds that Guy offered. They had been kept for perhaps decades behind a rolled-up Turkish carpet.

"They look ancient," Marshall said.

"*Mais oui.*" Guy began rummaging excitedly through some cabinets in the back of the store. He went back and forth searching. Then he found what he was looking for, a roll of dark fabric.

"This was to line the curtains, to shut out the light. I am surprised myself to find this. Maybe it is left from the wartime, because people couldn't afford to buy it."

"Exactly what I want."

"You will keep the light inside at night, Marshall. And in the day the sun will stay away."

Marshall flicked dust from the black roll. "I hope you're not charging antique prices."

Guy shrugged. "For you, just what it's worth."

"I'll try it," Marshall said. He paid for his purchase, declining to have it wrapped. Laboriously, Guy wrote out a detailed receipt.

"See you next time, Guy. Where do you take your vacation?"

"I go to the Languedoc in August." Guy shut his cash drawer and straightened some knickknacks on the counter. "My wife likes breathing in the country. That's what she says—in the country she can breathe. My two sons and daughter and my parents and my wife's mother and my grandmother come. My brother comes with his family. We're all there. *Bien sûr*, there is nothing like having all the family together. We do the picnics, the games. It is bliss!"

Guy's broad smile made Marshall wistful. He thought of the family picnics Mary had mentioned. The elaborate logistics of the outings had always annoyed him, smothering whatever "bliss" he might have felt.

Walking down the avenue du Général Leclerc, he thought how unlike a Frenchman he was, with his inadequate attention to things that mattered most here—food and wine and family. History, they didn't dwell on. Sex—well, maybe he could see eye-to-eye with the French on that.

The blackout curtain material was brittle on the edges, but he trimmed it and taped it to the windows. He wasn't sure it was authentic, but it would do. That night he slept peacefully, and the morning sun was high before he was fully awake.

39

ANNETTE HAD GIVEN HIM EXPLICIT DIRECTIONS TO THE VARIOUS places where she had guided the aviators, and now in his new hiking boots, he set off to find them. First, he went to Saint-Mandé to see where the Vallons had lived. He had been entirely wrong about the location. The building, made of handsome pale stone blocks, seemed less familiar than the one he had found on his recent walk. Yet there was a vaguely recognizable outline and shape to the neighborhood. Standing across the street, he let himself turn back in time. The entry. The bicycles. The stairs. He identified the window of the room where he had slept, facing the small side street. He remembered waiting hours alone, trying to keep warm by doing jumping jacks—in his socks. The window on the corner was the sitting room, which had a large ornate stove that burned coal, delivered through a chute to the basement. He spotted the chute now. Annette, Monique, and their parents had slept in two rooms on the other side of the sitting room, and when there were additional airmen visiting, the girls moved into their parents' room. On the street, staring up at the dining room window, he remembered the kitchen beyond it, where Mme Vallon miraculously concocted splendid meals from meager rations. He remembered the goose, the feathers flying.

After studying the building for a while, he had readjusted his memory. It seemed odd to him that memory was so malleable, that what he had thought was true could be revised, like a flight plan.

To break in his hiking boots, he walked toward the Jardin des Plantes, keeping up a good stride along the Seine, passing a variety of scenes—fishermen, industries, laundry. The weather was good, not too hot. The long botanical garden stretched out in front of the Museum of Natural History.

"Go straight past the garden to the grove of Christmas trees," she had told him just two days earlier.

He passed the statue, Rodin's *Thinker*. The guy was still thinking. Marshall recognized the general layout and the area where among the evergreens she had assembled airmen before sending them across the street to the Gare d'Austerlitz. He wandered around through the trees. The path meandered. On a bench by some bushes, an aged man sat reading *Le Monde*. Marshall sat on another bench to tighten his bootlace. He dimly recalled that Annette had escorted him and a B-17 waist gunner to some benches amidst public shrubbery. Later, she had distributed their train tickets surreptitiously, without speaking. The last time Marshall saw her, she was hurrying away down the broad avenue of plane trees. He had thought he remembered how the sunshine dappled teasingly through the great trees lining the promenades. It was spring. But now he realized he must have been here near dusk. He had taken the night train to Toulouse.

The Gare d'Austerlitz was across the street from the Jardin des Plantes. Marshall made his way there, passing the Métro stairs and entering the massive building. The high glass-and-wrought-iron ceiling was so distinctive that he did not see how he could have forgotten the station. He could almost locate in his spatial memory the exact quai where he had boarded the train. Robert had entered the car without glancing at him. So many memories were crashing through Marshall's head that reliving them made him exultant—the fear then, the relief now.

On the way out of the station, he remembered what Nicolas had said about the Gare d'Austerlitz. The Jews were deported from this spot. Marshall was glad the *Dirty Lily* had dropped at least a few bombs. If he hadn't been shot down, maybe he could have helped shorten the war. If, if only. You couldn't revise history with conditional clauses.

He pictured the blithe young man he had been—reckless but scared, overconfident, out of his element, filled with longings, strangely detached from home, walking tentatively in a foreign country. He reflected upon his youthful brazenness, his naïveté. He wondered if Annette found her youth embarrassing too. Maybe the primary difference between youth and adulthood was the capacity for embarrassment.

40

HIS BOOTS GAVE HIM BLISTERS, BUT THE LEATHER WAS GROWING more pliable, and after five days of exploring the city, he considered the boots broken in, ready for action. Everywhere he went he thought about Annette, wanting to see her again, looking forward to seeing her mother again sometime in the future. He missed M. Vallon. Annette had said he had a weak heart.

The week passed quickly. One night he dined with Jim and Iphigénie, who were back from the Dordogne and already planning an August retreat in Switzerland. They sat at a small table on the sidewalk, jammed between two other tables. Marshall was all elbows, and the pedestrians crowding past annoyed him. Jim, however, seemed habituated to Parisian life, charmed by the way Iphigénie constructed an area of privacy around their small table, although they sat precariously perched on the edge of traffic. This was Paris. Marshall gave in. He let the wine stoke up his little glow—the miniature furnace of desire and hope that was burning inside him. His pilot light, he thought ridiculously.

"The Swiss go to Provence in the summer," Iphigénie said. "But I prefer Switzerland. It's peaceful. Paris gets too hot."

"I'd like to go to Tenerife," said Jim. "I flew there a few times."

"I would go to Morocco, to Algiers," said Iphigénie. "I adore the scarves, the jewelry. But I must wait for that."

"Iffy's working on a new line of clothes," Jim explained. "I tried to get her to call it 'Iffy.' She's full of brilliant ideas."

"The young people dress despicably," she said. "There is no respect, no style."

"You are right," said Marshall.

They listened attentively as Marshall recounted his success finding the girl in the blue beret, and Iphigénie smiled.

"You must take her a beautiful gift, Marshall. I will help you select."

"I met another woman too." He told about meeting Odile.

"How does she expect me to find those guys she helped?" he said. Then he heard how ungracious he sounded.

"She seemed desperate?" Iphigénie asked.

"She made a great sacrifice," Marshall said. "For a couple of fool Americans like me." Absently, he let the waiter refill his wineglass.

"Those guys should have written her," Jim said.

Iphigénie touched Jim's cheek. "What would you have done, *mon chéri?*"

Later, after Iphigénie went home, Jim and Marshall stopped for a drink at a bar on Jim's street. Jim had insisted.

"Marshall, I wanted to tell you something I learned. One of Iffy's cousins told me this at the wedding. I don't know why. It was hardly a topic for a wedding day. There was a little village not far from Iffy's family's house. In 1944, just a few days after D-Day, the Germans decided to destroy this village—out of sheer cussedness, I guess. It was Hitler's scorched-earth policy. They were in retreat, but as a farewell gesture, they rounded up everybody there and massacred them—in the church! Babies and all. Little kids. They machine-gunned them, then set fire to the place and set off explosions in two or three other places. Over six hundred people got killed. The whole town."

"The whole town?" Marshall turned to face Jim straight on.

"How can anybody to this day understand that?" Jim said.

Marshall lifted his drink halfway. "The woman with the parachutists said the German officer was very correct. That's something I've heard often. They were so correct. It meant they were precise. But barbarians also. It makes no sense."

"Here's what I wanted to tell you, Marshall. One of Iffy's aunts lived in that village. She had married a shoemaker, and they lived on the main street. Iphigénie has never told me about them. It was her cousin, a serious kind of guy, has a pharmacy or something in Limoges, who told me about it. He seemed hung up on it. He said that de Gaulle decided to leave the village exactly the way it was, a ghost town. This guy said you could go there and see where Iffy's uncle's cobbler shop was, and that the man's sewing machine, the one he stitched the shoes with, was still standing there, all rusty and forlorn-looking. That gave me the willies, just hearing about it." Jim paused and sipped his Scotch. "Good old Iffy. She's been through more than I gave her credit for at first."

Jim drained his Scotch and surveyed the room. Marshall stared toward the mirror behind the zinc bar at the reflection of a young waiter with a tray of drinks. Marshall could not see himself in the mirror.

"I'll get this, Jim," he said, reaching for his wad of franc notes.

41

Marshall planned to return to Angoulême after the weekend. On Thursday night he received a telephone call from Sonia Ford. Her father had died. She wanted to thank Marshall for the call he had made. It meant a lot, she said.

"Would you let the other crew members know?" she asked. "I don't think I can locate them all."

"Leave it to me," Marshall said.

Al Grainger answered on the second ring, and Marshall told him the news.

"Heavens to Betsy," Al said. "I didn't even know he was sick."

"We should have had a poop sheet for the crew. Loretta used to send out stuff and keep everybody in touch."

"It was Ford's time," Al said. "It's the Lord's will."

"I spoke to Ford last week. I had no idea he was that far gone."

They shared a few memories.

Marshall said, "I was wondering if you could make a couple of calls there in the States to let the others know, to spread the word."

"Sure thing."

"I'd be much obliged."

"The war seems like yesterday, doesn't it, Marshall?"

Or today, Marshall thought. He explained briefly that he had been looking up people from the war years. They talked for a while about Odile and the parachutists.

"We were lucky we didn't bail out and fall in a tree," he said. "Get an arm torn off."

"We were both lucky you landed the plane, Marshall, even if I did have to spend my vacation at Nasty camp in Germany. By the way, did you get my letter about the idea for a reunion?"

Marshall said that was a fine idea. "We should do that, Al."

"Yeah. I'm counting on it."

MARSHALL HAD TROUBLE sleeping that night, despite the blackout curtain. Ford was too young to die; they were all too young yet. Campanello and Cochran and Hadley were still busy with careers, and Marshall himself had found a way to keep moving, going off on a wild tangent. He had to seize the moment. Otherwise, he faced a countdown to oblivion.

More awake, he dreaded the idea of a reunion. Such a get-together seemed like a nightmare. Why should they celebrate their ancient debacle? He shuddered. What would Neil Armstrong do? Armstrong, a man who had disappeared from the limelight, was no superman, he thought. He had read about the time Armstrong brought the X-15 in wrong. He held the nose too high and bounced her off the atmosphere, overshooting the landing zone by miles and miles. Once he got the plane turned around, he almost crashed. He barely cleared the trees at the end of the runway.

MARSHALL BOARDED THE Métro for Saint-Mandé and went straight to see Caroline. She was arranging shiny green apples, polishing them with her apron. Her crooked smile acknowledged him, as if she had expected him. Bobby was in his basket, looking grumpy, and the kid was unloading oranges.

"*Bonjour, Marshall! Quoi d'neuf?*"

He had news. He had found the woman whose family hid him in 1944, near here, and she knew Caroline's father. He reported what Annette had told him, adding that he expected to learn more.

"Don't give up on your father, Caroline."

"Does your daughter treat you badly, the way I disown my father?" Caroline asked, frowning.

"No. She's a good daughter."

"And I'm a bad one?"

"No. Please. I don't mean that. It's just more complicated. Things are always difficult between parents and their children."

She nodded thoughtfully.

He said, "I have it on good authority that your father was very brave in the war. I feel sure there had to be goodness in him."

She resumed rubbing one of the green apples industriously.

He continued. "Anyway, I also wanted to say I'm sorry I was so overbearing with you—how do you say, too much the commander?"

"You're sweet, Marshall. Are you sure you won't marry me and take me to America? To Kentucky?" She grinned and squeezed his arm.

"The dog would be a problem," he said.

HE REVISITED THE COLONNADE on the rue de Rivoli, where Annette had taken him to have his photo made.

"It was the *photomaton* at the Louvre store on the corner at the rue Marengo," she had said last week. "I took the pilots on the Métro to the Palais Royal stop, and you waited in the Tuileries, across the street."

He tried to get that straight in his mind, but standing here again, he realized that the corner where the *photomaton* had been was not directly across from the Tuileries, as he had recalled. The gardens were some distance down the street. It made little sense that she would have him wait so far away from the *photomaton*. With millions of people misremembering a war, could anyone ever get straight what had happened?

At the Colonnade, he stopped at a souvenir shop and on a whim purchased a blue beret for Annette. He bought a black one for himself—to commemorate 1944, when he was Julien Baudouin, stonemason.

42

"I DON'T REALLY REMEMBER YOU, YOU KNOW," SAID THE DELIcate woman at the café table. She was carefully stirring two lumps of sugar into her tea. She wore a thin gray scarf knotted at her neck, as if she might be slightly chilly.

"I do remember you—just a little," Marshall answered. "I lived at your apartment for about two weeks."

"*Bien sûr.* There were so many of you. But I am very happy to make your acquaintance once more." Her smile was genuine but her eye contact uneasy.

Annette had said that her younger sister, Monique, lived in Paris, and she had suggested that Marshall call her. Marshall had been hesitant. This morning, however, only a couple of days before seeing Annette again, he decided to look her up.

Monique had a soft, shy manner. Her hands were nervous, and her voice was thin. They chatted about Paris in the old days, Monique's parents, and Marshall's flying career. Marshall told her about finding the Alberts, and Monique mentioned her husband, two children. Their daughter was at Boston College.

"I'm glad you have found my sister," said Monique, touching her lips with her small napkin. "She has had a very difficult way."

"Losing her husband must have been hard. But she seems to be emerging, don't you think? I admire her spirit. She's full of life, like I remember her. There was a special quality—"

"That's not all, *monsieur,*" said Monique, leaning forward. "She won't tell you about it, probably, unless you probe. I can see you don't even know."

Marshall was at a loss. "What do you mean?" he asked.

Monique paused. Then, spearing him with her eyes, she said, "In the spring of 1944, not long after you say you were with us, Annette and our parents were arrested and sent to the concentration camps in Germany. I was left behind. I did not see my mother and sister for more than a year. And my father did not return."

Marshall froze. He stared at his hands. He had never been so shocked. For long moments, he heard and saw nothing. He couldn't remember later what he had said then. Monique's eyes seemed haunted. They were the color of Annette's eyes. He remembered only what Monique said as they parted.

"I'm sorry, *monsieur.* I can't talk about it. Perhaps my sister will tell you, but it is very hard for her. You comprehend? Even if you ask her, she won't offer it easily."

43

ON THE TRAIN TO ANGOULÊME, HE STARED OUT THE WINDOW, hardly seeing the landscape. Having risen at five, he arrived at the Gare Montparnasse in time for an early train. But even after he bought his ticket he thought maybe he should turn back, postpone this trip until he had gathered himself. He had no idea what he should say or do when he saw Annette. Nightmare newsreels ran though his mind. Piles of skeleton people, bulldozers coming toward them, one or two arms waving feebly. A young girl and her mother, shrunken and curled. He saw skeleton people stuffed in bunks, skeleton people dressed in stripes. He saw gaping mouths. In a sealed room vapors hissed from the ceiling.

He knew so little—mainly headlines and film clips, the shocking revelations at the end of the war. Gold teeth and fillings yanked and stockpiled. Adolf Eichmann. Himmler. Barbed wire. The open pits, the bulldozers, the poison-spitting showers, the monstrous ovens. How did she ever survive?

He carried a copy of *Le Monde* but did not read it. Next to him a middle-aged woman with a feather in her hat was reading a paperback. Across the aisle were two teenagers, an amorous couple jumpy with the freshness of physical attraction. A dozen or so smartly dressed people were returning from Paris, laden with packages, exchanging tales of museums and theaters. Marshall's mind emptied them out, emptied out the rough plush seats, turning the car into a slow, creaky thing with slats on the sides to allow livestock to breathe. In this car he positioned how many? A hundred? Two hundred? Standing pressed together, unable to move. Darkness. His mind relentlessly measured out the space. Two hundred, three hundred?

He looked out at the scenery flashing by. The farmland was lush and green—patterned fields with artfully drawn hedgerows. It seemed so calm and orderly. When he rode the night train from Paris to Toulouse in the spring of 1944, he saw at dawn the vacant fields, tinged mint green, and he was sad that the farmers had to grow food for their enemy, not their own people. He thought he remembered feeling this. But maybe not. His thoughts then centered on saving his own hide—staying quiet, keeping a wary eye on the German soldiers on the train, steeling himself to show no surprise if there was a loud noise. He was supposed to be a deaf-mute. He remembered how he had hidden his head behind a newspaper. He dozed and pretended to doze. Another airman was at the rear of the car. They were to have no contact, pass no signals. Robert was in the front of the car, and another girl guide, who seemed a bit older than Annette, rode in the car behind. The other airmen in the group were scattered throughout the train.

Now the conductor operated on Marshall's ticket. The station of Tours was already being called, and the train would arrive in Angoulême soon. For a moment, Marshall saw in the conductor the outline of a German officer asking for his papers.

Monique said Annette might talk if he asked, but he didn't know whether he should. It was time he did something right, he thought, but he didn't know what that was.

44

"YOU ARE HERE AGAIN!" ANNETTE SAID, OPENING HER ARMS WIDE like her smile.

While she performed the three-cheek kiss, he breathed in the lavender on her skin, in her hair.

"I use lavender for everything," she explained. "My husband used it on the animals. It was good for their coats. It assassinated the insects."

She approved of his new boots.

They sat on her terrace again, and Bernard, who had greeted him happily, established himself on the stones between them.

"We are at leisure!" she said. "We have nothing that must be done. We are here, and we have a beautiful summer day."

Her twinkling eyes contained irony, humor, history, depth. She was full of laughter, and her hands were animated, her manners less formal than before. Something had changed. Just as he was drawing back, she seemed to be advancing.

She stared into his eyes. "It is still hard to believe that you came to find me so many years after the war. You are the only one. I couldn't search for any of you. I wanted to let the past go. I was in my life, each day—a son, a daughter, a husband, the animals.

"There was only one of the boys who was contemptuous of our circumstances. He demanded his cigarettes. He complained about our food." She laughed. "I took him on a tour of Paris. I showed him the Eiffel Tower, the Arc de Triomphe, everything, and he was disdainful. I asked him, 'Do you have anything like that in America?' and he said, 'No, but if we wanted stuff like this, we would buy it!' "

"An exceptionally ugly American," Marshall said. "We're not all like him."

"No." She smiled. "I do not know what happened to him. I did not go forth to find any of you. I had enough warm memories, and I wanted to keep them."

"You and your family took a lot of risks," he ventured.

"It was as though we had started on a rough crossing together, my parents and I, and we had chosen the most arduous course. As if we had a rowboat when we needed a battleship."

"You were just a girl," he said, after a moment. "How could your parents involve you? I mean, sending a young girl out to do Resistance work. It seems much too dangerous."

She laughed. "My parents were very strict! At the table with adults, we did not speak. We listened. But during the war, my parents released me! They set me free! Ironic, is it not? During the Occupation, when no one was free, I was freed!"

Her exuberant tone shifted, and she leaned forward.

"My parents understood the perils, but it was, for them, the greatest emergency. Young or old, we had to do whatever the war demanded. Our shame is that many French people did nothing. Or even worse, some aided the Germans."

She paused. "Some of the *aviateurs* were with us only a day or an hour, and some—like you—for longer. When you were with us, the Gestapo had a thousand eyes. It was very dangerous to move you south on the train, even though the snows were melting and the passage through the mountains was easing. But the Gestapo was behind every bush, and they had broken some of the escape lines. The Bourgogne survived, when others did not. We had to wait for the right moment to send you out."

"I was stupid," he said. "I didn't really know the risks you ran."

"It makes me chill," she said, holding herself against imaginary drafts. "And yet it makes me glow with warmth to have you here, to remember the good moments. We were young. We were open."

Her smile made him see the young girl in her again. He looked away.

She said, "When you first appeared from Angoulême in that large Citroën, I thought I was dreaming. Could it be true that one of my boys had returned and was looking for me? I had often thought of a path back to that time, with those pilots we helped. And yet it was so hard.

"I must confess—when you first came from Paris, I wasn't even sure I remembered you. I mean, I knew who you were, and I recall your stay with us. But I wasn't sure I recognized you. Then the next day on our drive, I remembered how you laughed. It was very specific, and it filled me with joy and anticipation. When I saw how eagerly you listened to Odile tell of her parachutists—how fervently you wanted to know the past, I was so glad you found me! This week last, while you were away, I turned it over in my mind. It is very complicated. The war is always with me, and yet it is not with me. I have wanted to remember and wanted to forget. Is it not true for you, as well? My own past seems like a stranger's sometimes. It has so little to do with how things are now. Now I live normally. Then, nothing was normal.

"I began to look forward to your return today. I grew more eager. In my mind I began reliving what had happened. And I kept telling it in my mind. Again and again I was insistent in my mind. I made you listen. I am not sure you wanted to listen. I could not stop myself."

Marshall tried to speak, but he stalled again. He thought about the men of wartime France—defeated, unable to protect their families. The humiliation must have been excruciating. He thought about M. Vallon, his elegant brown suit.

Marshall thought Annette would have told him everything then, but she grew quiet, and he did not press her.

THEY HIKED AT A PARK near Cognac. The trails were wooded and moderately inclined. The hike was vigorous, and his boots were fine.

The day was balmy, not hot, and walking offered them a growing intimacy—the two of them together, out in nowhere. When the trails ascended, she went ahead, and conversation dwindled. He regarded her energy and enthusiasm with wonder, not able to square it with the dark imagery in his mind.

She had made a small picnic lunch, which he carried in his new backpack. He also carried a canteen of water, but she wanted wine with a meal, with glasses, so he carried those too. She had fruit and cheese in her little pack. He had not yet given her the beret he had bought for her. He was still unsure how appropriate the gift was.

They paused near a waterfall that emptied into a churning green pool. The rush of the water obliterated the sounds of other people on the trail, and the faint spray cooled them as they sat on a flat rock and spread the picnic on a blue floral-patterned cloth.

"This is a romantic spot," he said carefully. "We should be young again."

"*Pfft!* In France, remember, age is different. The old are always young in their hearts."

"I hope so." Caroline had said something like that, he recalled.

Annette poured the wine and they clinked glasses. The wine was astringent. It puckered his mouth slightly.

She apologized. "I like it, but my sister always finds it treats her that way. She prefers the Bordeaux."

He hadn't yet told her that he had seen Monique, and when he mentioned it now, a flicker of a shadow crossed her face, but she brightened again immediately.

"Monique works very hard with her students—the disabilities with hearing and reading, the children who read back to front. She teaches them music."

"*Dyslexique?*"

"Yes. She is a very good teacher, always helpful. Her students adore her."

"So she is like her sister—someone who helps."

She laughed and turned aside. She cut two thick pieces from the baguette and handed one to him.

They were silent a moment. Then, averting her face, Annette said, "Monique told you, didn't she?" She was staring at the waterfall. "I could tell that you knew. It is in your tone, and in the way you observe me."

He was startled, embarrassed. He wanted to see her face, to see what this moment meant. But she kept her face turned away.

"She told me very little," he said. "I didn't want to ask you about it. If it's too painful, don't say anything."

"Oh, I can tell a story!" She waved her hand and looked at him. "I can make it very dramatic. But it is so worthless."

"I doubt that."

They locked eyes. "You don't need to hear it."

"No, I don't have to hear it."

Dropping her eyes, she sliced a piece of cheese for him. The waterfall was loud, intrusive.

She said, "I don't tell it. I had asked Odile not to speak of it to you when we went to see her, and she understood. It is of no use to anyone. You have no interest in this." She sighed. "My life is so small."

He set his bread and cheese on the cloth and placed his hands on her shoulders. He said, "No. Your life is not small. You are a heroine. You saved men's lives. You were active when others were afraid. Your life is not small."

He saw tears coming in her eyes, and she allowed him to hold her. For a moment, he saw them with a passing tourist's eye: lovers beside a waterfall, entwined in a romantic embrace, exactly the sight one was supposed to see on a scenic trail by a waterfall somewhere in France.

MARSHALL HELPED ANNETTE WITH HER EVENING CHORES — taking grain to the horses, shutting in the chickens. Birds were twittering and trembling in the vines on the wall, and the peacock was roosting in a small tree. Annette fed the dog and cat.

"I should probably go find that hotel in Cognac," he said, with a hesitation that left open a question for her.

"Do not go, please," she said, touching his arm. "We must dine later. I have prepared some dishes. And I want to tell you what happened. Wait, please."

She showed him where he could wash up, and he grabbed a clean shirt from his bag in the car. In the mirror above the sink his face was blank, he thought. He combed his hair and went to the terrace. She was still in the kitchen, and then she brought some cold Perrier and an open bottle of wine. She excused herself again to bring food from the kitchen, refusing his offer to help. The dog went with her. Marshall drank half a glass of Perrier, then sipped some of the wine. It had a metallic taste. He watched the cat washing her face. It was just after sunset, and the sky was still bright. A 727 was going over, a domestic flight, maybe from Bordeaux.

Annette returned with a small tray and sat down across from him. He shifted his chair so that he could see her clearly in the late light. She had changed into blue pants and a tight V-necked shirt. She seemed fresh and delicate, not like a country woman who had just hiked five miles. Bernard lay down on the tiles between them, his head on his paws.

"Am I a threat?" Marshall asked, regarding the dog.

"No, no. Bernard accepts you," she said. "He approves."

She leaned to stroke the dog. "Bernard knows the story I will tell you now. At least I think he does."

Bernard groaned and stretched out on his side.

Annette spread some pâté on tiny pieces of toast and laid them on a plate between them. The table wobbled slightly, and Marshall got up to adjust it with a chunk of wood he had spied in the grass.

"So much happened," she said, arranging her napkin on her lap. "I can't repeat it all."

"Don't tell me if you don't want to," he said.

"But I do." She absently folded her napkin and set it on the table.

"One day everything changed," she said. "I haven't told it often, except to myself, and there inside I've told it so often that it has worn grooves in my mind, like the tracks of a tire rolled through wet cement. In the years since my husband's death, these memories seem to be stirring."

She clasped her hands together, intertwining the fingers, and laid her head against the tall back of the chair. Gazing skyward, she continued.

"It was April 27, Maman's birthday, only a week or two after you left us. We had two more Americans with us, one from New Jersey and one from Michigan. We had completed the work on their papers, and Robert arrived at our apartment just after I returned home from school. He spent some time explaining to these two Americans all their instructions. There was much to remember—the little pine grove at the Jardin des Plantes, the tickets, the walk to the Gare d'Austerlitz, where Robert would meet them. I told you about the pine grove recently."

"Yes, I went there this week. It was just as you said."

"My mother was making sandwiches for the boys. Robert had brought some good ham, and she had a small Camembert. She had two small apples. Papa was at work. Then the priest arrived. I do not know if I told you about the abbé, Father Jean. He was our liaison to the Bourgogne. He helped young people like Robert to avoid the forced-labor exile to Germany.

" 'I came to warn you,' Father Jean said. 'There has been a betrayal. I don't have time to explain, but you must leave. *Allez, allez!* I have warned Monsieur Vallon.'

"Immediately, Maman ran to the balcony, where she set a plant in a certain position to warn Papa if he came home. Father Jean put his hand on Robert's shoulder. Robert was his protégé, the young man he had hoped would enter the priesthood. The priest departed, but he was still in the corridor leading to the downstairs door when the *milice* arrived, followed very soon by Papa, who saw the flowerpot and should have stayed away! But he had to know what the danger was—and he stepped into its midst, the maelstrom. The *milice*—the worst of the French police, as bad as the Gestapo—were there, in those dreadful dark navy berets."

Annette spoke rapidly, as if scuttling the hard memories down a dark street.

"The intrusion was brutal. They threw Papa against the wall. I could see that worse than the physical pain was the assault on his pride. The *milice*, so puffed up with power, arrested us—Robert, the two Americans, Papa, Maman, the priest, and myself. Monique, as she knew to do, was hiding in the cupboard near the door. One of the officers pulled that cupboard open and saw her huddling there with her *poupée*, her dear worn ragged doll, terror on her face, and he kicked the door shut again. They left her behind and drove the rest of us to the police station. We were questioned, but we refused to answer. They had searched the apartment and found the incriminating equipment before we had a chance to dispose of it out the back window. After fifteen minutes or so of confusion at the station, the police separated the men from Maman and me. They led us down a corridor and locked us into a cold cell. Maman held her arms around me to make me warm and to comfort me. What was burning into my mind was the sight of Monique, grasping her *poupée* in the same way Maman was holding me, Monique with her face in terror. I had only a glimpse before the policeman slammed the door shut and we were gone.

" 'Will the little door open from the inside?' I asked Maman. 'Can she get it open?'

" 'Yes,' Maman said. 'Don't worry.'

"Monique had the address book of all the *aviateurs* we had helped—about fifty of them. We had been prepared, and she knew what to do. She had hidden the little book in the clothing of her doll. Your address was in there. I thought about all of you a great deal after our detainment. I hoped that you would arrive home and that after the war you would have a good life. We were arrested long before the BBC would send its coded message that you had arrived safely.

"There in the prison cell I was frightened for Monique, and for Robert and my father and the priest. And the two Americans we barely knew. I remembered their new false names better than I remembered their actual names.

"Father Jean, who was very courageous, had been recruiting students for the *réseau* Bourgogne." She paused. Her hands unfolded and fluttered up beside her ears like birds at a window. "Robert had been a student of Father Jean's, but he didn't have a heart for the priesthood. He was too worldly. The life of the escape line was for him irresistible. Everyone thought so highly of Robert. He was handsome, courteous, vivacious . . ."

Annette faltered then. Marshall waited quietly for her to continue. The summer light was fading, and bats were beginning to flicker above the courtyard. He had told her that he wouldn't probe her with questions. He didn't want to say something insensitive. He hadn't known before that Robert had also been arrested, and now he realized that Robert had probably been sent to the concentration camp too—and that Caroline perhaps did not know. His view of Robert Lebeau kept shifting, like light and shadow flitting across the face of a mountain.

Annette sipped her wine and continued. "My mother and I never again saw the men who were arrested with us. We were told no news of them.

"In the middle of the night we were transferred to a large stone prison called Fresnes, south of Paris, and there we stayed in an overcrowded cell with three other women. We were all French, all arrested for *résistance*. The other women had left their children, all small children, I think, and they were frantic with worry. My mother commiserated with them, but she would not give up her belief that Monique was safe with our friends. 'She had her instructions,' Maman would say. 'She knew where to go.' The image of Monique and her *poupée* would not leave me. Eventually we managed to exchange messages with her, and the other women received messages smuggled in from friends, along with some small parcels of food, which they shared with us. We formed a bond then, after an uneasy start. Yvonne, Marcelle, and Jacqueline—three women we began to know intimately. In prison, the bonds become very strong. You have no one else, do you see?

"We maintained our dignity despite the closeness of our quarters. Yvonne began to withdraw, working herself into a ball and moaning now and then. One morning my mother ordered her to straighten herself. 'You can't wash yourself if you stay rolled up like that,' she said. We had managed to create some privacy by hanging up a bedsheet in a corner by the *toilettes*—if you could call it that. Well, never mind. Marcelle told us again and again about her three children who were at her mother's when she was arrested, how she was innocent of any political activity. She was confused with someone else, she insisted, although her insistence began to break down eventually, and we never knew if she was truly not *résistante*, or if she had come to believe she was, weakening out of fear.

"Three times Maman and I were taken from the prison in an armored truck to the Gestapo headquarters on the rue de Saussaies for questioning. That was a frightful place. We had to wait for hours in a damp cell, where they had kept horses. The stone floor was covered with filthy straw, and there were no chairs. One day, about the third time we were taken there, I was waiting in the cell while my mother was being questioned, and when she returned, she was smiling. She whispered under her breath, 'Robert left a sign that he was here.' She explained what she saw: in his handwriting, on the wall of the waiting room, some lines from Villon." She paused, seeing the past, her eyes distant. "He was always quoting Villon because we were Vallon."

"A poet?" Marshall asked.

"A poet, yes." Annette stopped to spread a dollop of the pâté on a piece of toast. She stared at it and handed it to Marshall. He couldn't eat it.

"I cannot dwell on how we were treated at the Gestapo head-quarters." She shuddered. "We could hear the sounds of street life outside, mostly German sounds but now and then a French word called through the air, or a child singing. We clung to those French words; we always spoke French to the officers who questioned us. We refused their words. We wouldn't repeat them.

"A German officer would say, in halting French, something like 'Did you have a notebook of contacts?' He would hold up a note-book, a *carnet*. And he would use the German word. And instead of repeating the German word, we'd say *carnet*. It was almost funny. It was as though he was teaching the German word and we were teach-ing the French word. I liked to speak quickly and excitably—nothing incriminating, just something to confuse them.

"They were a type without humanity," she said harshly. "You would think that in their position, with all the fine accommodations they had in Paris, and the privilege of the finest restaurants and other enjoyments, they would be easier in their sentiments, but no, evidently no. For our part, my mother and I, we had to grab at any stray bits of wit in order to know that we were alive, that we were still ourselves."

Annette wasn't looking at Marshall as she talked. She was staring across the courtyard as if waiting to see the moon rise above the rooftop.

"At Fresnes, there were frequent air-raid alerts, and once some bombs hit a factory nearby. The prison was in an uproar. The anticipation was so great that we became riotous as the sounds died away, as the aircraft receded. We knew the Allied planes—we recognized the sounds.

"All the while, my mother held me and reassured me. I realized I was still a child. I clung to her as I did when I was five. I had been so happy going about with Robert. He had told me his wishes for the future. He was determined to fight the Germans. He vowed to join the Free French army if he ever received the opportunity, although he did not want to leave France because of his parents. He was devoted to them and always went to them on Sundays. In his heart, Robert was a man of peace, but it was thrilling to hear what he would sacrifice, how he would dare to change if necessary to regain freedom for France.

"It was dark in our prison. And so hot, with no air circulating. The noises were unending, day and night. Cries, pounding and clanging, boots tramping up and down. We heard rumors and snatched morsels of news. We knew that the *débarquement*, D-Day, had happened. We heard the bombers. We believed the liberation of Paris was imminent. We heard shouts and fights, and the guards who brought our food taunted us with false, twisted stories, lies. The food was hardly food. Yvonne was rolled in a ball again. Our clothes had become worn, but still we tried to wash them and keep them as clean as we could. At times we were thrown into an exercise yard for some free movement, though there was little we could do. They wouldn't let us have *boules*—too much like weapons. For the most part, what we did was cast around for news; we exchanged life stories and gossip. We learned to talk through a system of signals we tapped on the pipes that connected all the floors. Oh, the prison was dreary and bleak and isolated. We could see in the distance the gray ceiling of Paris, as if it were empty and deserted and we were at the end of the world, looking back.

"*De Gaulle is coming*, we heard. *The Free French are coming.*

"*The Germans are going home.*

"*Au revoir, les Allemands!* We made it into a song. *Au revoir, les*

Allemands, and then it seemed appropriate to learn some of their words, to taunt them and mock them. So we twisted those ugly words, *Auf Wiedersehen, Deutsche*, singing them vengefully. In the exercise yard, we would burst into spontaneous songs and shouts, but we were quickly dispersed and returned to our cells.

"What happened next is unspeakable. I have gone over and over it my mind, and I never comprehend it. There were two things I held closely for the duration: the image of Monique and her doll, and the presence of my mother, holding me in the same way Monique held her doll.

"I clung to my mother like a baby, and she held me in her strong arms and sang lullabies."

Bernard lifted his head toward her, but Annette went steadily on.

"Paris was liberated on August 25, although the war did not end for many months yet. I have seen the films. Oh! Such scenes! When the Allied tanks roared into Paris—led by Frenchmen!—there was jubilation, and de Gaulle strode down the Champs-Elysées like a man on stilts, wearing the military hat that always reminds me of a *gâteau* box. 'La Marseillaise' was sung everywhere. There was so much joy. The church bells rang again. The champagne came out of hiding."

Annette folded her hands across her breasts and continued in a soft monotone.

"However, we were not there. Ten days before, the Germans—who were in retreat from Paris—sent off the last convoy to Germany. My mother and I were in one of those cattle cars, creeping out of Paris toward Germany as the sun was rising."

46

IT WAS DARK. ANNETTE WENT TO THE KITCHEN, TAKING WITH HER the plate of toast and the pâté. Bernard followed her, and in a little while she returned. She brought candles but did not light them. Marshall tried to speak. He did not know if, in telling her story, she was offering him a gift or transferring a burden. His ears and eyes and heart were not sharp enough to catch fully all that Annette was telling him. He could not grasp the depths of her story. He felt that his mind was cemented over. She replenished the wine, and the wine made him feel easier with her, drawn to her like someone reaching across an abyss.

When she touched the inside of her forearm, he tried to remember if she had worn long sleeves throughout their visits. It was ironic, he thought, that the Nazis had kept such meticulous records, branding their victims while knowing the numbers would disappear, flecks of ash floating through the air.

He took her hand and—boldly or tenderly, he did not know which—pushed her sleeve up, nearly to the elbow.

"No, there was not a number," she said. "We wore a cloth patch with our numbers, on our clothing."

Gently, he kissed the spot where he thought the Nazi mark would have been, and she enfolded his head with her arms.

She held him close to her breast, an endless embrace. There was no time, just this breathless communion. The courtyard was silent.

Eventually, slowly, he raised his head.

"And that was the price you paid for helping us—for helping me." Marshall was near tears. "I can't bear it."

"It was the same—you aided us and we aided you," she said,

touching his face gently. "It is no matter. Whatever I did for you, I also did for myself, for my family, for France. We were crushed, Marshall. Defeated. You cannot know the shame. Whatever any of us did, we did for ourselves—so that we could have still a little self-respect. Just a little."

"I didn't know that any of this happened to you," he said.

"I didn't want you to know. I have told very few."

"I was safe back home, and you were still going through the war."

She rose and gathered the napkins and wine. "I must check the dinner," she said. "And then I want to tell you the rest."

He didn't know if he had had too much wine or too little. Food would not have occurred to him. He opened the kitchen door for her, bringing his glass.

"Please stay here tonight," she said with a smile. "There is a room upstairs that can be yours. It will be like the old times. You will be in hiding, and I will take care of you."

47

THEY MOVED INSIDE, WITH BERNARD, TO HER SITTING ROOM. Marshall noticed that the dog seemed to trust him now, enough to leave Annette's side and go to his bed in the corner. A table was set in the adjoining dining room, and Marshall could smell food cooking. She said they would eat soon.

They sat on a divan, side by side, and she resumed her telling. It seemed that she was telling her past to him as she had told it to herself for years. It came even more easily as they became more comfortable together. Intermittently, her expressive hands touched him, making contact, drawing him in.

"I don't speak of it," she reminded him. "But now I tell you. I want to tell you. I trust you, and you are part of my past. A good part.

"I know you are well aware of the Jews, their terrible fate under the Nazis. There were also thousands of *résistants* like us sent to Germany during the war. We were sixty women in a train carriage that had room for forty. The train journey was five days, with little food or water or other necessities—space, air. . . . On the way, through the small vents on the wooden sides of the car, we glimpsed the bombing damage to Germany.

"We expected to go to a labor camp. We also expected that the war would end soon. Maman reassured me. She said, 'We're strong. We can work. It won't last. The war is almost over.' Her reassurances gave me strength, and my acquiescence and obedience gave her strength.

"We still had not heard what had happened with my father and Robert and the priest and the two *aviateurs*. Fear for our men had haunted me all the while we were at Fresnes. If the *aviateurs* were lucky, they would go to a stalag as prisoners of war. But I had a profound apprehension about the others. I did not know what might happen. My mother insisted they would not be shot, but I had seen the posters on the street stating clearly that anyone caught helping *aviateur* evaders would be punished; the men would be shot, the women would go to prison. At Saint-Mandé we had lived under this threat, and we took the risk willingly. But now the reality of our situation was very bitter."

Annette fell silent for a moment. Then with a shake of her head, she said, "Others suffered so much worse than we."

She clasped her hands together, as if to squeeze something out of her memory. "We arrived at Ravensbrück, a camp for women north of Berlin. Ravensbrück was in a beautiful part of Germany. There was a lake and beautiful trees. But then the sight of the camp struck us with terror. We could not comprehend what this place was. There was a high wall all around it, with electric barbed wire strung along the top. Inside were many long rows of rough wooden buildings—like warehouses, with bars on the windows. They were overflowing with thousands of women—women starving, despairing, fighting for survival. It was shocking and so bewildering that we thought we must have lost our sanity.

"The prisoners worked in the Siemens factory, which made armaments. And there were many workshops. We were put to work first filling in a swamp with sand, then hauling wagons of manure to a field. The barracks was terribly overcrowded, and there was not enough food. We were slaves. Women were dying. And more kept arriving.

"I didn't expect Ravensbrück. The world didn't know of such places. We didn't know.

"We were in the night and the fog—*la nuit et le brouillard*. We were meant to disappear." She stopped. "The *résistants* were supposed to vanish."

She rubbed the material of her sleeve.

"There were no uniforms," she went on. "We had to sew a cross on the front and back of our clothing, to identify us as prisoners, and we had to sew our numbers on our clothing. I still have my number. I often thought about being a number, whether a person can be reduced to a number—at once the most specific and the most abstract of designations."

She clasped his knee and continued, "I wasn't tortured. I was beaten, but . . . oh, that's no matter. So many women suffered more.

"The women SS guards, the *Aufseherinnen*, were monsters. They were brutal. Well, I won't go into that. Those women—they had a cruel sense of humor. They laughed at us, knowing how that would humiliate us. We were in Block 22, with the French, and the other blocks were Poles, Slavs, and other Europeans. Gypsies. Sometimes our own block leaders, chosen from among us and given privileges, were more difficult to deal with than the SS women themselves. To receive their petty rewards, they closed their hearts to us, their compatriots. But the SS women . . ."

Annette sighed heavily.

"There were so many of us in our block that we had to form alliances to allocate resources, to protect each other. My mother and I had formed a close attachment to the three Frenchwomen with us at Fresnes, and we were all of a sympathy as women. We slept so close together that we were each other's blankets and pillows. There was so little food that to save your life you had to steal; to save your humanity you had to share. I must emphasize that although we were in an *enfer*, there was a goodness in the women who helped each other. This goodness was our survival.

"Each day Maman said we were going to remain brave.

"Then a group of the most able-bodied of us were transferred to Torgau to make ammunition, but many of us refused. The Geneva convention forbade us to make ammunition. So in retaliation we were sent to another work *Kommando* in Koenigsberg. Torgau and Koenigsberg were satellites of Ravensbrück. Ravensbrück was Heinrich Himmler's baby! His pet project, you might say. He would sell the women's services to factories all over Germany."

Once again Annette stopped speaking. She seemed to summon up courage before continuing. "This is difficult," she said.

"Do you want to wait?"

"No. Please listen."

Marshall visualized the young girl Annette at his hiding place in Paris. He remembered seeing her as she bent her head to flip her hair forward, positioned a hair ribbon, then lifted her head and tied the ribbon on top. She shook her hair so that it fell into place, her head beribboned like a package. That memory made him ache.

"We were sent to Koenigsberg-sur-Oder, across the border in Occupied Poland, where we leveled an airstrip for the Luftwaffe. The hangars were disguised so the Allies wouldn't see them from the air. We worked on a plateau, in fierce wind and snow. All I had to wear was a thin cotton dress, no gloves or coat or hat, and it was the coldest winter I had ever known. Oh, but perhaps you think I'm exaggerating. It is no matter. As you want. After the first snow they gave us coats. Some were nice and some were ragged. You can comprehend how they collected such garments. Each morning I stuffed my clothing with the straw from my mattress.

"The *appel* began each morning outside the barracks at four and then again after work. They had to make sure no one had escaped, and they would call the roll again and again. But there was no guard tower there, for it was too cold to escape. We had to stand still in the cold for the *appel*. We tried to stand as closely together as possible. During the *appel* we had to be sure to stand straight. If you weren't strong enough to work, you might be shot. We don't know why we weren't shot. There were five hundred women, half of whom were French. At Ravensbrück where there were so many women, the *appel* went on for hours. The *appel* was smaller, so we didn't have to stand for so long, but sometimes they made us stand naked, and they turned the water hose on us. It was the winter. They made us stand there while the water froze on our bodies."

"My God, Annette. How did you survive?" Marshall blurted.

She didn't answer that. "The work *Kommando*—the airstrip," she said. "We cut out large blocks of frozen sod and lifted it into wagons that ran on rails. The rails were short, and from time to time we had to move them with our hands and then lift the wagons to fit onto the rails. We were moving the sod from one place to another. We were cows!

"We tried to work crowded together, for warmth. We took turns shielding each other from the wind. We hugged and huddled. As our hands began to freeze, we thrust them into each other's clothing to thaw. We fashioned a system for keeping our blood warm. We blew warm breath on each other and rubbed each other. If someone began to whimper or fall behind, we quickly surrounded her and circulated our meager warmth around her. Our model was the herd animal, the clustering that keeps deer and cattle alive in the winter.

"A truck arrived with soup at midday, and we scrambled to fill our bowls. Sometimes it was hot, but unless you managed to be first in line, the soup quickly became cold. It was watery, just a few scraps of potato or rutabaga. At night there was a piece of bread and sometimes a bit of ersatz cheese. In the morning we had something they called coffee. It wasn't coffee. It was watery and tasteless. We suspected it was soaking water from old leather.

"The women were all thin and hungry. In our miserable section of the barracks there was a little fire where we could cook what food we could find—that is, if we could find wood or coal. Sometimes we burned our own bed slats. One day Jacqueline smuggled to us a goose egg one of the kitchen workers had let her have. We hunched over the little stove, and we boiled it so we wouldn't spill any. But when we cracked and peeled it, we found a little goose inside, formed perfectly, boiled alive. For only a second we retched in horror, but then we tore at the food, sharing it equally among the five of us. It was a delicacy!

"The water was usually frozen, so we had little for cooking. We couldn't wash ourselves. As each day went by, we weakened. We were growing too weak to be useful as labor. We saw so many people die. In their beds during the night, or in the snow on the plateau.

My mother fell ill and was allowed to stay in the infirmary for two nights, and two of our friends shared their food with her. She was returned to the plateau during a heavy snowstorm. We found that the snow acted as insulation. We pushed it up to make a little fort that shielded us from the wind.

"After several weeks of this *enfer*, the commandant asked for volunteers to work in the woods. We could see the forest in the distance. It would be farther to walk, and the work would be more difficult, but the trees would shield us from the wind. It was five kilometers in the direction of Gdánsk. My mother and I and some of our friends trudged to the forest, and our work there was to dig out stumps. The Germans had forced some Russian prisoners of war to cut down trees to make a road through the forest. We dug the stumps out. We had the wagons and the rails, and we had to dig trenches for the rails, cutting through the roots. The ground was frozen, and we hacked and hacked. We had only shovels and axes."

Marshall laid his arm around her shoulder, a brief embrace. She went on, "It is not a sequence in time. It is a collection of sensations. Time blurred; it was like sleep. When you have only a scrap for sustenance and you must labor until the dark, then you are already almost dead. My mother, who could hardly walk because of vitamin sores, labored alongside me, and she tried to conceal her sufferings from me, until there was a time when she could not continue. She breathed in sharply and lowered her head and closed her eyes. She clutched her hoe and said, 'Don't lose heart, Annette.'

"On the plateau, the *gardiens* watched us like those birds that feed on the dead. When a woman collapsed, the *gardiens* ran to grab her and throw her onto a cart. We were being worked to death. Our numbers diminished, and the bodies disappeared. There was no *four-crématoire* at Koenigsberg. I could not let my mother fall. I had to keep her upright until we could reach the infirmary.

"From the beginning, my mother was my strength. I had the *hantise*, or—how do you say it?—the anxiety to be separated from my mother. We were close, so physically close, her arms around me as if

I were still balled—*roulé en boule!*—inside her. And in time, it was re-versed, when I had to hold her, when she curled up in her weakness, the loss of strength, and the illness of which she was surely dying. In the infirmary I kept her warm. I gave her my soup. I mashed the bread into a little gruel, a *panade*. Bread and water heated on a fire felt so much more nourishing—to have something warm in our stomachs. She could hardly swallow, but she tried her best to eat, for me. It dribbled from her mouth, and she could not swallow. I lifted her head so she would not choke, and I caught the dribbles from her mouth in her spoon and saved it until she rallied and could get the breath again to try to eat."

Annette's voice cracked.

Marshall held her, and he caressed her hair. She turned her head away.

"You are good," she said, pulling back from him.

"One morning at the work camp we saw a man come from the forest and speak with a *gardien*. Then the *gardiens* pushed us out on the road, but we didn't march five by five in lines, as usual. It was chaotic, and we did not know where we were going. There was tur-moil among the *gardiens*, as if they couldn't agree on anything. Their discipline was crumbling. Finally, they marched us back to the camp, and they locked us inside again. We did not return to work that day.

"There was no *appel* that evening. There was no noise during the night; usually there was much noise. In the morning also there was no noise. No guards were there!"

Annette rose from the divan and paced back and forth, unable to contain her energy.

"We crept out of our barracks and rushed around. The *gardiens* had disappeared! We ventured farther. There were no Germans any-where. We broke out of the camp. We went into their headquarters across the road and saw that they had left. They had abandoned everything. They had been living there with their families. There were bottles for babies. And food! We found food!

"We began to eat everything we could find. And we carried all we could back to our quarters, fearful that the Germans would return at any moment. They had left in the middle of a meal—lovely vegetables and meat. We ate everything left on their plates. To see how they had been living—with their families, in luxury—so near to us, it filled us with rage. They had their children there! Can you imagine bringing children to such a place? The children would surely know how we were treated. There were toys and sports equipment—tennis rackets, skis.

"We raided the women's closets. I found sweaters and coats and blankets, and wool jackets and skirts. I found a beautiful navy wool coat and put it on immediately, for it was freezing that day! I took an ensemble back for my mother, who was too feeble to join the raiding party, but I was still strong enough. I brought back an enormous tin of peaches! I wore the coat back and forth—and filled its pockets with food.

"The water was frozen, but we made a fire and heated ice. We had hot water! We washed ourselves. We changed clothing. In luxury and liberty, we walked out in the sunshine. I can't explain the joy. We were all together."

Her arms opened wide, as if to embrace all those she remembered. "We were so happy! It was sunny! We felt free.

"Then at dark we returned to our barracks. A Polish girl wanted to escape—to leave—but we pulled her back. 'Don't go out there,' we urged her. 'It is too cold. You have nowhere to go. We have plenty of food here now, and the Russians will come to liberate us.' Some Frenchmen who were prisoners of war at another camp had been exchanging messages, clandestinely, with us at the *Kommando* in the forest, and they had received hints that the Soviet army was coming. But we were afraid the Germans would return, and so we hid carefully all our stolen goods.

"Two Russian soldiers on a bicycle stopped at the camp. One of our women, who was Russian, told them we were 'partisan,' the

Russian word for *résistante*. The soldiers left. We knew their units were advancing and they would find us. We waited, praying for liberation. We could hear their cannons in the distance.

"We had two days of freedom. Then a German patrol appeared in the night. We had been sheltering two escaped Frenchmen—two of the prisoners I mentioned—but the Germans discovered them and shot them instantly, then left abruptly. The Frenchwomen had been so happy to have the Frenchmen there. Now our hearts were breaking.

"In the morning we heard shouting and shooting, shouting and shooting. It was thunderous, murderous. Explosions. Yelling. It was dreadful. The SS from Ravensbrück had arrived, and they were pulling everybody out of the blocks."

Annette had been speaking with Marshall in English most of the time, but now she lapsed into rapid, excited French. Gently, he guided her back.

"Slowly," he said. "You're going too fast for me."

"*Désolée.*"

"Go slowly."

She sat down beside him and took a deep breath. "The SS made everybody who could walk go out on a forced march back to Ravensbrück," she continued, in English. "I could walk, but my mother could not walk, and I could not leave her! I could *not* leave her. I hid in the infirmary with her. We were in the room with a nurse who was very good with my mother. She had been arrested for falling in love with a German. She was a nice girl, and when the Germans routed everybody, she warned them away from the infirmary.

" 'They have the typhus!' she cried. The Germans backed away then.

"There were only a handful of us left behind in the infirmary, and all the others were sent back to Ravensbrück, on foot. Eighty kilometers. I knew they wouldn't live.

"The SS put out the fires in the stoves and removed the fuel. Then, with the fuel, they set the camp on fire. They locked the doors and left. Our little group, left behind in the infirmary, was going to die in the fire! Frantic, we managed to break the door. And then"— Annette clasped her hands together in a quick gesture of thanksgiving or prayer—"it began to snow, and the snow stopped the fire! Our infirmary survived the fire. But six of us died. We had to bury them, and the two Frenchmen. It was true. We did have the typhus.

"We waited. There were so few of us. The nurse, who stayed behind with us, had reserves of strength, and she built a fire to keep us warm. And she cooked for us. But I slept then for two days. I slept through the Battle of the Oder! The Russians and the Germans were shooting at each other across the camp, near the infirmary. But I was so sick I didn't care."

Annette's hands flew up, quivering, then lighted in her lap. Again she had spoken rapidly, mixing French with her English. It had taken Marshall a moment to decipher "typhus," which she pronounced *TEEF-us*. He took her hands and quieted them down. She turned her head away from him for a time.

"After two days the Russians arrived, with their tanks and their large guns, and they liberated the camp. It was such joy for us! Oh, they were very good with us. They spoke some English.

"We spent three weeks at the camp with the Russians. They were like children with us. Playing, laughing. One of them shot a cow so that we could have meat. But the nurse told me that my mother should not eat meat because of the typhus—it would make her bleed more. She was losing blood, leaving a trail. But the Russian, a big high officer, wouldn't obey the nurse. He ordered a soldier to cut a *bifteck* and barbecue it for her. We couldn't make him understand. He insisted.

"There are two images that stand out in my mind the most strongly now. One is my sister and her *poupée*—dressed in baby-chick yellow!—on the day the *milice* came. And the other is my mother with the *bifteck*—her joy at having it, and the Russians' delight with themselves for providing it, and my own despair that it was bad for the typhus. It made her dysentery worse. We all had the dysentery from eating so much when we plundered the abandoned German quarters. So much jam! And beautiful vegetables and cans of asparagus and boxes and boxes of crackers."

She sighed. "I was *increvable*. Indefatigable." She laughed, then hid her mouth with her hands. "So much had happened." She paused, looked at him, then turned away. "I can't go further now."

Marshall's feelings were whirling. He could scarcely comprehend how she had survived, or that she was here now with her strength and her beauty. He didn't know how to respond to her words. No response could possibly be adequate.

He put his arms around her. He felt her body relax, and they held the quiet embrace for several long moments.

"We will eat now," she said, smiling up at him. "And talk of other things. You will tell me about your airplanes."

"I T WASN'T UNTIL LATE JUNE THAT WE RETURNED TO PARIS," ANNETTE said later, after the dinner was finished and they were again in the sitting room. "We were in a Polish hospital for three months. From there, we traveled through Germany, then Holland, then Belgium. The journey was slow because of all the destruction. We were in a *camion*, a transport truck, and the route was difficult, with many detours. In Germany, the people regarded us with awe. They were reserved and subdued, their land so beaten, but the ordinary people were kind.

"We arrived at the Hôtel Lutetia, where the lobby was now a center for returning *déportés*." She paused. "The Germans had used this fine hotel for interrogations. But now the boulevard Raspail, with all its air of normality and ease and *bonheur*, was our lovely prewar Paris again. Yet we felt out of place, so humiliated and crazed and ashamed. There were very nice people at the Lutetia, and they tried to be helpful. They had set up tables in the lobby by the fireplace, under a magnificent chandelier, but the place clashed with the memories fresh in my mind such that I was in shock. We were desperate for news of my father and Monique. We had to fill out forms. We put notices on the wall. We read all the notices, people searching for loved ones, wanting news of the returning prisoners. Pictures and pleas. An agreeable young woman at the desk said, 'Oh, yes! We had news of a Monsieur Vallon, returned from one of the camps.' Oh, we were so happy! I clasped my mother. We embraced in the lobby and wept. It was an eternity before the young woman returned, and with a long face she apologized again and again. She had made a mistake. It was not Monsieur Vallon, she said. It was Monsieur Ballon."

Annette lowered her head.

"But soon we learned certain things."

She ticked off a list on her fingers.

"We learned that my father died at Buchenwald on February 6, the very day the Russians had liberated my mother and me at Koenigsberg.

"That the abbé, Father Jean, had died there too.

"That Robert had survived Buchenwald and was in Paris.

"Much later we learned that the *aviateurs* who had been arrested with us, as I had suspected, went to the stalag and were liberated at the end of the war."

She paused and looked into the air, as if trying to remember more. *Robert. Buchenwald.* The words sank into Marshall's mind. After a moment she shook her head and went on.

"Not long after we arrived, Monique came to the Lutetia to find us. We had managed to send a letter to her, carried to the embassy by a French officer who arrived in Poland when the war ended. For weeks, Monique had come by Métro from Saint-Mandé to meet the arrivals of the *déportés*. Our hope of seeing her had helped my mother survive in the hospital. When we saw her we could hardly speak. She had not only grown tall and elegant—now eleven!—but we could see the suffering on her sweet face, as if it had been continuously taut with tears and worry. Her embrace was so tender, as if she thought we might break. We were still extremely thin and weak, and she could not hide her shock.

"Monique had been with our friends, the Mauriacs, and they had cared for her, and she had continued in school. The Mauriacs had managed to retain our apartment, and thus we were able to return to the same home where you were sheltered. The Germans had plundered only the paintings and some of the furniture.

"When we walked into that apartment, my mother, for the first time in the year since our arrest, broke into tears. All her emotion of the year—her fear and worry—had gone into survival, into protecting me, keeping up my spirits, calculating means of survival, enduring the diverse hardships, hating our tormentors. She had never allowed her grief and sorrow to flow until now. My mother dropped to the floor, swooning with release but also with grief—for Papa.

"For some time I had been mother to my mother, and now I found I had to be the mother still and to hold her and caress her and assure her. And I had to do the same with Monique, who must have been both overjoyed and frightened at the sight of us.

"It wasn't until some days later, when we had resettled into our old lives in this stunted way, that I permitted myself to let go. Or maybe I didn't permit myself—it took hold of me and I had no choice. The grief was true, and I could no longer contain it. I cried and raged until I ached."

She stopped and sighed deeply. Marshall expected her to cry now, but she did not.

"Marshall, I am so grateful that you will listen. When we returned to that forlorn apartment, where our 'boys' had hidden, where they had helped us with the daily affairs, they seemed like ghosts there. We kept waiting for Papa to return from his office, or for Robert to arrive at the door. There were vacancies in our home. Nothing could be quite right again."

She stood, went to a sideboard, and poured something from a bottle into two glasses. The room was warm and dark; only a small lamp burned. She gave Marshall a tiny glass of cognac. The brandy hit him like fire. She sat beside him again.

"We wanted to see Robert, but he was slippery. He did not want to see us. We could not understand. He had been in the habit of calling my mother *tante*, a term of affection, but now he would not answer our calls. We were very anxious. We wanted for him to give us details of Papa. Monique kept advising us that perhaps we did not want to know. It was clear that *she* did not want to know. We realized that Monique had had to be strong while we were away—living daily with uncertainty and fear and no news at all. Maman and I, who had seen everything, thought we could not be shocked. But we became distressed for dear Monique and Robert."

She leaned lightly against Marshall. "Telling about coming home is for me as hard as telling what happened in the war."

"Do you want to save the rest for another time?"

"No." She smiled, sitting erect again and sipping her cognac. "If you live in Cognac, you must drink cognac. Or so they tell me. Is it well with you?"

"It has an after-burn!"

Bernard moved from his bed in the corner, circled in front of them, then threw himself down on the rug. Annette bent forward to pat his head. Then she resumed.

"When we returned to Paris, it was an anticlimax. We had been taken away ten days before the liberation of the city. Paris was happy. It had celebrated! De Gaulle had marched down the Champs-Elysées to Notre Dame. Even though the war continued through the winter and spring, Paris was free of the dreadful Nazis. And now the war was truly over, everywhere. Most of the *déportés* had already returned some weeks before we arrived, and we felt that we had been passed by. It was as if the *déportés*—and the awful knowledge that was beginning to surface about what had really happened—had disrupted the way of life for everyone else. Paris didn't want to know what we had been through. They did not want to hear about us. Since then, all my friends have been the *déportés* and those who were in the *Résistance*. There is a deep bond. We don't have to speak of the deportation because we know. There is that bond of memory.

"We had to resume our lives. We had very few resources, and it was two years before we received anything from the government. Maman returned to teaching, and she cared for Monique and me. She was strong again. Something in her was destroyed—do not misunderstand. She never overcame the loss of my father. But she went forward. Of course, what else was there to do?

"As for me, I attended special classes for the *déportés* and the Jews who had been hidden. I passed the *bac*, then studied at the Sorbonne, and then I met Maurice! And here I am now."

She turned to Marshall and smiled.

"There is not a day when I don't rejoice," she said. "It's the small things that give me most pleasure. I can see a butterfly on the window and think I'm in heaven. And yet . . . I don't know how to explain. I know I am never quite myself ever again. I am not *her*." She gestured at a portrait on the far wall. "I am not the woman *she* would have been, if life had been different."

Marshall arose and crossed the room to study the portrait, a framed drawing.

"It's you," he said. "That's how I remember you. That's how I see you now."

In the drawing, made with free-flowing charcoal lines, she was lovely and delicate—her twinkling eyes, the teeth he loved.

She shook her head and stared at her hands, folded in her lap.

IT SEEMED NATURAL that they would lie in each other's arms that night. It was what they both wanted. They needed to be together. Physical comfort was what he had to offer her, not words. He sank into her, in her downy bed, alighting smoothly, rushing and then slowing, and she was affectionate and generous. For a long time afterward, they clasped each other tightly. They couldn't get close enough. He had no sense of what came next.

"It is warm with you," she said.

"I want to protect you."

"You are good to me."

"You are nice to hold."

"Just hold me."

49

WHEN MARSHALL AWOKE NEXT MORNING, SHE WAS NO LONGER beside him. It was late, past nine. The kitchen was cleared of last night's dishes, and the cat was at the door. He found a box of pellets for the cat, a striped gray thing with a notched ear, and filled her dish on a shelf on the terrace. When Bernard greeted him with an elegant bow, Marshall talked to him like a friend. The day was calm and clear. The chickens were out, scratching in a patch of grass. A horse whinnied. Annette's car was absent from its spot in the recess of a building in the courtyard. He heard a car pass on the street. A 727 flew over. The captain would have taken off from Bordeaux and was gaining altitude. Perhaps he was on his way to Berlin, or Düsseldorf.

The aftereffects of the wine and cognac made Marshall feel fuzzy. His eyes were burning. He could not stop thinking of Annette curled up with her mother, her mother near death. He imagined lice-infested hair, rat-bitten skin, rags, bodies stacked in dirty, crowded beds. In the shower, he sobbed. He shaved with his new electric razor, but there was no mirror near the outlet.

Hearing Annette's car, he crossed the courtyard to close the gate behind her.

She greeted him then with a smile and kisses.

"I had to go early to the market," she said, retrieving a large basket from the seat beside her. "I had to check for the peaches, and the freshest fish arrives on Tuesdays."

Her hair was feathery around her face, and she appeared well rested. He carried the basket inside for her, and she began unloading it on the worktable in the kitchen.

"It was too early for the peaches," she said. "But I found sweet cherries!"

"Georgia peach," he said. "In the States peaches grow in Georgia. A pretty girl in Georgia might be called a Georgia peach."

"That's nice. Would I have been a peach if I were a girl in Georgia?"

"Of course. You are always a peach, no matter where or when."

They were giddy.

"ISN'T THE BREAD LOVELY? Do you want some bread?"

"Yes, thank you."

"Do you want butter?"

"Yes, please."

"And *confiture*? I also have croissants, two kinds. Sit."

"Yes."

"You Americans like butter on your bread around the clock, but we have butter on the bread only at breakfast."

"I know. I've been to France a time or two."

"And I didn't know you were here!"

Her lively gaze shifted around the terrace—to the ivy-covered wall, to the stone steps where the cat was washing her face, then to Marshall's face. The coffee she gave him was strong and satisfying. He drank it in small sips. He was enormously lucky—to be here, in this place, with her. He wanted to take care of her. What was a man for but to offer protection and security to a woman? He breathed deeply.

50

THROUGHOUT THE DAY SHE CONTINUED THE TELLING. HER French was too fast for him, so she indulged him by speaking English. In the kitchen, in the chicken house, in the field with the horses, she spoke—insistently, passionately. Walking down the lane to the river, they guided each other, arms around each other's waists. He was holding her in a half embrace even as she was launching a carrot at a horse or drying a bowl in the kitchen. He felt rooted in Annette's courtyard. He was at home with her chickens, her horses, the exuberant yet patient dog.

He followed her around, trailing in the wake of her story. She made elaborate dishes that required both precision and intuition. She seemed to do this automatically, as if cooking were only a background accompaniment to her voice. She whipped eggs for a quiche Lorraine. She pitted cherries for *clafoutis*. She minced parsley.

They were in her garden, in bright sunlight. She was showing him how to deadhead a flower bed. Holding a handful of dead flowers, Annette stood beside a bank of zinnias, the palette of colors virtually jumping against the dull landscape of the work camp she was describing.

"At Ravensbrück, we were digging potatoes. It seemed to me that the *jardiniers* were experimenting with some esoteric principles of 'biodynamic' gardening. I learned more about this later. At the time it was of little interest."

She laughed and flipped a dead flower into a bucket. She snipped some more flower heads and continued. "The Nazis wanted purity in their lives. They wanted pure food, pure art, pure blood. Hitler would not eat animals. That was the only good idea he had! Oh! Also

he liked dogs. The Nazis used animal manure only in a certain way
that they thought natural and compatible. In the garden, they set us
to labor—to grow food for them, nothing for us. We did not know
where we were or how much of eternity we would be there."

Letting the dead flowers fall, she grasped his arm and lowered
her head.

"What I hated most about the German soldiers and officers was
the way they could be perfectly polite in one moment and coldly
brutal in the next, as if that were the rule. They followed rules. Now
you will be correct. Now you will be violent. The French love rules,
but of course we mean the rule of civilization, not of barbarity. The
Nazis behaved as if barbarity could follow rules, and that therefore it
could be normal. That's the difference. Or, that's what I used to
think, but . . ."

She let go of his arm.

"Marshall, I know I shouldn't hate the Germans. But even now
when I'm in the presence of someone German I feel a little cold
shiver. I'm ashamed to say that."

"How can you feel ashamed after what you've been through?"

"Think, Marshall. Their barbarity called forth our own savagery.
There is atrocity everywhere. The blame is not just on Germany. It's
on all of us."

"I see."

"But I'm going on with opinions. It exhausts me—the weight of
my opinions. My mother is telling me, urgently—she told me when
I was in Saint Lô last week—that I must conquer my refusal; that I
must assemble some scrapbooks and begin to visit the schools. People are beginning to do that—as Odile is doing. Maman says if I
don't go out to be a witness, the young people are never going to
know how it was."

LATE IN THE AFTERNOON they rested indoors, in the bedroom. She
closed the shutters, muffling the outdoor sounds. The workmen had

returned to the courtyard to lay a stone walk between the house and the former carriage house, where she stowed her car. Their voices were unintelligible, punctuated by occasional curses or loud bursts of laughter. The room had large, ornate furnishings and portraits of ancestors, and fresh flowers.

"I haven't been in a French home since the war," Marshall said, then remembered Iffy and Jim. He had forgotten all about them.

"That armoire was in the Paris apartment when you were there," she said, pointing to a somber, heavy piece of furniture opposite the bed.

"It's big enough to hide a couple of flyboys," he said.

"Indeed. That's why it's called an *'homme debout.'* A man standing!"

"I just realized why French doors are double doors," he said, thumping his forehead. "To move the giant furniture."

She laughed. "I tell you horror stories, and I expect you to make me laugh."

"I do my best."

STILL ENCLOSED IN EACH OTHER, they lay on her soft, lavender-scented sheets. It was too warm, but he didn't want to let her go, and she did not move to release him. Quietly, she resumed the telling, parceling out more from her store of turbulent memories.

"There are some things that will keep repeating somewhere in my consciousness always, till my last breath. The throes of child-birth are like birds singing at dawn compared to the harshness of wearing broken shoes in winter as I lifted my ax again and again to work the ground. And now you arrive to me, like a ghost, stirring me until I could think I was eighteen years old again. Since that time I have never known misery. I have never felt discomfort on a train, or waiting a long time for a seat, or in a line. I am never bored. I never feel that a minor discomfort is insupportable. I know what I can bear."

"I'm amazed at what you had to bear."

"Maman had to protect me from the depravity. Oh, it was so horrible. What they did to her— No, I can't visit that. It's gone."

Annette threw her hands up to cover her face for a few moments. He thought she might be crying, and he pulled her to him, but then she resumed in a soft, low tone.

"I cannot tell of the worst things. You will think it was all like that. The friendships with so many wonderful women—I don't want to say that was the happiest time of my life, certainly not. But in a way it was the best time, the most important."

"Tell me what you mean—the best time."

"You had to have a best friend in order to survive. For me, it was my mother. But there were so many women willing to help. We helped each other to live. At some point a person stops helping and thinks only of herself. But I knew women who never gave up their willingness to help. When I arrived at Koenigsberg, I had an ear infection. A girl who was a nurse stole some medicine from the infirmary and gave it to me. 'Don't say a word,' she told me. She could have been shot for that simple kindness." Annette paused. "And in fact she was shot, later, on the Death March."

"So with the friendships came loss."

"Yes. There were some very brave English girls at Koenigsberg with us. They were British agents who had parachuted into France to work with the *Résistance*. They were sent back to Ravensbrück early. We hoped they would be liberated, but we learned much later that soon after they arrived at Ravensbrück they were shot. I had been deported with those girls, and I had worked beside them at Koenigsberg, and the news of them made my heart so heavy."

She paused. "I apologize," she said, squeezing his hand.

"The idea of shooting a woman . . ." Marshall couldn't finish the thought.

"Of the two hundred and fifty Frenchwomen I was with, fifty-six of us returned to France." Pausing, she took a deep breath.

Her eyes focused on the *homme debout*.

"There were moments of pleasure. In the evenings we talked, we shared our lives. We made *poésie*, songs. On Sundays we had *prières*. On Christmas a very nice Polish girl who was *artiste* made a pretty Christmas tree, using every little scrap to decorate it. The German directress, who was so cold and brutal, liked our tree. It brought a little smile to her face, but she wouldn't admit it. Her eyes were blue and hard like metal. She was terrible, but she was a simple woman.

"We had the *poux*—I don't . . . what is the word? In our hair—oh, you know what I mean. I won't go into that."

"It's all right," he said.

"But it was one of the good times!" she said. "On Sundays we helped each other pick out the *poux* from our hair. We found the greatest pleasure in this!" She smiled.

"I'm running on, in all directions," she said.

They were now sitting side by side on a divan by the window. She was quiet, and he reached for her, holding her shoulders and resting his cheek against hers. She resumed.

"Earlier at Ravensbrück the pregnant women weren't allowed to keep their babies. The SS women, the baby-catchers, they were called, seized the newborns and drowned them by holding them upside down, their heads in a bucket—in front of the mothers. I didn't see this. When I was there, they were allowed to keep the babies, but how could these babies survive? Some women saved their meager rations for them, or sometimes they got packages and shared the cans of milk. I knew of three babies kept hidden under the clothing of the mothers. They had no milk. One day I saw the book where the block leader listed the births in our block. And beside each name was the word *Mort*. But there were three names unmarked. I saw one of these babies, glimpsed it beneath a Polish woman's rags. She was a slip of a girl, with no possible milk. Yet her baby survived as I survived with my mother, hunched under her wing.

"That was the worst thing in the war—what the Nazis did to children." She turned her gaze out the window. She whispered, "It takes a newborn baby a long time to drown."

She separated herself from him to study his stricken face. She offered an encouraging smile.

"The day I lost my husband, almost five years ago, I was possessed with uncontrollable grief for perhaps one hour, until I recalled how wise and hard I had become. I could endure. I was afflicted with an odd sting of happiness then. I was so thankful that I had lived to have a husband and children.

"At first, when the news came about Maurice's accident, it was as though I were once again scrambling in the mud and the wet snow, clutching at roots, craving that awful soup. Oh, that dreadful soup girl! We called her *la Vachère*. The cow keeper. We were cows! She would spill soup in the snow and laugh while we scrambled to lap up the snow. And then, oh, the happiness when the Red Army arrived and found just a few of us, delirious, starving! Because the buildings had burned, we could not explain to them clearly that there had been five hundred of us, that many had died and the rest had been marched away to Ravensbrück. They had no idea what we meant by Ravensbrück.

"There were nine of us at Koenigsberg with the Russians for about three weeks. Then they sent us on a two-day trip to a hospital in Poland. Two of the soldiers accompanied us in an uncovered *camion* to the train station. The landscape was ravaged, but we were happy to see that the Red Army had already routed the Germans along the way. We were arranged on some good bedding salvaged from the ruins of the German quarters, and we kept each other warm. My soul and spirit had been badly bruised. I had seen so many women die. I had seen some of my friends marched away, and I was certain they would not live. I did not see how any of them could survive the walk to Ravensbrück—eighty kilometers. Even as they left, the last straggling rows were holding each other up. I saw a Polish woman being dragged by her companions, who did not have the strength to lift her. I learned much later that a train had taken them part of the way.

"If I had not connived to stay with my mother, I should have been on that march, since I could walk. But I could not leave her. *Never*.

"At the end of the train journey, they put us in a *charrette*, a little wagon, and we arrived at a hospital in Poland. That was the most welcoming place I had ever seen. A group of women in nun's dress appeared before us, and one of them, Sister Roza—she was so lovely! Our savior! The nurses there wept when they saw us. We held their hands in joy—even my mother, who managed smiles of gratitude to them. She could hardly raise her hand; she could not rise. I had fear that she would die during the journey. She was so weak, and she hardly had the strength to eat, even though we now had food. The dysentery had subsided, but with the typhus she had lost so much blood. Sister Roza bent over her with the most angelic smile. She stroked Maman's brow and whispered gently to her, and I made her understand that this was my mother, all I had in the world. I held back my tears as this magnificent woman held her and, with the help of another nurse, gently lifted her onto a little rolling bed.

"Maman and I had our own room. The most luxurious chalet at Grenoble would not have surpassed this little room. It was bright and warm and clean. There was warm water. There were towels. We could wash ourselves! There was a little desk with writing materials. Of all the things in the room, that little desk seemed the most civilizing! Possibly we could write letters, I thought wildly. Oh, would the war ever be over?

"The Germans had been living in one wing of this hospital, and when one of them was sick, they called upon the nurses to help them. I thought Sister Roza must have witnessed so many incidents of cruelty that I wondered how close she came to surrendering her faith. The Polish people had seen so much suffering. When the Germans retreated, and our little band of skeletons arrived, she learned that the Nazi barbarity was even more widespread than she had thought. She threw herself into helping us.

"She had fear that my mother would not survive, but she nursed her devotedly. She slept in the basement in a little cell. To have nothing during the war must have seemed natural to convent sisters. I did not see the sisters take much nourishment, but they always brought it to us. There were three sisters, a doctor, and two younger nurses, novices. Me, I had lost my faith, but with the example of Sister Roza I was tempted to try to retrieve it. Then I realized I had faith only in the individual, people like Sister Roza and so many courageous women at Koenigsberg—pulling the plow in the mud, sharing their food, sheltering each other. Some people could do this. Others, as you might expect, reduced themselves—I was going to say they became animals, but that is unfair to animals. Animals don't share, unless it's a mother animal with her young, but animals have a great dignity—a sense of self, I want to say. They do not betray their nature. They do not practice self-deceptions. Humans have a great capacity for the diabolical. Oh, Marshall, the Nazis invented so many unimaginable crimes. You see I have had time to think all this through!

"We had to speak German there, but Sister Roza had some notions of French from her school days, and she had a worn Polish-French dictionary—a treasure!

" 'Where is Ravensbrück?' she wanted to know. 'You had friends there? Are they there still?'

"We could hardly explain. After Sister Roza said, 'I have a brother in a labor camp and I have not heard from him in several months,' we refrained from revealing the horrors of our camp. We wanted to erase it from our minds for her sake.

"In April, Sister Maria rushed in with news that the Russians had the Germans in retreat from the Oder River.

" 'It may be possible soon to write a letter,' Sister Roza said.

"Maman was rallying. Her cheeks had regained some color and were filling out. She weighed nothing. Sister Roza brought us clean rags to use for our menstruation.

" 'We haven't done this,' I said. I stopped. We did not have our *règles.* None of us did. I did not want to tell Sister Roza a hundredth part of what had happened.

"Sister Roza smiled as she tucked the rags into a cabinet. 'For when you need them,' she said.

"And then one day I found a blotch of blood issue from me. It was only a small bit. I told Maman, and she rejoiced. I think she ate with better appetite then, and she was sitting up more easily. She still wasn't walking.

"I was *increvable*! If I had not been in fine health at the start and so young, perhaps I could not have lasted. I was so fortunate. I do not know why I was so lucky and others were not. I was quite ill, but the doctor there gave me a drug that helped. I think it must have been penicillin, which was new then. The injections were very painful, but pain was nothing to me anymore. It was a miracle. In two weeks I was recovered from the typhus. I was gaining weight, and I was feeling almost rested. I would not have come through so quickly if I had not been determined to live for my mother. I could not bear the possibility that she would lose me. Of course I could not bear the possibility that I would lose her, and I think her principal feeling was that she wanted to live so that I would not be abandoned.

"For a long while after we were back in Paris, we still shared the same bed. We always awoke in the night and clutched each other, and we would moan reassurances. Eventually it was my mother who pushed me to be independent again. At first I was uncertain, but she said, 'Annette, we have been through this and it will always be there. I will always be there, in your heart, even after I'm gone. Just keep me there. You don't have to remain a child. Go, go.'

"That was the wisest thing she did for me. It is the truest mother love to trust her child to be free. I think the independence she forced on me restored me—more than anything else after our return. I felt that whatever happened I could manage. Anything.

"Sister Roza was older than my mother. Maybe she has gone to her rest by now. She was a large woman, rather gaunt. I could tell that she might have filled out her frame during better times. But she was strong, and she could lift my mother. She had a kind face. The headdress she wore was flattering. She was pretty, I thought. Her skin was so white and soft. With her powerful hands, she massaged us, for the circulation. One of our companions, called Jacqueline, from Fresnes, had racking pains in her bones, like growing pains, and Sister Roza massaged her thin legs, sometimes in the middle of the night.

"Then on a beautiful spring day the news came that the Russians had reached the heart of Berlin. Hitler had been defeated. Perhaps he was dead. We hoped he was dead. Even the nuns prayed that he was dead.

" 'France! We will have France!' we cried.

"I held Maman and said, 'Hitler is no more, Hitler is no more.'

"She smiled and fell back peacefully on her bed. 'A darkness has lifted from the world,' Maman said.

" *Vive la France!*' I cried, the exuberant schoolgirl again. We cried and held each other, and then Sister Roza brought out a cake she had been saving. The occupants of the hospital gathered in a large room that had a piano—brought by the Germans, requisitioned from someone's home. By then we had been joined by several refugees of varying states of debility. We were all improving, and most of us were able to circulate. They had rolling chairs for Maman and for two of the other women.

"*Vive la France!* We made some decorations. We made a flag for Poland and one for France. The nuns sang hymns, their heads lifted to the heavens. One of us French could play the piano, and so the Frenchwomen burst into 'La Marseillaise,' with *joie de vivre*. We made the nuns weep with the sentiment of it. It was a joyous time! We even tried to dance. But of course you know it was terrible for the Polish people after the Russians came. But the nuns celebrated with us.

"But since then, I have wondered many times about the old camp at Koenigsberg, which is now in East Germany. I ask myself, would anyone ever know what had happened there?"

51

HE COULD STILL HEAR HER VOICE AS HE DROVE THE RENTED Citroën down small country roads. He meandered along the lay of the land, with no compass headings, no map check. He was flowing aimlessly through the countryside. He circled and wound through vineyards and villages. It was a soft, gray day.

Not far from a military base, he parked on a side road while trios of fighters screamed overhead, mad birds against a gray sky. He stayed a long time and watched for more.

Then, at a small café in a village twenty kilometers south of Angoulême, he studied the Michelin map of the Charentes and drank an *express*. He had been drinking a great deal of coffee. The strong European coffee agreed with him, sharpened him. The waiter, a small middle-aged man in horn-rimmed glasses, glanced his way.

"*C'est tout?* Anything more, *monsieur?*"

"*Non, merci.*"

He had to think. He couldn't think. In his mind, Annette was the young girl again. He saw the gentle outlines of her innocent face, her spirited teasing, her panache. The horrors she described had been inflicted on that young girl. As she related her sufferings, he became the young guy she had risked her life for. He had known so little then. There were only faint whispers, averted eyes. He had been ignorant. Maybe he had never learned anything truly important until these last few days.

He was in the car again, driving.

A girl in a summer dress digging sod in the snow, hacking out stumps, shivering with ragged, hungry women. The blasts of icy wind cut through them. They chopped through ice and slogged through mud, making a bed for an airstrip. Annette and her mother, balled together like a pair of socks tunneled into each other. Crowds of shriveled women like flocks of chickens scratching in dirt.

Monique and her doll; Annette and her mother. Mother and child *roulé en boule*, the mother almost dead but refusing to die, the daughter refusing to abandon her mother. So many women packed together—filthy, debilitated women dragging one another on the Death March. The Russian soldiers offering a cow, in kindness.

She hadn't told him everything. She balked at some of her memories. She spoke of the "depravity," as if one ugly word could sum it up, but she wouldn't say more. He had to fill in the blanks. Rape? Mutilation? She mentioned the young women at Ravensbrück who were called "rabbits." Nazi doctors carved up these women's legs to study gangrene. She described the *Walzkommando*—a giant roller for smoothing roadbeds. Women who were being punished had to pull it until they collapsed. What she wouldn't say about the colossal chimney behind the kitchen at Ravensbrück made him cringe. She dismissed that strange burnt odor greeting new arrivals. She had not told him the worst.

He wanted to scream, hit, crush—something. His own past was splintered by her tale. It was falling into a new design. He wanted to see his long-dead mother again. He wanted to apologize to Loretta, to make up for all the slights and indiscretions, anything he had ever done wrong. He wanted to tell his children all his memories of the war, and all of Annette's. His breathing was like the labored gasping of a rickety antique machine. He couldn't fill his lungs. Highway markers danced in the periphery of his vision as if fractured by raindrops.

A team of red-clad bicyclists passed him, rushing and melting together like a swarm of birds. He thought of bombers forming up. As an obtuse youth, he had crashed into a strange land. And thinking only of himself, he had fled the scene, alone.

Annette.

She had saved his precious hide. And her reward was the hell of Ravensbrück and Koenigsberg.

He pulled over to the side of the road, his body shaking. He parked beside a vast vineyard. The grapevines—spindly, twisted trunks held by posts and wire supports—were disciplined like soldiers in straight rows. He examined the vines, the way their tendrils wrapped around the wires and even around themselves. Some of the tendrils waved in the air, seeking a hold.

If Mary or Albert asked him how his summer in France was going, where would he begin?

Starting up again, he was scarcely aware of the car or the road. Annette would meet him later at the train station in Angoulême, in her small blue Renault. He was returning the rental car.

She had borne two children; she had grandchildren.

She was beautiful.

He writhed in sympathetic pain. The women, crowded and cold and starved.

The sky was clearing, and clouds were drifting in from the Atlantic—white puffs, the kind of cloud that was so satisfying to see from above. An infinite, rolling field of white.

AT THE TRAIN STATION, he sat in the car, the engine off. He listened to the whistle of an approaching train. It was her idea that he return the rental and use her car, but she hadn't insisted.

Her voice was still echoing in his mind—her fervor in telling him things she had stored up for so long, the pitch of her voice rising as a memory overcame her. She trusted him enough to tell him more than she had ever told anyone else. It was a special honor, an obligation he couldn't calculate.

He thought about the nurses at the Polish hospital, and he pictured the piano that the Germans had stolen from someone's home.

52

MARSHALL HAD HESITATED ABOUT GIVING HER THE BLUE BERET. But after they returned from the train station, he fetched the berets from his bag upstairs, carrying them behind his back as he entered the kitchen, where she was snipping the ends from thin green beans.

"Something for comic relief," he said, handing her the blue beret.

She stared at it for a moment, then laughed with pleasure. She wiped her hands on her apron and set the beret on her head, pulling it down to one side. He followed her into the sitting room, where there was a large mirror above a sideboard. She adjusted the beret to a jauntier angle.

"Oh, if only I had had my beret at Koenigsberg! I had the red socks I was wearing when we were arrested. But soon they were thin and faded."

"I bought myself a beret too, like the one I had in '44." He slapped on his black one, and she reached up to position it for him.

"That's better," she said, touching the back of her hand gently to his temple.

"Julien Baudouin," he said, saluting their images in the mirror. "Stonemason, from Blois. Or was I a bricklayer?"

"I'd recognize you anywhere."

They stared into the mirror together and laughed at themselves.

"I hope this isn't inappropriate," he said. "I heard that a fascist youth group wore blue berets. Can that be true?"

"They were not significant," she said, brushing away the idea. "And the blue beret was only my school hat."

"I remember in the Pyrenees, the Basques wore their berets laid flat on top of their heads," he said.

"That's the Basque way. I think their beret must fly off." She laughed and removed her beret. She set it on a chair and smiled up at him, maybe remembering the day she guided a young pilot out of the train station.

He felt at ease with her. He wanted to hold her all day. But she awed him. What would she expect of him?

She finished the green beans and led him out to sit on the terrace with the omnipresent Bernard, who seemed to stay closer to her since last evening. Marshall sat in a wicker chair, and she sat in a chaise longue with her feet up, her hands folded.

"I have a proposal," she said, her smile holding a hint of mischief. "For us."

"What?"

"Our hike the other day was like an excursion for schoolgirls. We need something more vigorous!"

"Where to?" He shaded his eyes from the sun's glare.

"A *real* hike. Across the Pyrenees to Spain!"

He was flabbergasted.

"*Mon Dieu*, Annette, why would I want to do that again?"

"We could go together."

"The last place on earth I'd want to take you! It was torture."

"It would be different now. You had to sneak over at night on smugglers' paths, while pursued by Germans!" Her hands were moving enthusiastically, like butterflies courting.

"It was an adventure, *bien sûr*!"

"Didn't you tell me it was a 'breeze'?" she asked teasingly.

"I was being macho, I guess. You know—manly."

"*Eh oui*," she said.

"But why would we want to go there now?"

She rose from her chair and leaned close to him, her hand on his shoulder. "My family sent so many boys over the mountains—the *aviateurs*. And we didn't know how the crossing went for them."

"Oh. You want to go through that?"

"Oh, it wouldn't be the same thing—the trails are very good now—but it is the idea of going to that place." She ruffled his hair. "We will search for some maps. It will be a breeze."

"Are you serious? Could you do it? Could I?"

"Dédée de Jongh did it more than thirty times in the war. In the dark! She was young, to be sure, but we must not surrender to age. She followed the route with the roaring river to cross, but we can follow a different way. You know about Dédée, do you not?"

"Yes, I do." He recalled Nicolas telling him about the Belgian woman who organized one of the first escape lines for airmen. "Won't we need a clandestine, a *passeur*—one of those mountain guides?" he joked.

She laughed. "But we don't have to be smuggled, Marshall! The trails are good now, and well marked. We can join a hiking group. And now is the best time to go. The snows are melted. People will be out on the trails. It will be merry!"

She sat on his knee for a moment and hugged him, then jumped up and stood facing him. Her face glowed in the late-afternoon sunlight.

"We could go to the national park," she said. "We could even go through Andorra. Or we could take the easiest way, down below Perpignan along the Mediterranean. You see, I have studied this matter."

"Will there be Coke stands?" He laughed.

She smiled, and in the bright light he could see tiny scars on her chin, faint little zigzags. They did not interrupt her loveliness.

"I'm glad I bought those berets," he said. "We'll get cold at night."

"*Ah, bien*, I did not doubt your spirit of adventure. This will be a test. And thereafter we can say with pride, 'We did that!' "

"How long have you been thinking of this?"

"About five minutes. When you mentioned the Basques." Her smile dissolved. "But really, those mountains have been on my mind for years. I do much hiking, but I always avoided the high mountains. All the boys we sent across . . ." She frowned, then touched his shoulder affectionately. "But with you, I thought suddenly—now is the time. I would like to cross the mountains with you."

Marshall was pacing the length of the terrace now. The Pyrenees had troubled his sleep for years, dark images of rugged heights and rocky canyons, cold and unforgiving.

"I would worry about you," he said. "The Pyrenees are dangerous. I don't want anything to happen to you."

"*Pfft!*" she said, flipping her fingers outward. "If I could build an airstrip with my bare hands, I could hike up a mountain!"

"That was long ago," he said.

"And this is now," she said.

"AT YOUR AGE? You've got to be kidding, Dad."

"I've got new boots."

"Still, if the airlines won't let you fly, then what does that say? I never knew you to be an athlete."

Albert had driven from Manhattan to the house in New Jersey and had arrived just as the telephone rang.

"I've done nothing but walk since I got to France," Marshall said, almost defensively.

"What about altitude sickness?" Albert said. "Oh, sorry, I guess you've spent half your life at high altitudes."

"This is not Mount Everest," Marshall said. "There are official hiking trails and rest stations along the way. And I won't take the most strenuous crossing—not like I did in '44."

Besides, he was going with a woman who was an experienced hiker, he told Albert.

"Aha!"

Genial banter moved along the edge of accusation. Marshall ignored it. Everything had to be reconsidered now, he thought. He remembered Albert and Mary in Halloween costumes. He was guiding them down the block, and the evening was growing dark. Mary cried because her witch hat kept falling off. Albert dropped his candy in the dirt and kicked it off the curb. Then, in no time at all, it seemed, they were in graduation gowns—Mary's hat flying up like a Frisbee, Albert flapping bat wings—and then they were gone.

Albert relayed telephone messages from two of the crew: Chick Cochran and Bobby Redburn. Cochran had heard from someone in Hootie Williams's hometown who would be writing to Marshall in Paris.

"That's good," Marshall said. All the crew was accounted for now.

Hootie. He had thought he was free from the memory of Hootie, but Hootie kept coming back, like the soldier in the old story of Martin Guerre, an impostor who returned to a family that wasn't his.

IN THE WEEK of busy preparation for the hike, Annette told him nothing more about her deportation to the camps. The book seemed to be closed. "I've told you enough," she said. "Now we can go forward."

Her resilience, her insistent good nature reasserted themselves. She seemed unburdened now. But he knew that she was willing herself to be strong. He could not look at her now without seeing, behind her mature grace, the thin girl working on the airstrip—hungry, latched to her mother, fighting snow and wind. Death all around her, bodies in the snow.

Annette consulted guidebooks, located a hiking club, and reserved a hotel room at the edge of the mountain pass. By driving up to the pass, they could hike across the border in only a day. It would be simple, she said. He did not want to read the guidebooks. He did not want to go trekking across those mountains again, but he wanted to please her.

He fed the animals, gathered the eggs, cleaned out the horse shed. There was more flower deadheading. Lost in the immediacy of the chores, he relaxed and was content. She would not let him help her snip the ends of green beans, because the task had to be done a certain way with the fingers, and his were too large and clumsy. He wondered at himself as he trundled a wheelbarrow of compost to a fenced-off pile. Back home, his aversion to yard work had been notorious.

At meals, he marveled at the everyday calm of her life now, the ease and expertise of her hands in the kitchen. She fed him well. She was generous but not wasteful. She gave him the last stalk of asparagus. Carefully, she stored the leftovers. The bread would go to the chickens. At the end of each meal, she presented three cheeses—a wedge, a flat slice, and a small round—like treasures brought out on special occasions. Marshall was agog—gorging and lounging in a way he didn't remember ever doing at home.

Every day, to build up their stamina for hiking, they walked for several miles. They walked early before having coffee and again late in the day. On the terrace, Marshall read a Japrisot mystery novel from Annette's study shelf. And he browsed through her histories. The workmen had finished the stone walk, and the courtyard was quiet, except for the bees in the ivy. Bernard began sitting at his feet when Annette was busy elsewhere. She arranged for her son and daughter to care for the animals and the garden while she was away. They did not ask suspicious questions, and Marshall suspected they would not be surprised even if their mother planned to learn deep-sea diving, or decided to go to Africa to nurse lepers.

Annette promised to invite Marshall for a grand family Sunday after they returned from the mountains. It would be an important occasion, she cautioned. Her mother, impatient to see him again, would come from Saint Lô. He met the daughter, Anne, briefly, the day before he and Annette planned to drive toward the mountains. He had been apprehensive about meeting Anne, for fear he would see in her the young Annette who was sent in a cattle car to Ravensbrück. There was something familiar in her eyes, but Anne had a less delicate face, straighter hair. She seemed to be the new liberated woman, with her hair cut severely short, her manner brisk.

"Maman, I plan to take Bernard home with me," she said. "We will come every two days, and Georges will come the other days. Don't worry. Everything will be just as you want."

"Bernard, you poor thing," Annette said, bending to hug the dog. "You would insist on going with me over the mountains if you knew. But now Anne needs you."

"I'm going to give his face a trim," Anne said, ruffling the dog's fur. "Maman, he can hardly see through that curtain."

"Don't tease him, Anne."

53

THEY WOULD HIKE INTO THE MOUNTAINS ON A WELL-DEFINED trail in the general region where Marshall had crossed the border in 1944, southwest of Oloron-Sainte-Marie. Marshall never knew the exact location of his night crossing.

They drove straight south down from Bordeaux, through an expanse of farmland and villages with gray spires and red-tile roofs. Annette's car needed brake shoes, so Marshall had rented another car, a small Citroën 2CV. It was like driving a snail, he thought.

They were easy driving companions, and for long stretches they were quiet, only now and then murmuring over scenery or road conditions. She praised his driving, and he congratulated himself on his new alertness at the wheel. He was starting to appreciate the pace on the small French highways—the numerous stops and detours and villages, alternating with straight stretches of earnest speeding. When they stopped for a picnic, he contemplated the leisure of it, the pleasure of the food. She was teaching him to be French. He was Julien Baudouin, grown up.

Marshall had not counted on plunging in so deeply. Getting together with Annette turned out to be both simpler and far more complicated than he had imagined. He faced something that demanded uncommon understanding and intimacy. He was inexperienced. With Loretta he had simply turned the marriage over to her. She ran the marriage, the home, the children, while he flew away.

OLORON-SAINTE-MARIE was an old town lodged in the foothills of the Pyrenees. An ancient church was perched on a hill within the old

ramparts. As they drove down the main street a second time, having
missed the turn for the hotel, Marshall noted the *tabac*, the *boucherie*,
the *épicerie*, the *boulangerie-patisserie*—the essentials of a French
town. A group of schoolchildren was blocking the street, protected
by two guides directing traffic. Marshall recalled a flock of sheep in
a road once when he was driving with Loretta and the children in
Scotland. He remembered his impatience then, but now he could
wait.

They would start their hike in two days. It would be fun, not a
hardship, she insisted, as they climbed to their room on the third
floor of the small hotel. The wooden steps were scarred and creaky.

"We should have had the fourth floor," she said. "For practice.
We're mountain climbers."

"We can trot up and down the stairs a few times," he suggested.

"Oh, I forgot my little kit behind the seat," she said when they
reached the room. "It has my sewing thread, and I see you have a
loose button."

"I'll get it."

"We'll both go. Trot, trot."

FROM THE WINDOW of their room they could see past the town to
green forests, golden farm fields, scattered goats. The line of mountains beyond was obscured by clouds.

"I like this view," she said. "Maurice and I came here to Oloron-
Sainte-Marie for a week one summer. I remember it was so restful."

Maurice had been a prisoner of war in Germany. Early in their
marriage, she said, they had vowed not to dwell on the ordeal of
their imprisonment. Together, they forged a life, pushing the past
into oblivion.

"It was like after the horror movie ends and the lights come on.
We French have a way of going on; the past is past. There had to be
a forgiveness. Maurice and I, we never told each other the whole
truth. My feeling is that there was more. He may have thought the

same of me. Maybe we should have spoken more. But now I am telling you."

"He didn't get to know a side of you that I knew—the schoolgirl with the leather book satchel."

"That time was ours," she said, busying herself with his loose button. "That is what you have given me again. And with you it is bearable."

In a few minutes she came to him at the window, her thread extended between the shirt in her left hand and the needle in her right.

"I need more light," she said.

She finished the button decisively, then sat down on the bed and kicked off her shoes. She sat cross-legged against the pillows and tugged at her bare feet. She was like a young gymnast, he thought.

"You're staring at me," she said.

"Every movement you make is extraordinary," he said. "Annette, how did you manage to come out of the camp with your good nature intact?"

She brought her knees up and hugged them.

"At Koenigsberg many women kept their spirits alive by making things, writing, sewing little things, dolls. It was all clandestine, of course, but as long as we could express ourselves with our hands, we still knew we were women."

"You were very strong."

She shrugged. "I was always the optimist," she said, adjusting the pillow behind her. "Speak about your wife. Was she pretty? Were you proud of her?"

To his surprise, he was glad to talk about Loretta. Framing her in a way that brought her to life for Annette helped him to see her more clearly himself. It occurred to him that his marriage had been similar to Annette's—two people agreeing not to reveal the worst of themselves, being strong for each other. He was glad to have this thought.

"I couldn't have had with my wife what I have with you. She could never have understood. I feel bad about that."

"You will feel guilt over your wife for a long time," she said. "That is most ordinary—even when there is no reason."

"You're probably right."

"Grandchildren," Annette said. "It is very sad to me, Marshall, that you have no grandchildren."

LATER, THEY WALKED OUTSIDE. They found a long stairway up to a high promenade leading to the medieval church at the top of the hill. From the promenade they could see the mountains, a natural fortress rearing along the border between France and Spain. Marshall thought he could see snow but decided it was only the glitter of the afternoon light.

"It is beautiful," she said.

"Yes, from a distance." He shaded his eyes and stared toward Spain.

"Are you sure you want to go?" she asked him.

"I'm willing to go—with *you*."

"But do *you* want to go?"

No, he didn't, but he didn't say so. He just pointed and said, "It *is* beautiful."

54

MARSHALL WAS BECOMING ACCUSTOMED TO WINE IN THE evening. He liked red wine better than white. Annette had taken a brief nap, and she seemed refreshed, quick-witted, and positive. Her throat was soft, her voice a murmur punctuated with sharp little pings of enthusiasm.

They were drinking aperitifs at a small table in a faintly lighted corner of the hotel terrace. They had ordered their dinner, and she had selected the wine. A thick hedge sheltered them from the side street, and they had a view of the waning moon over the dark, silhouetted hillside to the south. Specters of the mountains lay in the back of his mind.

"Tell me more about Robert," he said. The abruptness of his question surprised him, and he regretted asking when he saw the pain on her face.

"I can't help wondering," he said apologetically. "He is such a grand figure in my imagination."

"Robert. Robert. Robert." Her hands flew up as if to hold a headache. "He is such a trouble to me."

"To everyone, it seems," he said.

"I knew the real Robert," she said. "Your Caroline may never understand this history, but I know it well."

"Maybe she should hear it from you."

Annette sipped her drink. She said, "One of his other daughters came to me once, pleading for information about him. She passed the night with me. She had come on the train from Paris, and we stayed up until late. She was troubled because she had seen him in the hospital. I did not know how I could help her. I was trembling. I could not visit the past for so long."

"Can you speak of him now?"

She nodded slightly. "You may remember him enough to know that he was *gentil*, and sincere, and passionate about his work for the Bourgogne."

She spoke slowly, her face pale in the candlelight.

"I told you that Robert hid at our apartment once because the French police had arrested him on his way back from Perpignan. They were suspicious of his papers, but they let him get away. We were afraid someone had followed him, but he assured us that he had taken several Métro trains, crisscrossing the city, and he had walked a random route before arriving at Saint-Mandé. He was hungry and frightened.

"But Robert was a bold person. He had a tendency to court danger, even though his emotions were in turmoil. On an earlier occasion, a terrible thing happened that haunted him dreadfully. He had escorted a group of *aviateurs* to Perpignan, and after they were transferred to the local *convoyeur*, he went on a mission to set up a new safe house in a village outside Perpignan—one of those hilltop villages, very remote. Apparently the Germans were not bothering themselves with that town. The family—a man and woman and their three children—had very modest means, but they were eager to shelter our *aviateurs*. Their house was conveniently set near the bottom of the hill, away from the street. Robert was satisfied, and he left to meet his ride on the main road. As he made his way in the darkness, he heard a foreign vehicle approaching. He jumped back from the road into a bank of bushes, and he wasn't seen, but he could identify the car—a grand chauffeur-driven Horch touring car. *Mon Dieu*, it was likely the Gestapo. Robert saw the auto proceed into the village, and in a while he heard loud noises. He heard gunshots. He reached the main road, and in moments an old Citroën appeared, his ride to the train station at Perpignan.

"Robert didn't know until some time later that the Gestapo had shot the family that night—the mother, the father, and the three children. He didn't know why."

"The Nazis didn't always need an excuse," Marshall said.

"Someone, probably a resident in the village, had denounced the man. The family must have resisted arrest. I don't know the whole story."

"For the Nazis, it might have been random," Marshall said. "Or something to do that evening."

"*Bien sûr.* And I ask you, what kind of neighbor would willingly see his neighbors killed? How could such a person live with himself? Did he even think of the children? For Robert, the torment was all-consuming. He had been with that family only five minutes before."

"If I thought a massacre like that was my fault . . . I'd never get over it," Marshall said. "Imagine—an entire family."

"It was not Robert's fault. He learned later that the man had been involved with some other project of the *Résistance.*"

"But wasn't the Bourgogne exposed then?" Marshall asked.

"No. Robert was confident that he had covered his own tracks because he had given no names. Oh, I don't know." She passed her hand over her head. "But he was ravaged by the memory of that family in that village! And he did not even see the reality. It was in his imagination. I remember how he prayed and prayed over that. 'Why?' he kept asking. There was a certain fragility in Robert, although he took chances. As long as he was successful in his projects, he had confidence, but when something bad happened, I think he crumpled in his emotions."

Annette paused, and Marshall reached for her hands, but she moved them away.

"What was it about Robert?" he asked. "What drove him?"

"His religion. Both good and bad, it was his religion." Her sigh seemed to take an enormous space on the terrace.

"His parents wanted him to be a priest, but he had self-doubts. I think he looked up to our priest, the abbé at l'église de Saint-Roch,

Father Jean, so much that he could not imagine himself in so lofty a spiritual position. Father Jean was very gentle with Robert. He desired to see him become a priest, but Robert feared a hollowness. He felt unworthy.

"Robert's parents had said, 'Go to the seminary! You'll make a priest!' "

Annette laughed. "I cannot imagine Robert as a priest. He was devout, yet he was so worldly! He liked to draw and go to the cinema. He liked to draw pictures of women. He showed me pictures of nude women he drew in art class! Should I have gotten mixed up with him? I ask myself. Maybe he wasn't so good for me.

"He confessed to Father Jean his doubts about the vow of celibacy. He said, 'When I desire something, my reason is attacked!' He emphasized his fantasies of women! But Father Jean had a solution for him, something for Robert to do so that he could serve usefully.

"Father Jean had recruited a group of students from the Lycée Henri-IV, near the Sorbonne, some *khâgneux*—students who were preparing for higher learning. They were desperate to avoid the work-service in Germany and they were filled with anger. That was such a difficult situation for many young men. Robert's father wanted to send him to hide with an uncle in Lyon, but Robert did not want to hide. He wanted to be active.

"The abbé sent him with those students to the Bourgogne network, so that's how Robert began to escort *aviateurs*.

"When he first joined the Bourgogne, his parents did not ask questions, but they allowed him to have supplies from their *épicerie* to help people like my family who were trying to feed a great many very large Americans!"

She paused and smiled at Marshall as the waiter poured the wine.

She went on. "Father Jean was an extraordinary man. Not many priests would take such risks. Priests were such likely suspects. They knew the secrets of the confessional! But even though the Germans were watching them, there were a few courageous priests."

"Was it because the Germans had their eye on your priest that you were arrested?" Marshall asked.

"Oh, no, Father Jean came to warn us. He had already warned my father at his office. Papa rushed home because he could not bear to stay away while we were in danger. Robert was there too. Our fear caused us to cluster instead of scatter. Of course that was a great mistake, but to the last moment we could not truly conceive the danger that was befalling us. How could we grasp that our world—everything we knew—was ending?"

She sipped her wine. "We were betrayed by someone who gossiped—a waiter at a café. He knew us and he made a careless remark to the wrong person. You never knew whom you could trust. The *collabos* were despicable!" She quavered. "There's nothing more to be said about that." She paused and drank from her glass. "Father Jean had lovely brown eyes and a ringing voice like the church bells. I can hear it now. When I go along the rue Saint-Honoré, I stop at the church where he was abbé, but there is no remembrance of him there, nothing on the walls. I notice that, and I wonder if Robert would be better if Father Jean had survived."

She was quiet then, as though she were finished.

Marshall tried to pull his thoughts together. He said, "I hadn't realized how precarious the Bourgogne network was, how much it depended on trust."

"Yes, of course. You knew this."

"I never really thought about it."

"It was not necessary for you to know our difficulties or the real dangers you faced. There were *Résistance* agents arrested right here in Oloron-Sainte-Marie in the spring of 1944, when you crossed the mountains. But the Bourgogne was very successful, very tightly organized."

Marshall asked, "The guy who ran the thing—did you know him?"

"Georges Broussine—yes. In fact we knew him, and the abbé, but we were not supposed to know anyone else. Georges had a genius

for building a network of trust. When the Comète line was infiltrated, the Bourgogne had to take over, and that is why you had to
wait so long in Paris. There were so many pilots waiting it was hard
to find enough safe houses for them." She smiled and shook her
head. "Today Georges is reserved—perhaps too much so. Few knew
of him then, and few know now what he did in the war. He trained
in London with the Free French, you know. And he parachuted into
France with radio equipment to start the Bourgogne. He made
many escapades!"

Marshall wanted to ask if she had named her son after Broussine,
but the waiter interrupted then, and after some exchanges over a *con-
fit* of some kind, she resumed.

"When my mother and I returned from Poland, we were anxious
to find Robert. Why did he not search for us? As soon as Maman felt
well enough, she went to see him. I did not go. I did not know what
I would say to him, and I sensed that he would feel the same toward
me. We were both in a state of shock, I believe, and each of us in our
own way had retreated. My mother had at Koenigsberg exhausted
herself in her protection of me, and when she was so sick I had exhausted myself in my care for her. 'Why does he not come to see us?'
she would say, agitated. He would not even speak to us on the telephone.

"Anyway, she was strong enough of spirit to go to see him first.
She returned in tears. 'He used to call me *tante*,' she said. 'They have
destroyed him.' He told her a little about Papa, only a little. Robert
was apologetic and tormented with guilt. He had the guilt to be the
survivor.

"Robert said to Maman, 'The *avis*, the posters on the streets,
promised to shoot the men who aided the Allies. Why didn't they
just shoot us upon arrest? It would have been better.'

"Robert told her he had been tortured at the rue des Saussaies in
Paris before he was sent to Buchenwald. Fragile though he was, he
would endure torture rather than reveal any of the safe houses or betray anyone in the network. He wouldn't tell Maman what the

Gestapo did to him, but I knew that they beat their prisoners with a whip made of woven rattan. The heavy stone walls muffled the sounds. I wasn't tortured when I was there, but I know about the instruments of torture. On the fifth floor where they made the interrogations, there was a bathtub like a coffin, with a lid."

She hid her face in her hands for a moment, then went on. "Maman was terrified that I might be tortured, and I was terrified that she would be, but we knew so little. We knew not to betray Robert or the priest or Papa."

"Or Broussine," Marshall said.

"*Bien sûr.*" She lowered her voice.

"After Maman's visit, I went to see Robert myself. His mother allowed me in, but she regarded me up and down with disapproval. I was still a student, and my clothes were modest. I was glad Madame Lebeau survived the war with her dignity intact, but I felt right away that she was not good for Robert. Robert appeared in loose garments, not what one would wear on the street, but I did not think he was an invalid. He was pale—and shockingly thin.

" 'Can you tell me anything?' I asked him, after we made some confused greetings. We were both ashamed and filled with pain. I was happy his mother was not in the room.

"He shook his head.

" 'Was my father with you?'

"He gazed at his feet. 'I lost him,' he mumbled. 'I did not see the end.'

" 'Robert,' I said. 'Look at me. Remember what we shared.'

"He turned his head away. I saw the drawings he was making and wondered what his mother thought. I tried not to look at them. There was one that was lurid, and grotesque, and horrible, but also erotic. It was a nightmare. I did not have to ask more. Robert lifted his sleeve and showed me the small black number tattooed on his arm. I put my hand on it and squeezed his arm. I laid my head on his chest.

" 'I'm so sorry,' he said. 'I have nothing.'

"That's what I remember, 'I *have* nothing.' He seemed to mean, 'I *am* nothing and so I have nothing for you.' I remember that it seemed not a rejection of me but a rejection of himself. It broke my heart."

Annette looked away, toward the hedge, and cleared her throat.

"I saw him again at his parents' *épicerie* several months later. We sat and talked in the back room. Robert was not in full health, and his spirit remained low. He was drawing in a sketchbook, and I could see that he was drawing more frightful images like the shadows of hell. His mother interrupted us. 'Robert is going to take over the *épicerie* very soon,' she said with pride.

" 'I will sell rutabagas,' Robert said.

" 'No, you will never sell rutabagas!' his mother said. 'No one in France will ever eat a rutabaga again.'

"He was indifferent. He bent over his sketchbook.

" 'Rutabagas are for pigs!' his mother said with scorn. 'Rutabagas tear out the insides.' She clenched her abdomen and said she still had trouble.

"Robert had a half smile playing on his face. 'I am useless,' he said to me.

" 'Robert is going to marry Hortense,' his mother said. 'Hortense is the daughter of Monsieur "the Hat King." He has his shop on the rue de Vaugirard. The most chic *chapeaux*!'

"Robert grunted, as if it did not matter to him whether he be married or not. Or with whom. I did not see how he could marry with anyone, in his bad state of mind. But his mother insisted on the marriage with mademoiselle the daughter of the Hat King. Oh, how his mother complained about the rutabagas she had to endure in the war! But I know she managed to eat well; it was at the camps that the rutabaga reigned supreme. It was her son who was entitled to denigrate the rutabaga."

Annette's elaborate gestures as she mocked Robert's mother would have amused Marshall, but he saw that for Annette the scene was present and alive in her imagination.

She continued. "At the insistence of his mother, I have no doubt, he married this Hortense and proceeded to reproduce like a rabbit! The poor wife—all those children, one after the other, and at the same time Robert fathered an equal number with the mistress! Just think. If he couldn't be a priest, was he working overtime, such to say, in his secular operation?"

Annette did not laugh at her bitter witticism. Her head sank slightly, and her voice lowered.

"About ten years after the war, I met a man who knew Robert at Buchenwald. I met him at the school where I was training apprentice teachers. Philippe and I had a long talk. He said he knew Robert well, but he did not remember the priest or my father. 'Oh, Annette,' he said, when we had gotten to know each other, 'Robert was the most admired young man in the block. He was thoughtful of everyone. He gave up his food. He wrote little passages of scripture and sent them around for people to share. Uplifting quotations. He helped everyone through.'

"I could hardly believe this to be true. I thought about Philippe's words for a long while."

"You thought perhaps Philippe had the wrong guy?" Marshall asked.

"I wondered. But then I thought perhaps it was as if Robert had become the priest he hadn't believed he could be. This is how I interpreted Philippe's words. This was how Robert survived, I decided. He sacrificed, and the act of sacrifice filled him with strength."

"And then when he came back, he collapsed?"

She nodded. "He may have believed that my father and the abbé had sacrificed themselves for him at the camp. That would have given him guilt. But it was normal for Father Jean to offer spiritual comfort, and he would have given Robert his food. Many of the older ones gave their food to the young ones. I know this was so. Father Jean would have done this. My father would have also. In fact, my father's heart was not strong, and he would have not lived anyway under those circumstances. It was normal for the old to help the young."

"Did you see Robert again?" Marshall asked.

"I kept in touch with him a little over the years. Eventually, he was able to tell me about my father."

She bent her head for a moment. "I can't. . . . There's nothing to say."

"It's all right."

"From time to time I went to the *épicerie*. Sometimes Robert's wife was there, and she always seemed tired. She wore an apron—and no hat! She certainly didn't impress one as the chic and privileged daughter of Monsieur the Hat King."

"Do you know where Robert is now?" Marshall asked. "Caroline seemed to think he was in a mental hospital."

"He spent some time in an institution, it is true. But it was a sanatorium, not a psychiatric hospital. About ten years ago he disappeared for a year, and his family was ready to consider him dead. But then he returned. And since then he has had the tendency to disappear for long periods. It is a good thing he provided that *épicerie* in Saint-Mandé to this Caroline. I do not know why he gave it to her and not to one of the sons, a legitimate one. But Robert always had some kind of obscure reasoning in the back of his mind." She sighed. "Or do I know him at all?"

The waiter brought their food then. Annette straightened her back, looked directly at Marshall, and smiled. "I've talked too much!" she said. "Let us enjoy our dinner."

55

UPSTAIRS IN THEIR ROOM, THEY STOOD BY THE WINDOW LOOKING at the moonlit street. Marshall was not sleepy, and he anticipated that the moonlight, if not thoughts of Robert Lebeau, would keep him awake. Annette seemed wide awake too.

"Robert always worked hard," she said. "He worked intently on anything he did. His *gentillesse*, his sensitive character—his sensibility was perhaps his weakness. He couldn't achieve a balance with the torment. Maybe he couldn't refuse it as I did."

Annette rubbed the fabric of the curtain between her fingers, as if to feel the essence of the material. She said, "No one ever knew how I loved him, except Maman. She knew everything. I loved his hair, and the quiver in his upper lip when he smiled."

She turned away from the window. The light in the room was dim, and her small frame seemed to fade into the shadows.

"I believe his disappearances are his way of regathering his strength," she said. "I remember that when I used to go out with him to meet a group of *aviateurs* at the train, or to escort some of them to a safe house somewhere, if we passed a church and we had time, Robert would always go inside. It was a way of focusing his will, reconstituting himself. It was humble; he was a servant. Maybe his disappearances are periods of retreat, another way of being like the priest he couldn't be.

"I believed in the church too, before the war, but it left me. Perhaps it left Robert also. I often wonder where he is. Sometimes I can imagine him in one of the spots that we went, our own little bowers, or escape places when we went out on our missions."

"Are you still in love with him?" Marshall asked.

"That is not a practical question," she said sharply.

She switched on a lamp and began preparing for bed, searching through her suitcase. Her clothing was perfectly organized and folded, but she seemed flustered. She closed the case and disappeared into the bathroom. He heard the roar of the bidet.

Later, when she was in her silky gown, he drew her to him and embraced her tightly, feeling her warm breasts against him. He held her while she cried, her tears running onto his shoulder. In a while, she drew back to speak.

"You know, I must think of what Father Jean did for the Bourgogne. I must find Robert and confront him. We cannot let the abbé disappear into oblivion, without being acknowledged. We must commemorate him somehow."

"Is that what your mother wants?"

"Maybe. I think she despairs of Robert, but I must get him to remember how he loved Father Jean."

"If he lost his religion, wouldn't he be reluctant?" Marshall said.

"Oh, that doesn't matter," she said almost dismissively. "The abbé was a person, and he sacrificed his life. He loved Robert. I must remind him."

Marshall imagined setting out with Annette to find Robert Jules Lebeau. He had searched for the bright young man Robert had been, only to find that the trail had taken a dreadful twist—Robert damaged by the war, the young lovers split apart. It would serve him right, Marshall thought, if he helped reunite the two now.

"Thank you, Marshall," she was saying. "Thank you, thank you."

"For what? Don't thank me," he said. *Not me.*

He held her and she did not cry more. He thought she felt an immense relief in knowing him. She snuggled with him, letting him hold her a long time. She kissed him deeply. He was right to hold her close.

"Do I have a chance with you?" he ventured to ask.

"When we get over the mountains," she said.

"Then what?"

"We will know."

Later, he tossed around in bed, wondering where he was headed. He had come to France hopefully, pie-eyed, imagining a pleasant jaunt down memory lane. Now the faces of the absent characters —Annette's father, Robert and all his children, Robert's mistress, his priest, even the mysterious chief of the Bourgogne—paraded through Marshall's waking dreams.

At dawn, hearing water trickling somewhere, then birdsong, he felt his mind clearing. Annette was lying close to him, curled toward him, her fine hair tangled, her lips hanging open. Were they thrown together inevitably, or had he imagined them into a couple with a destiny? After the war, Robert was crushed, but Marshall had been rescued, and he thrived. No matter what else he might feel, he was indebted to both Robert and Annette. The logic of that was undeniable. He wept inside for the priest—Marshall, whose religion ended when he was eight and heard that an old woman's house had burned down with her picture of Jesus over the stove and her grandbabies sleeping on a pallet nearby.

56

ANNETTE AWOKE LIVELY AND PLAYFUL, RISING SWIFTLY FROM
the bed to throw open the shutters.

"How did you sleep?" he asked.

"I slept completely," she said, smiling.

Marshall had slept little. He hadn't thrashed and flailed as he
often did. Instead, trying not to wake Annette, he had lain quietly,
trying to capture his runaway thoughts.

Coffee and croissants arrived. Annette hurried to the door to accept the tray from the young woman in a blue smock. A flurry of *bonjours* and *mercis* followed. Marshall was glad to see the large pot of
coffee.

"I really should try to find Robert," Annette said later, emerging
from the bathroom with a towel on her head. "For the sake of Father
Jean."

"I believe you could march over the Pyrenees and then get right
to work."

She laughed. "It would be necessary to march back across the
border first.

"I don't know," she said after a minute, falling into doubt. "Perhaps Robert is beyond rescue. Since the war, he has led a life of dis-
sipation and irresponsibility. I don't know if his true nature can be
reawakened."

Marshall was suddenly tired of hearing about Robert.

"Maybe we'll find him behind a bush in the mountains." His attempt at humor fell flat, he saw by the startled expression on her
face.

He touched her moist cheek. "I'm sorry. But I have to point out that I feel insanely jealous."

"*Peuh!* Do not think that way." She was combing her hair, carefully easing a fine-toothed comb through her wet curls.

"I'm sorry."

"I have the idea that someone sympathetic should go to him, with something from the past. I will take *you*. You are a success story. A success for him. And for me," she added quickly. "Everything we did—we are confirmed, in seeing *your* success."

He was embarrassed. "You and Robert, both of you, made a terrible sacrifice," he said.

Annette would not accept such thinking.

"What were we to do?" she asked. "Just sit there and let our country be stolen? Not just our buildings and our churches and our lives, but the very culture that is our life! To see it all replaced by German beer and sausage? My family could not abide it. Whatever we did, regardless of the risk, we *had* to do it. For my parents, it was automatic. For me also. We simply did it. You would too! Absolutely." Her voice was vigorous, almost shrill.

Not every Frenchman had taken such chances, Marshall thought. Would he have taken them? He had been willing to bomb Germany—not only factories but, inevitably, citizens—and then to sneak through Occupied France, thinking only of his own survival. But Annette . . .

She twisted the towel around her head and placed her hands on his shoulders. Gazing into his eyes, she said, "Once, during the war, from our window in Saint-Mandé, we saw two parachutists. An Allied plane was shot down. I think the target was a factory at Pontoise. The plane was far away and we didn't see it fall, but we could see the parachutes in the distance. Then we saw the men being shot as they drifted down. German soldiers on the ground shot them as they descended. We were hiding a pilot, and he watched this with us, and he began to cry when he saw the shooting of his comrades." She paused, as if replaying the scene in her mind. " 'Poor men!' he said. 'Poor men.' "

"My God."

"Yes," she said.

"*I'll* cry now," he said.

"No, you will not do that."

"Did Monique—"

"Yes, Monique saw it."

Annette touched his cheek. "You have encouraged me so much," she said, waving her hands for words. "I cannot explain how your return has affected me. What I just said about France—that is what I should tell my students. Maman wants me to make a scrapbook for them." She smiled. "Do I make sense? I could make an exhibit of you for the students—my *aviateur*!"

"Would I have to wear my old flight suit?"

"For us, this project could be *jubilatoire*!"

"Come here," he said. "If you're not careful, I'll fall in love with you for sure." He lifted her hand and kissed her palm.

57

THE DRIVE UP TO THE MOUNTAIN PASS WOULD BE SIMPLE, Annette had said, pointing to the map. Marshall had given no thought to the squiggly line leading up into the mountains, but as he drove the route now, he felt the mountains closing in. The cliff-edge road twisted alongside steep woodlands, and it seemed to become narrower with each hairpin curve.

"You must have been a very good pilot," she said, patting his arm. "I trust you to drive me anywhere."

"How far is it to that hotel?" he asked.

"Thirty-two kilometers. Not far."

He was aware of the deep valley on the right, but he kept his eyes on the road, the spiraling climb.

Some bicyclists came hurtling past the car, curving and zipping downhill, as smoothly as fish in water.

Some of the curves were bordered by foot-high stone guardrails, but some equally precipitous were not.

"The whimsical placement of these little walls is entertaining," he said.

She laughed.

He pulled over slightly for an oncoming car. His tires skittered on gravel.

"The view is breathtaking," she said.

His eyes were fixed on the winding road ahead. They climbed higher. He was guiding a lumbering aircraft through an insane corkscrew ascent. After a while, the switchback turns became rhythmic. Higher up, the day turned gray, but visibility was still good.

The lip of the valley beside him, five feet away, opened onto an abyss.

The stone barriers were even less frequent at higher altitudes, and the road was barely wide enough for two small European cars. Good thing he had rented the smaller Citroën, he thought.

"I'm enjoying the view," she said. "*C'est magnifique!*"

They drove for nearly an hour. His fingers were stiff, and his eyes were burning.

"It is only another kilometer," she said, rustling the map.

A small settlement appeared ahead, complete with a church, and soon he was scooting into a parking area beside a faded hotel that seemed to be waiting patiently for them.

"I'm glad it wasn't rush hour," he said, setting the parking brake.

THE HOTEL HAD a white stucco façade and an unpronounceable Basque name that sported an *x*. The lobby was pleasant, inviting, with landscape paintings and a fireplace. The *propriétaire*, a rugged woman wearing large beads and a red sweater, was writing the evening menu on the dining room chalkboard as they entered.

"You are with the hiking group?" she asked. "I was expecting you! Your guides are already here."

The guides had walked over from the Spanish side that afternoon, she said. She finished writing the menu and moved to the small desk in the minuscule lobby. Marshall made some small talk with her as she was checking them in.

"Okey-dokey!" she said. "I am very happy to welcome an American."

Annette explained that they would be leaving their valises at the hotel in the morning and would return for them in two days.

"Okey-dokey. Not a problem," said the *propriétaire*. "We get many hikers this summer!" She handed Marshall a large key with a metal tag shaped like a sheep. "I do not go over the mountains anymore. My husband and I used to keep cattle and sheep in the mountains, and twice a year it was necessary to search for them. But no more."

The room, up a flight of stairs, had two narrow beds placed close together, a tall lamp, and a window seat. The toilet and shower were down the hall.

Annette began unpacking, sorting items for her hiking pack—cotton wool, Band-Aids, sunglasses, her canteen. Marshall found his eyedrops, and he began searching for the little foam blister preventers he would stick in his boots.

Annette wound her arms around him affectionately.

"The mountains are bothering you," she said. "The drive—it reminded you."

"I like mountains better from a cockpit—preferably at thirty thousand feet."

"You were elegant behind the wheel," she said.

They sat on one of the beds and laughed. The bed was lumpy and squeaked.

"We don't have to stay here," he said, teasing. "I'm sure there's good straw bedding in the animal refuges up in the mountains."

"Oh, good. We can sleep in a barn if it snows."

"Don't worry. It won't snow."

He scrutinized the room—the worn carpet, the weighty drapery, the freestanding coat rack next to an armoire bedecked with carved birds. There were thumps on the wood floor above, apparently someone jumping. The bells of the church across the road rang, although it was no special time of day. Marshall's watch said 4:37.

"Happy bells," she said. "Perhaps a marriage."

Accordion music drifted in from the road.

"What luck," he said, groaning. "Wild dancing and music all night long."

"Well, we will not linger here long," she said, shutting her bag. "Should we swim?"

"I don't have a suit."

"If they had a pool, we could swim."

"Let's don't swim."

"I didn't want to swim anyway."

"Okey-dokey."

They laughed again.

IN THE EVENING THERE was a good dinner. They sat with the hiking group at a long table, and the conversation was convivial, although a Canadian couple who spoke no French seemed forlorn. The mountain air was chilly, even indoors, but Annette was wearing a blue dress of some flimsy material and no stockings. She looked healthy, lovely. Marshall liked to see her in a group of people, the best-looking woman in the room. His eyes had stopped burning.

The guides, Marie and Roland, moved with the fluidity of flirting youth. Their muscular bodies were tanned. Marie's hair was short and curly, while Roland's long locks trailed down his neck.

"One of us will take the lead and the other will follow at the rear," Marie told the group. "We have the *talkie-walkies*, and if you require aid, we will be there."

"You'll be right there if we fall off the mountain?" Marshall joked.

"Absolutely," Roland said. "We never permit our guests to jump!"

"We'll be O.K.," said Marshall, wondering what the young people made of his age.

After dinner, Annette wanted to go outdoors. She said she didn't mind her legs being bare, but she got cold around her neck and chest. He dashed upstairs for their jackets.

She was chatting with Roland when Marshall returned to the lobby, but she said a quick smiling *au revoir* to the guide. Marshall held her jacket for her, taking care as she slipped each arm into its sleeve. He had brought their berets. They walked out the side door, past the parking spaces, and sat on a small ledge across from the church. There was no sign of a wedding, and the accordion music had ended. They could see lights far down the valley. An intermittent, moving flash in the distance seemed to be a car driving up the road they had come.

The foothills made Marshall think of the squeezed-together hills of Kentucky, which could trap the smoke from someone's woodstove and send it circling through the holler, the scent lingering until morning.

"The mountains are bothering you," Annette said again. She ran her hand along his arm reassuringly.

"Mountains are deceptive," he said. He stopped her hand with his. "There's no horizon—no level land to get your bearings. And the perspective keeps changing. There's no objective view."

"Is there ever, anywhere?"

"I always want things to be clear," he said. "I get impatient if they aren't."

"You would not be impatient behind the wheel of an airplane. You must have been a very precise pilot."

"Yoke, not wheel."

"Oh, *pardon, monsieur.*" She was teasing him. "Just be with me," she said. "Isn't this good? We have the night. There is no war. My dog is safe with Anne and Georges."

"Did you name your son for Georges Broussine?"

"*Bien sûr.*"

"Does your son know?"

"Oh, yes. However, I think the original Georges may be a little embarrassed."

"A modest man, you say."

"Yes." She laid her hand on his knee.

"I named my son Albert," he said. "After the family that helped me in Chauny."

"Yes, you told me."

"The name means 'courage.' "

The waning moon resembled a hat hanging in the sky. He pointed it out to her.

"A beret," she said.

"Aren't you glad I bought this chic headgear from the stall on the rue de Rivoli?"

"Yes. My beret is warm," she said.

"It feels strange to be in the Pyrenees again," he said after a moment. The rocky peaks were out there, somewhere in the dark.

"Tell me about the time before," she said. "I know it has been on your mind."

He stared into the darkness, toward Spain.

"What are you seeing?" she asked. "I would like to know."

A meteor dashed silently across the sky then.

58

MARSHALL GAZED AT THE SKY AS HE BEGAN TO SPEAK.

"When I crossed the Pyrenees in '44, I thought if I could just get to the summit, it would be like flying. To get back to my base, I was prepared to face whatever dangers lay ahead. The train was the first hurdle. I think Robert was my guide on the train."

"Yes. After Perpignan, he had begun making journeys to Pau."

"And there was a girl, a girl with blond pigtails."

"I think that was my friend Hélène. She was two years older than me, and she had an aunt in Montauban, so she could travel on the pretext that her aunt was sick. Her parents didn't know she was *résistante*!"

"The night train to Toulouse was miserably slow. The tracks had been sabotaged in several places. Now and then the train jolted on a bad roadbed, and sometimes we stopped for a long time. It was hard to stay awake. I had to be fully alert, but I was dead tired and miserable. It was dark and the windows were covered, so we couldn't see the terrain. I carried a newspaper—the one your mother had pressed into my knapsack before I left to meet you."

"At the Jardin des Plantes."

"Yes. I went there last week. Didn't I tell you?"

"*Oui, oui.*"

"In the daylight on the train I kept reading the newspaper, and I tried to play 'deaf and dumb.' I had to make sure I was never startled by a noise. It was a useful discipline. People now are going to meditation classes to learn how to be mellow." He laughed. "By noon I had learned all the French in the collaborationist news, but my companions in the compartment probably thought I was an exceptionally slow reader. No one really spoke. Under German eyes, everyone kept to himself. No one wanted to speak or even offer common courtesies to the enemy. I have to admit I was terrified. Any minute and their pistols could be at my head. Your mother had made my hair dark, and I hunched down to conceal my height. But one thing I hadn't thought of. When I went to the lavatory, the floor inside was wet, and I made boot prints down the aisle when I walked back to my seat. After I turned to open the door of my compartment, I faced the other way and I saw my footprints—a trail of little USA insignias, written backwards! The letters 'USA' were in the rubber on the heels of my boots. I must have turned red as a cherry at the sight of that. I retraced my path, sliding my feet to blur the prints. The next time I went to the lavatory, I dried my boots off before leaving."

He laughed, telling this, and she laughed with him.

"Your calling card," she said.

"It's funny now, but the whole trip was nerve-wracking. I almost had a heart attack when I saw that incriminating trail. I was with three other airmen, and two of them were in different cars. Robert was at the head of my car. He was reading a book and paying no attention to me. Our group got off at Montauban, and the girl guided us to a park."

"I'm sure that was Hélène."

"In the park we could scatter out and pass the time for a while. Then, I think to confuse the Germans, she took us on by bus to Toulouse. Robert didn't go to the park, and I lost sight of him. But there he was on the quai at Toulouse. The train to Pau was due in just a few minutes. Robert went to the lavatory, and the girl was reading a book on a bench. The train was late. That was a miserable hour! We couldn't talk, couldn't buy anything to eat or a newspaper, for fear of betraying ourselves. We all sat on various benches, checking the departure board from time to time. I concentrated on not hearing a train approaching. I wondered just how deaf I was supposed to be. Would I hear the vibrations of the train when it was still far away? Was I totally deaf or partially deaf? Why didn't I know sign language? And would that be the same in French? I was crazed with all these questions."

"All the Allied *aviateurs* who fell into France were deaf and dumb," she said, laughing. They laughed together. He had not imagined his tale would be so entertaining. She said, "The flu epidemic of 1917 left many people deaf and dumb, so it was plausible."

"Still, the Germans must have been stupid not to notice," he said. "The French would have noticed us, wouldn't they?"

"Oh, they did. And no one denounced you! This was the passive *résistance* of the French! They say most people collaborated, but this was an example of how we resisted when there seemed to be nothing one could do. The Americans were obvious—and everyone knew! We kept quiet. Oh, excuse me, I've launched into my opinions. Continue, please!" She hugged his arm.

"I had eaten most of the food your mother gave me. I tried to eat my orange the way a French workman would. Anyway, an orange was messy enough to keep people at arm's length. Two of the men in our group—I didn't know them at all—were behaving rather strangely, talking to each other. Although I wasn't seated near them, I was determined to have nothing to do with them. They were going to jeopardize the whole operation. One of them went to the kiosk and bought something to eat, and he started toward me signaling that he wanted to give me some of it. I stood up, turned, and walked away. The fool. I was afraid we were going to attract the attention of the German officer who was standing at the exit to the street, checking papers. In the lulls between trains, he strolled around, gave everybody the once-over, and entertained himself by throwing pebbles at pigeons. Then a new set of guards arrived and they *heil*-Hitlered each other with great fanfare. I imagined them practicing that in front of the mirror. I thought about Hitler looking in the mirror and wondered what he saw.

"Robert returned and we all boarded the train to Pau. We got there uneventfully. The Germans at the checkpoint glanced at my papers without asking any questions. I thought they probably couldn't read French anyway, so the papers you and your mother had created worked just fine, I am happy to tell you."

"Maman filled them in with her left hand. She insisted on that method of disguising handwriting."

"It worked, and I was thankful to the bottom of my boots. I had been chiding myself for not taking a knife to those USA initials on the boots. How could I have been so careless? By the time we arrived at Pau it was the middle of the night, and Robert passed us off to a man and woman who drove us to a safe house, where there were some other airmen sheltered. We were given cheese and some kind of bread and soup. But here was the biggest surprise of all. I was totally unprepared for this. You remember that I told you about the crew of our plane. The pilot—Lawrence Webb—died at the scene, I was sure. And there was another guy, a waist gunner called Hootie Williams. I thought he was hurt pretty badly, and I didn't know if he was captured. I was almost certain he had died. He looked bad. All during my trip through France I was nagged by thoughts of Hootie and what happened to him. Well, believe it or not, there was Hootie! In this house, sitting at the table eating soup. I can't tell you the greeting we gave each other.

"He was calm, though. He said, 'Hey, Marshall, what took you so long? I've been waiting on you!'

"I was astounded. And thrilled. You can't know.

" 'Well, Hootie,' I said. 'I always said you were the smartest one of us all. I should have known you would find your way.'

"Hootie told me that Webb was dead and had been buried in that little village in Belgium. And he said three of the crew had been arrested."

Marshall paused, remembering how Hootie, his mouth stuffed with chewy bread, had praised him for the landing. Hootie hadn't bailed out, as Chick Cochran did. *Oh, no, Marshall. I knew Webb was a goner. When he said "bail out," I knew we were too low. But Chick jumped anyway. The dope.* Hootie shook his head and grinned like a hyena.

"Many *aviateurs* became separated when they were shot down," Annette was saying. "Then at the safe houses they might find each other again, or receive some news. Sometimes there were long waits."

"We didn't know at the time that everybody else from our crew had survived and would eventually make it home." Marshall laughed. "Hootie told a tale about a woman who guided him on a train, and when the German officers were approaching, this anonymous woman pulled him into a headlock and kissed him, smothering his face with her hair. She figured the Germans wouldn't break up a pair of lovers, I guess. I didn't know whether to believe him, but Hootie said, 'Marshall, that kiss couldn't be repeated in heaven! I never found out who she was. She got me to where we were going and then she took a run-out powder.' "

"That was a strategy," Annette said. "Robert and I played sweethearts, so no one would suspect—"

"Hootie stayed with a family in Belgium who kept him out of the hospital where the Germans would have found him. He had been wounded, but not seriously, as I had thought. He was soon on his feet. While he was with the Belgian family, he started helping the Resistance! He worked with the explosives.

"Hootie told me the family was named Lechat. I did not run across that name again until this spring when I went back to the crash site. And, Annette, the people told me that a boy's father was shot for convoying one of our crew. It was Monsieur Lechat. He paid with his life for taking care of Hootie."

Marshall paused, recalling Hootie's crazy laugh. "I didn't know this until I went back to Belgium this spring."

"These are difficult recognitions," she said, leaning on his shoulder. "Go on. It is hard, *n'est-ce pas*? I am listening."

"Hootie had gotten word that Campanello, our navigator, was one of those who went to the stalag. We weren't too worried about POWs because of the Geneva convention. We didn't know that the Germans were starting to get a little loose on that point and were sending some POWs to Buchenwald. I only heard about this years later."

"Yes," Annette said. "That was so."

"Hootie had made his way through France by taking chances and pulling his wheeler-dealer ways. He was charming that way. He was the biggest daredevil I ever knew. He claimed he never went hungry in France.

"The next afternoon four of us were picked up in a dilapidated truck and driven through miles of foothills. We were let out at the end of a farm and told to walk down a stony path through some trees. We were off the road, so we were relatively safe. There was a French guide with us who would bring up the rear and be the translator. I don't remember that he had much to say, though.

"It was growing dark, and the trail started to get twisty, so we were glad when we met the guide who would lead us across. He was a Basque who knew only a few English words and apparently had little interest in anything except getting us to follow him at breakneck speed in total silence. He had some rope sandals for us, some clumsy strung-together things that I refused to wear. First, he demanded it; then he shrugged his shoulders as if to say, 'It's your funeral.'"

"Espadrilles," she said.

"I called them Basket shoes. The other guys took them because their shoes weren't so great, but I wouldn't part with my USA boots. The night before, I had gouged out the letters with my knife.

"We carried small knapsacks. I still had a few items from my escape kit sewn into my pants legs, and some soap your mother had given me. The Basque guide, a big fellow, carried a huge pack on his back that seemed no more troublesome to him than carrying a pillow. The French guide, coming along behind us, was smarter. He had only a small backpack."

Marshall paused, remembering the tension that oppressed the group, and the profound darkness.

"The trail was narrow, like an animal track, and we couldn't see. There was a misty rain, and we all had the sniffles. The walking was easy at first. We were told to be absolutely quiet. We weren't any-where near the border patrols or guard posts, but we still had to be quiet. Then it got *very* dark—I mean pitch-black—and we had to hold on to each other by the belt or the jacket.

"Trying to be quiet, trying to stay awake, and not breaking the pace—it was worse than boot camp, that's for sure. It was cold, but we were moving so vigorously that we were sweating. As we walked, I kept up my strength by telling myself I was responsible for the oth-ers. It was my duty. I was an officer. There was Hootie, and two guys who had bailed out near Bordeaux—enlisted men. And then there were two others, British civilians. I hoped they weren't spies. If we got caught with spies in our group . . . But among us Americans I had the highest rank, so I tried to make sure we kept moving along in good order.

"After a few hours, we came to a long swinging bridge across a ravine. Somehow I could tell the ravine below was really deep. There was a sound of rushing water, but it was very faint, far away. It could have been half a mile down, I suppose.

"The crossing was slow. It was like being on a chain gang—a snif-fling, blind chain gang, inching ahead. We just felt our way. Some-one up ahead—I think it was one of the Englishmen—stumbled and we all swayed, holding on to the guide rope with one hand and the coattail of the guy ahead with the other. I doubt if the Basque guide held on; he was sure-footed as a mountain goat. But the rest of us were saying our prayers, swaying out there over nothingness. It took us so long to get across, the sky was getting light by the time we all made it.

"Soon after that we came to a barn and bedded down for the day. In the light we could see where we had been, and where we would go that night. We could see that the side of a slope ahead was a steep jumble of rocks. It seemed so treacherous we could not imagine how it could be crossed.

"It was cold in the barn," he said. "I was probably dressed more warmly than the others because your family had outfitted me so well, and I had a sort of wool neck warmer that I kept in my jacket pocket. I had brought it with me from England.

"After resting that day, we took off in the dusk and plodded up one peak after another; zigzagging up switchbacks, then coming down in order to go up again. A misstep and we'd go ass over teakettle. All night again we were climbing and climbing, and the track twisted around on itself, and the guides wouldn't let us stop.

"The trail was steep and cobbled, and even before we gained any altitude, we slipped and slid through patches of snow. Mostly it was great sweeps of scratchy vegetation that tore at us. Then it got rocky. The Basque didn't slow down at all, but we were dog tired. I can tell you that a guy can be a pilot of a jumbo jet and yet be afraid of heights. I've never confessed that before. But I was afraid of heights that night, and I guess I have been ever since."

"That is reasonable," she said. "Go on."

He took a deep breath.

"At dawn we were in a clearing, and soon we arrived at a farmhouse. We learned that we were still in France. This was a Basque family. None of us could understand their language. But they were generous, and they fed us.

"We fell asleep on straw mats in a sort of lean-to behind the house. We slept till dusk. They gave us some more food, and then we hit the rocky road again.

"We were bushed, and our feet were sore and torn up. If it hadn't been for the pace of that Basque guide, and if we'd had good equipment and enough food and rest, we might have done better. But we had to rush along in the dark. I couldn't have done it without some Benzedrine from my escape kit. All my life I've always thought I could make it, whatever jam I was in. But on those mountains there were times when I *knew* I wasn't going to."

Marshall laughed ruefully, ashamed of himself.

"But you're here," she said gently, laying her head on his shoulder.

"I'm not sure how to tell this next part. I know it doesn't begin to compare to what you went through, but . . . Are you cold?"

"No. I'm all right. But yes, your arm around me feels good."

The young guide, Roland, appeared in the half-light outside the hotel. "Do you need anything?"

"*Non, merci,*" said Marshall.

"We will be on the trail at eight in the morning."

"*Merci. Bonne nuit.*"

"*Bonne nuit.*"

Marshall continued. "The trail was treacherous, but despite everything, I was glad to be on my way. The cold, misty rain stopped when we got to the snow. At first it was just a dusting, but soon we got to places where it was up to our knees. Our guide just mushed on through and left us to hop in his footsteps. Then it got even deeper. Sometimes we sank in to our waists, but we got through it. And then we trudged down the other side of the mountain. Hallelujah, I thought. We're in the home stretch. But we only went down a short way before we started climbing another slope. And that's how it went for hours. Up and down. We had hardly any food, and we didn't stop to rest or eat. The aim was to cross the border while it was still dark so we wouldn't be seen out in the open above the tree line.

"The border was near, and there were sentinels and a German guard post two hundred yards from the narrow path where we had to sneak across. There was a dim crescent moon and enough re-flected light to see the path—just barely. The nearest sentinel was moving back and forth ahead of us. We had to wait till his back was turned, when he was moving away, and then two of us could make a break for it. Then the rest of us waited until the sentinel came back; when he turned away again, two more of us could go.

"The Brits went first, when the Basque signaled. We waited. The sentinel returned. We could see his silhouette and the guard post on a promontory. We were up pretty high, but we were still below the guard post.

"The other guys sneaked through. I was hanging back with Hootie, and it came our turn. We had just climbed a steep path to the side of a precipice, and we were panting. It was steep, and the air was getting thinner. I started ahead, toward the path that I could barely see. I saw the shadow of the guide. Hootie was just behind me, I thought. Suddenly there was a burst of light, and then gunshots. My instinct told me to run. I ran like hell, toward the path ahead, toward the Basque.

"I heard a whimper and a clatter of rocks. I looked back and I couldn't see Hootie. He wasn't there. Behind me was the cliff we had just climbed. A searchlight was sweeping across, and there were more gunshots. I couldn't run back. The rear guide, the Frenchman, was herding us on, into a thick grove. There was nothing we could do, he said. I wanted like hell to go back, but he wouldn't let me. And I could see he was right."

"That is what the guides did," Annette said. "They just kept going. It was necessary. It was too dangerous otherwise. I know of such journeys."

"So we were across the border, but Hootie was gone. And before long the guides were gone, too. The French guy slipped away near the border. He headed off to the side, to cross back into France somewhere farther along the border. The Basque led us a mile or two into Spain, but then he picked up speed and just left us behind.

"We were in Spain, but we had no food, and we weren't really sure what to do next. And my head was whirling because of Hootie. I don't think I've ever been so heavy-hearted. I had reached my goal. I had made it out of France, finally, but it felt like the worst day of my life."

Marshall quit talking, and Annette waited. They sat quietly, side by side, for several minutes before Marshall took up the story again.

"It was less rocky there, and then it was grassy and we came tumbling down, sliding on the fresh grass. There I was, in Spain with four strangers who might have included spies for all I knew, but we were still in mountainous terrain with no clue to what was ahead for us.

"I won't bore you with our wanderings. You know how we were arrested by some Spanish border guards and detained. But that was pretty much just for show. We wound our way through Spain and then to Gibraltar, where we were processed back to England.

"I never saw Hootie again. He simply vanished. Except for that one whimper, there was no noise, no cry. It was just darkness. I don't know if he was shot or if he simply fell from the cliff. That episode is something I've played over and over, as if it had a meaning, some symbolism for my life. What could I have done differently?

"I was able to tell his family what happened—how he seemed to disappear. I wrote to them. After that, I tried hard never to think of that night, but it kept coming back to me. How could I be sure he was dead? I wasn't sure the shot hit him. I assumed that slipping over that ledge was fatal. But I don't know. I wondered—should I have gone back?"

She laid her head on his chest. "Was his body ever found?" she whispered.

"No. Surely someone will find his dog tag one day. You remember, we kept our dog tags in our boots. Of course, I always imagine I'll run into him somewhere."

"No one is to blame," she said.

"*C'est la guerre?*"

"*Oui.*"

"Understand, I've never talked much about this, not since the war. Annette, I know you saw much worse—much worse than you can ever tell me. But you told me a lot, and I—I owed it to you to tell you my own small story."

Annette cupped his face in her hands. "Marshall, I think you are a person who has rarely divulged his heart. But now you have. Thank you."

He rose and walked a few steps away. She was still sitting on the ledge.

"Loretta and some of the others made a fuss over me," he said. "The 'hero.' I made it to Spain and back to England when so many others didn't. But *I* was no hero. What did I do in the war? Nothing. *De la merde.* Got shot down, then saved my own ass."

He paced a few steps, then punched his fist in his palm.

"I didn't even do that," he added. "You and the others saved me."

She started to speak, then tightened her lips and turned her head.

"There are no heroes," she said after a moment. "We both got caught. You were shot down, I was deported."

She stood, smoothed her lap, and moved the few steps to him. The moon was high now.

"We were both caught." He repeated her words.

"Now, we begin again," she said.

Her fingers were so slender, her hand warm in his, her cheek warm on his.

59

"ARE YOU AWAKE?" ANNETTE ASKED, REACHING FOR HIM ACROSS the narrow crevice between their beds.

"Sometimes I don't know the answer to that even when I *am* awake," he said.

"Can't you sleep?"

"No."

"I can't either. I want to tell you something more," she whispered. She scrunched across to his bed, bunching back the covers, and snuggled in with him.

"What is it?"

"It's Robert. You see, the war brought us closer," she said.

"I see. But that is normal, *n'est-ce pas?*"

"Maman trusted Robert. She wanted me to be safe, and Robert kept me safe when I went with him to Chauny or to Noyon on the train. At first we played the lovers, a common *stratagème*, so no one would suspect our mission. But then we found retreats, places to be alone."

Even in the dark Marshall could tell that she was glad that he could not see her face.

"It's all right," he said, pulling her closer to him. "I don't have to know."

"It is such a small thing. It is not important. But I want you to know."

Her voice was low, the whisper of a secret.

"On one Friday afternoon, Robert and I went to meet *aviateurs* at Noyon, but they were not there. There was some slippage in the network. We had made our contact, and then we were told to stay the night in a barn in order to convoy the men the next day. *Oh, la la la la,* the barn was cold! But we kept each other warm. We did manage to fulfill our duty and guide the *aviateurs* to Paris the next day. We did our job well, but . . ."

"*C'est la guerre,*" he reminded her softly.

She was silent for a long moment, her hands pulling at the covers.

She said, "We would have had a baby—but it wouldn't grow in me."

She nestled her head against his neck, and he encircled her shoulders—clumsily, with the two sets of rumpled covers intruding.

"I loved Robert, but our hope was destroyed."

"But *you* weren't destroyed," he said, feeling her tears. He stroked her hair, trying to soothe her.

"I was always an optimist, as you know. And I was happy, relieved, that I lost the baby. I could not have had it taken from me and murdered. To lose it naturally, this was more acceptable. But still the ache of loss has never dissolved." She laughed softly, sarcastically, through sobs. "There was a law encouraging family expansion! But there was no food! And then the deportation. The babies born in France had the *rachitisme*. I don't know the English word. It was so cruel. I'm sorry if I trouble you."

"It's O.K. Go on."

"Before the war, girls didn't wander about unchaperoned, but in the war, anything could happen. To misuse my liberty distressed me—the betrayal of my parents. Maman understood, though."

"Did you ever tell Robert?"

"No, I never told him. I didn't tell Maurice. I was so content to have a husband who didn't probe or pry, who loved me, who worked for me. I was so glad to have a son and a daughter. I was so privileged."

"Did Robert love you?"

"*Bien sûr.* I know he did. He promised me . . . he gave me such gifts. He was *artiste*, you know. He made the pastel portrait of me that you saw in my *salon*. It survived the war."

She spoke in whispers, into his ear. He stroked her hair, her cheek.

"When Maman and I arrived at Fresnes prison I was with child, but I did not know it yet. Although I did not have a healthy glow or signs of swelling and bloom that would be natural, Maman soon knew. We lived so closely, and she saw that I did not bleed after we arrived at the prison. On the train out of Paris to Ravensbrück, some weeks later, it pushed from me quickly, with pain no worse than the pain of blisters on the heels, or the frostbite on my nose and fingers. I knew I should have suffered deeper cramps as the little creature tried hard not to let go. But the scraps of food we were fed in prison could not sustain it, and it withered and sloughed from my body. My mother held me as it happened. Later, at Ravensbrück, we learned the fate of the children there. Women had to watch their children starve, or they were forced to see their babies killed. The SS women smashed a newborn's head against the wall.

"In the end, I felt that so many children died, my not-yet-made being inside me was only a small loss. Yet it was mine, mine alone, and after we were liberated I still felt its empty little spot inside me for a long time. It is still there."

She lay on her side, facing away from him, curved into him closely, and he held her, steadied her shoulders against her sobs.

"It is very painful to tell you this," she said.

"I know. It's all right."

"I want you to know."

Annette grew quiet. He had expected more tears, but there seemed to be none.

AS THEY WAITED for sleep, in each other's arms, he made a mental survey. The field in Belgium. Henri Lechat's father shot on his bicycle. The woman who taught him French in a barn. The women in black. Claude blown up in his barn. The cat Félix. Chauny and the remarkable Alberts, still there. Nicolas wearing the Bugs Bunny jacket. Pierre offhandedly taking out the "isolated *boche*."

The valiant Vallons.

Robert, the ardent youth smuggling costly nutriments to the fallen flyboys.

Odile ordering the schoolboy to tell his parents to cut down the tree to rescue the airman whose arm was torn off. Marshall tried to reconstruct that incident in his mind. If the parachutist's arm had really been torn off, he would have bled to death before the tree was down, but the guy lived long enough to ask for a cup of coffee. Marshall could almost feel the excruciating twist at the shoulder as the arm caught on a pine branch and the man's body flipped.

Georges Broussine. Annette had told him more about this elusive figure who had himself crossed the Pyrenees more than once. He was a Jew, she said. A Jew in German-occupied France.

Broussine, the Vallons, the women in black, the Alberts, Odile, Robert Lebeau, the priest, all of them working to save airmen. Now Marshall had to help Annette, even if it meant reuniting her with her sweetheart, Robert. He couldn't forget the pleasure on Robert's face when he brought the goose to the Vallons. That eager young face got burnt out, a light gone dark.

So many thousands of stories. Lost. Disappearing.

Webb. The brusque Basque. Hootie.

He intended to search for Odile's parachutists somehow. But he wouldn't leave Annette. Sleep was coming. He would figure it out. He knew he would.

Annette had sheltered him; now maybe he could assist her. He looked ahead to helping her bear witness. He saw her standing before a blackboard in a classroom, writing essential words for schoolchildren to remember, showing them the symbols. The ration card. The swastika. The cloth number sewn at her breast. She could speak, firsthand, of the unspeakable.

He could be there.

A soft peacefulness settled over Marshall. The *Dirty Lily* was fading away, like a mishap in his youth. But the war itself had grown more real to him—so many new questions, like newly discovered photographs. The decades that followed the war, when he went winging around the world dressed up in a blue suit with a gold-braided cap, seemed like a bubble now—an illusion, a fleeting interlude between the war and his retirement, when he circled back to Europe and to the war and to Annette.

He thought about James Ford meeting the sweethearts—Annette and Robert—at the Gare du Nord. Marshall could picture the youthful *résistants* on bicycles, speeding alongside the Seine, laughing, the breeze snapping her Scottish scarf, her blue beret snug on her head, her cheeks rosy. The boy is looking back to make sure the girl is there.

Le petit Albert, he thought as sleep finally came.

WHEN THEY WOKE AGAIN, she said, "Are you dreaming?"

"I don't know. Are you?"

"I was remembering the joy I felt when I heard from you, my big American." She kissed his cheek lightly.

"Are you warm?"

"*Mmm.* After today, we will remember the Pyrenees fondly."

60

"WE WILL BE IN SPAIN FOR DINNER," SAID ROLAND, WHO HAD clustered his flock of trekkers at the start of the trail, just beyond the hotel. He issued pairs of metal walking sticks, then gave a brief talk about the old smugglers' trails, long used to transport contraband. He did not mention refugees or wayward American airmen.

Their group was small—an Australian in a tam who described himself as a *bon vivant*, a sturdy couple from Denmark, the Canadian couple, and a French woman with her recently returned big American.

The climb was not arduous, although the footing was uncertain. Marshall discovered that he needed both his walking sticks for balance on tricky patches of sand and gravel. They were walking on a narrow path through a forest, the light coming through thick growth. Marie was walking point and Roland brought up the rear. Now and then Marshall heard them on their *talkie-walkies*. He walked close behind Annette, to catch her if she slipped. But she moved with graceful confidence.

The path ran along a ledge above a stream. Below, two cows were nibbling at tree branches. On the path ahead were more cows, one with long horns.

"They are peaceful cows," called Marie to the group.

"Watch your step," Marshall said to Annette.

"This is beautiful," she said.

"Are you out of breath yet?"

"No. I breathe well. And you?"

"I'm O.K. This is exhilarating."

He could hear the flat metal sounds of cowbells, several of them clanking randomly.

"Listen to the cowbells," he said. "Strange music." *Familiar music.*

The ground leveled for a time, and the trail narrowed as it passed among boulders spotted with lichen. He remembered the grand rock at the zoo in Saint-Mandé.

Robert Lebeau was Marshall's better self. Annette was his better half.

He put one foot in front of the other. The awkward atonal music of the cowbells grew fainter. He recalled cowbells in the Kentucky mountains, cattle roaming, foraging, their bells like cracked voices singing folk ballads.

Time was a bellows, opening and closing. He remembered himself as the young boy who first saw a biplane flying above the mountains and wanted desperately to sprout wings. He had watched buzzards and hawks soaring through the valleys and rising over the tops of small green mountains, borne beyond wraiths of fog.

Now the Canadian couple was chattering about Biarritz and how clean it was, how they hoped they would have a better bed at the hotel in Spain than they had last night. The Australian man was telling Annette about hiking to the top of Pic du Canigou in the Catalan region. There, at the summit, he came upon two men cooking paella.

"Right on the top!" he cried. "They brought the whole kit and there they were—cooking paella! Unbelievable. Barely standing room on a pile of rocks, and they're cooking paella."

"*Mais oui, bien sûr!*" Annette said. "Paella is much, much better in the open air."

"Why not?" said Marshall.

After a while, they emerged from thinning trees, and the view opened out. The sun was brilliant, but it gave little warmth here, in the heights. Marshall spotted a glint of snow on a distant peak. Ahead, he could see vague misty clouds swirling in front of dark, enveloping mountain faces. The group spread out on the trail, with their young guides positioned fore and aft. The climb was becoming steeper. At a narrow curve, Roland waited until all the hikers were in sight, and he signaled to Marie. He was leading their formation now, and Marie was Tail-End Charlie.

Roland advanced around the curve. Marshall was following Annette, her blue beret rising and falling in front of him as they climbed into the haze ahead.

They were gaining altitude.

THE END

ACKNOWLEDGMENTS

THIS NOVEL WAS INSPIRED BY THE WORLD WAR II EXPERIENCE of my father-in-law, Barney Rawlings (1920–2004). He wrote his memoir, *Off We Went*, in 1994, to leave a record for his family. Our conversations and his book were the springboard for my imagined story.

I was also inspired by the wartime experience of Michèle Moët-Agniel, who as a teenager was an escort for Allied airmen shot down in Occupied Europe, 1943–44. Her family worked for the Bourgogne escape network and directly assisted Barney Rawlings. Mme Agniel graciously welcomed me at her home in Paris and shared her memories with me.

I read widely in memoirs by American airmen who were evaders, and I also read books about Europeans who aided Allied airmen. Essential to my story was the captivating diary of Virginia d'Albert Lake. She was one of the few survivors of the slave-labor camp—a satellite of Ravensbrück—outside Koenigsberg-sur-Oder in Occupied Poland. After her release, she wrote a vivid account of the ordeal, published in *An American Heroine in the French Resistance* in 2006. Michèle Agniel, also a prisoner at Koenigsberg, wrote an emotional account of her return visit to the site (in what is now Chojna, Poland) in 1995. In her conversations with me she recalled the camp at Koenigsberg, which I imagine was far more brutal than she was able to tell me. She refers to Koenigsberg as "Petit-Koenigsberg," to distinguish it from the Prussian city of Koenigsberg, which became Kalinigrad under the Soviets. She was imprisoned at Ravensbrück and Koenigsberg with three British Special Operations Executive (SOE) agents—Violette Szabo, Liliane Rolfe, and Denise Bloch—who were executed by the Nazis as spies. These agents have been memorialized and celebrated for their service to the French Resistance in preparation for D-Day.

I am grateful for the cooperation, conversation, correspondence, published interviews, reminiscences, and friendship of Michèle Agniel.

I am thankful also for conversation and the unpublished memoir of Jeannine Fagot, who aided American parachutists in 1944.

Thanks to other generous friends in France:

Francis and Marie-Isabelle Agniel, Jean-Marie and Nicole Moët, Elise Agniel, Geneviève Camus, in Paris.

Jean and Marie-Thérèse Hallade and their large, welcoming family in Bichancourt.

Catherine and Andrew Smith in Cognac.

Winnie Madden and Philippe Chavance in Paris.

I am grateful to the residents of Solre-Saint-Géry, Belgium, and its environs who generously welcomed me in 2008. Several of them had witnessed a B-17 crash landing there in 1944—the *G.I. Sheets*, co-piloted by Barney Rawlings—and they had assisted the crew, at the peril of their own lives. In 1987, local citizens honored the crew by erecting a handsome memorial at the crash site. Benoit Dorignaux and Françoise Stiernet graciously hosted me during my visit. Roger Anthoine, whom I met elsewhere, told me how members of his family had risked their lives by sheltering two members of the crew.

The Air Forces Escape and Evasion Society is active in preserving the memory of those times and in honoring the special friendships formed between aviators and their European helpers. I am grateful to members of AFEES, including Larry Grauerholz, John Katsaros, Roger Anthoine, and the late Clayton David, who shared their memories with me.

In this novel, Georges Broussine (1918–2001) and Dédée de

Jongh (1916–2007) are historical figures. Georges Broussine was the mastermind of the Bourgogne network, which sheltered and convoyed more than three hundred Allied aviators to safety. In reading of his brave exploits, about which he was extremely modest, I am in awe of his courage.

Several books, such as *The Freedom Line*, by Peter Eisner, recount Dédée de Jongh's heroism and bravery with the Comète escape line, which she founded.

My husband, Roger Rawlings, was named for the #3 engine of his father's B-17, the *G.I. Sheets*, which crash-landed in Belgium on January 29, 1944, two years before Roger was born. Roger owes his life to the brave Belgians and French who helped his father successfully evade the Nazis. This book owes its life to Roger's careful eye and loving support.

Thanks to Jim Alpha for the cars, Roger Rawlings for the airplanes. My sister LaNelle Mason was my enthusiastic companion on several exciting trips to France. Lynne and John Drahan and Catherine and Trevor King were my excellent guides over the Pyrenees mountains.

I want to thank Millicent Bennett and Beth Pearson at Random House for their tireless attention to the manuscript. My appreciation also goes to Robin Rolewicz, formerly of Random House, for her early encouragement.

Thanks to Karen Alpha, Mary Ann Taylor-Hall, and Sharon Kelly Edwards for emotional support and critical reading of the manuscript, Cori Jones for friendship and Paris, Binky Urban for her enthusiastic encouragement, Kate Medina for her generous readings and enduring confidence in the story, and Monique Roman, professor *extraordinaire*, for the French language. Any mistakes in French are mine. Special thanks to Philippe Chavance for his careful reading and pertinent advice.

SELECTED BIBLIOGRAPHY

ESCAPE AND EVASION

Air Forces Escape & Evasion Society. Paducah, KY: Turner, 1992.

Bennett, George Floyd. *Shot Down! Escape and Evasion*. Morgantown, WV: MediaWorks, 1991.

Broussine, Georges. *L'evadé de la France Libre: Le réseau Bourgogne*. Paris: Editions Tallandier, 2000.

Conscript Heroes. www.conscript-heroes.com.

David, Clayton C. *They Helped Me Escape*. Manhattan, KS: Sunflower University Press, 1988.

Eisner, Peter. *The Freedom Line: The Brave Men and Women Who Rescued Allied Airmen from the Nazis During World War II*. New York: William Morrow, 2004.

Nichol, John, and Tony Rennell. *Home Run: Escape from Nazi Europe*. London: Penguin Group, 2007.

Ottis, Sherri Greene. *Silent Heroes: Downed Airmen and the French Underground*. Lexington: University Press of Kentucky, 2001.

Rawlings, Barney. *Off We Went*. Washington, NC: Morgan Printers, 1994.

The U.S. Air Forces Escape and Evasion Society Communicator, a quarterly bulletin.

de Vasselot, Odile. *Tombés du ciel*. Paris: Editions du Félin, 2005.

THE AIR WAR

Gobrecht, Harry D. *Might in Flight: Daily Diary of the Eighth Air Force's Hell's Angels 303rd Bombardment Group (H)*. San Clemente, CA: 303rd Bombardment Group (H) Association, 1993.

Kaplan, Philip, and Rex Alan Smith. *One Last Look: A Sentimental Journey to the Eighth Air Force Heavy Bomber Bases of World War II in England.* New York: Abbeville Press, 1983.

O'Neill, Brian D. *Half a Wing, Three Engines, and a Prayer: B-17s Over Germany.* Blue Ridge Summit, PA: TAB Books, 1989.

RESISTANCE AND DEPORTATION

d'Albert Lake, Virginia. *An American Heroine in the French Resistance.* Ed. Judy Barett Litoff. New York: Fordham University Press, 2006.

Guillemot, Gisèle, and Samuel Humez. *Résistante, Mémoires d'une femme, de la résistante à la déportation.* Neuilly-sur-Seine: Editions Michel Lafon, 2009.

Morrison, Jack G. *Ravensbrück: Everyday Life in a Women's Concentration Camp 1939–1945.* Princeton, NJ: Markus Wiener, 2000.

Rameau, Marie. *Des femmes en résistance 1939–1945.* Paris: Editions Autrement, 2008.

Tillion, Germaine. *Ravensbrück: An Eyewitness Account of a Women's Concentration Camp.* New York: Doubleday, 1975.

Weitz, Margaret Collins. *Sisters in the Resistance.* New York: John Wiley & Sons, 1995.

THE GIRL IN THE BLUE BERET

BOBBIE ANN MASON

A READER'S GUIDE

BEHIND THE BOOK

BOBBIE ANN MASON

———

My father-in-law was a pilot. During World War II, he was shot down in a B-17 over Belgium. With the help of the French Resistance, he made his way through Occupied France and back to his base in England. Ordinary citizens hid him in their homes, fed him, disguised him, and sheltered him from the Germans. Many families willingly hid Allied aviators, knowing the risks: They would have been shot or sent to a concentration camp if they were discovered by the Germans.

In 1987 the town in Belgium honored the crew by erecting a memorial at the crash site, where one of the ten crew members died. The surviving crew was invited for three days of festivities, including a flyover by the Belgian Air Force. More than three thousand Allied airmen were rescued during the war, and an extraordinarily deep bond between them and their European helpers endures even now.

My father-in-law, Barney Rawlings, spent a couple of months hiding out in France in 1944, frantically memorizing a few French words to pass himself off as a Frenchman, but his ordeal had not inspired in me any fiction until I started taking a French class. Suddenly, the language was transporting me back in time and across the ocean, as I tried to imagine a tall, out-of-place American struggling to say *Bonjour.* Barney had a vague memory of a girl who had escorted him in Paris in 1944. He remembered that her signal was something blue—a scarf, maybe, or a beret. The notion of a girl in a blue beret seized me, and I was off.

I had my title, but I didn't know what my story would be. I had to go to France to imagine the country in wartime. What would I have done in such circumstances of fear, deprivation, and uncertainty? What if my pilot character returns decades later to search for the people who had helped him escape?

Writing a novel about World War II and the French Resistance was a challenge both sobering and thrilling. I read many riveting escape-and-evade accounts of airmen and of the Resistance networks organized to hide them and then send them on grueling treks across the Pyrenees to safety. But it was the people I met in France and Belgium who made the period come alive for me. They had lived it.

In Belgium, I was entertained lavishly by the people who had honored the B-17 crew with the memorial, including by some of the locals who had witnessed the crash landing. I was overwhelmed by their generosity. They welcomed me with an extravagant three-cheek kiss, but one ninety-year-old man, Fernand Fontesse, who had been in the Resistance and had been a POW, planted his kiss squarely on my lips.

In a small town north of Paris I met Jean Hallade. He had been only fifteen when Second Lieutenant Rawlings was hidden in a nearby house. Jean took a picture of Barney in a French beret, a photo to be used for the fake ID card he would need as he traveled through France over the next few months, disguised as a French cabinetmaker.

And in Paris I became friends with lovely, indomitable Michèle Agniel, who had been a girl guide in the Resistance. Her family aided fifty Allied aviators, including Barney Rawlings. She takes her scrapbooks from the war years to schools to show children what once happened. "This happened *here*," she says. "Here is a ration card. This is a swastika." She pauses. "Never again," she says. The characters in *The Girl in the Blue Beret* are not portraits of actual people, but the situations were inspired by very real individuals whom I regard as heroes.

QUESTIONS AND TOPICS
FOR DISCUSSION

1. Discuss the special bond between Allied aviators and their European helpers. Why did it take so long for many of them to re-unite after the war?

2. What does flying mean to Marshall? Discuss Marshall's failed B-17 mission and the effect it had on his life.

3. Re-read and discuss the images of flight throughout the novel. How does the final sentence tie in with these?

4. What is Marshall's feeling about the young man he remembers as Robert? Does Marshall romanticize him? Why is finding Robert so important to Marshall?

5. Love and war. There are two main love stories in this novel—the younger couple, Annette and Robert, and the mature couple, Annette and Marshall. How are these relationships different from each other? What does war do to love and romance?

6. Why is Marshall so unprepared for what Annette reveals to him? How does he deal with her story? What possibilities lie ahead for him?

7. The name Annette Vallon is inspired by a historical figure, a woman who was William Wordsworth's lover during the French Revolution and the mother of his illegitimate child. What suggestions are being made by the use of the name here? What else can you learn about Annette Vallon from further research?

8. What do you make of the epigraph by William Wordsworth? Is it appropriate? How does it connect with the use of Annette Vallon's name?

9. What do mountains mean to Marshall? Trace the importance of mountains at different stages of his life.

10. How does Marshall look back on his war experience? How does his perspective change during the course of the novel?

11. How do the experiences in the book compare with your own experiences of war? Have you ever known anyone captured during wartime?

12. What is meant by second chances in the context of this book?

13. How do you interpret the ending? Review the emotional developments that lead up to the last lines, especially Marshall's thinking as he falls to sleep the night before. Based on your understanding of the characters and their situation, what do you imagine they are likely to do next? How does the aviation term, "gaining altitude," apply here?

BOBBIE ANN MASON is the author of *In Country*, *Shiloh and Other Stories*, *An Atomic Romance*, *Nancy Culpepper*, and a memoir, *Clear Springs*. She is the winner of the PEN/Hemingway Award, two Southern Book Awards, an award from the American Academy of Arts and Letters, and numerous other prizes, including the O. Henry and the Pushcart. She was a finalist for the National Book Critics Circle Award, the American Book Award, the PEN/Faulkner Award, and the Pulitzer Prize. She lives in Kentucky.

The text of this book was set in Janson, a typeface designed in about 1690 by Nicholas Kis—a Hungarian living in Amsterdam—and for many years mistakenly attributed to the Dutch printer Anton Janson. In 1919, the matrices became the property of the Stempel Foundry in Frankfurt. It is an old-style book face of excellent clarity and sharpness. Janson serifs are concave and splayed; the contrast between thick and thin strokes is marked.